Critical acclaim for Jeff Gulvin

'So detailed, so accurate in its depiction of terrorist and counter-terrorist activities, that had it been written as a piece of non-fiction, the Government would almost certainly have tried to ban it' *Time Out*

'*Storm Crow* is that rare bird – a meticulously researched thriller with a gripping and ominously plausible plot'
Dr Bruce Hoffman, Director of the RAND Corporation's Washington Office

'This rattles along at a fine pace, yet has time for the detail which not only adds authenticity but demonstrates the author's thorough research and sound knowledge of his subject' *Shots*

'With spine-chilling realism, the world of international terrorism is exposed in a tour de force thriller from an author rapidly gaining comparisons with masters like Frederick Forsyth. Definitely a candidate for thriller of the year' *Aberdeen Evening Express*

'. . . the labyrinths of betrayal and personal responsibility are as important as the mechanics of the thriller plot. Gulvin's main aim is to keep the pages turning (and here he scores a palpable hit), but he is fastidious in his characterisation and his villain in particular is something of a unique creation' *Good Book Guide*

Jeff Gulvin is one of the most exciting young British thriller talents around, with critically acclaimed best-sellers such as *Storm Crow* and *The Covenant* already behind him. He was born in 1962. He has travelled extensively and lived in the USA and New Zealand.

By Jeff Gulvin

THE
PROCESSION

JEFF GULVIN

ORION

An Orion paperback

First published in Great Britain in 2002
by Orion
This paperback edition published in 2003
by Orion Books Ltd,
Orion House, 5 Upper St Martin's Lane,
London WC2H 9EA

A CIP catalogue record for this book
is available from the British Library

ISBN 0 75284 943 3

Typeset at The Spartan Press Ltd
Lymington, Hants

Printed and bound in Great Britain by
Clays Ltd, St Ives plc

This book is for my sister Lyn

Acknowledgements

The author would like to thank:

Special Agent Mike Kirkpatrick, Assistant Director FBI, CJIS; the Organized Crime Squad – New Orleans FBI field office; the FBI Resident Agency, Clarksburg, West Virginia.

Robert Hecker, Chief of New Orleans' Harbour Police; Chief Clayton, Bridgeport Police Department, West Virginia; William J. Null and Frank Palestina, Department of Corrections, New Orleans.

The staff of the Criminal Justice Information Services Division, FBI, West Virginia; the skipper and crew of *Apache Eagle* tugboat; Gary Hirstius and Coco Robicheaux.

one

Christmas Eve

Snow lay crusted and brown, bloody almost in places.

Maxwell Carter stared out of his bedroom window with a sense of unease in his gut. During the night he had been disturbed by the sound of a truck idling right outside his house: it was only there for a matter of seconds before driving away.

Fresh snow had fallen yesterday morning but nothing since; the front lawn was still a bed of virgin white, but Carter had beaten a path to the door and the driveway was mussed and muddy. He stared at the end of the driveway where it dipped into the camber of the road and he could see a set of tyre tracks that hadn't been there yesterday.

He sat on the edge of his bed, naked still, the mass of white flesh crumpled at his belly and thighs. He got up, rubbing the small of his back, and waddled along the landing to his computer room. His mother's Christmas card lay on the filing cabinet: he traced a forefinger over the padded velveteen front and read the message he had written.

Outside he crunched across the snow, still flecked with slivers of ice in places where yesterday's sun hadn't been able to penetrate. He could see the tyre tracks plainly now, wide and deeply treaded, much fuller than those made by his own car. It was as if the driver of the truck had half pulled in, wanting to turn. But he hadn't turned: he had just backed out again and carried on in the same direction.

Why would somebody do that?

The sense of unease grew now. It became a finger of fear as he stood, his massive booted feet sinking into the snow. He bent, wheezing slightly with his weight, dragging the air into his lungs, his hair untied and hanging low over his face. Somebody had half pulled into his yard then backed out again.

His breath came in short clouds of steam as he stared at the tracks. Stupid, he told himself. You're being stupid: they made a mistake is all. Whoever they were, they just made a mistake.

Back inside he kicked the snow off his boots. The furnace was going full blast and the house sweated with the heat. Carter opened the door to the basement and looked down into the darkness. He switched on the light, listening for any irregularities in the humming of the furnace. It was old and he always feared it might break down on him at this time of year. Right before Christmas, that would be just too bad.

Coffee bubbled in the pot on the worktop behind him. Carter swept dank hair from his face and was about to close the basement door again when something caught his eye. Gooseflesh prickled his skin. He stared at the bottom step. Half a bootprint marked the yellow wood.

Carter's heart was pounding now. He stared at the print then reached into the closet for his baseball bat. He started down into the basement, moving slowly, each step creaking under his weight. At the bottom he bent and inspected the footprint more closely. A set of tyre tracks and now a footprint. His mind was turning cartwheels. For the first time he began to regret starting all this. He scanned the basement for any sign of an intruder, but the tiny window had not been forced and the only other way in was through the kitchen. He looked at the print once more, then he frowned and with one hand on the rail he upturned his right foot. The relief was tangible as he realized the print was his own.

Upstairs he poured coffee into his big mug, his hand a

meaty paw with overlong nails like claws that scratched the plastic. The steam played over his face and he closed his eyes, took a noisy sip and sat down at the kitchen table. There was nothing to worry about, just a little paranoia setting in. With what was at stake he was entitled to feel a little paranoid. But the sound of that engine rattled in his head still. Why would somebody half pull into his yard in the middle of the night then drive away again? There could be any number of innocent reasons and he went through them mentally while he straightened his bed, his coffee cup on the nightstand. He puffed up the pillows like his mother had always done, pulled the comforter up and tucked it in at the sides. He liked a neat bed: with his massive bulk he didn't want the bottom sheet to crease because the ridges got stuck in the folds of his flesh and rubbed him raw. It was the same when he dried after bathing, he was always careful to leave no damp places and used copious quantities of baby powder. He really ought to lose some weight, but he had been telling himself that since he first ballooned in his twenties. That was twenty years ago – what chance did he stand now?

Satisfied with the bedroom, he went into the computer room where the monitor sat silently on the desk. Later he would talk to Jeannie-Anne. Jeannie-Anne Rae, whom he'd first met in a chat room and now talked to every night. It was a gradual relationship, neither of them very good at this sort of thing, neither of them very able emotionally: physical appearance counted for so much in society. They had no confidence, it was one of the things they had in common. But the internet enabled them to talk, to begin to build something before they met. They were not at the meeting stage yet and it was a long way to Tallahassee. Carter wouldn't go until they were both ready.

He stood musing for a moment, staring out the window at the tyre tracks, clearly visible now the sun was up and bathing the yard in a white light, refracted through icicles

3

that clung to the trees. His inner silence was complete, oblivious to the sounds from outside; his own silence where he could sit and think and contemplate all that he was doing, what it might mean for the future.

His CJIS identity card was lying beside the computer and he allowed himself a wry smile as he inspected his picture. He *was* big, way too big. His mother had told him. His two older sisters told him every time he saw them, which was infrequently now they had moved to the Shenandoah Valley. His hair was matted and long, matching the black of his beard so when he went to work he looked like a biker in sports jacket and tie.

He sipped more coffee then set the mug down while he took a shower. The water was hot and he had cleaned the showerhead with lime-scale remover only the other day, so the needles rattled his flesh. He soaped himself down, paying attention to the great fatty creases in his flesh, his genitals and his bottom. He liked to be clean and he always had fresh towels and bathrobe.

He powdered himself and slipped on a robe then padded through to the computer room for his coffee.

It wasn't where he'd left it.

There was a mark from the bottom of the cup on the desk, but it wasn't there now. His heart began to beat a fraction faster. Sweat gathered in pinpricks at his hairline. He looked round the room, stepped on to the landing and listened. No sound, he could hear nothing except the hum of the furnace and his own heart beating.

His coffee mug was sitting on the vanity unit in the bathroom. He stared at it. He hadn't put it there. Had he? He thought he'd left it in the computer room. Again he moved on to the landing and listened, but he heard no sound, sensed no presence other than his own.

Paranoia, he told himself. It was bound to set in sooner or later. Suddenly the stakes had risen, he was in a new game altogether and was still finding his feet. But everything was

OK: all the necessary precautions had been taken, this was just absent-mindedness brought on by waking in the night. Sleep disturbance – his head was always in a fug when his sleep was interrupted.

Downstairs the phone rang. A glance at the caller ID told him it was from out of the area and he looked at the black receiver with the hairs prickling the back of his neck. This was stupid, all because of a set of tyre tracks in the yard. He lifted the receiver from the cradle.

'Hello?'

Silence. Yet somebody was there: he could sense the rhythm of breath without actually hearing anything.

'Hello.' A sharper edge to his voice now, a hint of agitation.

Nothing. Nobody said anything and nobody hung up.

Carter put the phone down, feeling the sweat damp against his skin. No voice, no sound of breathing, just the density of silence.

Upstairs again he dried his hair and told himself he was being foolish. He thought about making a call to Charleston but decided against it. Charleston knew nothing about this so what would be the point? He was paranoid; there was nothing more to it than that. A truck and a wrong number. Get a grip, Max.

He whistled as he made French toast, the sound fracturing the heaviness of the atmosphere. He had no work today, which was just as well given it was Christmas Eve and he had promised his mother he would be at her house for lunch tomorrow. He still hadn't bought her a present. He'd meant to do it last Saturday, but had never got round to it. He was bowling in the league now, had been on a roll of late and the guys on the team had elevated him to mini superstar status. It had taken up all his thoughts, bowling like that: he had never bowled like that.

That was before CJIS, however. Everything was before CJIS. *BC-JIS.* He laughed at his own joke then heard a

5

truck on the road outside and went to the window. Lifting back the drapes, he peered at the black Chevy that rumbled down the street. The windows were tinted so he couldn't see the driver. He felt the knot of unease in his stomach, the movement of hair on his arm.

It was time he went out: if today went by and he hadn't bought his mother a Christmas present the hurt in her face would haunt him the rest of his life. Taking his coat and his car keys, he locked the door behind him then set about scraping the packed ice from where it crusted the windshield of his Dodge. The car was new, white with leather seats, one of the luxuries he had allowed himself since things started getting better. He was a single guy, nobody would raise any eyebrows: single guys could afford decent cars. He loved the smooth lines of the Dodge. He found it a little hard getting in and out, the seat never seemed to go back far enough, and he swore he *would* lose some of the three hundred pounds he was packing around these days.

Still, he was over six feet tall and with his hair, his beard and the darkness of his eyes he never had any trouble from the kids that hung out in the mall. His eyebrows were thick and shaggy and the set of his mouth twisted his beard in such a way that people looked away when he stared. He liked that, gave him the kind of rush that had been missing from his life since childhood.

He backed the car out, bumping over the packed brown snow, erasing the tyre tracks in a moment. Skirting the northern end of the park, he headed south on James to Philadelphia Avenue, before crossing Simpson Creek. Main Street was busy and he had to wait at the intersection before he could pull out.

Mrs Annabel Carter gazed across the frozen surface of Maple Lake beyond the children's playground to the ice-clad diving platform, cast grey all at once with the sun passing behind a cloud. The sky promised more snow

6

although none had been forecast on the weather channel. She liked the weather channel: in a way it kept her abreast of what was going on better than the news did. She gauged the world by the weather. The clouds seemed somehow ominous and she saw again the expression in Madame Josephine's eyes, that quick and darting movement before looking away.

That had been Friday, her fortnightly visit. Today was Sunday and she had been to church already. Tomorrow was Christmas Day and she had prepared the bird and all the trimmings and would make the thick brown gravy her son liked so much. She had dressed the tree and the lights still worked, and that nice boy from the printers on Main Street had fixed up a set on the front of her house.

Everything should be wonderful: this was her favourite time of year. It was a pity the girls and her grandchildren couldn't make it over from Virginia but she planned to see them for New Year. Everything was fine, Maxwell was coming and she would look forward to that. Why then did she have this terrible sense of foreboding?

She had been going to Madame Josephine for years now. The reader had a little salon just a block up on the highway, and ever since her husband Larry died, Mrs Carter had sought some solace in her readings. The girls were long since married and busy with their lives, but she still had Maxwell living close by. That had been a comfort to her when death came so suddenly but now she wished Maxwell would get married. He was almost forty-three and he should be settled with someone by now. She had suggested Weight-Watchers but he had just laughed at the idea. He was a strange man and didn't make friends very easily, not really the kind of son that her husband had hoped for after the two girls – introverted and preferring his indoor games to going hunting or fishing.

That had been the only bugbear between them in fifty years of marriage, that and Maxwell's apparent lack of direction. She had told Larry countless times that it wasn't a lack as such, just that some people didn't find their feet till later in their lives. That had been how it was with Maxwell, leaving high school with less than adequate grades, flunking out in college then drifting from one job to the next till they built the new FBI facility just off the interstate. Larry had lived to see his son get a job with the FBI and that had thrilled him: it was Annabel's one consolation when he died.

She would phone Maxwell now, he wasn't working today. She hadn't spoken to him since she met with Madame Josephine and she had been meaning to call him. She picked up the phone and dialled, but he wasn't there. She hesitated when his answer machine clicked in but she didn't leave a message.

Carter drove through Bridgeport on Highway 50, past the gas station and the hair-replacement centre, up towards the intersection with I79. He pulled up in the parking lot of the giant K-Mart store and as he locked his car he had the feeling that somebody was watching him. The hairs lifted on his neck and he stood with the key in the lock of the Dodge. He glanced quickly behind him. Rows and rows of vehicles, men and women with shopping carts and children, but nobody looking at him, nobody taking any notice of him at all. His breathing came a little easier, but he was sweating and his hair matted against his scalp. He stuffed the keys in his pocket and glanced across the roof of his car. Right at the end of the lot he saw a black Chevy pickup with tinted windows, exhaust fumes rising from the tailpipe.

Carter moved between the shelves, picking up a massive bag of peanut brownies and another of starburst candy. He dropped them in his cart and paused at the refrigerated section before selecting a case of Samuel Adams beer. He preferred the imported Newcastle brand but it was more expensive.

8

Lingering briefly in the hunting section, he thought of his father and his passion for the sport. A video was running, some Virginian kid who'd shot his first white-tailed deer at the age of five, holed up in a tree, waiting for another deer he could bring down, probably from miles away given the nature of his rifle.

Carter felt a sudden presence. Slowly he turned. The aisle was empty, and he took a moment to calm himself. This was ridiculous: he was jumpy as hell and for no good reason. So somebody thought about turning round in his driveway, so what? He exhaled heavily and pushed his cart into the next aisle, saw a friend of his mother's from Maple Lake and nodded to her. His mother. That was why he was here. Tomorrow was Christmas Day and he'd better not show up without a present. But he had no idea what to buy her, he never did. Come to think of it, he'd missed her birthday completely. He'd never once given it a thought. Not so much as a card. He thought about the card he had for her now. She would treasure it all the more: she never threw cards or letters away. All the more reason to get a good present, though, make some kind of effort given it was Christmas and all.

He shambled between the aisles, half thinking about his mother's present and half about later tonight when he would be talking to Jeannie-Anne. She was his girlfriend: that was how it felt even though they hadn't actually met. It was a delicious feeling, like he was wanted, and he had never been wanted before – never in high school and not since high school. Idly he picked up a table lamp sculptured from cheap glass in the shape of a turtle: $16.99. He put it in his cart.

Jeannie-Anne Rae was working Christmas Eve: Tallahassee was hot as hell, which it shouldn't be at this time of year. It should be warm, sure, but not this hot. Maybe there was something to global warming after all. She was a checkout girl at the Winn Dixie supermarket and the stool they gave her to sit on was uncomfortable, with her buttocks splaying out on both sides. Her armpits were already soaking, and she could feel the stickiness in her groin. All day she punched numbers on the cash register, ran barcodes over the scanner, dreaming of cool showers and talking to Max Carter.

What a difference to her life. Now she was like all the rest of them, she had her man out there though they were yet to meet. They talked, though, shared intimate conversation, and that alone was sufficient.

'You put that through twice.' The customer, a blue-rinse woman, looked across the counter, a hawkish expression on her badly painted mouth.

'Excuse me?'

'That bleach right there. You ran it through the scanner two times.'

Jeannie-Anne looked at her. She might have done, daydreaming like she had been.

'You ought to be more careful. Overcharging people like that.'

'If I did I'm sorry.' Jeannie-Anne flicked the cover off the till roll. 'I'll check it for you now.'

Carter always carried his bowling ball in the trunk of his car. He bowled as often as he could, especially since he'd been on such a winning streak. The clouds had given way to a thin blue in the sky and the diluted presence of the sun. The snow had been cleared from the parking lot, just the odd crust remaining here and there, yet it was mushy and damp underfoot. There was plenty of the day left and Jeannie wouldn't log on till this evening so there was nothing to do at home except watch television – he could wrap his mother's present later. He'd forgotten to buy paper at the store, but he would swing by again on his way home. Right now his winning streak would wait no longer: Carter was going bowling.

He bowled well, not as well as he could and not as well as he had been doing lately, but well enough to leave around five that afternoon with a certain sense of satisfaction. He stepped out into the parking lot, where the darkness was almost complete, and stamped his feet in the cold. He was a little disappointed, however. Howard Bentwood had been in the lane next to him and had bowled better than he did, but Carter had beaten him only last Saturday. Besides, he had more important things on his mind now and was anxious to get home.

Highway 50 was busy, Christmas Eve shoppers heading for K-Mart or Valley Hills. He got held up at every set of lights and drummed thick fingers on the steering-wheel. Vaguely he listened to the news on the radio. Nothing much was going on, some woman complaining of civil rights abuse from a Nutter Fort police officer after she was involved in a car wreck on Saturday night. Carter listened disinterestedly and headed for Bridgeport and home.

As he drove the loop of Compton Park he saw a black Chevy pickup parked by the side of the road: the windows were tinted and the plates were from Tennessee. He slowed as he drove by but he couldn't tell if there was anyone inside.

It was fully dark now and the snow had a luminescent glow to it from the streetlamps. His front yard was still virginal and he paused a moment as he switched off the engine to admire the perfect smoothness.

He had left the furnace on low and now he hovered by the door to the basement as he powered up the thermostat. He placed the Sam Adams in the refrigerator, then uncapped his last cold one and took a long pull before wiping his mouth with the back of his hand.

The man sitting in the basement heard him at the top of the stairs. He picked up the 9-mm pistol where it lay at his feet.

*

Carter thought the house was quiet today, too quiet for his mood. The street outside was deserted, people scurrying home early to be with their families for the holiday, and the temperature plummeting. He switched on the radio to break the mood, twiddled the knob looking for some country and western. He found a station where Kenny and Dolly were singing 'Islands in the Stream', and he hummed along with them as he took cheese and crackers and the bag of peanut brownies and made his way upstairs.

He stripped for the shower: he always liked to be clean when he spoke to Jeannie-Anne. It felt like a proper date if he was showered and changed, even if it was only into a fresh pair of sweatpants or a bathrobe. He stood in front of the bathroom mirror and shifted his belly so he could inspect his genitals. It was a long time since he had been able to look on them directly without the use of a mirror. He shook his great body and the rolls of white flesh shuddered with a life of their own. His buttocks hung in great gobs of fat and his thighs folded like snakes twisted round saplings. He was too fat, three hundred pounds was dangerous, particularly with his thirty Marlboro and twelve pack of beer a day.

But that's how he was. He'd told Jeannie-Anne that was how he was and knew she carried a similar problem. It brought them closer, made them more like confidants. She said she liked him regardless: his size wasn't a problem. It was the man inside that counted. That had given him the kind of thrill he'd never thought he'd experience. No woman had looked at him before and if they couldn't get beyond that they would never know him. Their loss, he'd told himself. But it had been hard. Life had been lonely. Women had been indifferent, some of them openly disdainful, and there had been times when a look or whispered comment produced such sadness he had contemplated suicide. At work the women avoided even sharing the elevator with him if they could help it, such was their disgust at his bulk and his hair and his beard. The bosses at CJIS had wanted him to get a haircut, but he assured them you didn't need to be the all-American hero to punch a few keys and scan a fingerprint card. They probably feared he'd file if they hassled him too much and now they let him be. His work rate and ability did all the talking for him.

The man in the basement smoothed the black gloves more tightly over his fingers. He took the ski mask from his pocket, set the gun down and pulled the mask over his head.

Carter showered for the second time that day, taking his time, washing his hair with shampoo and conditioner, running the flat of his hands through the tangled locks so that strands came away, littering the tub and clogging the plughole. He always waited till the water was completely gone before he hooked the lost hair out. He could tell by the thickness of the clump whether he was losing more than usual. He figured he wasn't: his hair was still thick and black, a little less in front these days but barely receding at all. He finished towelling off, put on a robe and went downstairs, where he pumped up the furnace. It was very cold again tonight, too cold maybe to snow.

Upstairs he checked the contents of his bank account: that always gave him a thrill, to see how much he had accumulated over so short a period. What a difference to two years ago when his tax deductions had all but wiped clean his pay check. He glanced at the notes he had scribbled, ran a thumb down the spine of a textbook on Louisiana history and congratulated himself on his internet investigation. It was his perfect choice of words, his assumed identity that had worked this particular miracle. Never had a voice gone so quiet so quickly. Never had he been taken so seriously. Once this was over he'd quit. There would be more than enough money to go to Tallahassee, perhaps he would move there for good. Maybe even get married. The future was bright and the possibilities were endless.

The man in the basement stood up, dressed all in black, masked and with a gun in his hand. In the pocket of his coat he had a roll of duck tape. He had a length of cheese wire.

The feelings of paranoia that had plagued Carter the whole day were banished as he waited for the appointed time to log on and talk to his girlfriend. He decided they would have to meet sooner rather than later and thought he might pose the question tonight if the opportunity arose. He had an e-card ready to mail her for Christmas. He'd designed it himself and had considered exactly what he would write for a long time, much more time than he'd taken with his mother's present. He glanced at the – as yet – unwrapped turtle lamp and a pang of guilt pricked him.

Jeannie-Anne logged on to the internet, bathed and per-fumed and as feminine as she felt these days. She thought briefly of the comments she received every day, her flesh wobbling against the material of her sweatpants, watch strap lost in the reddened folds of her wrist. Two chins, three chins, the sniggers she had suffered at school, the sniggers before she dropped out of college and the two chairs they set for her in the staffroom at work. They knew nothing about her, who she was or what she thought. All they saw was a mass of white flesh, rolls of lard, her back, her bottom, her breasts. But she didn't care. *Here* she was herself, here she was alive with every sense in her being, and the anticipation was delicious. She knew Max felt the same way. They were two lost souls forced to moved spectrally in the world of virtual reality, passed over by the living.

But it didn't matter. They were who they were and such had been the depth of their communication that she was more hopeful about the future than she had ever been. Soon he would suggest they meet up: he had already hinted at it, but not come right out with it. Still shy about his weight probably. It was the same for her – dating had never been easy. She had not pushed the issue when he dropped the hints, just letting him build up to it. She liked a man to be the man in a relationship. The very word *relationship* delighted her: it was something she had been denied until now.

Carter logged on and sat back, waiting for her reply. He completely forgot about the tyre tracks and the sound of the engine and the paranoia high stakes had generated. He forgot about Christmas, about sealing the card and wrapping the sculptured turtle lamp for his mother. He lost himself in the screen and Jeannie-Anne and the rush of conversation like a release valve in his soul. He told her about his day, how he would be spending tomorrow and how he wished they could spend it together. It was the biggest hint he had dropped yet, but it was Christmas Eve and he was feeling bold tonight.

He didn't hear the man on the basement steps.

He didn't hear the door open and close.

He didn't hear the loose board on the stairs.

He heard nothing till a shadow fell across the screen and the pressure of a gun barrel was cold against his cheek.

Jeannie-Anne read what he had written, felt the thrill rush through her and typed in her reply.

That would've been great, to spend the holiday together just you and me. I'll probably be on my own tomorrow. My mom lives out of town and I've got to work on Tuesday. It doesn't matter, so long as we can talk tomorrow night. Can we talk tomorrow night?

She waited, willing him to suggest getting together, maybe for the New Year or something. She looked at the screen, the flickering cursor like a video printer waiting for racing results. But he didn't reply. The seconds felt like minutes. She bent over the keyboard again.

Can we talk tomorrow night?

Carter sat perfectly still, sweat flecking his brow as the masked man traced the barrel of the gun round the base of his skull. Like fingered caresses he drew lines across his neck and shoulders, easing the gun over sagging male breasts exposed by the gap in his robe. Carter's eyes remained fixed on the screen.

Max?

Max, are you still there?

He couldn't reply. She was talking to him and he couldn't reply.

The man in the mask pressed the gun against his forehead. He handed him a roll of silver tape and pointed to his feet. Carter looked at the screen as Jeannie spoke to him again.

What's up, Max? Have I said something wrong?

Carter was trembling, literally quivering, and all his flesh moved. He tied his own feet to the swivel stem of the chair. He tried to speak, but the man lifted a finger to the gash in the mask where his mouth was. Now he took Carter's arms and wound tape about his wrists, tying them behind his back. When he was done he spun him round and round, slowly at first so that Carter could still see Jeannie trying to contact him. He imagined her confusion, such intimacies then suddenly nothing. He spun faster and the words began to blur.

Max, Max, are you there?

Jeannie-Anne stared at the stillness of the screen and felt her hopes for Christmas begin to fall apart. Why didn't he answer? Was he playing games with her as others had done before him? She didn't think she could stand that. He had seemed so genuine. Again she tapped the keys.

Carter stopped spinning, tape over his mouth now, revolving before his captor like meat on a spit. He looked at the masked face and the gun and the screen.

Max, why don't you answer? Don't play games with me, please.

His breath stuck in his chest as the man dangled a length of cheese wire in front of his face. The man threaded the wire under his flabby left thigh. He waited a moment then crossed the wire and slowly began to tighten, the wooden handles gripped in black-gloved hands. Carter's eyes were on stalks. He felt the sharp, stabbing pain. The wire was tightened and tightened and the flesh puckered white and blue. It broke the skin and blood flowed. Then the artery burst and the scream died in the tape over his mouth. Blood leapt in ropes to spatter the desk and keyboard. Blood spattered his robe, the carpet; it soaked the leg of the desk.

His killer stood straight then bent his face close. He touched the barrel of the gun to Carter's temple then moved to the door. For a moment he looked back. Carter strained to see him. Then he was gone and Carter was left helplessly staring at his leg, where the artery had been severed and his life was pumping from him in thick red spurts. He stared at the screen, unable to move, barely able to breathe.

And Jeannie tried to talk to him.

Max, Max, are you there?

two

Christmas Day

Harrison sipped coffee, standing on the porch of his rented house with the morning sun on his face. The field before him was covered in thick uninterrupted snow that encircled the foot of the lone Douglas fir and carried to the fence and the highway. The farmer who leased him the place had guests for the holiday, but his house was way back up the hill and all Harrison could hear were a couple of ravens calling across an empty sky.

He finished his coffee and considered what Christmas Day would have been like if Santini hadn't been on her own and asked him over for lunch. He had never looked forward to this time of year, it only served to accentuate his aloneness. He hesitated to use the word loneliness even to himself, because to admit to being lonely would be a final indictment of the way he had lived his life, which at fifty years of age was now beginning to bother him. Santini's company was good for him. She was forty, divorced twice and feisty; originally from Clarksburg, one of the forty per cent of Italians that made up the population. She was dark-eyed and acid-tongued and attractive in a European sort of a way. Harrison knew that he liked her a lot: he just wasn't prepared to admit it.

He tossed the dregs of his coffee into the snow where it steamed in a splatter of smoking holes. Setting the cup on the post, he plucked a single Marlboro cigarette from the pocket of his shirt. Always the one smoke scraped out of the box. To an onlooker it appeared they were loose in his shirt. He snapped his service issue Zippo and drew smoke into his lungs for the fifty thousandth time in his life. He hadn't taken up the habit before he'd gone into the army and he blamed the Viet Cong for the state of his chest.

He took his time scraping the ice from the windshield of his new Chevy pickup while the engine warmed the cab. He had kept his old one for years, a classic with a bench seat and three-speed shift on the column. When he sat in the driver's seat of the new one, however, he realized it was about time he offered some comfort to his worn-out bones.

He drove slowly into town. Santini lived on the far side of Clarksburg, and as he had volunteered for call-out duty he decided he would swing by the resident agency and see if it looked any different on December 25th.

He cruised the handful of miles to Bridgeport and nodded to the state trooper parked by the BP station before he crossed the railroad tracks. Heading into Clarksburg, he left the highway at Joyce Street and pulled onto East Pike from the slip road where the state police *Drive Safe* poster adorned the wall of the parking lot. The light was red and he sat, engine idling, and fingered the length of his hair.

Harrison twisted the rear-view mirror so he could see his face and thought he looked weather-beaten and old. His hair looked thin where it was so long and tied back, stretching the skin on his forehead. Iron grey and straight like an Indian's. The light hit green and he gunned the motor, delighting in the simplicity of an automatic after years of the three-speed shift. No judder, no lurch, no moan of protest from the clutch. Little things, he told himself. Most everybody took it for granted but the little things in life had always pleased him the most.

He rode gently down East Pike, past the Mission thrift store where a couple of toothless old-timers sipped from bowls of soup. Harrison touched his finger to his temple in greeting. He crossed under the shadow of the highway as it passed over the city and glanced at the battered buildings to the left and right: Stonewall Jackson's home-town no longer benefited from the industry it used to.

Further down the street he noticed that the door to Bobby T's barber shop was open. The life-size cardboard cut-out of James Dean was pressed up against the window and the barber, a black guy of about forty, was sitting on the step wrapped up against the cold and sipping a glass of wine. Harrison pulled over and rolled down the passenger window.

'Merry Christmas,' he said.

'Merry Christmas to you.'

Harrison squinted at the open door. 'Don't you got no home to go to?'

'Don't you?'

'I'm working. You working?'

'I figured I might. You want a haircut?'

'You figure I need one?'

'That's up to you.' The barber swallowed more wine. 'I reckon if I had a go at that it'd not be so much of a haircut as a change of life.'

'You might have a point.'

'You want to go for it, then?'

'Might as well.'

The barber stood up and carried his glass inside. Harrison locked the truck and followed him.

He poured Harrison some wine and they toasted Christmas and then Harrison sat in the chair, his hair hanging well below his shoulders, and looking at himself in the mirror. He glanced at his watch – plenty of time before Santini was expecting him. He set his Nextel communicator on the counter and sat back. He was fifty years old and he'd had hair like this since he quit the border patrol back in 1974.

The barber told him his name was Mike and he had been cutting hair for only six years. Harrison watched him in the mirror and figured that his right eye was prosthetic, as it didn't work in quite the same way as the other one. Mike caught him watching and grinned.

'You want me to pop it out?'

'That your party piece?'

'Sometimes. Now and again I go to a lap-dancing club, you know, for a little recreation. I like to set it on the counter so I can get a better look.'

Harrison laughed. 'Bet the girls just love that.'

'I reckon they see pretty much everything in those joints. Don't figure my glass eye's gonna bother them.'

Mike told him that he had been in the army and Harrison listened, watching his hair and his past fall away in the mirror. Mike had been big on basketball and had played for the army team. One day an opponent accidentally poked his eye out and his team-mates had to hold his arms at his sides so he couldn't touch it where it lay on his cheek. The opponent was so upset about it that for weeks afterwards he followed Mike round like a puppy: in the end it got so bad he had to go and see the sergeant to get the guy off his back.

Mike cut his hair to his shoulders and stopped. 'The weight is off – you look younger. You want me to keep going?'

Harrison barrelled his lips and exhaled. 'Nope. That'll do for now. Don't want to give myself a heart attack, man of my age.' His Nextel rang where it lay on the counter. He picked it up. 'Harrison.'

'This is the SAC, John. Where are you?'

'A barber's shop in Clarksburg.'

'I just had a call from Captain Rollins of the FBI police at CJIS. There's been a homicide.'

'At CJIS?'

'No, in Bridgeport. Rollins is reporting it to the locals now.'

'Do we know who the victim is?'

'Maxwell Carter, he worked as a fingerprint analyst. His mother found him dead at his home this morning. She called Rollins because he's the first person she thought of. Not our jurisdiction really, but a federal employee. Get yourself over there, will you?'

'OK.' Harrison switched off the phone.

Outside he called the Bridgeport police headquarters located behind the Holiday Inn just off Highway 50. Then he called Santini at home.

'Hey, Francesca, it's me. Can we eat lunch for dinner?'

'Why, what's going on?'

Harrison told her and they arranged to meet at the victim's house in Bridgeport. He turned his truck around, fixed the blue light on the dashboard and raced through town to rejoin the highway by the cemetery.

When he pulled up outside the white clapboard house on Zappia Drive two Bridgeport PD cruisers were bumped up on the kerb. In the distance he could hear sirens, which he figured was either Santini or the crime scene unit from Clarksburg. Two patrolmen he didn't recognize were spreading tape across the yard to keep people out – a number were already gathered on their steps and porches opposite or peering through condensation-soaked windows. Harrison approached the tape and a young patrolman in a tan-coloured uniform looked up at him. He had the dark brown Bridgeport issue turtleneck under his shirt.

'You the Feds?'

Harrison flashed his shield and stepped under the tape. 'You got a detective coming?'

'Tom Proud.'

'I bet he's just delighted. Christmas Day and all.' Harrison rested a fist against the roof support on the porch. 'What do we have inside?'

'Maxwell Carter in his bathrobe and tied to a chair upstairs. Looks like he bled to death.' The young officer's face was pale green at the jawbone. Harrison could smell the residue of vomit on his breath.

'Your first one, huh?'

'Yessir. You don't expect too many in this neck of the woods.'

Harrison laid a hand on his shoulder. 'It's why I came up here, my friend. Lowest crime rate in the country – allegedly.' Nodding to the other patrolman, he went inside the house.

He was careful where he trod, keeping well to the sides of the tiny hallway. The killer may have entered or vacated the scene by that route and he would have walked in the middle of the floor unless he was very professional. Beyond the hall a glass door opened into the living room and dining area. The kitchen was separate and off to the side, overlooking the front yard. Harrison paused and looked around. The house was neat and tidy: no dust on the wooden arms of the chairs or the telephone table, everything looked in its place, nothing appeared to be disturbed. This didn't look like a robbery.

The stairs were wooden boards with a section of light blue carpet stretched across the middle of each step. They rose steeply to a landing before doubling back on themselves. Harrison moved in an arc across the living room floor, picking out the details as he went. Not bad, he told himself, for an aging guy with attitude who had spent more time with the bad guys than the good. He tried to remember the last time he had actually worked as a case agent.

Sirens signalled two cars pulling up outside and he turned before the stairs and went back to the kitchen. Santini parked her police package Impala behind his truck and Detective Proud of the Bridgeport Police was climbing from a Suburban. He looked pissed off. Who wouldn't? He had a family and it was Christmas. Harrison waited to one side of the stairs as they crunched across the packed snow to the door.

'Johnny Buck with nothing better to do,' Proud greeted him. 'What we got here?'

'A DOA who worked at CJIS is all I know. He's upstairs.

Your boys outside have made their obvious death determination. They tell me he bled to death.'

'They called the doctor?'

Harrison shrugged. 'I never asked.'

Santini came in behind Proud and smiled at Harrison. Harrison had liked her as soon as he'd met her. She had been his friend and confidante ever since he arrived back in the job after nine months out. He had left the Bureau just over a year ago, but headquarters had talked him back so he could teach recruits at the academy. He said he'd do the odd class, but if he was coming back he still wanted to be out in the field. West Virginia was a quiet resident agency only four hours' drive from DC so they offered him that on the proviso he would come into Quantico at least once a month.

He had been a civilian for the first time in years, trying to get some kind of life going other than working for the FBI. He went to London with a Vietnamese doctor called Jean Carey. He had met her while working special operations out of New Orleans. The relationship hadn't worked out, though, or at least not in the way he had hoped, and when the legal attaché in London told him he was being courted again by the suits, flattery got the better of him. He still talked to Jean from time to time but given he was back here the chances of anything working out long term had dwindled. They had met in extreme circumstances and like so many cases, when the danger was over so was most of what had attracted them. He had seen it too many times to lick his wounds for long.

Santini moved round the edge of the living room. 'You had a haircut,' she said. 'I never thought I'd see the day.'

'This morning.' Harrison fingered the ends of his hair.

'Don't tell me you're going all Establishment on me. I was just getting used to the hillbilly look. And how did you manage to find a barber working on Christmas Day?'

'I just drove by. Bobby T's on East Pike. A one-eyed ex-soldier called Mike. We shared a glass of wine and a little Christmas spirit then I let him loose on the locks.'

Detective Proud was watching them. 'Another guy as sad and lonely as you, huh?' He packed the chew under his lip with his tongue. 'Let's get on with this, shall we? I got a houseful to get back to.'

'Take off now if you want to,' Santini told him. 'We can always make this federal right from the get go. Ten bucks says we steal it from you anyways.'

'You can kiss my hillbilly ass, Santini.'

Proud led the way upstairs, being careful to keep to one side. He wondered where he was going to get some electronic gear to lift any prints from the carpet. Harrison guessed his thoughts. 'We got equipment in Pittsburgh, Tom. Oh, and the boss has already offered our evidence response team if you want it.' He exchanged a wicked glance with Santini. 'We know how tough these *real* crimes are on you small town departments.'

Proud looked sourly at him, shifted the tobacco in his mouth but said nothing.

Harrison could smell blood from the landing. It was thick and metallic in his nostrils as if it was not quite dry. He could see the limits of the pool where it had spread in rivers, little muddy bayous running out of the room. The carpet was light blue like the stairs, but beyond the second doorway it was heavily stained. The door stood wide open. Proud went in first, and Harrison heard him take in breath. He glanced at Santini and followed.

The victim was slumped in a chair at his computer, huge and white and naked save a bathrobe that gaped open. The bloodstain ran from the door right to the body. It gathered round his left foot, which was hooked up on the toes like a ballet dancer and tied to the swivel stem with silver duck tape. The flesh was caked with flaky dried blood below the knee. Harrison crouched on his haunches. Santini stood next to him.

25

'Skinny mother, is he,' Harrison muttered.

'A real regular waif.'

Maxwell Carter had been a huge man: Harrison considered his bulk, drained of every drop of blood now. His head was slumped to one side, beard on his shoulder like an extra growth of hair, eyes half closed. Duck tape bound his wrists, which had been wrenched so hard behind him, bruising showed at the shoulders. A sliver of tape silenced his mouth like a shiny gash in his beard.

Harrison glanced at Proud who squatted down next to him. He was concentrating on the left thigh where the wound seemed to have been inflicted. Harrison looked more closely and at first the wound itself disguised it, but the two wooden handles gave it away.

Cheese wire.

He stood up suddenly, the breath tight in his chest.

Santini stared at him. 'Take it easy, cowboy – are you OK?'

He didn't answer her. In his mind's eye he saw another length of cheese wire, another wound, only the flesh was young and black and it was the neck that had been torn open.

'There's no other sign of injury.' Proud straightened up with a crack of his knees. 'Guess we better wait for the doc, but it does look like he bled to death.'

Santini was bending over the desk. 'Take a look at this,' she said. 'His computer's switched on.'

Harrison moved alongside her and studied the spiral of lights that was Carter's screen saver. Santini pursed her lips and pulled on a pair of tight-fitting surgical gloves. She pressed the space bar on the keyboard.

'He was logged on,' she said, a little edge to her voice. 'He was logged on to the internet.' They all stared at the screen now, where Jeannie-Anne's last words were still visible.

Max, Max, are you there?

Proud was leaning next to Santini now, staring at the

screen. 'He was talking to somebody. Some kind of chat room, maybe?'

Santini scrolled higher up the text. 'It looks more like a one-to-one. Whoever it was, they're no longer logged on. It looks as though they could've been when whatever happened happened, though.' She pointed to the screen. 'It looks like he just stopped talking. I can check the internet provider and find out who it was.'

Harrison was taking in the rest of the room, twin heavy filing cabinets to one side of the computer, a closet, an aged bureau of drawers. A K-Mart bag lay on top of it and he nosed the contents with a pencil: some peanut brownies; a glass lamp made in the shape of a turtle. On one of the filing cabinets was an envelope with a Christmas card, padded and depicting a rose, lying on top. Harrison looked at the inscription inside: *To my mother, keep safe, Maxwell*. He assumed the lamp was for her as well. $16.99. Cheap-assed sonofabitch.

He decided he didn't like Carter and then he wondered at himself. What a great advert for the job. The poor guy had just been murdered and he decided he didn't like him. He glanced at the contents of the bag once more and decided it was just as well he'd spent most of his career in the special ops group. He looked over at Santini who caught his eye and smiled. It stirred him, that smile: it had right from when they'd met. Now Santini *was* a good case agent: she'd originally trained as an attorney, been top student in her class at the academy and dealt with all the bullshit women could get in a field office. She watched him watching. 'What are you thinking, Harrison?'

Harrison looked at Proud. 'I'm thinking this is Bridgeport PD jurisdiction. I want to know what he's thinking.'

Proud let go a stiff breath. 'Well, obviously this guy was a surfer. Not the sleekest guy on a board but rode the waves nonetheless. I don't know, maybe he got his kicks on that way.'

'I don't see any web cam,' Santini said.

'Well, whatever.' Proud stuck his hands in his pockets. 'Do you know what else I think? I think this is Christmas Day. I think I'm gonna stick around long enough for the doc to do his thing, then let Clarksburg crime scene pat the place down. You two guys do me a favour so I can get back to my family before midnight, will you?'

'Go see the mother?' Santini said.

'Yeah. Help me out there, would you?'

Harrison patted his shoulder. 'Sure thing, partner. We'll see you tomorrow.'

He and Santini left the house as the crime scene van rolled up with its blue light flashing and the rubbernecks still across the road. Proud was right, there was nothing they could do today. A patrolman would be posted and they'd all be back in the morning. Carter would still be dead and his mother would still be grieving.

They took both vehicles and drove out to the address the patrolman had given them at Maple Lake. Mrs Carter lived in a two-storey house on the far side of the lake down the little hill from the highway. There was a small cannon in the garden – for ornamental purposes, Harrison assumed. The house was blue with maroon shutters, and a small Toyota sedan was parked in the drive, snow still clinging to the roof in places. Harrison guessed Mrs Carter drove very slowly.

She answered the door – a diminutive woman, her flesh folded at the neck, wearing cat's-eye glasses set in pale blue frames. Harrison was reminded of the carpet in her son's house. Her eyes were puffed red, and her pale skin streaked where tears had run with powder. She peered out at them and blinked. 'Can I help you?'

'We're from the FBI, Mrs Carter,' Santini said gently.

'Oh, yes, of course. Please do come in.'

The house was stifling, it felt as though the furnace was turned up full. All the windows were closed and the air was thick with dust particles that danced where light creased the windows. They stood in the hall and Harrison looked down at the old woman, so tiny, sparrow-like almost, delicately attired in a grey suit and matching grey shoes. She looked like she had just come back from church.

'Mrs Carter, I'm special agent Santini and this is agent Dollar. We're so sorry for your loss, ma'am.' Santini spoke softly, taking the old woman's hand lightly between her palms. 'We'd like to talk to you for a little bit then we'll leave you in peace. Is that OK?'

'Yes.'

Santini smiled. 'Do you have any other family?'

Mrs Carter nodded. 'I've got daughters in Virginia. I called them. They're driving over.'

'Good, you won't be on your own, then.' Santini still held her hand. 'You found him. That must have been a terrible shock.'

The old woman sank into a chair. 'It was. Awful. In his bathrobe and all that blood.' She choked a little on the words, tears misting her eyes. 'I suppose he must have just taken a bath. He was always one for being clean, often he would bathe or shower twice a day. He was sitting at his computer.'

'We think he was talking to somebody,' Harrison said, 'on the computer. Would you have any idea who that might have been?'

Mrs Carter shook her head. 'I'm sorry. I don't know much about computers. Is it important?'

'It might be. Don't worry. We'll find out.'

Santini sat on the couch opposite her and glanced at the selection of framed photographs on the walls and the bureau and the mantelpiece above the fire.

'Is there a Mr Carter?' she asked.

The old woman shook her head. 'He died.'

'And these people are the rest of the family?'

'My daughters and their husbands and children.' She

forced down a sob. 'I knew something was going to happen. I just knew it. All day yesterday I had the feeling.'

'You knew?' Santini looked at her. 'Did your son say anything to you? Was he frightened or concerned about something? Was he in any kind of trouble?'

'No, he didn't say anything to me, but I knew. Madame Josephine knew.'

'Who is Madame Josephine?'

'You mean the reader?' Harrison sat down on the couch. 'The psychic lady?' He drove by here every day and he'd seen Madame Josephine's advertisement many times. 'Up on top of the hill there?'

Mrs Carter nodded. 'I go there now and again. For comfort mostly, though my pastor wouldn't agree with it. I miss my husband, you see.'

Harrison nodded. 'And Madame Josephine told you something about your son? I didn't think readers did stuff like that.'

Mrs Carter shook her head. 'She didn't tell me in so many words. I had a reading, my tarot. You know.' She paused and looked for a moment out of the window. The sun was high, casting strands of rainbow-coloured lights off the ice that crusted the lake. 'She laid the cards. She saw something. I always watch her eyes when she lays the cards. I know she saw something.' She looked at Harrison again. 'Something in the cards.'

'Did your son have any enemies, Mrs Carter?' Santini asked her.

'Enemies?'

Santini nodded. 'It didn't look as though the house was disturbed. We don't know for sure yet, but it didn't look like anything had been stolen.'

'I don't think he has any enemies. All he does is go to work and come home. He goes to the bowling alley now and again, but he's not the sort of man to have enemies.' She broke off and looked at his picture framed on the mantelpiece. 'I only went round when he was late this morning. I called and called on the telephone, but he didn't answer. I was worried in case he got sick. He has high blood pressure, you see, the weight and everything.'

'And you just found him like that in the chair.'

She nodded and her eyes buckled at the corners. 'He leaves a key for me under a flowerpot by the step. You know, for when he's away. I let myself in and called out to him. He didn't answer me, though.'

They left her then and called in next door, telling the neighbours, a middle-aged couple, what had happened. They said they would look after Mrs Carter until her family arrived.

Santini lived beyond Nutter Fort in a single-storey house that smelled of fresh flowers. She grew a whole garden full of them, her one and only passion, she told Harrison. Even in winter there were fresh flowers in the vases. Harrison hung up his coat and inspected his hair in the mirror. It was a hell of a lot shorter, but still beyond his collar.

'It looks good,' Santini told him. 'Makes you look younger, lifts your face.'

Harrison rubbed a calloused hand across his jowls. 'That'll work, then. Cheaper than the surgeon.'

'You wouldn't want to lose all those lines, Harrison. Nobody would recognize you.'

'Santini, you always did know how to make a guy feel good about himself. You know that?'

She laughed. 'I try my best. Seriously, though, you've had long hair ever since you joined the Bureau – why now to get it cut?'

'I don't know.' Harrison leaned on the worktop. 'I just fancied a change, I guess.'

She passed him a long-necked bottle of beer. 'Not a mid-life crisis, then.'

'Are you kidding me? I passed mid-life years ago.'

'What're you talking about? You're still a bitty kid. You'll go on for ever.'

He laughed. 'You keep telling me that. My bones are getting old, I can feel it.'

'Creaky gates always last the longest. That's what my grandma always told me.' She clinked his bottle with hers. 'Merry Christmas, Harrison.'

'Merry Christmas.' Harrison kissed her lightly on the lips and for a moment they looked at one another, then he averted his eyes.

'You know, I often wonder about you,' Santini said.

'What about me exactly?'

'Being a regular case agent now. You haven't done that for years. Everybody knows you as the original undercover agent. Don't you miss the work?'

'Nope.'

'You mean not at all?'

'Nope.'

'Will you do it again?'

'No, I'm way too old.' Harrison plucked a cigarette from his shirt pocket, menthol this time. He alternated between Marlboro and menthols, a pack in each shirt pocket. 'Undercover work's a young man's business.'

Santini offered him a match. 'And you're not young any more.'

'I don't feel young. Put it that way.'

Santini started preparing dinner. 'Do you want to work this case?' she asked him.

'I don't know. It's reactive squad stuff. I'm not really reactive squad.' He looked through her and saw Carter's empty body and the dangling handles of the cheese wire in his mind's eye.

'Do you want me to work it?' Santini said.

'Do you want to?'

'You took the call, Harrison. You were the one who volunteered to work Christmas Day.'

He made a face. 'I guess we could work it together. You want to work it together?'

'Sure, why not.'

He sipped beer. 'Do you figure we should have done more at the crime scene maybe?'

'I don't think so.' She went to the stove and tasted gravy from a teaspoon. 'By the time the medical examiner's through and the evidence response team, there's not much more we could do. The Bridgeport uniforms will be conducting a neighbourhood search. The body will be in the morgue and nobody's going to disturb anything at the crime scene. It's Christmas Day, Harrison. Let's enjoy ourselves like regular people. Besides, did you see Tom Proud busting any blood vessels out there?'

Harrison sat on a high stool, resting his elbows on the work counter, and finished his beer. 'She was a sweet old lady,' he said. 'The asshole only spent seventeen bucks on her for Christmas.'

Santini stared at him. 'What?'

'Mrs Carter. Her son only spent seventeen dollars on her Christmas present.'

'How do you know?'

'Because I saw what he bought her – a turtle lamp from K-Mart. Seventeen dollars bar the penny.'

'How do you know it was for his mother?'

'Who else would he buy a turtle lamp for?' He shook his head at himself then. 'See what I mean about getting old. Listen to me, cantankerous sonofabitch.'

Santini squinted at him, a light in the back of her eyes. 'Maybe you just need to feel young for a while again.'

'You think?'

'Don't you?'

'Depends what you got in mind exactly.'

'Who said I had anything in mind? It's you we're talking about.'

'Is it?'

'I don't hear anyone else bitching and whining.'

Harrison laughed.

They ate dinner and watched some TV then Santini put a match to the coals she had ready in the fireplace and lay down on the rug like a cat. She shifted the weight of her hair from her eyes. It hung loose now and thick about her face, where normally it was scraped back from her head. Her shoulder rig and ankle holster were laid over the back of a chair. They were both issued Sig Sauers but Harrison had preferred the stopping power of a .45 since he went in deep. A 9-mm shell could go right through a person without them knowing they were hit. A hollow point .45 would stop a bear.

He lay back on the couch with his boots off, ankles crossed on the coffee table, sipping red wine and smoking.

'How come you never got married?' she asked him.

'How come you did it twice?'

'Now, that's a good question.' Santini sat up again and crossed her legs. 'I guess I fell in love twice, or thought I did at least. I guess I decided to risk it. I may have trained as an attorney, Harrison, but I'm Italian. We take risks. I think I like the risk factor.'

'Which is why you joined the FBI instead of some corporate law firm.'

'Exactly. That and the money. I just couldn't live with myself if I earned that much money.' She made a face and sipped wine. 'Two husbands, two divorces and no kids. I got something right at least, didn't leave quite so much of a trail of debris behind me. I tell you what,' she went on, 'let's change the subject. Why do you figure someone would want to kill Carter?'

'I have no idea.'

'What did he do at CJIS?'

'Worked as a fingerprint analyst.' Harrison sat forward. 'The boss will have notified Fitzpatrick by now. I'm surprised he hasn't called.'

'Fitzpatrick the assistant director at CJIS?'

'Yes. I worked for him when I was in special ops in New Orleans.'

'You want to work the CJIS end, then?'

'I guess it makes sense, if you don't mind hanging around with Proud.'

'I don't mind.' She smiled. 'Not till tomorrow, though, eh? Today is Christmas.'

Harrison looked at her. 'I never got you anything. A present or card, I mean.'

'I didn't either.'

'That's good. We're even, then.'

Still he looked at her, the firelight casting shadows that darkened the flesh beneath her cheekbones. He could smell her scent, delicate in a way which was most unlike her: she was brassy and in your face, but she looked and smelt very feminine.

'Would you like to go to bed, Harrison?' she asked him.

He sat up straighter, face suddenly red. 'Excuse me?'

'You heard me. It's Christmas, you need to feel younger and I'm asking if you want to go to bed?'

'But I'm old.'

'You only think you are.'

'How do you know?'

'Call it women's intuition.' She stood up, shook her hair out and stretched. 'I'm getting older myself, so I guess we're both running out of time.'

Harrison stood for a moment then he took her in his arms a little awkwardly. 'Even so,' he said. 'Just be gentle with me. OK?'

They took a shower together and the water ran between her breasts, high and full with firm dark nipples. Her skin was the dusky hue of her Mediterranean ancestry, dark hairs licked her forearms and massed pubic hair ran now with water. Harrison pushed stiff fingers through the dampness of her hair. He kissed her neck, bruising her with hard lips and tongue. He took her there in the shower, up against the tiles, his chest against her back while the warmth of the water flowed between them.

Dried and robed, they sat again by the fire, a fresh bottle of red wine between them. Harrison smoked and flicked ash into the flames.

'It doesn't mean anything, does it?' Santini said.' What we just did, I mean. It was just – you know – sex.'

'I guess. Unless you want it to mean something.'

'You think that's a good idea?'

'Who knows? Probably not.' Harrison sipped wine. 'I mean, we work together, don't we.'

'It's not against the rules. Working together. I know married couples that work in the same office.' Santini put wood on the fire. 'Probably best if we leave it where it's at, though, huh?'

'Probably.'

She looked at him. 'I don't mean to sound hard.'

'You don't. We're all grown up, Fran. We're friends who got it together one time.'

'Just the once, then.'

He looked at his wine and then in her eyes and then they both burst out laughing.

'Listen to us,' Santini said, 'two hard-assed cops egg-shelling around like a couple of kids in high school.' Her eyes softened. 'Let's just see how it goes, shall we?'

'Sounds good to me.' He crushed out his cigarette.

'Can I ask you something?' Santini sat back and her robe parted from the neck to her navel.

'Of course.'

'Back there in Carter's house when you saw that cheese wire for the first time, you looked really troubled. I know it was a homicide and everything but you've seen homicides before. I mean, your eyes were all busted up.'

Harrison was silent. He bit his lip and for a moment he was in Bill Chaisson's office in Jefferson Parish, Louisiana.

He was looking at pictures that disturbed him much more than they should. He blinked the images away and glanced at Santini again. 'It was nothing,' he said. 'You forget I've been undercover for years. I don't see that many homicides.'

Santini looked unimpressed but she didn't push the point any further. Instead, she stood up and slipped off her robe. Naked, she held out her hand and led him into the bedroom.

three

The black kid wearing a thin red jacket was annoying the jazz quintet who had set up on Royal Street and St Peter in the French Quarter of New Orleans. The quintet was a regular fixture when the road was closed off, two blocks east of the Vieux Carré 8th District police station. The old-timer on the double bass was trying to play but the kid kept jumping off the kerb and getting in his way. The singer was a black man with one finger missing, a silver ring in his right ear and his hair receding in tightly knotted curls. He wore red trousers and a multicoloured waistcoat, his aging portable amplifier on the sidewalk at his feet.

'Hey, kid, quit doing that.' He grabbed the young boy by the shoulder and spun him round. 'Come on, son. Be a man. Behave like a man.'

'I ain't no man, am I. You just said I was a kid.'

'You is a kid, boy, but I'm axing you to act like a man.'

The kid flipped him the bird, then sauntered through the crowd of tourists and snatched the purse from a woman's bag as he brushed past her.

Junya sat in the doorway of an art gallery, smoking a cigarette and watching. He had one last rock in his pocket and he worked it between his fingers. The boy moved away from the quintet now as they struck up once again, trumpets and bass and a small piano fastened to the back of a cart. The boy moved his way, shoulders swinging, baggy jeans flapping at the ankles. It was cold for this time of year in New Orleans. Junya had spent Christmas Day on Grand Terre at the southern tip of the Barataria with Marie and the others. Today he was working and the wind nipped at him, down as low as thirty degrees, or so Marie said. Any alligator not hibernating out in the swamp would be dead. Podjo told him that just before the crew split for the holiday there were sections of ice on the bayou.

The kid came swaggering towards him. Junya dragged on his cigarette and lifted his hood over his head. The boy looked just like *he* used to only he was darker, more obviously black. Junya figured he himself was mulatto, though he had no real idea where he came from. He remembered that his mother was black but had never met his father. He looked the boy up and down, ten or eleven maybe, just the age he had been when he started.

'What's up, brother?' he said, as the kid moved past.

The kid paused and looked back, stuffing the stolen purse further down in his pocket

'How much you figure you get?'

The kid frowned.

'The pocket book, how much you figure?'

'What pocket book?'

'Come on, my man.' Junya stood up and hunched his own baggy jeans higher up on his hips. 'I saw what you did – real cool, brother. Couldn't do no better myself.' Junya stepped closer to him and brushed knuckles. 'Step this way, my man. They gonna figure it was you just as soon as she finds out it's gone.'

He led the kid down towards the back of St Louis Cathedral and into Jackson Square.

'What's your name, brother?'

'Spix.'

'Spix?' Junya stopped, hands on his hips. 'What kinda name is that?'

The kid shifted his shoulders. 'It's just what I get called. What you all called?'

Junya took a pack of cigarettes from his pocket, lit two and handed one to Spix. 'You just call me Nonk.'

'Nonk. What the fuck kinda name is Nonk?'

'It's a Cajun name, my man.'

'Y'all is Cajun?'

'Nah. I know it means uncle, though, and I figure I'm yo' uncle today. Getting yo' out of trouble and all.'

'What trouble?'

'Spix, my man.' Junya slipped an arm round his shoulders. 'You was about to get busted. You took that pocket book not two blocks from the 8th District is what yo' did. Your old nonk here took you off the street. Right about now that lady is describing you to the po-lice.' He headed off along Decatur.

'Where you going?' Spix called after him.

'I'm getting off the street, of course. I don't want no cop busting my ass.'

Spix scratched bitten-down nails over his short-cropped hair. Junya looked back at him. 'You not coming, suit yo'self, my man. I'll see you around.' He crossed between two mule-drawn wagons. The boy would follow; he knew he would. He was like Junya had been himself – he could spot them a mile away, on the street and on their own, just like he had been.

'Hey, Nonk, wait up.'

He paused and looked back as the kid skipped between a taxicab and a biker. 'What we gonna do?' he asked as he ran up.

Junya looked at him then and smiled. From his pocket he took out the single rock of crack.

'You got any money?'

The kid fished in his pocket for the purse. He opened it and counted the bills. Fifty-seven dollars. Then he grinned from ear to ear. 'I got money,' he said.

Junya put an arm round his shoulders and they set off on the French Market side of Decatur and crossed back again.

40

They walked the full length to Esplanade where the people traffic thinned and they sauntered up the grassy median of the road, where cars were parked on either side.

'You wanna smoke some of this?' Junya said, indicating the crack.

'You kidding me?'

Again they brushed knuckles.

'You got a place to go?' Spix asked him. 'We can't smoke it on the street.'

'Oh, yeah.' Junya nodded slowly. 'I got a place.'

At the corner of Esplanade and Bourbon they turned left and Junya led the way back towards the centre of the Quarter.

'Where we going?' Spix asked him.

'We here.' Junya stopped at the back of a silver panel van with the back windows blacked out. He rapped the side and the back doors popped open. He gestured to the cushions laid out on the floor and Spix climbed in. Junya glanced behind him, to make sure they were not being overlooked, but this was the residential end of Bourbon Street and the houses were shuttered and barred against intruders. He climbed into the van and shut the doors behind him. Then he settled down next to Spix and took the rock of crack from his pocket. 'You got a pipe or you want me to make you one?' He tapped the panel behind his head and the engine started. Spix rubbed his palms together as the van pulled away from the kerb.

four

Harrison met Santini at 7.00 a.m. the day after Christmas. Their office was housed in the Federal building on West Pike Street and they shared the floor with both the District and US Attorneys, which saved a lot of time when they were looking to indict a suspect. Ray Somers, the supervisor, was in his office and called them both in.

'What do we know about this murder yesterday?' he asked them.

Harrison sat down and rested an ankle on his knee. 'Not much. The DOA was a guy named Maxwell Carter who worked at CJIS. His mother went round to his place on Zappia Avenue when he didn't show up for his lunch Christmas morning. She found him taped to a chair in front of his computer.'

'With a cheese wire slicing his leg to the bone.' Somers picked up a faxed sheet of paper. 'Bridgeport police sent this over. The medical examiner reported the cause of death as acute blood loss due to the severing of the femoral artery, some time between seven and eight p.m. on Christmas Eve.' He laid the paper aside. 'The report says the DOA was playing on his computer or at least it was switched on at the time.'

'The connection was broken but he had been on the internet,' Santini said. 'He was talking to what appears to be his girlfriend. I'm going to check with his internet provider for an address. That's if you want both of us to work on this, boss?'

Somers pressed his fingers to his chin. 'For the time being I do, yes.'

'I'll get on to the computer end of things now, then. Harrison was going to work CJIS.'

'Fine with me.' Somers looked back at the police report. 'The crime scene's intact. The Bridgeport chief has asked for our evidence response team to take a look at it. I don't think he's got much faith in the Clarksburg unit.'

The Criminal Justice Information Services Division of the FBI was state of the art: completed in 1995, it was the only facility of its kind in the world. Space-age-looking buildings housed the uprated National Crime Information Center, and formed the central repository for fingerprints in the United States. It had revolutionized crime-incident reporting since the inception of the idea.

Built amid nine hundred and eighty acres of rolling hills and woodland, it had become one of the largest employers in the area and cost the Bureau nothing: virtually all the funding had been raised by the local senator in exchange for his proposed site being chosen. There was a nine-mile perimeter, unfenced and patrolled by uniformed FBI police in trucks and on quad bikes. They were, according to some, the third largest police force in the state of West Virginia.

Harrison left I79 at Jerry Dove Drive and thought about the agent it had been named after. He thought about him every time he saw the exit sign. In 1986 two suspects in a stolen car in Miami had gunned Dove down: he was one of the FBI martyrs whose pictures were posted on the wall of every field office in the country.

Flashing his shield to the cops at the gate, Harrison drove the mile or so further to the facility itself. Snow covered the hills and deer clipped at what meagre grass straggled between the rocks. He passed the day-care building and parked in the lot out the back of the main facility. Kirk Fitzpatrick, the assistant director, met him in the lobby. He was a tall man with grey hair, the only agent in New Orleans who had worn his gun openly at the field office. His office had been closest to reception, which meant if they ever got troublemakers he was the first to respond. These days he wore an ankle rig like everyone else.

They shook hands. 'Captain Rollins called me about Carter yesterday,' Fitzpatrick said.

'Have you spoken to our SAC in Pittsburgh?'

'Briefly.'

'They're sending evidence response agents down this morning. Ought to be arriving about now.'

They took the elevator and Fitzpatrick showed him into his office. 'Are you the case agent, Johnny? That'd be a first.'

Harrison shrugged. 'That's what I do these days. There are no special ops in the resident agency. I'd have to go to Pittsburgh for that and I'm all done with cities.'

'All done with undercover work too, from what I hear. I have to tell you, I'm surprised you let them talk you back at all. What did they do – promise to stack up your pension?'

'Something like that.'

Harrison sat down on the mock leather chesterfield and Fitzpatrick settled in an armchair. 'This Carter thing is a local PD beef at the moment,' Harrison told him. 'A detective from Bridgeport will probably be along on his own account later.'

'What do we know so far?'

'Not a whole lot. The locals did a pretty good house-to-house yesterday afternoon, but there don't seem to be any witnesses.'

'What about enemies? Family?'

'We don't know yet. As far as family goes, there's his mother. An old lady, she lives out on Maple Lake. She had a premonition something was going to happen.' He told Fitzpatrick what Mrs Carter had told him.

'Mumbo-jumbo, the lot of it.'

'I figure. I'm going to speak to the reader anyway.'

Fitzpatrick sat forward. 'What do you want from us?'

'Just the usual. I'm going to need to speak to his colleagues, you know the kind of thing. Who he was, who he hung out with, etcetera.'

'You figure this might be work related in some way?'

'I don't know, Kirk, it could be.'

Fitzpatrick went to his desk and picked up a blue paper folder. 'I've got Carter's file right here. He was good, John. Started when we first arrived, went quickly from fingerprint analyst to supervisor then into the special processing unit.'

'Did he have much responsibility?'

'Some.'

'Access?'

'To the system, total.'

'Then that's where I want to start.'

Harrison was *en route* to the fingerprint floor when Santini called him.

'Where are you?' he asked her.

'I'm at Carter's house. The body's gone to the morgue, and the techs are here from the field office.'

'They turn anything up yet?'

'Not yet, they've only been at it a half-hour. I've got something, though.' Santini told him that Carter had been logged on to the internet from 7.30 p.m. till the connection broke by itself around 8.15 p.m. 'It seems he did have a girlfriend, of sorts,' she said. 'They met in a chat room and it was she he was talking to when whoever hit him hit. Her name is Jeannie-Anne Rae and she lives in Tallahassee, Florida. We've got a couple of agents on their way to the food mall where she works right now. There's a chance she can tell us something.' Santini told him she would call him again when the Florida agents got back to her. He snapped his phone shut and hung it on his belt.

The special processing unit was located at one end of the spacious floor occupied by the fingerprints analysts. Harrison spoke to Stephen Daly, the general manager, who gave him some background information. Since the facility had been built every law enforcement agency in the world had the opportunity to run a match for prints they picked up at crime scenes. Every set of felon prints in the US going back to 1924 was housed on the massive computer system that had been designed specifically for the purpose: forty-one million of them in total. The prints came in from all over the country, sometimes electronically and sometimes on a card, a rough 50–50 split. They were scanned into what was termed the integrated automated fingerprint identification system in the data centre. After that they were sent to the fingerprint comparison unit where an analyst would look for an 'ident' using the descriptive information on the card – name, sex, race, right hand, left hand and so on. If they found a match they would check it for actual physical identification via the unique minutiae of the prints themselves. With a confirmed 'ident' they would put it back into the system where it would automatically be reconfirmed or queried by another analyst. That was random, analysed on one workstation, then back into the queuing system to be looked at by somebody else.

'Tell me about Max Carter,' Harrison said.

Daly shrugged his shoulders. 'He was good – very good, in fact. Right from the get go. I came over from DC when the facility was relocated. Carter was a local guy, looked pretty weird for a government employee but he was always very good, very thorough indeed. He worked for me for about a year, I guess, then he got promoted.'

'Into special processing.'

'That's right.' Daly got up. 'I'll walk you over there, let one of the analysts talk you through what they do.'

Twenty people worked in special processing. All of them had at least three years' fingerprint analytical experience and all were very good. Harrison could sense the sombre atmosphere. The desks were laid out in modular office fashion, cubicle compartments where somebody was working all of the time. CJIS never closed: they ran three eight-hour shifts seven days a week, three hundred and sixty-five days a year.

Harrison wanted to speak to all the analysts, find out who was working and when, who knew Carter well, who knew him only a little. Daly went off to find the duty roster and Harrison sat down in Carter's empty space. Taking his tin of chew from his jacket pocket, he pressed a finger full under his lip and sucked the juice.

Carter's desk was as neat as his home had been – an office tidy pen and paperclip rack stuffed with pens in order of colour, all the right way up, a bottle of liquid paper, a sheaf of blank notepaper and a box of fingerprint cards. Harrison picked up the cards and began to leaf through them.

'The analysts in this section get to walk the whole process through.' Daly's voice came from behind him. 'Special processing: they deal with fewer cases, but they're the really urgent ones, you know – unidentified bodies, somebody trying to assassinate the President, that kind of thing. These guys sometimes get prints sent in electronically but more often than not it's the original card from the law enforcement agency.'

'How do the cops that send them in get notified of the result?' Harrison asked him.

'On the regular floor it's done automatically through the data centre. Here,' Daly said. 'The analyst calls them up on the phone.'

'So Carter dealt with cops.'

'Oh yeah.'

'Anybody else?'

'Everybody else. DEA, ATF, Secret Service, Department of Corrections, Immigration, Customs, State Department, you can pretty much name it.'

'So he talked on the phone a lot.'

'Certainly.'

'Are records kept, his phone calls and so on?'

Daly smiled. 'Are you kidding? CJIS *is* records. We monitor everything that goes on here.'

Harrison looked at Carter's blank computer screen. 'Do you monitor what they're doing on the system?'

Daly nodded. 'We can instruct a keystroke investigation which will give you chapter and verse of everything Carter ever did here. Why? Do you think that might be relevant?'

Harrison stood up. 'I don't know. Depends on what he was working on, I guess. It's an avenue we need to think about. So is the possibility he had a bust-up with the wrong guy in a bar.'

'Carter was working on cold cases,' Daly told him. 'He had been for eighteen months or so. He ran a small team looking at cold case latent prints, not normally what they would do here, but we've had some pretty grisly unsolved murders over the years. Before CJIS there was no easy way to cross-check unidentified prints picked up at the crime scene. They've only just transferred the cold case stuff over from DC.' He smiled. 'We needed to play catch up, I suppose, so the boss instructed me to form this team. Max Carter was running it.'

Harrison stared at the box of fingerprint cards. Cold case latents: he knew all about cold case latent prints.

He needed to interview everyone on the floor, but he didn't want to start that without the Bridgeport police being involved. They'd only have to do it again and Fitzpatrick wanted the place as undisturbed as possible. Notwithstanding the sensitivity of his work location and the fact that Carter was a federal employee, the FBI had no jurisdiction in the investigation: they were along for the ride by invitation only. Harrison called Santini and told her what he had so far. Nothing had come in from Tallahassee yet, and she agreed to meet him at Carter's house.

The evidence response technicians had finished up by the time Harrison got there. A Bridgeport cop in uniform guarded the entrance and Harrison found Santini upstairs at the computer desk. The blood had dried completely now, but the stain would be there for ever and the place had that immovable odour of death which clings to your clothes no matter how much you wash them.

Harrison surveyed the room, taking in the bookshelves and the rack of computer CDs. Twin metal filing cabinets with a book on the history of Louisiana lying on one of them – he could see where its place had been on the shelf. He looked for other history books but didn't find any. Why specifically Louisiana? he wondered. He moved to Santini's shoulder. 'You turn anything up?'

She shook her head. 'Not really, this place is as neat as a Pleasantville kitchen.'

'Anything stolen?'

'I don't really know. There's no sign of breaking and entering. Proud thinks either Carter let the killer in, which means he probably knew him, or he found the spare key. His mom would have to verify whether anything was missing. I doubt it, though. His wallet is in his pants in the bedroom – there's three hundred dollars in it.'

Harrison made a mental note to find out how much a CJIS supervisor got paid.

'There is one thing I've come across, though.' Santini beckoned him to the desk and pointed to a notepad of tear-off paper. The top sheet was blank.

Harrison looked closer. He could just about make out the faint ridges of an indentation. 'You got a pencil?' Santini passed him one and he sat down and very lightly began to shade the paper. Two words took shape in the faintest of lines on the page.

'White Camelia,' Santini said. 'A camelia's a flower. I grow them in my yard.'

Harrison sat back, took a cigarette from his pocket and lit it. 'Carter tore off three or four sheets after he wrote this – if it *was* Carter. Why would he tear off three or four sheets? He was a meticulous kind of guy. I bet he hated wasting paper.'

'Unless he was deliberately trying to hide it,' Santini said.

'The name of a flower – beats me as to why.' Harrison stood up. 'Come on. Let's go get your palm read.'

Madame Josephine operated from a little storefront on the hill opposite the Gables Apartments on the eastern side of Bridgeport. Harrison didn't know what to expect, having never visited a tarot reader or psychic before. He found a pleasant-looking woman in her early forties, well dressed and bubbly. She introduced herself with a rush of conversation and then poured some coffee.

'Now,' she said, sitting down, 'are you both wanting readings – individually or together perhaps? I can work just as well with couples as individuals, you know.'

'Actually,' Santini said, 'we wanted to know what you saw in the cards when you gave Mrs Carter her last reading.'

Clouds lifted in Madame Josephine's eyes. 'What I say to a client is confidential,' she told them. 'I can't possibly divulge a confidence between myself and a client.'

Harrison sat forward. 'We're from the FBI, Madame Josephine.' He flipped open his shield. 'I'm sure you've heard that Mrs Carter's son was murdered on Christmas Eve. Maybe you could divulge a confidence to *us*.'

Madame Josephine stared at him. 'I don't know anything about what happened to poor Maxwell.'

'You knew him?'

She shook her head. 'Only through his mother. I never met him, but she used to talk about him all the time. So much so that in the end I felt I knew him.'

'You never did a reading for him.'

'No, but more often than not his mother wanted to know about *his* life rather than her own. If he would marry, what the girl would be like, that sort of thing. I think she craved some normality for him.'

'Did you get the impression that she thought he was abnormal in some way, then?' Santini asked.

'I didn't say that. I don't know. Maybe.'

'But you saw something,' Santini went on, 'in the cards – Mrs Carter's tarot. Was she asking you about her son on that occasion?'

Madame Josephine didn't answer.

Harrison looked evenly at her. 'You disturbed her, you know. It's the first thing she told us.'

Madame Josephine sat back and sighed. 'Sometimes,' she began, 'being psychic, being able to see things others cannot, places you in a position you would rather not be in. You have to be responsible, especially with your regulars. Most of the time I see nothing out of the ordinary. Daily readings are just that, they're run of the mill. But then . . .' She stared for a moment then tailed off and looked a little helpless.

'What did you see?' Santini asked. 'When you were with Mrs Carter, what exactly did you see?'

The reader looked at Harrison with sudden questions in her eyes. 'You don't see *things* as such,' she said, 'not specifics. You feel things, you can sense things.'

'Like happiness perhaps? Or sadness?' Santini said.

Madame Josephine was still looking at Harrison. 'Disturbance is a good word for it, things that are undone, things unresolved – sometimes in the past, sometimes in the future.'

'So what did you see when Mrs Carter was here?'

'Trouble. I saw great disturbance ahead.'

Harrison shifted the plug of tobacco in his cheek. 'But you didn't know Maxwell Carter personally?'

She shook her head.

'He didn't come here? Not one of your clients?'

'I've already said so.'

'What about people who did know him?'

'You mean other clients?'

'Anyone.'

'I didn't know anyone who knew him.' Madame Jose-

51

phine looked at him again. 'I'm sorry I can't help you any more, but I really don't know anything. I saw symbols that indicated trouble, nothing specific, and I didn't say anything to Mrs Carter.'

Outside, Santini buttoned her coat. It was snowing again, the sky grey and scarred above their heads, the town blanched by the cold. Ice hung in stalactites from the roof of the tarot reader's building. Harrison shivered and climbed into his truck. Santini got in beside him. 'What do you think?' she said.

'I don't know.' He took a cigarette from his shirt pocket. 'You believe in any of that stuff?'

'Do you?'

'No.'

'It must be just coincidence, then.'

Harrison started the engine. 'You mean rather than our psychic knowing more than she's telling us? Yeah, I'd say so. I don't put her down for anybody's killer, do you?'

'No, but I wouldn't have put Jeff Dahmer down as one either on first meeting him.'

Harrison drove back to the resident agency after dropping Santini at the crime scene to collect her car. The supervisor was on the phone and Harrison sat down at his desk.

He thought about Maxwell Carter. He was a big, fat, probably awkward guy, and from the little he had learned so far from the man's work colleagues he was also quite shy. It didn't appear that he had many friends and his only pursuit outside his work and his net surfing was the county bowling league. Harrison swivelled in his chair and looked out of the window. Snow fell in soft flurries; the three old guys who were always messing about in the open parking lot across the street were nowhere to be seen.

Restless all at once, he went to get a bagel and coffee from the Country Kitchen. Santini had just pulled into the parking lot and he indicated his intentions and she nodded.

She took her coffee with cream and sugar. He got two cups to go and two bagels and crossed the street again. She was waiting for him beyond the metal detector in the lobby of the federal building.

'What's up?' he asked her.

'Tom Proud just called. He wants us to run up to headquarters.'

'He turn something up?'

Santini nodded. 'Carter's bank accounts. It seems there was a lot more money going in than there should have been.'

They drove up to the Bridgeport police headquarters, a brown, flat-roofed building next door to City Hall. It was just off the interstate, behind the complex that housed the Holiday Inn and Maxy's restaurant where Harrison liked to get a beer after work.

Proud was one of only two detectives in the twenty-man Bridgeport force and he was alone in the tiny office he shared with a colleague. He looked up when Harrison and Santini arrived.

'What've we got, Tom?' Harrison sat down opposite him.

'See for yourself.' Proud handed him a sheaf of papers, photocopies of Carter's bank statements. 'Check out the cash entries, three this year and four the year before that.'

Santini moved closer to him and Harrison could smell the scent of her hair, the residue of the shampoo she liked to use. She never wore perfume to work but he often noticed her hair. He scanned the papers and then passed each one to her. Three cash entries during the past year, November, June and March: a total of thirty thousand dollars.

Harrison looked at Proud. 'This is interesting.'

'It's all we've got, JB. The house is clean. Your guys just verified what our guys already figured: no prints, no hair, nothing – no sign of B&E, no busted locks or forced windows. This guy was either known to Carter or he studied the place long enough to find the spare key.'

'Or Carter killed himself,' Santini said wryly.

Harrison looked again at the bank statements. 'Carter was working cold case latents, Tom, unidentified prints lifted from unsolved murder scenes. I don't know if that tells us anything, but I figured you'd want to know.' He gestured with the papers. 'Can we take a copy of these?'

'Those are for you.' Proud stood up and swung his jacket over his shoulders. 'I'm going to see his mom, find out who he hung out with. Then I'm going to check the lanes. He was on a bowling team – somebody might know something. I guess you guys are headed back to CJIS. Let me know what you come up with.'

Harrison drove, Santini scanning the bank statements once again. 'I already asked his boss to get us the details of what he was looking at,' Harrison said. 'We know he worked in special processing, Fran. Walked the sequence through from start to finish. I figure it's the only real way you could abuse the system if you wanted to. Normal fingerprint analysts make their ident from the descriptive material given. When they come up with a match their work is automatically checked.' He turned off the interstate for the second time that day. 'The analysts have no contact with the agency that send in the prints, that's done automatically through a different section.'

'But not in special processing?'

Harrison shook his head. 'The top guys are in that department, they do the whole thing themselves – check the prints, make their ident from minutiae as well as descriptive material, then they call the investigating cop with the results.'

Kirk Fitzpatrick gave up part of his office for them. As soon as Harrison showed him the bank statements he cleared his conference table and set them up. 'You'll want to talk to his colleagues,' he stated.

'Just special processing to start with.' Harrison picked up the phone and dialled Daly's extension. 'First up we want to

54

look at his caseload. It's getting late now. What time do you take off?'

'Don't worry about me,' Fitzpatrick told him. 'You stay all night if you want to.'

Harrison spoke to Daly and reminded him he wanted everything Carter had been working on going back to the beginning of the previous year. Ten minutes later he had four boxes of paper files on the floor at his feet and the most recent ones laid out on the table. Santini took a call on her Nextel and moved to the far end of the office.

Fitzpatrick sat down with Harrison and picked up a paper file. 'Here's a blast from the past,' he said. 'Jesuit Bend, Jefferson Parish Sheriff, the boy in the bayou murder.'

Harrison felt a chill work through his veins.

'You remember this, JB?' Fitzpatrick said.

'Yeah, I remember.' Harrison stood up. 'Just going to the bathroom. I'll be right back.'

He left the office, walked the corridor to the men's room and stood in front of the mirror. Weary grey eyes looked back at him. His face was seamed and weathered, the skin burnt brown by years in the sun and the lines deep and pale round his eyes. His hair was shoulder length now, the ponytail of so many years finally cut away, but not the part of his life that went with it.

He leaned on the sink. The boy in the bayou, his body found in a trainasse, a muddy line of water, a portage trail stretching into the swamp. Jesuit Bend, a tiny hamlet off Highway 23 in southern Louisiana. He could see the water, smell the damp reed and the mud with the previous night's rain washed into it. The grass was yellow and brown, drifting back a few feet before the channel wove its way into float top and a stand of live oaks draped with Spanish moss. On the edge of the Barataria, where two hundred years earlier the pirate Jean Lafitte sold stolen African slaves for one dollar a pound.

Harrison splashed his eyes with cold water. It had not

been his case. In fact, it had nothing to do with him: he was not even attached to Jefferson Parish during his time in New Orleans. In those days he lived in the back of unmarked vans in the Calliope and Magnolia projects, or was a customer in the coffee shop the organized crime squad opened to clean up La Cosa Nostra. Now and again he hung out in Lafourche Parish, if he was looking at some redneck from the rigs. But the boy in the bayou still haunted him: he had visited the dumpsite on his own long after the corpse was gone.

That case had been part of the reason he had quit the job. The boy was about ten years old when he died; his body never claimed, never identified, not even by dental records. A throw-away black kid found naked in the bayou with one sneaker on his right foot and a length of cheese wire twisted so hard round his neck his head had almost been severed.

He went back to the office where Santini was talking to Fitzpatrick. She looked up, caught his expression and frowned. 'You OK, John?'

Harrison felt the sickness in his gut. 'Just dandy. What's going on?'

'I talked to the agents in Florida.'

'And?'

'Jeannie-Anne Rae *was* talking to Carter when it happened. They were talking about Christmas then he just stopped replying. She thought he'd dumped her or something. She got one hell of a shock when they told her he was murdered.'

They got coffee downstairs in the refectory. Harrison sat opposite Fitzpatrick with Santini on his left. Their table was close to the window and he gazed out on the snow-blown hills, the shivering cedar trees stripped of their foliage, pressing naked broken fingers towards the sky. A uniformed cop rode by, spindrift lifting in a grey haze from the wheels of his quad bike. Harrison drank his coffee. He was with them but not with them, their conversation blurred into a murmur as he stared out the window, unable to get the image out of his head. He could remember exactly how the boy had been lying, face down in the bayou, one foot caught in the mud, the other leg bent so the knee was against his stomach.

'You remember the details of that Jesuit Bend case, Kirk?' he said quietly.

'Who doesn't?' Fitzpatrick glanced at Santini. 'It was three years back, when Johnny Buck and me were in New Orleans together.'

'Did you work the case?'

'No, it was a Jefferson Parish homicide.'

'Bill Chaisson worked it.' Harrison glanced at her. 'Twenty years a detective – Houma for ten of them, then Jefferson Parish. He works for the Department of Corrections now, a probation and parole officer based in New Orleans.'

'The kid was a throw-away,' Fitzpatrick told Santini. 'You know what I mean, a project kid probably, father unknown, mother a crack whore who had him at fourteen or something, dumped him when he was five or six or younger even maybe. No school, living on the street. They're a dime a dozen down there.'

Harrison looked at the grounds of his coffee in the bottom of his polystyrene cup. 'The autopsy showed he had been sexually assaulted, and he was naked except for one sneaker. The other one was found at a fishing camp in the Barataria. Some guy from Georgia owned the camp, a driller from one of the rigs out in the gulf. He only used the place a few times a year, left it locked up, way out in the middle of the swamp, the sort of place you'd never find unless you knew exactly where it was. There are thousands of them out there.

'Anyways, that guy called the Jefferson Parish Sheriff a couple of days after the boy turned up. The one sneaker was the only identifying mark on him so Chaisson used it in his press release. The oil guy must have seen the TV or read it in the *Picayune* or something because he called up saying he'd found a sneaker in his camp. It had been broken into, he hadn't reported it at the time because nothing had been stolen, but he found the sneaker on the deck outside.' He broke off and glanced at Fitzpatrick. 'It matched the one the floater was wearing.'

'And that was about it,' Fitzpatrick said.

Harrison nodded his agreement. 'Chaisson worked himself to death over that case. He never got anywhere with it, but it still bothers him now.'

'It sounds like it bothers everyone,' Santini said. 'Why that particular case? There must be a hundred and one floaters down there in the bayous.'

'There are.' Harrison sat forward. 'Plus another hundred never found, chewed by the alligators or just rotting away with the vegetation. There's hundreds of thousands of square miles of swamp and marsh and nothing much else. If you want to hide out or dump a body – go there.'

'Louisiana's a weird place,' Fitzpatrick put in, 'a melting pot of people. Along the gulf coast there's no work except in oil and gas or seafood. In the late seventies the Bureau reckoned there were at least fifty thousand fugitives living under false names in Terrebone and Lafourche Parishes alone. It's bayou country, the most dangerous place in America to be a fish and game warden.'

'Oh, yeah. That job comes with a health warning for sure.' Harrison tapped his knuckles on the table. 'To answer your original question, Fran, it was just one of those cases. You know what I mean – sometimes one of them gets to you. A young kid, raped and murdered and no way to tell who he was. Nobody seemed to have lost him. According to any known record, he didn't even exist. Only he did exist or he had at least, till somebody put a cheese wire round his neck and garrotted him.'

*

Back in the resident agency office he called up the Bureau's copy of the file from the database of the violent criminal apprehension programme. The evidence response team had been to the camp owned by the oil worker and gone over it with a fine-tooth comb. It was a big, well-kept camp, stocked with tinned food and fishing gear, dry wood for a fire; one large room maybe thirty feet square with an alcove at the back. They had dusted the place from top to bottom, inside and out, and come up with two sets of unidentified prints. The full five of a right hand, including part of the palm, had been lifted from a rail which split the main room from the alcove, and various other prints had been picked up from the floor and the doors and the rail out on the deck. Those all belonged to the same person, but neither of them had ever been identified.

Harrison knew Bill Chaisson well, having carried out some undercover surveillance for him on the suspect on Bayou Lafourche. They were the same age, both had fought in Southeast Asia and they had got drunk together on many occasions, sitting up into the small hours telling war stories. Chaisson had worked that case like nobody worked a case. It had marked his soul in the same way it marked Harrison's and yet Harrison had had nothing to do with it. Maybe it was the victim's age, the brutal way he died or the way he was just left for the alligators. Maybe it was the fact he was naked or just that he was unknown. Harrison had never asked for Chaisson's specific reasons.

Some things just got to a man. With him the boy in the bayou brought the past back to haunt him, mock him from thirty years ago. It almost cost him his job and it was all he could do to shove unlooked-for emotions back in the box. He had left the Bureau but now he was back and the same cold case had risen to haunt him again. It felt as though old wounds had never been allowed to heal properly.

Santini was sitting next to him: she was going through

some of Carter's other papers. 'This thing has really gotten to you, hasn't it?' she said.

'Not especially.'

'Come on, Harrison. You can't bullshit a bullshitter, especially one you've slept with.'

Harrison closed the screen down and rubbed his eyes. 'I'm beat,' he said. 'You wanna grab a beer?'

The following morning Santini asked for a complete key-stroke check on everything Carter had been working on for the past twelve months. Harrison took the boy in the bayou file through to special processing himself. He sat with an analyst who had worked closely with Carter, and asked him to go over Carter's work. The file was marked as a non-ident on either set of prints – in other words there was no match with anything on record at CJIS and the Jefferson Parish Sheriff's Office had been informed that was the finding.

Santini began to check Carter's phone records and looked at who – if anyone – had visited him. She called Proud and asked him for any address book or list of telephone numbers located at Carter's house.

Harrison watched as the analyst worked: a middle-aged man named Jim Parker, balding on top and red-faced with broken veins in his nose. He sat at Carter's workstation and called up the information on the two sets of unidentified prints. Harrison looked on, arms folded, as the first set, the ones from the floor and the doors and the deck, came up on the screen. He watched the analyst click on 'Search' and sit back.

'You might want to go get some coffee or something,' he said. 'This could take a while.' He smiled, though he looked a little nervous. 'There's forty million prints on this baby.'

Harrison went to the coffee machine. When he came back Parker was tensed over his keyboard.

'What's up?' he asked.

'This is very odd.' Parker tucked his seat in further and Harrison bent over his shoulder. 'I've got a possible here on the system.' Parker improved the image on the screen and then he began to work. Harrison watched him, the tip of his tongue protruding marginally from his mouth as he checked the screen again and again. He changed the density, the contrast, heightening certain aspects of the image, overlaying prints and removing them again.

'This is really weird,' he said. 'It's not the definitive sixteen-point match, but that's an ident right there.'

'You sure?'

'Positive. I've been doing this job for twenty years, and that is a confirmed ident.'

Back in Fitzpatrick's office Harrison found Santini on the phone: she was sitting by the window, watching two white-tailed deer picking at bunch grass through the snow. Harrison laid the file on the desk and sat down. Parker had run the second set of prints for him and had come up with a non-ident, as was recorded previously. Santini came off the phone.

'How's it going?'

'I think we have something.' Harrison squared the file and passed it to her. 'Two sets of cold case latent finger-prints,' he said. 'The Jefferson Parish Sheriff was informed that there was no ident with either of them. A Detective Muller pulled the cold case and sent the prints up here. I didn't get to talk to him because he's retiring. A gal down there confirmed the non-ident call coming in from CJIS.'

'So?'

'So Carter was lying to them.'

There was silence as Santini took in what he was saying.

'The ubiquitous set of latents,' Harrison went on, 'doors, deck etcetera. An analyst ran them for me just now and within ten minutes we had a confirmed ident.' He paused and sucked breath. 'And not just any old ident either.' He passed Santini the rap sheet that Parker had printed from the National Crime Information Center. 'Take a look at the jacket.'

Santini read aloud: ' "Marcel Call, two-time loser, served time in Pensacola, Florida and Angola, Louisiana for assault with a deadly weapon. Currently on parole in Orleans Parish, Louisiana." ' She looked across at Harrison. 'You know this guy?'

'Let's say I heard the name. Do me a favour, Fran. Call up the parole officer for me, will you? Find out if anybody's been asking about Call in the last couple of months.'

He left her and went outside the back entrance of the facility, where the main parking lot stretched. He plucked a menthol cigarette from his shirt pocket and struck a match on his heel. He blew smoke from the corner of his mouth as the implications of what he had discovered began to sink in.

Marcel Call was a bit part player with a self-styled Cajun Mafia run by one of the most dangerous men in New Orleans. A man the organized crime squad had been after for years and never got within a whisker of in terms of any evidence. He divided his time between a condo in the French Quarter and a camp on the Grand Terre Islands.

'I thought I'd find you here.' He started at the sound of Santini's voice. 'You're jumpy, cowboy,' she said. 'What's bugging you?'

'Nothing's bugging me.'

'No? So where were you just now?'

Harrison half smiled. 'Actually I was thinking about St Louis cemetery in New Orleans. Marie Laveau is buried there. You ever hear of her – the original voodoo queen?' Harrison dropped his cigarette and mashed it under his heel. 'Marcel Call hangs with a Cajun crew, Fran. It's run by Augustine Laveaux.' He let air escape his lips. 'Now, there's a name to conjure fear in the soul. It's spelled differently but I always thought it was no coincidence that he was the namesake of the voodoo queen herself.' He paused and looked beyond her for a moment. It was a long time since he had experienced such deep-seated unease, but he could feel it now, there on the steps of the building with snow covering the trees. 'I did some work for Bill Chaisson one time,' he told her, 'the guy that investigated the Jesuit Bend murder. It was down in Lafourche Parish.'

It had been a long day, and Harrison had been cooped up in the back of a van watching Chaisson's suspect down at the Fourchon, the last deep-water port before the Gulf of Mexico. He drove home through Golden Meadow and stopped at a bar for a beer.

The interior was dark, not quite happy hour and room for him to belly up on one of the stools set at the large square counter that dominated the middle of the floor. A very attractive Cajun girl was serving. Harrison ordered a bottle of beer and a shot of Jim Beam. He didn't try to strike up any conversation with the girl. Cajun men were very protective of their womenfolk and he knew better: an out-of-town worker, keep it quiet and keep it clean and they *should* leave you alone.

His fellow drinkers were oilfield workers or shrimp fishermen, their occupation given away by the white rubber boots they always wore. Conversation was thin and nasal, some of it in French. Only one guy across the bar was busy. He was talking to the bartender, trying to catch her eye, sipping alternately on a beer and a glass of sour mash. Young, dark haired, clean cut compared to the rest of them; he sounded like he was from somewhere up north. Harrison watched him for a moment. He recognized Ignace and Cristophe Laveaux seated on either side of him.

Harrison took another cigarette from his pocket and looked back at Santini. 'It's pronounced "In-yass" but spelled Ignace. He and Cristophe were brothers. Cousins to Augustine.' He stared beyond her. 'I should have figured it then, those boys don't enjoy the company of anybody that isn't family.'

Cristophe was younger than his brother. He ran his own shrimp boat while Ignace was the skipper of a feeder tug for the rigs. Collette, the girl behind the bar, was Cristophe's girlfriend, only he hadn't told the Yankee sitting there with them. He hadn't told the Yankee anything. He was enjoying the spectacle, sitting there with a balsa-wood pick stuck in the gap between his teeth.

'Come on over here, sweetheart,' the Yankee was saying. 'Come and talk to me. I'm lonely, baby. A long way from home.' He had been in the bar since four. It was six now and the Yankee had been drinking steadily, a beer and a shot, a beer and a shot ever since they got here. Cristophe and his brother had arrived at four-thirty and the Yankee was already hitting on Collette.

Collette ignored him. She was at the other side of the bar, serving somebody else. She glanced at Cristophe now and then, indicating for him to say something, but he just grinned and slowly shook his head. He exchanged glances with Ignace behind the Yankee's head when he leaned on the bar and snapped his fingers to get Collette's attention.

'Hey, homeboy.' Cristophe rested a friendly hand on his shoulder. The young boy looked at him, his gaze slightly off to one side, the drink flowing freely in his veins. 'You been drinking a lot. Me and Ignace gonna get some grub. You wanna come with us maybe? Then we can drink some more.'

'Where you thinking of eating?'

Ignace laid a hand on his other shoulder. 'Oh, we'll find somewhere. We know all the good places.'

'But what about my girlfriend there?' The Yankee pointed across the bar at Collette.

'She still be here when we get back.' Ignace stood up. 'Come on. We'll pick up a twelve pack and go get something

64

to eat. When we're done we'll come on back. Maybe we can introduce you.'

'Really?' The Yankee's eyes lit up. 'That'd be great, guys. I haven't had so much as a sniff of pussy since I came down from New York.'

Cristophe squeezed his arm. 'Don't worry. We'll find you something to sniff.'

It was dark outside, winter coming and daylight saving had turned the clocks back so that night fell early. The darkness rolled in from the gulf to soak up the flat lands where the salt marsh had stripped away the trees. The horizon was grey and chill and only edged here and there by the odd fishing camp rising from the marsh. The Yankee fumbled in his pocket for the keys to his truck. Ignace shook his head. 'I'll drive,' he said. 'The cops are hot down here. They'll string up you Yankee ass in a heartbeat.'

Cristophe opened the passenger door of Ignace's truck and pushed the Yankee in ahead of him so he was squashed on the seat between the two of them. Ignace drove to the store and Cristophe picked up a case of beer and then they headed down to the bayou where Cristophe kept his boat. Neither of them spoke now and the atmosphere had dried inside the cab. The Yankee was beginning to sober up.

'Where we going?' he said. 'I thought we were having dinner.'

'We are. Down at my boat.' Cristophe jerked the ring pull off a can of beer and stuffed it in his hand. 'Drink up.'

Ignace drove down the highway to a dirt road that led alongside the bayou. He skirted the western levee for a mile or so and the Yankee sat between them, sensing the change in their mood, the edge that had come over the cab. Ignace looked sideways at him and showed his teeth. 'What's the matter, Yankee, cat got you tongue? It was wagging like a fishtail back there in the bar.' He nodded to Cristophe. 'My brother's girl was sick of hearing you shit.'

'Brother's girl?' The Yankee squirmed where he sat, a

shiver rippling through him and coming out as wind. The Cajuns laughed aloud, a harsh sound, abrasive in his ears.

'Didn't you know she was my woman?' Cristophe raised his eyebrows at him. 'Oh, yeah, she fine. Me and Collette been together for years.'

'Look, I'm sorry. I . . .'

Ignace stamped on the brakes. The Yankee jerked forward and cracked his head on the windshield. Cristophe jerked him back in the seat, and he sat there with both hands lifted to his face. Ignace had the driver's door open. He hauled the Yankee out. He was tall and wiry and immensely strong, and the Yankee was sent sprawling in the dirt. He came up on hands and knees, coughing, spitting the dirt from his mouth.

'Look. I'm sorry. Please . . .'

Cristophe kicked him hard in the backside, catching him in the coccyx and sending him into the dirt again. He yelled now, twisting and squirming on the ground, one hand to his bottom. He came up, caught in the glare of the headlights like a frightened rabbit. Ignace and Cristophe stood either side of him, Cristophe with a sloppy smile on his face, Ignace coiled like a spring, fists bunched into bony knots at his sides.

The Yankee rocked back on his haunches. 'Look, I'm sorry, OK. I had no idea. Really, I was just fooling around. I didn't mean anything by it . . .'

Dust danced in the beam of the headlights. Behind them Cristophe's shallow-hulled shrimp skiff shifted restlessly. Ignace went to his truck box and pulled out a towing chain. Cristophe started to laugh.

'Don't kill him,' he said. 'I still want him yet.'

Ignace coiled the chain round his fist then swung the hooked end. The Yankee rolled in a ball, arms and legs tucked in like a foetus, the heavy hook thudding sickeningly into his ribs and back, his thighs and upper arms. Ignace whirled the chain again and again. The Yankee tried to scrabble away. He lifted his head and the chain bit his flesh with a heavy clunking sound. Blood flew and his head lolled and he moaned where he lay.

Ignace was panting. He threw the chain to one side and Cristophe moved in. The Yankee groaned as Cristophe took his head and held his face to the light. His hair was matted against his forehead, blood already coagulating; the skin blue and puckered, broken under the hairline.

'Had enough?'

The Yankee moaned again, and spat a tooth into the dirt, trailing a gob of bloody saliva on his chin.

'No.' Cristophe stripped off his jacket. 'You ain't had nearly enough.' He pushed him on to all fours and sobs rose in the man's throat.

'Please,' he murmured. 'Please, I only . . .' Then he yelled as Cristophe yanked his trousers down. 'This one is for Collette,' Cristophe said.

Ignace stood back with his arms folded, laughing as his younger brother raped the Yankee.

When he was finished Cristophe got up and wiped himself down. The Yankee was lying with his face in the dirt, weeping like a baby, his bare bottom almost luminescent in the beam of the headlights. All the while the big diesel engine had been running and the sounds that came from his mouth were muffled by comparison. Cristophe leaned against the truck. Taking the tow chain, he aimed another blow on to the Yankee's back and he cried and rolled over, scrabbling to pull up his pants. Cristophe was panting. The Yankee lay on his back, his shirt open, belly exposed, smeared with dirt and blood and grime.

Ignace reached for his favourite alligator-skinning knife. He drew it from its scabbard, stood for a moment then stepped so one foot was either side of the Yankee's trunk. He dropped to his knees, looked in his eyes with a smile on his face and sank the knife hilt-deep in his stomach. The Yankee gasped and doubled up, a scream gurgling in his throat like a baby choking on milk. Ignace pushed him flat again, the knife still embedded, then he wrenched it to his sternum and split him open. Cristophe had his hand over the Yankee's mouth so his screaming was stifled. His belly was peeled back and his viscera exposed. Cristophe yanked up his head to make him look at it and the Yankee screamed again. He scrabbled to get up. Ignace climbed off his legs and Cristophe let him go. Somehow he got to his feet. He started to run, both arms clutched about him, holding in his intestines. Blood drenched his arms and Ignace balked at the smell. He stepped to one side and tripped him. The Yankee fell, one arm out to protect himself. And the squelch where he landed on his exposed guts was audible.

He was wailing now like a child, shaking his head from side to side, tears flowing, lying on his side desperately trying to keep his innards in place. The two brothers looked down at him, wolfishly, like competitors on a kill. Then Cristophe took him by the hair and dragged him to his knees. He took out his own knife and wiped the blade across his thigh. He stood behind the Yankee who held his guts and stared pleadingly at Ignace, terror and disbelief standing out in his eyes. Ignace looked on. Cristophe grinned at him then bent to the Yankee's ear.

'Say after me,' he hissed. 'Our Father.'

The Yankee just gurgled.

'I said *say after me*!' Cristophe yanked his head back. 'Our Father.'

'Our Father,' the Yankee mumbled through his tears.

'Who art in heaven.'

'Who art in heaven.'

'Hallowed be thy name.' Cristophe's voice was liquid now, spittle on his lip.

'Hallowed be thy name.'

Cristophe smiled at his brother, eyes like lumps of chilled ice, his lips drawn back over yellow and blackened teeth. 'Lead us not into temptation,' he said.

The Yankee opened his mouth and Cristophe slit his throat.

Harrison looked at Santini. The Yankee turned out to be a man named Peter Thomas, twenty-three years old, working offshore for the first time in his life. He had only been away from New York for a week. His body was discovered the next day dumped in the bayou. Bill Chaisson had told Harrison about it and he confirmed he had seen the two brothers in the bar with the man the previous evening. 'They were subsequently interviewed and Cristophe was charged with murder,' he said. 'His DNA matched the semen found in the body. Metal traces from the knife that Ignace used to open Thomas up were recovered but never the knife. No other evidence was found to put Ignace at the crime scene and Cristophe wasn't about to give him up.'

'How did you found out what went down?'

'Because Cristophe bragged about it in Angola. A guard got wind of it and informed the Lafourche Parish sheriff. Chaisson drove up to interview one of Cristophe's cell-mates who had recounted the story.' He paused and crushed out his cigarette. 'Before he got there, however, both the cell-mate and Cristophe were found dead. Stabbed. The word was they killed each other in a knife fight.' Harrison leaned and spat. 'The bragging talk could have led us to Ignace. If we got to Ignace we might have got to Augustine. But he wasn't going to allow that so now there's one less Laveaux in the world.'

Santini was quiet for a moment. 'Nothing was proved, though.'

Harrison shook his head. 'Augustine Laveaux doesn't leave loose ends. If he even thinks he's threatened, he kills. To him it's very simple.'

Santini chewed her lip. 'All of this is beginning to make sense,' she said. 'I spoke with Call's parole officer just now, Vincent Palastina in the West New Orleans office. He told me Call is working on a tugboat that runs from the harbour to the Gulf of Mexico.'

Harrison looked at her. 'I'll bet Ignace Laveaux is the skipper.'

She passed him the sheet of paper she was holding. 'The only enquiry New Orleans have had about Call was from another parole officer in Charleston. He wanted to check Call's whereabouts because his name had cropped up here in West Virginia.'

Harrison stared at the paper.

'There's something else,' Santini said. 'Carter's phone records. He's called the parole office in Charleston seven times since August.'

five

Harrison flew to Pittsburgh from Benedum Airport, on top of the hill overlooking the industrial area of Bridgeport. He drank coffee and stared at the seat in front of him, thinking about Augustine Laveaux. Maxwell Carter's murder investigation was a week old and ever since Laveaux's name had cropped up he had filled Harrison's head like a spectre. Two days previously Harrison and Santini had taken the shuttle to Charleston and paid a visit to Michael Campbell, the parole officer who had enquired about Marcel Call in New Orleans.

'Just hit the sonofabitch with it,' Harrison had said as they sat in the rental car outside his office.

'You think?'

'Yeah, I think. We've got his phone calls to and from Carter's desk at CJIS. We've got Carter calling him from home. We've got him calling his cellphone and emailing the sonofabitch. We've got Campbell calling half a dozen parole officers around the country, getting addresses for felons that have nothing whatever to do with his office.' He opened the car door. 'This guy knows Carter's dead. He'll be crapping himself, believe me.'

He led the way upstairs, showed his shield to the girl at reception and asked to see Michael Campbell, the supervisor. Campbell appeared from behind the glass door of his office looking a little green around the gills. He was in his mid-thirties, thin with lank brown hair and shaving hives on his neck.

71

They sat the other side of his desk from him in the cramped little office. 'So,' he said, with half a smile. 'What does the FBI want with me? Is there somebody I can help you with?'

'Yes,' Harrison said. 'Marcel Call.'

Campbell blanched. He tried to hide it, but couldn't. 'I don't recognize the name,' he said. 'Are you sure he's one of ours?'

'I'm sure he's *not* one of yours. He's a West New Orleans parolee. You called Vincent Palastina about him last November.'

'I did?' Campbell lifted his eyebrows.

Harrison leaned an elbow on the desk. 'Listen, Mr Campbell, don't be blowing smoke up my ass, I'm really not in the mood. Marcel Call was an ident made by Max Carter from the boy in the bayou murder. A Louisiana cold case, remember? You know all about it because you asked Palastina. He gave you an address and I guess you blackmailed Call to keep his name out of the beef.' He shook his head. 'Way out of your league, buddy, he's got serious friends.'

Campbell was staring at him.

'We figure that was your fourth blackmail attempt of the year, Mr Campbell,' Santini went on. 'You and Carter had quite a thing going, what with him in Clarksburg, having access to all those fingerprints, the National Crime Information Center. It must have worked really well for a while, Carter picking up prints from known felons then you getting on to your buddies round the country to see if the felons were on parole.'

'I don't know what you're talking about,' Campbell interrupted.

'Sure you do.' Harrison took out a cigarette.

'You can't smoke in here.'

Harrison ignored him. 'When you found a parolee I guess you made the call – what was it? Sort of, "Hey, Mr bad guy, me and my buddy can put you at the scene of a murder for which you'll fry, or do life in some godforsaken hell hole with the prize bull shoving it up your ass every day. On the other hand, if you pay us a few grand we might not let on that we know." ' He blew smoke in Campbell's face. 'Is that how it went?'

'I guess if they paid you then Carter doctored the prints on file at CJIS,' Santini said. 'He could do that, couldn't he? We've been through every cold case he worked over the last two years, and you know what? In the really juicy ones there was never an ident made.'

Campbell stared at her. Harrison leaned close again. 'We can do this the easy way or we can do it the hard way, Mr Campbell. We already have a grand jury looking at the evidence and it's only a matter of time before we indict you. You can get your lawyer and go to trial and we'll bust your ass anyway. Or you can help us out here and maybe get a plea bargain. Now, what's it going to be?'

Campbell looked shell-shocked. The colour had drained from his face but the hives on his neck burned red. He scratched at them.

'Tell us about Marcel Call,' Harrison said.

'I didn't contact him.' Campbell looked at the floor. 'It wasn't worth it. Max said there was no point. He'd only been out of prison a little while. His address was a flophouse in New Orleans. He wouldn't have had any money.'

Initially Harrison had thought Campbell was lying but on reflection why would he? As far as Campbell knew, Call was a lowlife nobody with nothing to his name and no chance of getting money to them. Carter, on the other hand, had the full file from the boy in the bayou murder and access to the National Crime Information Center. He was a bright man: he had proved that already and with a little digging he could have unearthed the bigger picture, i.e. Augustine Laveaux and his clan of Cajun gangsters. Perhaps he thought this was his chance at the big time. If he knew that Call was connected to the Cajun Mafia then he might have cut his partner out. One good shot at a retirement fund maybe – the money the two of them had amassed so far was a relatively small amount. If Carter did know of Call's connections he probably went for the big time, and when he did he got burned. It had occurred to both Harrison and Santini that perhaps Campbell found out Carter was double-crossing him and killed him for it. But Campbell had a watertight alibi: he had been attending an office party on Christmas Eve and at least a dozen people could vouch for him. Besides, Harrison doubted he had it in him.

Harrison thought about the statement the Florida field office had taken from Jeannie-Anne Rae, how the conversation just dried up. He imagined Carter concentrating on his computer screen, oblivious to his surroundings. He imagined his silent assailant carrying a cheese wire. That wire round the thigh was vicious. A straight professional hit would have been a 7.62 rifle round from six hundred yards up a hill. This was sadistic, and sadism was exactly where the likes of Laveaux got off. He had a whole clan backing him, brothers and sisters, cousins, aunts and uncles. The family could trace their roots back to when the Acadians first came down from Nova Scotia in 1764. Harrison was reminded of the Louisiana history book he had seen in Carter's room.

Laveaux kept a home in New Orleans and a camp on Grand Terre. That gave him access to the Gulf of Mexico and all the traffic through it; it also gave him access to the Intercoastal waterway via Bayou Barataria. He ran legitimate shrimp boats crewed by offshoots of the family. He ran oyster scoops and skiffs and he ran tugboats. He was linked to at least three inland waterway companies (all of which were legitimate) working from New Orleans to St Louis, a thousand miles upriver. He leased sections of Governor Nicholls Street Wharf from the Port of New Orleans, but regular visits from the harbour police had turned up nothing out of the ordinary.

Laveaux was six feet six inches tall, with the dark complexion of the Cajun, black hair and a scar down one side of his face, a souvenir from a fight with a boat hook in the days before he became the man about town he was now. The word was he liked to model himself on the nineteenth-century pirate Jean Lafitte who had ruled the Barataria much as Laveaux ruled it today. He had even tried to buy Lafitte's old Blacksmiths Shop Bar on Bourbon Street and St Philip, and often he could be found buying drinks for the tourists who sat round Johnny Gordon's piano.

If Carter had got to Marcel Call then he would by definition have got to Augustine or at least Ignace Laveaux and neither was good for his health. But it wasn't just that thought that plagued Harrison as he reclined on the Pittsburgh shuttle to New Orleans: the cheese wire smacked of the Jesuit Bend murder, and Marcel Call's prints were found at the camp where the missing sneaker was discovered. Call had no rap sheet in Jefferson Parish and the sheriff's office would have got nothing from New Orleans when the latents were first recovered. Call did his first stint of prison time in Florida and hadn't gone down in New Orleans till after the murder. Harrison was only too aware of how adjacent police districts didn't necessarily keep one another informed of what was going on, let alone two different parishes.

He opened his eyes, not sure whether he had been dozing or not, as the pilot called for the flight attendants to prepare for landing. Below them Lake Ponchartrain unravelled in brilliant blue, the sun high today, no hint of the storms that had been buffeting the gulf coast just after Christmas.

He had specifically turned down agent Penny's offer to meet him at the airport and he would not be going to the FBI field office when he landed. He had told his supervisor that he needed to fly to New Orleans to discuss the implications of what had turned up with the organized crime squad down there, given their ongoing interest in Laveaux. What he hadn't told him was the presence of spectres in his head, spectres that might just keep him in New Orleans longer than a few days.

The city had that old familiar feel about it, an atmosphere at once threatening and enticing. Harrison had worked in many cities round the United States and had done stints abroad in various attachments and guises, but there was nowhere like New Orleans, a place that both attracted and repulsed in equal measure. He picked up his bags then jumped the shuttle bus downtown to the Parc St Charles Hotel at the corner of Poydras and St Charles Avenue. It was not far from the old downtown location of the field office and a short walk across Canal Street to the French Quarter. For three years the Bureau had been waiting for their purpose-built facility to be completed out on Leon Simon's Boulevard, close to the university. Up until that point they had occupied three floors and various other offices in the Mobil Oil building at Poydras Plaza.

The shuttle bus dropped him and he tipped the driver and crossed behind the streetcar that rumbled from Canal down St Charles towards the Garden District. He checked in, dumped his gear on the bed and paged Matt Penny. Two minutes later his phone rang.

'Harrison.'

'What's with the cloak and dagger?'

'Hey, Matthew, sorry about all that. I'll tell you when I see you.'

'You deep again or something? You told me you weren't going there any more.'

'Let's not talk on the phone.'

'OK. Where and when do you want to meet?'

Harrison thought for a moment. 'The special ops office on Elysian Fields, make it about an hour.' He hung up. That was a good idea: he didn't want to meet Penny anywhere too public because you never knew who might be around. The special operations group carried out all the FBI's covert surveillance and did a good deal of work with police departments around the state. The agents did not work cases as such and rarely visited the field office: they operated from a small warehouse off Elysian Fields, which looked like any other industrial site in the area.

He took a shower and changed into his oldest jeans and boots. He wore a singlet under a faded Levi jacket and worked his hair back from his forehead. The TV babbled in the background. The governor was being interviewed on Channel Six, talking about the latest crime figures for New Orleans.

'Crime is down,' he was saying. 'That was my election pledge to the people of the southern parishes and that is what they've got. We've recruited over six hundred police officers in Orleans Parish alone and eradicated the notion that the NOPD is inherently corrupt. This is largely due to the Chief of Police, but it is also true to say that the state of Louisiana Legislature has backed him with the funding and wherewithal we promised before the election.'

Harrison looked at the screen and allowed himself a smile. Valery Mouton, a good old southern boy from the bayous, though sometimes he was apt to forget it. But it was true, what he'd said – the homicide rate in New Orleans was down to one hundred and sixty in the last year. That was still high but a hell of a lot less than the four hundred and sixty a few years previously. They had met once and only briefly. Mouton, as governor of the state, had been giving 'Colonel of Louisiana' medals to two FBI agents who had successfully broken up the budding Vietnamese Mafia in Shreveport. Harrison had led the surveillance operation and attended the ceremony, although he himself had not been cited for any honour. That was fine. Others could take the glory, he needed his anonymity.

Penny was waiting for him when he got to the special ops office. 'So how is West Virginia?' he asked him.

'It was quiet,' Harrison said, 'which was how I wanted it. Until the name Marcel Call cropped up.'

'Our Marcel Call?'

Harrison nodded. 'The one on parole right here in New Orleans, the one who currently works as a deckhand on Ignace Laveaux's tugboat.'

'OK, you got my attention.' Penny sat forward. 'What's going on?'

Harrison told him about Carter's murder and what he and Santini had subsequently discovered. When he was finished Penny shook his head. 'The boy in the bayou, that investigation was going on when I first got here. It was never solved, was it?' He looked thoughtful. 'So you want to round up Call for it, that and Carter both?'

Harrison tapped ash from his cigarette. 'There's nothing concrete to link him with Carter, apart from a motive, given that his prints matched those from the fishing camp of three years back. The fact that the sheriff's office in Jefferson was told there was no ident indicates that Call *was* contacted by Carter. But there's no forensic evidence at Carter's crime scene – no prints or fibres or hair. It was a messy but meticulous murder.'

Penny pushed the air from his lips. 'Messy and meticulous – you know who that sounds like, don't you?'

'Oh, yeah.'

'You know how many years we've been trying to get to him?'

Harrison didn't say anything.

'This has got to be some kind of opportunity.' Penny looked sideways at him. 'Is that what you've been thinking? Hence the secrecy, meeting here, and so on.'

Harrison put out his cigarette. 'I haven't been thinking anything. I just thought we should quietly pick up Call and take him some place safe for a talk.' He stood up. 'I got a couple of things to do, Matt. Can you get it set up then let me know where and when?'

'Sure.'

'It's probably best if the Feds are kept out of it, publicly at least. We don't want to go alarming anyone unnecessarily. Get somebody we can trust from the 8th District to pick him up. His parole officer works off Magazine Street, a guy called Palastina. Get him on it – a minor infraction of the rules, that kind of thing.'

They walked out to where the surveillance vehicles were kept in the indoor lot. A rusting Ford pickup was parked by the far wall: Harrison recognized it from his own days on the squad.

'I need some wheels,' he said, as Penny came alongside him. 'They still use that Ford?'

'I haven't seen it on the street in years. They use a lot of stuff we confiscate these days. Saves the department a fortune.'

'I'm going to take the pickup,' Harrison said. 'Fix it with the supervisor for me, will you, Matt? And I guess you better let the boss know I'm here.'

'You're not coming into the field office, then?'

Harrison laid a hand on his shoulder. 'Later maybe. I got things I have to take care of first.'

He wasn't going anywhere near the field office. With what he was beginning to plan he couldn't take the risk of being seen. The possibility was becoming a reality in his mind, yet he had spoken to no one, verbalized nothing, and there was no way they would go for it anyway. He was too old and too close to the situation. He wondered at his thought processes, how quickly and instinctually his mind worked. Could he go there again – to that place, drink from that particular chalice one more time? He was fifty years old and he wasn't sure that he could.

Sweat broke on his brow as he drove the Ford onto Elysian Fields and headed towards the crescent of the river. He rumbled along Claiborne Avenue through the run-down black district that was dominated by Interstate 10, passing overhead. Old men shuffled in worn-out shoes, young kids huddled in gangs watching him – a beaten-looking white

79

man in a beaten-looking truck. Harrison glanced left and right, the ragged nature of buildings that once had been smart middle-income dwellings now reduced to little more than shanties with all the middle-income families moving out of the city. Black faces stared accusingly at him and if he had stopped or popped a tyre he might have been in trouble. He felt the adrenalin tingle, enhanced somewhat by the .45 stuck in the back of his jeans.

He parked a block from the Port of Call on Esplanade and went in for an early dinner. He had not eaten since the ham and egg bagel he had had for breakfast and had forgotten about the Port of Call till he passed it: some of the best ground beef in the city and the finest baked potatoes outside Idaho. He ordered a beer and a burger, a potato with sour cream and bacon chips and chives. He ate at the counter, smoking a cigarette afterwards and watched five well-dressed black guys talking at a corner table.

One of them, a colossus of a man, rose to go to the men's room at the same time as Harrison, and for a moment their eyes met. The black guy was about six two, built like Schwarzenegger in his heyday, and his eyes were the coal black of a shark. Harrison could not help but notice the Star of David he wore round his neck. He knew that symbol and it had nothing to do with the state of Israel: that was the Gangsta Disciples signature. From Chicago they had spread their foul wings and enveloped a number of cities with a disease that ran through the African-American ghettos. Twice already they had tried to break into New Orleans, but the Magnolia project, St Thomas and the Calliope all had their own brand of gang-banging teenager that had spurned the more sophisticated advances of that organization and others such as the Crips and Bloods from LA. New Orleans street-gangs were family based and tough, they didn't need any Yankee infiltration.

But the GDs were here again, and he hoped it wasn't to stay. His eyes met with those of the colossus and Harrison was tempted to stare. But he let his gaze fall away like any regular person would. That was probably their worst mistake. To show weakness to people like this was to expose your soft underbelly when they'd tear you to pieces in a heartbeat, gorge on the aphrodisiac of your fear. The only people that looked right back at them were cops. If a person was in a tight spot and stared back they might think he was a cop. Chances are they'd leave him alone because all cops are armed, and even the biggest gangs avoid the heat. But right now he didn't want anyone thinking he was a cop so he looked away. What he had in mind was more suicidal than dangerous and he didn't want any more pressure on the hair-trigger than that of his own finger. As far as he was aware, only one person in the Quarter knew what he did for a living and he was on his way to see that person now.

Harrison was known to a number of other people in the Quarter, though they had no idea what he did. The service industry had its own society and he slipped in and out of their lives periodically: the longest he had lived there was six months when he rented two rooms in Burgundy and Toulouse. He was away and back, away and back, just long enough to have served a little jail time.

Dewey Biggs was the bartender at the Old Honfleur, formerly Nu Nus Café, formerly the Old Honfleur. It was part of the Hotel Provincial on Chartres Street, in the block that fronted Decatur and the French market. The ghost tour operators claimed the block on Decatur was haunted, having been a Confederate hospital during the civil war. Harrison didn't know if that was true and he didn't care. Dewey knew what he did for a living and had told no one. He was a stoic guy in his forties, having come down for the music from North Carolina. That had been twelve years previously and there was no way he could go back now.

Harrison parked on Decatur just as it was getting dark. The clouds were pressing the crescent, the wind stirring the greasy waters of the river and he could smell a gulf storm in the air. The meagre warmth of the day was gone and Harrison buttoned his jacket. He heard guitar music coming from the Margaritaville as he walked two blocks to the Honfleur.

New York Pete, a waiter from Frank's a block further on, was playing video poker and he looked up as Harrison stepped in off the street.

'Hey, Harrison,' he said. 'You been away again?'

'Does it show?'

'Only in your face.'

Dewey was watching from behind the bar, a smile parting his beard. He uncapped a sweating bottle of Miller and slid it across the counter.

'How you doing?'

Harrison shook his hand. 'Doing good, you old tar heel. What's going on?'

'Not much. Where you been hiding yourself?'

'Oh, here and there – you know how it is.' Harrison winked at him and Dewey shook his head.

'No,' he said. 'I'm glad to say I don't know how it is.'

They sat and bullshitted for half an hour. Pete went off to work and Harrison picked Dewey's brains about what had changed in the quarter. Kathleen, who used to look after the Sun and Moon guest house when Harrison had his apartment on Burgundy and Toulouse, was still around, her daughter still worked at Coop's Place a few doors down Decatur. The Duck Lady was going strong, though Salvador, her duck, was long since dead. Harrison already knew about the death of the Chicken Man a couple of years back: that had made the *Picayune*, a piece describing his exploits shaking chicken bones and shifting unwanted demons from business premises in the Quarter.

He told Dewey he was looking for an apartment and Dewey said he would ask around. He had heard word of a place not far from the Apple Barrel on Frenchman Street and he'd do his best to find out.

Harrison left him then, and walked up St Philip to Bourbon Street. The lights of Jean Lafitte's old Blacksmiths Bar were dim as usual, almost dark when he poked his head inside. He saw nobody he recognized and sat down at the bar for a drink; it was too early for Johnny Gordon to be entertaining tourists at his piano. Lafitte's was about the only bar on Bourbon Street that Harrison liked: quiet compared to the rest and at the better end, right on the lip of where it was safe to go north at night, however. Lafitte's had a payphone, and Harrison took a handful of quarters from his pocket and dialled. A gruff semi-Cajun accent answered the phone.

'Bill?' Harrison said.

'Who is this?'

'Johnny Buck.'

Silence for a moment then Chaisson let go a breath. 'Well, I'll be goddamned. How come you're calling all of a sudden?'

'I missed you. When're you next in the city?'

'I'm due at the US Courthouse at ten in the morning.'

'Meet me after, will you, Bill?'

'Sure. What do you want to talk about?'

'Jesuit Bend.'

Chaisson was silent; Harrison could hear the sudden rasp of his breathing.

'Where and when?' Chaisson said.

'Parc St Charles at noon?'

'I'll be there.'

Chaisson was a big man, six two and all of two hundred and thirty pounds. He was fifty-three years old, light brown hair cut short and combed to one side of his head. He had a cop's bearing and cop's eyes. Harrison had always liked him.

They first met when Harrison was teaching a class on undercover work to a group of certified police officers studying for their diploma from the National Academy at Quantico, the FBI's training facility in Virginia. Chaisson had been ten years a cop then and was the best student in his class. Harrison had sparred with him verbally, two grizzled guys in their early forties, not much that they hadn't seen between them. Harrison's appearance often gave the wrong impression: the classes he taught were to clean-cut career cops and he looked like a hobo. But he knew undercover work better than any other agent the Bureau had ever had and when he spoke about it other people listened.

He met Chaisson in the bar where the hotel served coffee twenty-four hours a day. The two men sat at a table behind the smoked-glass partition. Chaisson's face was red from the northerly wind that tore the length of the business district.

'Never known a January like it,' he said. 'The sun should be shining. This is the best time of year in the city.'

'Tell me about it. I just come down from West Virginia where we've had five feet of snow. I was looking forward to getting a little heat in my bones, but what do I find – more fucking winter.' They shook hands and Harrison poured coffee. 'So who was in court?'

'Oh, some weasel with interstate violations. Your boys picked him up at Lake Providence.' He unzipped his windbreaker and Harrison glimpsed the butt of a Casull 454 poking out from under his arm.

'You still carrying that cannon? Hardly the right piece for a concealed weapon.'

Chaisson laughed. 'John, with the shit bags I have to deal with I don't give a damn if the weapon's concealed or not.' He sat back. 'So how come you're back in New Orleans? And what's this about Jesuit Bend?'

Harrison finished his coffee and spat tobacco juice into the empty cup. He told Chaisson about the murder in Bridgeport, how they found Max Carter with a cheese wire twisted into his thigh. He told him what Carter had done for a living and how one of the last cases he worked on was the boy in the bayou murder.

'You remember those two sets of latent prints?' Harrison said. 'One of them was a messy set, the floor and the door and the deck, remember?'

Chaisson nodded.

'They belong to Marcel Call.'

'That coon-ass sonofabitch, he's on parole right here.'

'We like him a lot for this murder.'

Chaisson squinted at him. 'You like Call for murder?'

Harrison made a face. 'He's been to the big house twice for assault with a deadly weapon.'

'Two knives, yeah. He was packing them but nobody got stabbed. Call's a weasel, sure, John. But he isn't capable of killing anyone.'

'That's what I thought.'

'But you're looking to round him up anyway?'

'Well, we figure he's got a motive.'

'But?'

'Like you said, I don't think he's a killer.'

Chaisson cocked his head to one side. 'You're looking to reach out to him, aren't you?'

'I thought I might.'

'Because you know who he works for.'

Harrison nodded.

Chaisson took a roll of Lifesavers out of his pocket and for a long moment they looked at each other, neither of them speaking. Chaisson narrowed his eyes. 'Tell me you're not really considering this.'

Harrison made an open-handed gesture. 'I'm not considering anything. Except who those second set of Jefferson Parish latents belong to.' He poured more coffee. 'Call works for Laveaux and that's something I need to think about.'

'Something else you need to think about is staying alive,' Chaisson said. 'Laveaux is about the only man I know who'd kill a cop with no more compunction than spit. He doesn't care about the heat that comes with it.'

'That's what I figured. But I got a murder up in Bridgeport and a cold case in Jefferson Parish to think about. I figured if anyone would know how to get close to a man like that it'd be you.'

'Meaning I'm a coon-ass like him.'

'Meaning exactly that.'

Chaisson laughed. 'And if I know you I'm the first person you spoke to about this. None of this is sanctioned, right?'

'Bill, this conversation isn't even sanctioned.'

Chaisson sucked a Lifesaver and thought for a moment. 'You ever get that tattoo removed, like I told you?' he asked.

Harrison took off his jacket, revealing his upper left arm where a grinning rat, standing upright and holding a gun and a whiskey bottle, was tattooed in blue ink. Chaisson studied it for a moment. 'You know Augustine's brother was in the service.'

Harrison nodded.

'At the last count I think he actually had seven brothers, though he's closer to his cousin Ignace than any of them. Augustine was the second oldest in his family till Etienne was killed in Vietnam right about the time you and I were out there.

'Augustine worshipped Etienne. He was eight years younger and they were actually only half-brothers, but he worshipped the ground that boy walked on. The old lady had Etienne with her first husband who was stabbed to death in a bar fight in Cut Off. They'd moved to Lafourche from Opelousas, where the family settled when they first got here from Nova Scotia. Anyways, after this shrimper ripped the old man's throat out the old lady married again and had a whole brood of children.

'Augustine was the oldest of the second family but he loved his older brother. I guess he figured Etienne was a little special because he was older and having a different daddy and everything. He took it very hard when Etienne didn't come home from Asia.'

Harrison was watching him.

'Augustine is only forty-one now,' Chaisson went on. 'Too young to have fought in Nam, which was all he wanted to do when his brother bought the ticket. He's had a thing about the place ever since.' He was quiet again for a moment then he said, 'He's a cold, clever man, John. He doesn't make mistakes and you know what he's capable of when he's threatened. But if he's got a chink in his armour, which I doubt, it's his weakness for that godforsaken war you and I were in. He's been known to hand $100 bills to vets begging on the street and that guy does not do charity.'

'How come nobody ever got anything on him?' Harrison asked quietly. 'Like a set of prints, I mean.'

Chaisson looked at him carefully. 'He's too careful. You really think that second set are his?'

'It crossed my mind.'

'John, just because Call was at that camp it doesn't mean Augustine was. Even if he knew whatever was going down was going down, he'd be a million miles away. He doesn't leave his fingerprints anywhere. I've seen him wipe a glass he's been drinking out of in a restaurant. As far as I know, he's never had so much as a traffic violation. His businesses appear legit and he always files his taxes on time. He never gave anyone any good reason to look at his life too closely.'

'But you and I know he kills his own cousins, runs crack whores to the tankers, fronts illegal gambling and extorts politicians. Not to mention what goes up and down the river in those barges his boats push.' Harrison leaned across the table. 'Bill, our boys in 8 Squad have had a hard on for him for years. I don't know if he's got any connection to this thing or not. But Carter was killed with a cheese wire and so was the boy in the bayou. Call's been working for Laveaux on and off for years. If I can get a sniff at him I got to take the chance.' He was quiet for a moment, as if it was himself he was trying to convince and not Chaisson. 'I've got a motive for Call to kill Carter, but I don't figure Call for a killer. I also know he didn't have enough money to interest my fingerprint analyst.'

'But his boss did. Is that what you're telling me? You're thinking that maybe once upon a time Laveaux *did* have his prints taken and that somehow they wound up at CJIS.'

'It's possible.'

'And you're thinking that somehow this analyst matched the second set from the camp to Laveaux.'

'I don't know. Maybe. He matched them to someone other than Call, that's for sure. It got him killed, Bill, with cheese wire. Only not round the neck, round the thigh. Carter got to watch himself bleed to death.'

Chaisson leaned back in his chair. 'Does anyone else know you're thinking this way?' he said.

'I've dropped a hint with one of the guys from our organized crime squad. They want Laveaux very badly indeed, they have done for years.'

'If you did somehow manage to get someone close, the Bureau would look for a Cajun, wouldn't they?' Chaisson said.

Harrison nodded. 'Big mistake, huh?'

'No kidding. Laveaux is way too clever for that. That's exactly what he'd figure they'd do. His network is vast among his own kind. He could and would chase anybody down, find out who they really were. And when he found out he'd kill them. It wouldn't matter if they were a cop or a fed or a fucking navy SEAL.' He paused for a moment and looked at Harrison's tattoo. 'A Yankee tunnel rat might get away with it. He'd have to have cold eyes and a smart mouth, though. A man like Laveaux might get a kick out of that. That's what Etienne was like, as cold-eyed a killer as any of his clan, but with a real smart mouth.' He sipped his coffee. 'The Yankee would have to be good, though – as good as it gets, in fact. Because if he made a mistake old Augustine would have 'gator bait for years.'

Harrison could feel the hairs lifting on the back of his neck and all at once he wondered if he was too old for this. Thirty years ago he volunteered to drop into the darkness of a hole underground and crawl along with only a flashlight and six-shooting revolver to back him up. He worked on adrenalin alone, hunting soldiers of the North Vietnamese Army. He fought gun battles one on one, took a bullet in the thigh, had his eardrums burst by a grenade and still went back for more. He had to watch for booby traps, snakes and poisonous spiders. After that, any other kind of fear was no fear at all. But that was thirty years ago when he was young and had a hair stuck up his ass.

Chaisson could see his reaction. 'Are you nervous?' he said. 'You should be. You thinking maybe you're too old? Well, you are. You're not as sharp as you were either.' He arched his brows. 'Me, I quit being a cop because I wasn't sharp enough any more. Not in this neck of the woods anyway, not with guys like Laveaux. At one time maybe, but I knew when it was time to quit. I thought you did too.'

Harrison took out a cigarette and rolled it between his fingers. 'I'm not even sure why I'm sitting here, Bill. I don't know if it's because it's my job or because of that kid at Jesuit Bend, or because of something else completely.'

'Then go back to West Virginia. Give Call over to the field office and go home.' Chaisson stood up. 'That's my advice. It's not your fight. Let other people deal with Laveaux if that's who is behind this. So you got a stiff in West Virginia, so what. Pass it on to the field office and get back to the quiet life you were looking for.'

Harrison looked at him and Chaisson's face creased into a smile. 'On the other hand,' he said, 'if you decide not to – your boy has his office on the wharf right there in the Quarter. He works late but likes to get in the Margaritaville – especially on Wednesdays, that's when Coco Robichaux is playing.'

six

Penny called Harrison in his room. 'The boss wants to see you, Johnny Buck. Your supervisor has been on the phone from Clarksburg so we had to brief Mayer. He wants to know why you haven't come in and your super wants to know why your Nextel is switched off.'

Harrison rubbed the heel of his palm into his eyes. 'You still keep the NOPD surveillance van in the lock-up, Matt?'

'Sure.'

'Come and get me in that. Pick me up by the Confederate museum at Lee Circle.'

'John, there's no need for that. I know what you're thinking – even if we look to pitch Call, the boss has already said there's no way you're getting involved.'

Harrison smiled wryly at himself in the mirror. 'That's what I figured he'd say.' He sat up and the dog tags which he still wore from his service days jangled against his chest. 'Lee Circle, Matthew.'

Penny picked him up. Harrison got in the back of the van and sat on his bench till they were inside the underground parking lot at the new field office.

'Nice building,' Harrison said when Penny let him out. 'Beats fighting for parking space at Poydras Plaza.'

'You wait till you see inside.' Penny punched his access number into the lock on the door. 'We got more space than you could shake a stick at. The building's full of mould, mind you. Contractors screwed up somewhere along the line.'

He led Harrison up to the third floor and the offices of the special agent in charge. Charlie Mayer was nearing retirement; he had been Harrison's boss for three years before he left the job. The last time they met Harrison handed him his shield and his gun and they hadn't spoken since the suits at the Hoover building persuaded him to come back.

'John.' Mayer stood up and shook hands. 'Why didn't you check-in right away?'

'I did.' Harrison jerked his thumb at Penny. 'I checked in with him.'

'It's OK to come to the field office, you know.'

Harrison looked him squarely in the eye. 'Old habits die hard, boss.'

'Is that how it is?'

'I never quit smoking either.'

Mayer walked round behind his desk. 'Your supervisor wants to talk to you. He can't get you on your cellphone.'

'I'll call him.'

'Do that.' Mayer sat down. 'Penny filled me in on why you flew down here. You want us to pick up Marcel Call so you can interrogate him.'

Harrison sat on the couch. 'I want it done quietly, through his parole officer. Call works a tugboat that unloads on Augustine Laveaux's dock in the Quarter. I want him picked up there and taken to Vieux Carré.'

'OK.' Mayer pushed himself back from his desk. 'But that's it, John. Don't get any ideas about anything else. I know you're thinking we might be able to use Call to get close to Laveaux's operation, but if we do, which I doubt, it'll be a long-term investigation and won't involve you.'

Harrison laughed. 'Boss, I'm fifty years old. You really think I want to go through that level of shit again?' He stood up and shook his head.

'Take a desk in the squad room,' Mayer told him, 'and call your supervisor.'

Harrison talked to Santini before he talked to Somers. He used his cellphone and stood in the parking lot smoking a cigarette.

'Hey, cowboy, what's happening?' she asked him. 'Somers is popping blood vessels because you won't answer your phone.'

'He'll live. What's with the PO in Charleston? He still singing the same song about Call?'

'Yes, he is. He swears he never made contact.'

'You believe him?'

'Why would he lie? He gave us the heads up on the others. No, I figure Carter reached out to this one on his own and got his hand bitten off for his trouble.' Santini sighed. 'Why the silence, Harrison? Why didn't you check-in when you should have?'

Harrison didn't answer her. He was watching one of the SWAT team repacking the trunk of his car. He had a new Colt M-4 machine gun laid out with his carbine MP5.

'This has gotten personal, hasn't it?' Santini said. 'This Jesuit Bend murder really bit you bad. Harrison, you don't need me to tell you things shouldn't get personal.'

'Then don't tell me.'

'You're old enough to know it anyway.'

'I thought you said I was young.'

'I didn't say you were young. I said you needed to feel young.'

Harrison laughed. 'Don't worry about me, Francesca. I'm fine.'

'Are you?'

'Santini, quit mothering me.'

'I wouldn't dream of it, baby.'

He could hear the little edge in her voice. 'Anyways, I spoke to Bill Chaisson,' he said. 'You know, the original cop from the Jefferson Parish cold case.'

'Did you tell him about Carter?'

'I told him it all. That murder still bothers him, too.'

'I don't know why. The kid was probably some gang-banging shit bag who got himself burned in a drug war.'

'Santini, project-dwelling gang-bangers don't normally frequent the bayous. It's a bit damp down there and there's nowhere to plug in the boom box.'

'Ha, ha. Whatever he was, Harrison, you let it get personal and it'll be you frequenting the bayous, and I don't mean in a boat.'

'That's your warning, is it?'

'Just call me Madame Josephine.'

Harrison said nothing for a moment. 'Look, let's not fall out, uh? I hear you. Good enough?'

'Is that your best offer?'

'I figure.'

'Then I guess it's good enough.'

'I'd better talk to the boss. Keep him from setting his ass on fire.'

'OK. But keep me posted this end. I'm supposed to let Proud know what's going on.'

'He's still hanging in there. I'd have thought he'd be glad to punt this one downfield by now.'

'He's resigned to us taking over, John. But there aren't many murders in Bridgeport. If it hadn't been Christmas Day he'd have been delighted.'

She put Somers on the phone and Harrison told him what was going on. He told him he would keep him informed and, yes, he'd keep his phone switched on.

Penny talked to Vincent Palastina, Marcel Call's parole officer, who told him that the harbour police would pick Call up when the tugboat unloaded at Governor Nicholls Street Wharf the following Thursday. The harbour police would grab him on behalf of the New Orleans police for a minor parole violation, which meant Palastina calling in a favour from the 8th District, which in turn meant that the FBI owed him one. He would call Vieux Carré on Royal Street as soon as he'd seen the arrest warrant served. It was a three-minute drive from the wharf up to the station house.

Harrison got Penny to drop him back at Lee Circle where he jumped the streetcar and walked across Poydras to the Parc St Charles. He showered and changed his clothes then went out into the early evening. The wind had died away and the horns from the tugboats on the crescent warned of incoming fog. Harrison crossed Poydras and walked to Canal where he crossed again. Three young guys were hanging around the entrance to Burger King and they gave him the eye. Harrison stared right back at them this time, before heading east on Royal Street. He waited for them to come after him but they didn't. He thought about what Santini had said as he walked beyond the galleries where the skinny older guy was playing guitar. He always set his stool up east of Vieux Carré, and he had a pug-faced dog in a baby stroller. The man was about Harrison's age and looked and sounded like James Taylor. Harrison liked James Taylor so he fished five bucks from his jeans pocket and dropped it in the guitar case.

Santini was a good cop, and she was a good woman, and what she had said was right. This was personal and it shouldn't be and the irony was he didn't even know why it was so personal. It had taken a woman to voice it to him directly. He thought about what she had said about the bayous and again knew she was right. To put himself in the way of Augustine Laveaux was as dangerous as anything he had ever done in his life. The fact that he was an FBI agent made no difference. Laveaux would lose his body somewhere in the Barataria and go on about his business.

He walked toward St Philip, still thinking. A murdered CJIS employee had led him back to the boy in the bayou, a homicide that had shaped his dreams for three years, a homicide he had thought would remain unsolved till the file disintegrated from the weight of its own dust. Chaisson wanted it solved because it was a kid and it was a cold case and he hated unsolved murders. It was more of a professional thing. But Santini was right: with Harrison it was personal, and personal made it dangerous.

Beyond the 8th District station house at Vieux Carré he headed for the back of the Cathedral and came out on Jackson Square. Two stilt-walkers came towards him, but he shooed them away with a look and picked a path between the psychics and tarot readers. He thought of Madame Josephine and what she had seen in Carter's mother's cards then he thought again of what Santini had said. As he turned on to Decatur Street he almost walked into the vampire in the blue sunglasses who was just beginning one of his night-time walking tours. Too many Anne Rice novels, Harrison muttered to himself, and headed for the Honfleur and Dewey's stoic company.

Dewey was solid, ultra-reliable. A tar heel from North Carolina, he was the kind of guy that would stick in a fight and Harrison loved him for it. The fog was just beginning to settle under the haze of the gas lamp and the first damp fingers were tickling his collar as he stepped into the bar.

Dewey snapped the cap off a beer bottle and passed it to him. Harrison plucked a Marlboro from his shirt pocket and popped a match on his thumbnail. 'Dewey,' he said. 'Where does Gary Hirstius live?'

Dewey made a face. 'Can't tell you where he lives, but I know he's playing on North Carrollton tonight. The Wits Inn, right there on the Iberville corner.'

'What time?'

'Around nine, I guess.'

Harrison looked at his watch. It was just past eight. 'Reckon I got time,' he said. 'I'll see you later on.'

Outside again he turned on to St Philip and already his heart bumped in his chest. He had decided what he was going to do, although not quite sure why. He crossed Chartres Street and Royal and paused briefly to light a cigarette by Lafitte's Blacksmiths Bar, before carrying on north beyond Bourbon. Chaisson's words rang in his ears. He was too old for this. Nobody was sure if he could cut it any more, least of all himself.

The mist hung low and dense now, the gas lanterns barely cutting a hole in the yellow fog that gathered like mould round the scrolled iron balconies of the crumbling Quarter properties. Harrison kept to the side of the road and the shadows when only the middle of the street would do, or better still a taxi. He walked towards Rampart and Basin Street and St Louis No. 1 where the voodoo queen was buried.

He walked the length of St Philip Street without hassle. Only a couple of people passed him, tourists in a group on their way down to the relative delights of Bourbon Street. Big Daddy's and the Kasbah waiting, The Café Lafayette in Exile if you were that way inclined or just bad Cajun music, overpriced drinks and Rick's Café if you considered yourself a gentleman and didn't mind a ten-buck cover charge for your lap-dancing. He walked with purpose, much on his mind, and the quality of the buildings left and right deteriorated into lumpy shapeless shadows edging the mist.

He headed left on North Rampart in the direction of Canal Street and now he was in the part of town where – according to Bruce Springsteen – 'when you hit a red light you don't stop'. Was he too old for all of this? Were people like Chaisson and Mayer right? Fifty years old and on the street, not just beating the bricks but in there where it happened, where life and death dulled and blurred into each other. It occurred to him then that he didn't know very much else and for a moment couldn't be sure if that was a good or bad thing. He had bullshitted and played the mean guy when the suits in Washington had got hold of him through the legal attaché in London, but underneath the relief had been tangible. The FBI was home for him, this was family. Having witnessed life on the outside, he dreaded his fifty-seventh birthday, because without this job there was nothing.

But then again there was Santini. She was worrying about him, that much was obvious. He knew he could quite easily begin to worry about her if he allowed himself. And where would that leave him? Out on a limb somewhere or with a hope of a different kind of life. It had been so long he didn't know which it was. He felt a wafer of fear, though, like a damp sheet on his skin, the feeling accentuated by the hanging tendrils of mist that hovered above the streetlamps like visible ether to drown the already drowning. He didn't know where the fear came from, his immediate situation or what he thought he could be facing, or perhaps the certain knowledge that in order to have that other kind of life he had to go through this.

Two black youths stood outside a store that used to be a front for a massage parlour – and before the gambling boats and 'Harrah's Casino' – an illegal crapshoot.

'Need some company, my man?'

So it was still a skin joint. Harrison shook his head. 'Nope,' he said, and walked on.

'Be safe now.' The black man's voice lifted in mockery behind him.

Now he was on Conti and directly across Basin Street the chipped white blocks of mausoleum stonework lifted to cast the yellow fog as spectral. Harrison took a cigarette from his shirt pocket. He took a matchbook, split a paper match and struck it on his belt buckle. The instinct, the sense of professionalism began to work its way into his being, like a rusty tap slowly coming to life. A split match was a jail-time match and he was doing it without even thinking. He lit the cigarette and let smoke drift from his nostrils and then he crossed the street.

At the cemetery he looked beyond the barred gate, beyond the wide stone walls. The oldest cemetery in New Orleans, home to the voodoo queen herself, with the crosses scored on her stone. People came from miles around just to look at her final resting place. That's if she was resting at all. Take a cemetery tour with the vampire and he'd tell another story. The hype that was New Orleans, the only town in America where the cops encouraged you to drink.

Harrison sucked on his cigarette. There was hype on the one hand but on the other a current, a charge running through the place unlike any other town he had worked in. For all the laughter and parades and Mardi Gras there was an undercurrent of evil in this town, if such a thing existed of itself separate from those beings who put it to work.

Beyond the cemetery was the Iberville housing project and the squared three-storey tenement blocks rose in quadrangles through the mist. Rap music punched holes in the air, he could hear car horns blaring and even at this early hour the sound of a handgun going off. Harrison steeled himself. Beyond the Iberville was St Louis No. 2, a bigger cemetery housing such notaries as Dominique You who had sailed with Lafitte. Beyond that was the Lafitte project, much like this one, a black ghetto where the decent folk lived in fear of their lives and each block, each set of 'bricks', was ruled by some teenage gang lord, backed up and armed to the teeth. He would sit on his pile of turf until somebody blew him off it so they could sit there in his place.

Harrison worked the .45 looser in his waistband, checked his ankle rig and walked into the project. Whatever else, he told himself, this was the quickest way to North Carrollton Avenue.

seven

Frederico was driving, thin faced, black hair, a little Spanish amongst the Acadian of his ancestry. He wore a leather biker's jacket and a knitted black and white hat that hung down his back like a sock. Marie sat next to him, smoking a Newport cigarette. They had come up from Barataria to fetch Junya and Frederico was not happy about it.

'Piece of shit, kid,' he said. 'Arrytime we off the boat he want to go fooyay with stuff that ain't his bidness. He think he gonna be some kind of gang lord or something?'

'He's not fooling with anything, Frederico.' Marie tried to placate him. 'You know what he's doing. And it is his business.'

Frederico looked sideways at her, lip curled over teeth as if he was going to slap her. He would like to, but he needed both hands for the wheel so they didn't end up windshield-deep in the bayou. Cypress trees whispered in the mist on either side of the road and the cold dank fog penetrated the cab where Marie had the window rolled down.

'You just a crack whore, what the fuck would you know?' Frederico snapped. 'You don't know shit. The two of you don't know shit, now roll up the damn window.'

Marie did as he told her, leaving just a crack for her cigarette smoke. Frederico cursed under his breath and drove on.

Marie wasn't a crack whore any longer: she had been clean since Augustine gave her the kid to look out for. That was three years ago now and she was never going back to that dark place where she lived before the responsibility. Junya had saved her life: maybe Augustine had known that when he gave him to her. It was more likely he thought they would bring one another down so he could grind them both into the Barataria mud.

But there was something about the boy, barely ten years younger than she was. Something in his eyes reminded her of the brother she thought she might have had but could not recall, as most of her early memories had been wiped clean by coke and crack and anything else she could snort or smoke or shoot up her arm. Too many men bruising and battering her body, too many faces, eyes and teeth; too many mouths lusting for her, ravenous, voracious. The only way to block them out was to block it all out. She had learned the ability to remember very selectively.

Once she was clean other options appeared to her, though she had never taken them up. Pretty soon she realized she was just as much a prisoner of Augustine as she had been of the crack. Many times she had stood in the Quarter, considered the 8th District station house and thought about going inside and spilling what she knew. She knew cops from her whoring days, good cops and bad cops, cops that would give you a ride home and make sure you got there without getting raped, cops that would keep you out of the drunk tank. Then there were other cops, cops on a pad who arranged for the cabs to take you up to the Spillway or let you through the gates at Tchoupitoulas and Felicity so you could service the big ships. She knew cops who would get you to trick for them and cops that would beat you within an inch of your life if you crossed them. Many times she had considered seeking out the chief of detectives. But Augustine had thought of that, as he had thought of everything else: he had placed her in this van, given her money and this job to do, and because of that he owned her. She could no more go to the cops than fly in the air. Augustine owned her just like he owned the boy.

And now word had come up from his seclusion on Grand Terre to rein the boy in from freelancing in the projects. That was another demonstration of title, the freebies he handed out to Junya knowing where they would end up and that the proceeds would be in Junya's back pocket if he ever got picked up.

Junya was in the Iberville housing project, which backed on to St Louis No. 1 cemetery, where foolish tourists would wander among the graves looking for the voodoo queen while dusk fell and gang members watched from the top-floor windows through binoculars. Word would come via walkie-talkies to the ground and then there would be a dead or maimed but certainly robbed tourist lying out on Basin Street. The thrill of it was the proximity of the 1st District police station just two blocks towards the river.

Junya had no rocks left and he was just hanging, baggy jeans wet to the knees where the mist was thick with rain. He sat on a step with some of the kids he used to run with before he went on his own. Dylan was talking. Dylan was in a gang who bought crack from Junya and sold it on at a profit to the school kids during recess. He was leaning back with his elbows on the stoop, listening to a boom box spitting Puff Daddy and swigging beer from a long-necked bottle.

'We got GD in town again,' he said. 'I seen the mo'fuck-ers on Claiborne Avenue in their suits and their turtlenecks and their Jew boy necklaces dangling. I drove by with Clete and Stucky and I hollered, "Mo'fucker, get yo' nigger trash ass off my street. It ain't your bidness to be here. This is our town."' He laughed and his tongue hung out, pink and thick like a dog's.

'I seen GD in the Quarter,' another kid said. 'I told them to git back to Shitcago where they belong.' He yelped, too. Junya laughed with them.

He had run with this gang till Wendell got his head blown off three years ago on Canal Street. They had parked by the

101

radio shack, Wendell driving while he went in to get a battery for the boom box. Two gang members from Lafitte drove by in a Z28 Camaro and shot Wendell while he sat at the wheel. When Junya got back to the car, Wendell's brains were running like somebody's vomit on the inside of the passenger window. A woman was screaming and he could hear the cops coming so he jumped the streetcar, riding all the way through the channel and the garden district to the levee by Audobon Park. It was late afternoon by then and he hung out at the zoo for an hour or so. After that he went back to the levee and sat for a while on the batture land by the river. Then the crack whore showed up.

That had been the beginning of all this, and from that moment he had thought only of himself. Those Barataria boys might think they had him, but in reality he ran with no gang but himself. With what he had stored away nobody owned him. They could kill him in a heartbeat if they wanted to, but he figured he had been close to death all his life and he knew how to avoid it.

He figured he was probably eleven back then, but he didn't know for sure. Size wasn't a factor because he had never been very big and he had been living on the street for as long as he could recall. He wore his mother's ring on a chain round his neck, but he couldn't remember her face.

'GD won't come to this town,' he said. 'They done tried that shit already.' He got up, hitching his baggy jeans above his sneakers and fingering the roll of bills tied with an elastic band in his pocket. 'They got their ass kicked in St Thomas and Magnolia. They'd get whipped here, too.'

'I seen them today,' Dylan said. 'I already told you that.'

'On Claiborne.' Junya spat on the ground. 'Fuck the pussies on Claiborne Avenue. Claiborne was never worth dog shit. Y'all could take Claiborne from here.'

He looked up as two or three youths from the block across the street got to their feet, watching something going on down by the first row of wire.

'What's up, brother? What's going on?' Dylan was on his feet, older, taller and leaning an arm on Junya's shoulder. 'Well, fuck me,' he said. 'We got whitey walking the project.'

The first indication of trouble was a whistle, rising from a rooftop away to his right. Harrison didn't look round. He kept his eyes ahead, breath steaming now as the fog grew colder. Music thumped at every corner, the place alive with dealers and dope-heads and girls as young as twelve selling the only wares they had to get a hit of whatever it was that was hitting the streets tonight. You could just about make it through here in the daytime if you were quick. Dawn was good, even the dragon chasers slept at dawn. When he was on the SWAT team years ago, they always rolled at dawn if there was a take-down in the projects, but at night the gang-bangers ruled and Harrison was a white man in their midst.

He walked two blocks before the whistles got louder and the first cat call came from the squares of darkness that were the windows. They were like workers on a building site, whistles from every direction, only these whistles were full of malice.

The first of them materialized out of the gloom. Harrison saw him coming from the right, baggy pants and white football shirt, bright against the darkness.

'What have we got here,' the voice came at him, 'some saggy white pussy on the bricks?' Two of them now, young, woollen hats pulled low to their eyes, baggy clothing, heavy basketball sneakers with Michael Jordan soles. Harrison walked a little further then a whole group appeared in front of him.

Junya and Dylan made their way to the wire that separated their block from the next street. The white guy had slowed as five brothers approached him with three more coming from behind. Party time. Junya felt the saliva thicken against his lip.

*

103

Harrison paused, pulled a Marlboro from his shirt and snapped the rest of his jail-time match. With measured calm he lifted it to his lips and glimpsed his antagonists by the light of the flame.

'What you doing, old man?' The kid that addressed him was fourteen if he was a day. Harrison was not tall and this guy was smaller than him, hands bunched as fists in his jacket pockets; two taller guys hovered behind him. 'What you doing on the bricks, man? White meat like you.'

Harrison blew out the match, sucked smoke and exhaled without removing the cigarette from his mouth.

'Son,' he said. 'Not that it's any of your business, but I'm on my way to a gig.'

'A gig?' The boy swaggered in front of him. 'There ain't no gig, my man. We saw you looking at them gravestones. You on your way to a funeral.'

Harrison leaned and spat. The other kids were laughing now. He couldn't count them, voices around him, voices from the fence, voices rising as one from the weight of the mist. On his right he heard the metallic click of a switch-blade knife, far in the distance the wail of a siren.

'You a long way from home, whitey.' The young kid very deliberately stepped on his foot. Harrison let him press down with his weight then with the flat of his hand against his chest he pushed him away. 'And you, my friend, are a long way from your next birthday,' he said.

All at once a taller, much bulkier boy had a knife pressed to his cheek. 'You some kinda weirdo, man, coming through here at night. You looking for our girls, mister, you looking for some black pussy? Maybe you just looking to get stabbed.'

Harrison turned so the tip of the knife nicked his skin but he was face on to his aggressor, black eyes, the whites yellow with dope, red lines against his pupils. With more speed than he thought he could muster Harrison monkey-punched him in the sternum and he fell down like a tree.

The .45 was out and racked and pointed at the smaller kid's head before anyone else could move.

'I ain't looking to get stabbed,' Harrison said. 'But maybe y'all looking to get shot.'

They backed off. Maybe they could smell the adrenalin that lifted through his pores; maybe it was the look in his eyes. His brow was damp and his features a mask. He felt no fear now, just a surge of anger, revulsion that children this young could and would snuff out his or any other life as easily as he'd pop a match for a smoke.

'Now I'm going to cross the street,' he said. 'And you're going to move back and let me be. If you don't I'll cap away here till the clip is clean, and I won't be selective.'

He brushed the younger boy aside and the others parted before him. Harrison walked up the street and out of the project. He crossed Lafitte without incident and came out on North Carrollton Avenue. Only then did he put the gun away, realizing he had walked half a dozen blocks with it dangling by his side.

Junya watched him go, eyes half-closed, not quite believing what he had seen. He was thirty feet away and the mist was heavy, but he could see like a cat in the dark and he never forgot a face.

'That guy must be some nutcase out of the psycho wards at Charity,' Dylan said. 'Nobody but a ding brain would do a thing like that. Man, look at him go, he knows nobody's gonna shoot him.'

'He ain't no ding brain,' Junya said. 'A ding brain wouldn't do that.' He stared at the departing white man's back and spoke softly, more to himself than anyone else. 'Only a cop would do that.'

eight

Harrison pushed open the door of the Wits Inn and cut a path to the bar. He could feel the trickle of blood on his cheek where the blade had broken the skin. The bartender looked at him, then handed him a napkin and told him the bathrooms were out the back beyond the pool tables. Harrison ordered a beer and made his way through. The cut was bigger than he had thought and probably needed a Band-Aid. As if in recognition of the fact, the bartender appeared with a bottle of antiseptic and a box of waterproof plasters. 'Next time take a cab,' he said, and left him to his surgery.

Back in the bar Harrison took his beer to a stool at the counter that ran the length of the walls. Gary Hirstius had his band set up in front of the window, just himself, a bass player and a guy on pedal steel. He hadn't seen Harrison come in, bent as he was over his amps. Harrison lit a cigarette and blew smoke from the side of his mouth, the Band-Aid irritating the skin of his cheek. He nudged at it with the back of his hand and realized his heart was still pounding. But his reflexes were intact. He had walked through the Iberville, held his nerve and scattered a bunch of gang-bangers. He was quietly pleased with himself, though the adrenalin was still pumping.

He tried to determine exactly when he had made his decision to leave the corridor of FBI protocol and go his own way. He had always been a 'kiss my ass' agent, a term which described older guys like himself who were beginning to chip away at retirement age and who no longer cared about the suits and what they thought was important. He wasn't even sure he had come to a conscious decision; one thing had just led to another. It wasn't necessarily Laveaux's name that had started it, or the fact that the Jesuit Bend murder still haunted him after three years. Instinct drove him and right now he wasn't questioning it, though something told him he should be.

Gary Hirstius strummed the first few chords of a song while he set his mike correctly. Harrison stared through the audience at him. Hirstius was a fixture in the New Orleans music scene: he had been playing one club or another since he headlined at the strip joints when the mob had a hold in Bourbon Street back in the 1970s. Hirstius had been working towards a record deal for twenty-five years and to make ends meet, he'd wound up with a private investigator's licence. Harrison wanted to talk to him because he was a friend of Coco Robichaux.

Hirstius played 'Too far gone', the lyrics of which reminded Harrison of himself, then launched into some earlier numbers. He was good, very good, and Harrison could not understand why nobody had picked him up. Harrison bought another beer and sent one over to the singer. Hirstius took the bottle when the cocktail waitress brought it for him and squinted in Harrison's direction. For a moment nothing seemed to register. Harrison raised his own bottle and Hirstius picked his way through the crowd.

'Remember me?' Harrison said.

'Sure. You're the guy working security at McDonald's.' They looked at one another.

'I got promoted,' Harrison said. 'You still doing what you did before?'

'Afraid so.' Hirstius sat on a stool and sighed. 'I've been driving I10 for twenty-five years, my friend. Kinda hoped I'd be through with it by now.'

'No dice with a record deal, then?'

'Mister, over the past quarter of a century I've been promised the world. I believe nothing and trust nobody. Record companies want manufactured pop bands these days, not old blues players like me.'

'Feeling sorry for yourself, uh?'

'You mean *you* don't?' Hirstius sipped beer. 'What happened to your face?'

'Cut myself with the razor.'

There was silence between them for a moment then Hirstius said, 'I take it you didn't just show up for the music.'

'I could've done. It's good enough.'

'Thanks.'

'I mean it. You're good. You always were.'

'Like I said, thanks. What is it I can do for you?'

'Tomorrow night Coco Robichaux is playing the Margaritaville.'

Hirstius furrowed his brow. 'So?'

'So I want you to swing by and have a beer with me.'

'At the Margaritaville?'

Harrison nodded.

'You want to meet Coco or something?'

'Not really.'

Hirstius held up his hands in surrender. 'You got me, brother.'

'Just a beer, Gary, an hour of your time is all.'

'Why?'

Harrison bit his lip. 'I'll tell you one detail and that's it. Then either you come or you don't. Jesuit Bend,' he said.

Hirstius stared at him. 'You're talking about the Jefferson Parish cold case.'

'One hour listening to old gravel voice is all.'

'You'll owe me.'

'Of course.'

Hirstius slipped off the stool. 'I'll meet you in the Honfleur. Did you know Dewey Biggs was related to me?'

'No, I didn't.' Harrison pulled a face. 'That old tar heel, shit, I feel for you.'

Marie and Frederico picked up Junya on Basin Street. Frederico popped the rear doors of the van and Junya climbed inside. The van's windows were blacked out and he switched on the light. He shifted the little backpack he wore over his shoulders and squatted on the cushions as the van pulled away from the kerb. Back to the Barataria and the boat once more. He picked his nose, inspected his fingertip then flicked. Tugging open his bag, he took out his ring binder, sketchpad and his pencils. Carefully he leafed through the pages. Everybody was there, every one of them, right from the very beginning, face after face after face. He had seen a new face tonight, however – that white guy walking through the project. Junya frowned, tugging his mouth down at the corners and thinking hard. Taking up his favourite pencil, he began to shade the face from memory.

Harrison woke early, way before the alarm went off. He took a shower. The following day they were due to pick up Marcel Call via the New Orleans police department, but before then he had a hand to play, hopefully with Gary Hirstius's help. He called Santini.

'Checking up on me, JB?' she asked. 'I mean, it's barely seven.'

'You still in bed?'

'Of course I'm still in bed. I won't be at my desk till eight and it takes precisely fourteen minutes from here to the office.'

Harrison wanted to tell her what he was planning, but couldn't. What he was planning was out of line, and her knowing about it could compromise her position. When Somers and Mayer were presented with what was hopefully a *fait accompli* it was important that there was no one else on whom they could vent their spleen.

'We're picking up Call tomorrow. NOPD's bringing him in for a friendly chat. I'm pretty much kicking my heels till then,' he told her.

'There's not much going on at this end. Nothing you don't know about already. What're you going to do with Call when you get him?'

'Either book him or try and pitch him. I haven't decided which yet.'

'You talking about him going back as a confidential informant?'

'Maybe. It'll depend on what he can give us. Hopefully he'll have something on either of the Laveaux cousins and we can go after them. I figure Carter knew who the second set of latents belonged to. I guess I'm hoping it's Augustine. He's been a target down here for longer than anyone cares to remember.'

'Is that your wish list? Merry Christmas.' Santini yawned. 'Get your butt back up here soon, Johnny Buck. You may be an old-timer, but I miss your scrawny ass now that it's been in my bed.'

Harrison hung up the phone, aware of that tingling, the sense of excitement in his breast that could only ever be generated by the interest of a woman. It juxtaposed starkly with his other aspirations and again he felt the knot of sudden fear that had come upon him on Basin Street last night. His palms were sweating and he wiped them on his thighs. He lit a cigarette but it tasted foul. His reflection gazed back from the mirror as if to haunt him.

He did not go into the field office. Penny called him and confirmed their arrangement for the following day at the Vieux Carré station house on Royal Street.

At eight o'clock that evening Harrison was drinking a beer in the Honfleur bar when Gary Hirstius showed up. Earlier Dewey had told him the apartment on Frenchman was available if he wanted it, and Harrison wrote the name and number of the landlord on the back of a napkin.

He and Hirstius crossed the street to the Margaritaville, and Harrison could hear Coco Robichaux singing in his own unique fashion, a sound like rocks being dragged down a riverbed.

'He drinks tequila with Tabasco sauce chasers,' Hirstius told him. 'You watch him – he'll take a shot of tequila then follow it with a slug of hot sauce. People think he gets the voice from smoking, but it's tequila and hot-sauce chasers.'

They took seats at a table right in front of the tiny raised area that served as the stage and Harrison lit a smoke. Five Cajun men were gathered at the far end of the bar and a sixth occupied a table directly in front of them. He was long limbed and slim, wearing black jeans and shiny boots and a cotton shirt with no collar. His skin was dark and his hair black, his sharp fine-boned features split by a scar that ran from above his right eye to his jaw.

The evening was fine after last night's fog. The day had been clear and warm, no rain and no mist drifting in off the river, something more akin to the normal temperatures for that time of year. Hirstius got the drinks, nodding to the Cajuns at the bar. Harrison ignored them all and slipped his jacket off. He wore a sleeveless T-shirt underneath. His chest was well defined for his years and his arms taut and sinewy. The tunnel rat insignia was tattooed above his left elbow. He sucked on his cigarette as Coco rattled through a few covers, Bob Dylan, Woody Guthrie and the weirdest version of Leonard Cohen's 'Bird on the Wire' Harrison had ever heard.

Hirstius came back with the drinks. 'Who're your friends?' Harrison said without looking round.

'At the bar?' Hirstius raised an eyebrow. 'You telling me they're not the reason we're here. Eat shit, brother.' He tipped the neck of the bottle to his lips and nodded to Coco Robichaux.

There was a good crowd in now, the tables full, and the dining room beyond the stage where Coco was playing was heaving. Harrison finished his beer then carved out a path to the bar. He saw Ignace Laveaux leaning with his back to the counter, well-tooled arms folded across his chest like a Choctaw. His features were thin and pinched with pock-marks, his eyes black like his cousin's, hair to his shoulders. Both his front teeth were missing, giving his mouth a fanglike appearance. He glanced briefly at Harrison as he ordered.

Augustine Laveaux had got up from his table and was propped between his cousin and another man whom Harrison didn't recognize. He wore a Confederate flag bandana tied round his head. For the briefest of moments Harrison felt the intensity of Laveaux's gaze on his arm.

Back at the table Coco had finished his first set and was talking to the audience through the microphone. His voice was the same rasp when he spoke as when he sang. He sipped tequila and clamped a big black cigar between his teeth. 'I'm going to take a little break here,' he said. Then he paused while he lit the cigar and his eyes fixed on Hirstius. 'Gary Hirstius in the bar.'

Clapping started behind Harrison, which was exactly what he had hoped would happen. Gary shook hands with Coco.

'You want to play a couple while I freshen my glass, Gary?' Coco asked him. Again the clapping started, and Coco vacated his seat. Hirstius looked sideways at Harrison, who lifted one eyebrow. 'Go break a leg,' he said.

Harrison sat at the table on his own now with a vacant stool next to him. Hirstius played one song then picked away at the guitar strings for a moment before starting into a song. He finished up, began another and Harrison felt someone slide on to the stool alongside him. He didn't say anything and he didn't look round. But he could sense the size of the man and was aware of long black jeans under the table.

Augustine Laveaux held a glass in his hand and Harrison glanced at him, side on. Laveaux was watching Hirstius on stage, his skin dark, almost copper in tone like an Indian's, face split by that scar. Harrison thought about the second set of latent prints found in the oil worker's camp on the bayou. 'That seat's taken,' he said.

Slowly Laveaux turned his head.

Harrison held his eye for a long moment then nodded to Hirstius on the stage.

'He's busy right now,' Laveaux said quietly.

'Just so long as you know.'

Hirstius wasn't watching. He was deliberately playing with his eyes closed, distancing himself from their table.

Laveaux stared at Harrison a moment longer then took a black cigar from a silver case. Harrison watched him light it with an army issue Zippo, which he upended on the counter. Harrison recognized it: he had one just like it, issued when he landed at Lai Khe Base thirty years previously. He gestured to it with his cigarette. 'Where'd you steal that? You're too young to have earned it.'

For a moment Laveaux was still. Harrison could feel the tension in him. He had stopped tapping the lighter and Harrison could smell the sweat on his skin.

'It belonged to my brother,' Laveaux said very quietly.

'And he doesn't need it any more?'

Laveaux's eyes were black and cold in his face. 'He's dead.' He looked down at Harrison's tattoo. 'He was killed in Vietnam.' He sucked on the cigar and let smoke cloud from his mouth. 'If I find out that marker you're wearing isn't for real I'll peel it off you myself.'

After he was gone Harrison sat where he was, casually drawing on his cigarette and nodding to Gary Hirstius. Hirstius looked from him to Laveaux at the bar and back again. Harrison drank his beer then slowly he swivelled in his seat. Laveaux was standing next to Coco Robichaux. He passed his empty glass to the bartender and watched him wash it. Then he turned again. He still held the lighter in his hand and his eyes were fixed on Harrison. They were coal black and dead against the skin of his face.

nine

They picked up Call first thing in the morning. Ignace Laveaux's tugboat the *See More Night* was moored alongside Governor Nicholls Street Wharf and Harrison watched from a room in the Provincial Hotel. A harbour police cruiser pulled up on the dock with Vincent Palastina, Call's parole officer, in the passenger seat. Harrison could see Call waiting while a worker from the wharf moved the crane into place to begin unloading the barges lashed to the bows of the tug. Palastina and the police officer got out of the car and went up to where Call was standing with his back to them. Palastina spoke to him for a few minutes and he stood there shaking his head.

Ignace was watching, his hands on his hips, then gesticulating in frustration. He took a cellphone from his pocket and punched in a number.

Harrison was due at the 8th District about now, and he called Penny. 'They got him,' he said. 'I'll be along in a few.'

Across on the dock he could see Call arguing with the parole officer. Palastina took his arm and Call pulled away from him. The harbour cop stood with his thumbs in his belt, ready to move in if he was needed. A knock on the door made Harrison turn. A black lady smiled at him, her housekeeping cart stacked high with fresh linen.

'You all done looking at the room, sir?' she asked him.

'Yes, thank you, ma'am.' Harrison stuffed the binoculars inside his jacket. 'I'll go see the guys at reception.'

He took the elevator downstairs and walked across the courtyard and out into Chartres Street. The NOPD squad car rumbled past him as he walked up St Philip with both Call and his parole officer in the back seat. Harrison decided he would let Penny interview Call by himself initially, so he could study his reactions through the two-way mirror.

By the time Harrison climbed the stairs to the detectives' suite Penny had Call in the appointed interview room. He was sitting at a wooden table with an ashtray, a pack of cigarettes and a Styrofoam cup of coffee in front of him, which he looked at but didn't touch. Penny was in the observation room beyond the mirror and Call was staring belligerently at the opaque glass. His face was thin and battered by scars, his nose had been broken at least once and fluffy bits of beard clung to his neck and chin. He was dark skinned like the Laveaux cousins but much smaller; a vein moved like a worm on his neck.

Penny went next door and Call's attention was diverted from the mirror. He uncurled his skinny arms where they encased his chest and took a cigarette from the pack.

'What the fuck is all this about?' he demanded. 'I'm due on a tugboat that sails in one hour.'

'You're going to be late,' Penny told him. He stood, resting one fist on the table. 'I'm special agent Penny.'

Call squinted at him. 'Customs?'

'FBI.' Penny showed him his shield, then he sat down with the chair turned back to front and rested his arms on the back. 'I guess you were expecting customs, then, uh. Why, what's Ignace been smuggling?'

'He ain't been smuggling nothing. And I wasn't expecting nobody.' Call spoke through his nose. Harrison stood behind the glass, watching and listening. 'I'm on parole or didn't you notice the PO who came in with me just now?' Call said. 'I got a permit to work the river as far as the South West Pass and across the canal to Bayou Lafourche. I ain't done nothing wrong since I got out. I got a year left on my ticket and I ain't going back to Angola. No way, no how, no sir.'

Penny stared at him, his blue eyes colder now. 'Finished?'

'Yeah. I reckon.'

'Then tell me about Christmas Eve.'

'What about Christmas Eve?'

'Where were you?'

'Why?'

'Just answer the question.' Penny sat back, flapping his hand to clear Call's cigarette smoke.

'I was on the bayou, fishing.'

'Which bayou?'

'Bayou Barataria.'

'You mean you were poaching?'

Call shook his head. 'I work for Ignace Laveaux, in case you didn't notice. He got a whole stack of land in Barataria.'

'I thought all the land belonged to his cousin.'

'Augustine?' Call raised his eyebrows. 'I wouldn't know nothing about Augustine. I work for Ignace.' He folded his arms, chin thrust out, cigarette burning between his fingers. He was restless in the chair, shifting his position and nervously flicking ash from his cigarette so it missed the bowl on the table.

'They're partners, aren't they?' Penny said. 'Augustine and Ignace. Though the way I heard it, Augustine is the boss.'

Call twisted his mouth down at the corners and flicked more ash. 'I wouldn't know nothing about the bidness. I just work the deck. I's a deckhand is all. I work hard and don't ax no stupid questions.'

'You're not family, are you?' Penny said then. 'Most of the people working for Laveaux are related in some way. Isn't that how it is?'

'I guess it is. I ain't never thought about it.' Call looked musingly at the ceiling. 'Podjo'd be a cousin, I reckon. Jimmy Mesa the mate, he's related by marriage. I don't know about Frederico.'

'Tell me what you were really doing on Christmas Eve.'

'I done told you already. I was fishing Ignace's canals in my pirogue.'

'On your own.'

'Ban sure.'

'Speak English.'

Call curled his lip. 'Yes, then. Yeah, I was on my own.' He looked at the clock. 'You wanna tell me what this is all about? I gotta get to work or they gonna fire my ass.'

'Forget about going to work, Marcel. You won't be going to work today. The boat will sail without you.' Penny was on his feet now, pacing between the mirror and the table. 'You won't be going tomorrow either, or the next day. You'll be taking the bus back to the farm.'

Call stared at him. 'What y'all talking about? I ain't done nothing. Christmas Eve I was on the bayou.'

Penny shook his head. 'No, you weren't, you were in Bridgeport, West Virginia.'

Call's mouth hung open like a fish sucking oxygen from the water.

'You were tying Maxwell Carter to his chair so he could watch himself bleed to death.'

Through the glass Harrison was watching Call's reactions very carefully. No flicker in his eyes, no movement, nothing to betray he even knew Carter's name. That didn't necessarily mean anything, Call was already a two-time loser and had been in and out of holding cells most of his life. He was a low-level player, a grunt, a gopher for the crew, but he wasn't a user and he wasn't dumb. He had survived a stint in Angola, which was no mean feat in itself.

'I don't know what y'all is talking about,' he was saying. 'I ain't never been to West Virginia. I couldn't even find it on a map.'

'Oh, you found it all right, Marcel. You found the state and the town and Carter's house then you tied him to his chair and sawed through his femoral artery with a cheese wire.' Penny leaned across the table and looked closely at him. 'You like cheese wire, don't you? Kinda like your signature. We know you used it on the boy in the bayou.'

Harrison saw the fear flare in Call's eyes then, like oxygen rushing to a flame.

'Your prints were found at the fishing camp, Marcel,' Penny went on. 'Remember the camp? The one where you broke in, used that oil field guy's place to butcher the kid before you drug him off and dumped him at Jesuit Bend.'

Call was silent. He looked at his dirty fingernails and stubbed out the butt of his cigarette. Instinctively he reached for another one and Penny picked up his plastic lighter. He held it for a moment and studied it. 'The Jefferson Parish deputies couldn't pin those prints on you back then, Marcel. They'd never busted you, had they? At that time the only place you'd been arrested was Pensacola, Florida. That all changed, though, after you got picked up here in the city.' He handed him the lighter. 'Light your smoke, Marcel. I think you're going to need it.'

Still Call was silent and Harrison watched through the glass. 'I bet you thought you'd hear no more about it, that bitty kid in the bayou.' Penny sat down again. 'But then that analyst up at CJIS got hold of the prints you left and matched them to your rap sheet. But, of course, you know that already. He blackmailed you with the unsolved murder and you went up there and committed another one. You were a little more professional this time. You didn't leave quite so much forensic evidence behind you.'

Call sneered at him. 'I didn't leave any evidence, mister. Because I told you already, I ain't never been to West Virginia.'

They left him locked in the room and downstairs they drank coffee. Harrison watched the comings and goings of the 8th District: it was a long time since he had been in here and he didn't recognize anybody.

'You think he'll roll over?' Penny asked him. 'What's it look like from back there?'

Harrison held his cup between both palms. 'He knows the game, been playing a long time. I don't know. I guess it depends.

'We've got his prints at the fishing camp,' he went on. 'He had no business being there, no connection with the owner at all. All we've got to do is run a DNA test to see if it matches the semen found in the kid.'

'You said there were no forensics in West Virginia.'

'I don't think that'll matter. We can get him for the boy in the bayou. We got a motive for Carter's murder. That's enough to indict him, and combined it's more than enough to send him up the road.'

Penny looked at him then, a little smile on his lips. 'So why do you sound so unsure?'

Harrison sighed. 'Because he's a gopher, Matt. The worst he's got on his jacket is assault with a deadly weapon, though the weapons weren't even used. There's nothing to suggest child abuse or homicide anywhere in his history. Whoever got Carter was professional. I don't think it was Call.' He stood up. 'Let's go back and see what he's been thinking. Let me talk to him this time.'

He went in with Penny, took a cigarette from Call's pack and lit it.

'Who the fuck are you?' Call said.

Harrison showed him his shield.

'I want an attorney here.'

Harrison sat opposite him. 'You're going to need the best that Augustine can buy. We've got enough evidence stacked up to get you the juice.' He blew smoke from the side of his mouth. 'I wonder how many years you'll eke out on death row before they strap you down.'

'I ain't gonna be on no death row.' Call's eyes widened and Harrison could see the fear in them. He imagined Call's mind clicking over the details of what he had been told.

'Your fingerprints are all over that fishing camp,' he said, 'the one where the boy's sneaker was found, remember? They're going to love you, that jury, what with the cheese wire and how he was naked and butt-fucked and all. Not only a child killer but a paedophile.'

'I ain't no paedophile.'

'Well, we'll see about that in time. But right now we got you pegged as a child killer.' Harrison stood up, his hands on his hips, and looked down at him. 'We don't need to talk to you any more. We got more than enough to send you to trial already. Come on,' he said to Penny. 'Let's go call this roach a lawyer.'

They had the door open before Call spoke. 'Wait,' he said. 'Just wait a minute.'

Harrison looked over his shoulder. 'Wait for what, bubba? There's nothing you can tell us we don't know already.'

'Yes, there is.'

Harrison closed the door again.

'I didn't kill nobody in West Virginia. I swear I ain't ever been there. And I didn't kill no boy in the bayou either.' He looked viciously at Harrison. 'And I ain't no fucking paedophile. I moved the body is all.'

Harrison and Penny sat round the conference table at the field office. The special agent in charge was with them along with the organized crime squad supervisor. On the secure conference phone they had Somers and Santini from Clarksburg. Harrison sucked tobacco and spat the juice into an empty Coke can. He was listening and watching, saying nothing. Penny was doing the talking: the Laveaux cousins had been on his wish list for so long he was as excited as a child at Christmas.

'Call swears blind he did nothing more than move the body from the camp to the dumpsite at Jesuit Bend,' he said. 'He reckons he got a phone call from someone he thinks was Augustine Laveaux, telling him to go clean up the camp. He was told to get rid of the body well away from it, miles away, not just dump it in the bayou.' He looked at Harrison for support. 'Call's not even a minor league player. In any operation he'd be no more than a mule at best. He loaded the body in a pirogue and then he put it in his truck and drove around in a panic for two days. In the end he was sure a Jefferson Parish deputy was on his tail so he dumped it in the trainasse.'

'What about Carter's murder?' Santini spoke over the phone line.

'He claims to know nothing about it. He told us he couldn't even find West Virginia on a map, reckons he spent the whole of Christmas Eve fishing Bayou Barataria.'

There was silence in the room for a long moment then Harrison spoke for the first time. 'I believe him about West Virginia. The hit on Carter was carefully planned and very sadistic at the end. The parole officer in Charleston who was making the blackmail contacts for Carter told us he hadn't been in touch with Call, though he did make enquiries about him with Vincent Palastina.' He looked at the phone on the table. 'Fran, he had no reason to lie, right?'

'Right,' she said. 'He put his hands up and gave us all the others – why lie about this one?'

'Which means Carter must have got to Call himself?' Mayer said.

Harrison looked at him. 'Or someone else maybe.'

'The second set of prints at the camp?'

Harrison nodded.

'CJIS ran both sets of prints for us again,' Santini said, 'but the only match they came up with was Call. The other set were a non-ident, as before.'

Harrison looked at Mayer again. 'Carter worked in the special processing unit. He had the capability to alter things on the system, delete stuff if he wanted.'

'You mean erase a set of prints?'

'Or a rap sheet.' Harrison spread his fingers on the table. 'The original fingerprint card might still exist but if an analyst doesn't find prints on the system that's as far as he goes. The file cards for CJIS are locked in a cave somewhere south of DC and the law enforcement agency that sent them in holds a copy.'

Mayer chewed his lip. 'Which leaves us where exactly?'

'It leaves us with Marcel Call,' Harrison said. 'But I don't think he killed either Carter or the boy in the bayou. Like Penny said, he's a mule. He works as a deckhand on Ignace Laveaux's tugboat, claims he doesn't get to see a whole lot of what goes on. But Ignace is his boss and there's no one closer to Augustine than his cousin.'

Penny spread his fingers on the table. 'Right now Call thinks we can put him away for ever. Maybe even get him the juice. But, like JB, I don't think he did it. I do think we can get some leverage with him, though. He knows he's a two-time loser. He knows he's in a lot of trouble. That's a lot for a Cajun boy to think about.' He glanced at Mayer. 'I think if we're clever enough we can pitch him.'

'You mean as a snitch?' Somers said over the phone.

Penny looked at Harrison for support. 'I think we could do better than that. This is the Barataria Brigade, the Cajun Mafia. We've never had jack shit on Augustine Laveaux but Call putting his name to the phone call is dynamite. I think we can use Call to get someone in undercover.'

'With a bunch of Cajun boatmen?' Mayer shook his head. 'You're dreaming, Matthew.' He looked at Harrison. 'And you, don't even think about it.'

Harrison sat forward. 'I'm not saying anything. But we do have a potential angle with Laveaux.'

Mayer shook his head. 'I'm not sure I want to hear it.'

'He's as tight-assed as they come,' Harrison said, 'clever, cool and calculating. But he does have a weakness.' He looked at Penny who nodded. 'Vietnam,' Harrison said. 'He has a fixation with that war that borders on the obsessive. It began when his brother was killed. Augustine wanted to go fight very badly when anyone with any sense wanted to stay at home.'

'And that's an angle?' Mayer said.

'It could be.' Harrison rolled the empty Coke can between his palms. 'We all know how he is, the way he is about town, his spread on Grand Terre. Thinks he's some reincarnated Jean Lafitte. If he did ask Call to clean up the camp then the chances are he was there when the boy was killed. It's possible that his prints *were* at CJIS and Carter erased them. We don't know everything about Laveaux's history. We're told he's never been arrested, but we don't know that for certain. The US is a big place and he's been around. Maybe Carter blackmailed him without going through Call. With a little bit of digging he could find out what sort of money Laveaux was worth, and that would be the big one. Laveaux had his own cousin whacked in jail when he thought he might be threatened. Doing someone like Carter would be fun. Carter was killed with cheese wire. So was the boy in the bayou.' He paused for a moment and made an open-handed gesture.

'We could ask Call to try and get us a print from Laveaux, but I don't think he's up to it. Laveaux is very careful about leaving his marks around. He watches to make sure the bartender washes his glass when he's finished drinking.' Harrison set the Coke can down on the table. 'But he's a Vietnam junkie. His hero was his older brother and he carries his service issue Zippo like a talisman.'

Mayer looked sharply at him. 'How do you know all this?'

'Because I was sat right next to him in the Margaritaville last night.'

Mayer was quiet for a moment then he gestured at Penny and the supervisor to leave them alone. He spoke into the telephone. 'We'll call a halt to this conference for now,' he said. 'We've got some thinking to do at this end.'

When the others were gone Mayer stared across the

mahogany table at Harrison. 'I know what you're thinking, John. I know you've been thinking it ever since you came across that cold case up at CJIS. You'll tell me different but I know you too well.'

'I won't tell you any different. You're right. I'm bugged by that murder and this is the best chance we'll ever get to solve it.'

Mayer looked at him and sighed. 'Undercover work is a young man's game now.'

'I'm still the best we got, Charlie.'

'You used to be.'

Harrison spat tobacco juice in the can.

'Think about it, for God's sake – you're fifty years old.'

'Charlie, if we pitch Call and he works for us we might get Laveaux. That alone has to be worth it.'

'To us or to you personally?' Mayer said.

Harrison was tight-lipped. 'The bottom line is I'm the only guy in the whole fucking Bureau who stands any kind of a chance.'

'John,' Mayer said. 'You're not the man you were. Laveaux's crew are meaner, tougher and much younger than you. Tugboat crews are young men. They'd never put you on the boat.'

'Maybe I don't need to be on the boat. But if we don't give it a shot, we're never going to know.'

Mayer nodded. 'You have a point, of course you do. You think I'm not sitting here drooling at the thought of taking down Laveaux?' He leaned forward. 'But I think you're too old. I think putting you in is dangerous. And I really don't think you need that level of exposure any more.'

Harrison walked his fingers on the tabletop. Mayer was right. He didn't need it. He didn't need it at all. He felt the sweat on his brow again as he thought about it.

'You were starting to build a life up there in West Virginia,' Mayer went on. 'Get something going for yourself. That's why you chose the place. You really want to risk everything again?' He squeezed the air from his cheeks. 'Besides, they're tight-assed Cajun, and you're about as French as I am.'

'You're right, Charlie. I'm a Yankee and Laveaux will know it.' Harrison peeled off his jacket and showed Mayer his tattoo. 'He saw this last night. I was set in the bar minding my own business, listening to Coco Robichaux play music. Laveaux was there with his cousin and the rest of the crew. I didn't do anything, Charlie. I just sat there and the sonofabitch came right over.'

Mayer was silent for a few moments. 'You wouldn't be blowing smoke up my ass, would you, because you think you've got something more to prove out there?'

'Charlie, I got nothing to prove to anyone. I'm only sitting here now because the suits up in Washington persuaded me back.'

'To teach what you know at Quantico, not to hang your butt in the wind any more.'

'You're right. And under any other circumstances you'd be right about everything you're saying. But Laveaux has never got over what the VC did to his brother. When he saw this tattoo he threatened to tear it off my arm if it wasn't for real. That's how much the whole thing bugs him. He's professional, Charlie. Utterly. But he's got one weak link. And it's this.' He stood up and walked round the table. 'You tell me this is a young man's game, and you're right. But . . .'

'John, we've got plenty of Cajun agents in the Bureau.'

'Sure we do, but none of them are old enough to have been a tunnel rat in Vietnam. Charlie, this deal isn't a young man's game – you got to be my age to stand any kind of a chance. Laveaux is clever. He'd spot an attempt at putting in a Cajun in a heartbeat.'

Mayer sighed heavily. 'This isn't my decision, John. It's a grade 1, you know that. It has to go up to headquarters. There's a whole review board to go through.'

'There's no time for that. We got to pitch Call and we've got to do it now.' He smiled. 'You're about to retire. Make a unilateral decision. Get the stagehands to give me a past and get me some release papers from Camp J in Angola. Then call up Bill Chaisson in the West New Orleans parole office and tell him he's got a new client. He's the ex-cop that originally worked the boy in the bayou case and he's a graduate of the national academy. What better way to meet with your contact agent? Every ex-con's got a parole officer.'

The phone rang on the table and Mayer picked it up. He spoke for a few seconds and then hung up. 'We'll talk about this later. I have to go now. Val and David Mouton are outside. They've been due a tour of the place ever since we moved here.'

'The governor and attorney general?' Harrison lifted his eyebrows. 'Charlie, you're going up in the world.'

He followed Mayer outside into reception where the governor and his cousin were waiting. Mayer greeted them warmly and David Mouton shook hands with Harrison. They knew each other to nod to. Mouton was tall and suave and well dressed, his greying hair slicked back from his permanently tanned forehead. The governor was older and slightly shorter than his cousin; his face was equally tanned, however. He glanced at Harrison and cocked his head to one side. 'That's a familiar face right there,' he said. 'Did you get yourself a haircut?'

Harrison laughed. 'You got a good memory, sir.'

'I met you at the citation aware ceremony, didn't I? The Shreveport deal – those Vietnamese kids.'

'Yes, sir, you did.' They shook hands.

'How you been?' Mouton asked him.

'Just fine, sir, thank you.' Harrison stepped round Mayer and headed for the corridor.

'I'll get to work on it, Charlie,' he said.

Mayer glared at him. 'We'll talk later.'

Harrison called Santini. 'I'm going under, Fran. Tell Ray I'm out of circulation. Tell him I never existed up there.'

'Are you coming back first?'

'That's not how it works, baby.'

'Can I get in touch with you?'

'You know that's not how it works either.'

She was silent. 'Shit, Johnny, we'd only just got to know each other.'

'I know, but I'll be back.'

'Yeah, right, I won't hold my breath.' He heard her exhale. 'No more John Dollar, then, back to being Harrison again.'

'That's kind of become my name anyways.'

'That's not what I mean and you know it.'

'Ouch, that's sharp. There's that cutting edge again right there. Touch Santini and watch the blood flow.'

'It's not funny, John. You're too old to go back again.'

'You told me I was young – a bitty kid, I think you said.'

'That was bullshit. I was flirting with you then. This is serious. You're too old.'

'It's what I do, Fran. What I always did.'

'That's macho bullshit.'

He sighed. She didn't say anything more and for the first time he felt awkwardness between them. 'We're both beginning to care, aren't we?' he said gently.

'Sounds like it.'

'We said we wouldn't go there.'

'I guess we lied.'

'I guess.'

'Call me.'

'I will.' Harrison switched off the phone.

ten

The apartment on Frenchman Street was actually a studio with a separate bathroom and kitchen, but it was on the top floor between Café Brazil and the Apple Barrel where once upon a time Harrison had known the bartender. That was years ago, however, when girls used to lie on the glass-topped counter, which had hundreds of different coins pasted underneath, and guys would do belly-button shots and try not to spill the liquor. The place had always been a haunt for the French Quarter locals and the roustabouts and dockworkers from Governor Nicholls and Esplanade Wharfs. Dewey put Harrison in touch with the landlord, an English jazz promoter who had come to New Orleans thirty years previously for a holiday and never left.

The rent was reasonable, not that Harrison cared. Now that Mayer had got his head round the situation and persuaded the review board in DC that it was the best route, the Bureau picked up the tab. Their reservations had been largely about Harrison's age, given that most of the people in Laveaux's crew were young, and the fact that he had been attached to the New Orleans field office for three years. Mayer managed to persuade them, probably against his better judgement, that Harrison had only ever worked special operations and therefore had not been visible. A good proportion of that time he had been undercover anyway.

The one thing that really bothered them was the fact that

an old mug shot of his had been circulated on the militia websites, but Laveaux had no apparent links with radicals and Harrison looked very different now anyway. In the end, Laveaux's fascination with Vietnam won them over: Harrison was the only agent in the Bureau who had the relevant history.

The stagehands cleaned up his background so there was no chance of him being recognized and a number of 'hello' telephone lines were set up. These were back-ups, lines manned by 'relatives' or old 'cell-mates' that gave credence to his story. His story was simple. He was fresh out of Angola, still carrying his release papers, having done stints in both Camp F, which was where Marcel Call had been, and later Camp J, which was where the really bad boys were housed. That part was true. Harrison had done three months in Camp J to try and get some information from another inmate about a serial killer roaming the southern states.

The story with Call was that they had known each other to nod to and Harrison had bailed him out in a fight with three guys from Texas who hated both Cajuns and Yankees. That had been their only contact inside and they had been in different sections of Camp F: any closer a tie and Call would undoubtedly have mentioned him before.

The FBI monitored Call very carefully once they put him back on the street, but he thought he was looking at the death penalty if he messed up so they doubted that he would. He could tell them very little about Laveaux: Call spent his time on the tugboat so their contact was minimal. He told them that every now and then the tug would moor close to Grand Bayou at the bottom of the Barataria and take stuff aboard from fast-moving skiffs or the odd high-powered trawler. He had only been on the tugboat for a few weeks when they hauled him in, having spent most of his time on the dock. But he figured the boat was the key to their main source of income. He just didn't know what that was.

The cousins were very close and apart from Call the crew of the *See More Night* were all family and formed the top slice of the outfit. He was only a temporary replacement for another cousin who had been hurt in an accident while unloading at a rig. Call was always made to clean the engine room below decks or stay in his bunk when they met up with other boats. He never got to see anything and he knew better than to stick his nose where it wasn't wanted.

Harrison studied the crew from a distance. Ignace was thirty-nine years old and from the Barataria like his cousin; a swamp man through and through, hard drinking, hard fighting and carrying the bruises to prove it. He had been a skipper since his mid-twenties. He was married and had a house with a spotting tower built on it opposite the burial mound where Bayou Barataria met the Intercoastal canal. When the tugboat was docked in New Orleans he slept on board.

They gave Call six full weeks from the time he was picked up before they engineered a meeting. In that time Harrison hung around the bars in Decatur Street and Bill Chaisson, acting as his parole officer, managed to get him a job loading eighteen-wheelers from a forklift on Esplanade Avenue Wharf. It was located right on the bend of the river at the edge of the French Quarter and one block over from Laveaux's main unloading dock at Governor Nicholls Street. The foreman owed Chaisson a favour and he called it in, telling him if Harrison messed up once he'd gladly ship him back to the farm. Meetings with Penny, Harrison's contact agent, would be set up through Chaisson's office.

Harrison was glad Chaisson was on the team. He was Lafourche Parish born and raised and there was nothing he didn't know about the wetlands south of the crescent.

It was almost carnival time. Fat Tuesday was approaching with two weeks of parades and debauchery ahead of them, a field day for pickpockets and muggers. The city would be full of tourists and the police would be thick on the street.

Val Mouton had come down from Baton Rouge and he had made it clear he didn't want anybody messing with his crime figures. The last thing New Orleans could afford was for the tourists to stop coming.

Harrison worked twelve- and fourteen-hour shifts when a boat was being loaded or unloaded. He got the hang of the forklifts before he ever started on the dock, not wanting to give anyone reason to fault him. Chaisson fed his story to the foreman, the release from Angola state penitentiary just before Christmas and his ability to work long and hard hours. The waterfront men didn't mind ex-con labour because they knew that anyone coming from Angola was used to hoeing soya beans in a hundred degrees of heat. Half the guys on the dock had rap sheets as long as your arm.

Harrison worked with two black guys, Flunk and Digger. Huge men, the pair of them. Flunk didn't say much, he worked his rig with a hand-rolled cigarette permanently hanging out of his mouth. Digger kept earphones plugged in and the blues beating away in his head.

'Hey, Digger,' Harrison said to him one morning on the wharf as they broke for coffee. 'You ever hear the blues sung backwards?'

'Nope.'

Harrison smiled. 'Goes something like this: *I got my dog back, I got my car back, got my house back, got the kids back . . .*'

Digger laughed long and loud, as he did at the slightest joke. Flunk sipped on his coffee and stared across the muddy waters where the Mississippi bent in a crescent and the sun spilled flecks of gold on the whitecaps. Brown pelicans picked at the trash that drifted from the barges moored on the west shore.

The harbour area took in most of the crescent, twenty-two million square feet of cargo-handling area and six million of storage; the port was governed by a board of seven unsalaried commissioners. The nominees were put forward by local business, civic, education and maritime groups, and were appointed by Valery Mouton, the governor. New Orleans was the nation's number one coffee port, with fourteen warehouses totalling five and a half million square feet of storage space just for coffee alone.

Harrison sat down with his back to the warehouse wall, letting the sun play across his face, and took rolling tobacco from his pocket. He made a skinny cigarette, split a paper match and cracked it on his belt buckle. From the corner of his eye he could see Augustine Laveaux, dressed in black and very tall against the sky. He was standing on the Governor Nicholls Street Wharf talking into a cellphone.

The foreman came out of the warehouse and pointed to the Governor Nicholls end of the dock. 'There's a pallet been left up yonder,' he said. 'One of y'all go scoop it up.'

Flunk flipped away the butt of his cigarette and started to get up. Harrison jumped to his feet. 'I'm there, big guy. You take it easy.'

Flunk glanced at him, moved his shoulders and walked back into the warehouse.

Harrison got behind the wheel of a forklift and drove it along the dock towards where Laveaux was still talking on the phone. He looked up at the electric whir of the truck and his eyes met Harrison's across the short expanse of water. He said something into the phone then snapped it closed. Harrison sat in the glass cab and slid the forks under the pallet. He flicked the lever to lift it, pretended it jammed and flicked it back into neutral once more. Killing the engine, he got down and walked round to inspect the metal forks. Laveaux took a thin black cigar from his trouser pocket and lit it with his brother's Zippo. Harrison could feel the beat of his heart. Laveaux's gaze was intense. He straightened up and stared at him.

'Maybe you'd like me to get you a picture or something,' he said. 'So whenever you wanted to look it'd be right there on your wall.'

Laveaux chewed his cigar. His phone rang again and he stared for a moment across the pilings between them. Then he answered the phone. Harrison climbed behind the wheel of the truck.

After work he was in the Margaritaville. Wednesday night and Gary Hirstius had taken Coco Robichaux's spot under the Storyville sign. He had his pedal steel player with him and was halfway through his first set when Harrison came in with Digger. Laveaux was at his table near the bar, his cousin sitting next to him along with Frederico and Jimmy Mesa. Marcel Call was buying drinks; he had his back to Harrison.

The two stools closest to the door were free and Harrison swung his jean jacket over one of them. He stuffed ten dollars in Digger's hand and asked him to go get the drinks. Lighting a cigarette, he nodded to Gary Hirstius who had started into a track from his new album. Harrison rested against the wall and smoked his cigarette. Digger came back with the drinks then Call started towards the door on his way to the bathroom. He got level with their table then he stopped and squinted at Harrison. This was the moment. If this didn't gel it was over. And if it did gel, what then exactly? Harrison had left the Bureau because he couldn't do this any more. What was he doing here? He felt the weird sensation he had experienced on Basin Street wash over him once again.

'Harrison?' Call sounded very convincing and snapped him from his thoughts. 'Tell me that ain't you Yankee ass?'

Harrison squinted at him.

'It is you, you sumbitch.' Call stuck out his hand. 'Marcel Call, man, you remember me.'

Harrison could feel Laveaux watching them, his attention dragged from the guitar playing on the stage.

'You know, man, the farm.' Call leaned on the table and glanced at Digger. 'Don't y'all remember?'

'I remember you,' Harrison said slowly. 'The coonass that couldn't fight.'

Ignace was behind them now, pushing past Call to get to the bathroom. His cousin was still watching.

'Hey, skipper.' Call straightened up and grabbed Ignace by the arm. 'This is Harrison, man. The Yankee sumbitch saved my ass from three Texyans who were swinging their dicks at Angola.'

Ignace looked at Harrison and didn't smile. 'So what's he want – a medal?'

Harrison stared at him. Ignace curled his lip at Digger and headed for the bathroom. Call was building up the part. 'Let me buy you a drink,' he said. He glanced at the black man and Digger looked back, eyes dull and cold. 'You buddy, too.'

'I'm partic'lar who I drink with.' Digger swallowed the last of his beer and stood up. He brushed Harrison's knuckles. 'Later, man.' On the way out Ignace blocked his path. They stared each other down then Digger stepped to one side. Ignace showed the gap where his front teeth were missing and went back to the bar.

Call went to fetch Harrison a drink and Laveaux caught his arm. Harrison was watching Hirstius launch into another song. Laveaux spoke to Call for a few moments then he got up and started to walk over. His cousin stopped him and whispered something in his ear. Laveaux smiled, patted him on the shoulder and came over to Harrison's table, a whiskey glass in his hand.

'Is this seat taken?' His tone was one of sarcasm.

Harrison glanced up at him. 'Looks empty to me.'

Laveaux sat down.

Harrison said nothing.

Laveaux watched the music for a moment. 'You know, I haven't seen you before and then all at once I'm seeing you everywhere.'

Harrison didn't reply.

'First in here with him.' Laveaux jerked a thumb at Gary Hirstius. 'Then you show up on Esplanade Wharf.' His eyes were the same dead black they always were. 'And now I hear you saved Marcel's ass in the slammer.'

'Life's full of coincidences.'

'Not my life.' Laveaux sipped whiskey.

Harrison stared at him. 'Well, the thing of it is I'm American,' he said with the same note of sarcasm Laveaux had displayed. 'Which means I go where the fuck I please.' He finished his beer and pulled out his wallet to buy another and his release paper from Angola fell on the table. He went to pick it up but Laveaux put his glass down on top. Harrison held his gaze, his features expressionless, though the adrenalin tingled in his veins. He felt old and rusty, out of practice and scared.

Laveaux moved the glass off the paper then unfolded it using just the nail of his little finger. Harrison's heart beat faster. The paper had been an accident, but it might just work in his favour. Laveaux would either go for it or he wouldn't. Harrison watched him work the folds open just using the fingernail and the glass. Laveaux's care was beyond anything he had ever witnessed before – as if he knew he couldn't afford to leave his prints anywhere. Laveaux read the paper then sat back and stared at him again.

The whole crew was watching them now.

'You know what?' Harrison said, stuffing the paper back in his pocket. 'If you didn't have your girlfriends back there I'd kick your ass from here to Mississippi. What is it – Chaisson got you on my back, has he? Keeping tabs on me. Making sure I don't run off or fuck up. I done my time, pal, so leave me the fuck alone.'

Laveaux sat very still; Harrison could smell the tension in him. He was pushing it. He knew it. But it was now or never.

Laveaux waggled his glass at the bar for another drink

and Harrison could see he was bristling, though his face showed no expression. The crewman with the Confederate flag bandana brought the drink over and Laveaux handed him the glass. Harrison saw the crewman pass it to the bartender and make sure he washed it.

'You have a big mouth,' Laveaux said.

Harrison ignored him.

'You don't think before you open it. That's a dangerous habit.'

Harrison watched Gary Hirstius.

'The tattoo,' Laveaux said, nodding to Harrison's arm. '*Is it for real?*'

Harrison leaned so their faces were very close. 'Why don't you try and peel it off and we'll see?'

Laveaux was torn between his anger, his quiet outrage at Harrison's attitude and respect. Nobody spoke to him like this. They stared at one another.

'I'm going to give you a piece of advice,' Laveaux said. 'To survive down here is a delicate balance – like walking a tightrope, a case of watching where you step.'

Harrison didn't say anything.

'You're in danger of falling.'

Harrison got up to leave but Laveaux blocked his path. 'Remember the advice,' he said.

Harrison stepped out into the night. Decatur Street was busy and he lost himself in the crowd, walking away from the bar in the direction of Frenchman Street. He was shaking, trembling like an animal. He felt weak. Laveaux's eyes dominated his mind and he really wondered if he could do this. He thought of Santini and West Virginia and wondered why he even wanted to. He stalked back to his apartment with his hands deep in his pockets and his shoulders hunched to his neck. At the apartment he lit a cigarette then took his bag out of the closet. He stared at his clothes on the shelves, then at the bag. He could just pack up and go, put the clothes in the bag and walk out of here. He could walk right back to West Virginia and Santini, tell the Bureau they were right – he was no longer up to it.

eleven

Two months later Harrison was working for Augustine Laveaux. He operated the small crane on Governor Nicholls Street Wharf, loading and unloading the barges shunted up and down river by the tugboats. He had always been amazed by their power: the *See More Night* was only one hundred feet long by twenty-eight wide, but it could pull or push fifteen barges at a time. That created a vessel in excess of four hundred and fifty feet. The barges carried everything and anything and at any time there were literally thousands of boats working the river, all the way from the St Croix to the head of the passes where the Mississippi flowed into the gulf.

Unlike the bigger vessels, they did not need to take on pilots to negotiate the treacherous currents of the river. One of the most dangerous sections was right between the traffic light tower beyond Esplanade Wharf and the twin bridges connecting the west bank to New Orleans. Here the water swirled and eddied, and when the hurricanes blew, the salt water could reach this far up.

A month after he started on Esplanade, Harrison got in a fight with Digger, the Negro who had been his friend. It was a hot spring morning and sweat beaded on Digger's face as they rushed to load the trucks that lined the dock. A massive consignment of coffee from Brazil was due to be shipped all over the country and they were behind schedule. Harrison turned his forklift too quickly and ran into Digger's. The black man bucked like a bronco rider in his seat and cracked his head on the protective cage. Blood oozed on his face. Harrison got down to help him and Flunk came over. The foreman yelled from the steps to his office, but nobody paid any attention. Harrison reached up to help, but Digger flapped him away.

'Son of a fucking bitch, what you doing, man?' Digger jumped down, one hand to the cut on his head.

'It was an accident.'

'You fucking Yankee dumbass . . .'

'Hey,' Harrison said again. 'It was an accident.'

They were outside in the hot sun. The water slapped the concrete bulwarks and Flunk stepped between them, pushing Harrison out of the way.

'Get out of his face, white boy.' He looked at Digger. 'Oh, it's bad man. You gonna need a doctor.'

'Fuck doctors, I can't afford no doctor.' Digger glared at Harrison. 'You can pay for the fucking doctor. And you can pay me the money I lose when I go see him.'

'Fuck you, asshole. It was an accident.'

Digger swung at him and Harrison caught the blow on the jaw. He staggered back, lifting his hand to his face, but kept his footing. Digger came at him again, swung wildly and missed. Harrison punched him twice in combination, hard in the stomach. The muscles felt like bricks under his fists and Digger just laughed and swung again. This time Harrison got under the blow and took the big man behind the knee with a kick. Digger went down like a tree. The next thing Harrison knew a blade flashed in the sunlight and he stamped down as hard as he could on Digger's shin. Everybody heard the crack. The foreman was yelling. Digger screamed, dropping the blade, and Flunk kicked it into the river. Harrison stood with his fists bunched. The next thing he knew the foreman was screaming in his face.

Harrison was shell-shocked. None of this was part of the

plan: it had all got out of hand so quickly and he had just reacted instinctively to Digger going for him. The foreman jabbed him in the chest with stiff fingers. Harrison caught sight of Laveaux watching from across the pilings. The foreman jabbed him again and Harrison head-butted him.

Ten minutes later Bill Chaisson was frogmarching him off the dock. 'Nice going, Johnny,' he hissed. 'One month in and you're fired already. West Virginia's looking real good from here.'

The sun beat on Harrison's head. 'Don't make it look too good, dammit. You're breaking my fucking arm.'

'If that's all your boss breaks you'll be lucky. They are just gonna love this at the field office.' He let go of Harrison at the car and opened the back door. Then he manhandled him in, his hand pressing down on Harrison's head like a cop.

'Mr Chaisson.'

He knew the voice and he stopped, shaded his eyes from the sun and looked at Augustine Laveaux in silhouette. Laveaux walked slowly down to the car. He didn't look at Harrison but offered his hand to Chaisson.

'My name is Augustine Laveaux. I run the wharf next door.'

'Mr Laveaux.' Chaisson nodded. 'What can I do for you?'

'I saw what happened just now.'

'Did you?' Chaisson looked at Harrison. 'Well, you witnessed a man booking his bus ride back to the farm.'

Laveaux squinted at Harrison, who sat in the back of the car with his arms folded truculently across his chest. 'It wasn't his fault. Don't get me wrong, I'm not on the side of a felon if a felon he is, but he was provoked. I saw it all from my balcony.'

'It doesn't make any difference, Mr Laveaux.' Chaisson turned for the driver's door again. 'This guy's had all the chances he's going to get. The ramrod up there'll make his complaint and Harrison's heading for the bus.'

'I'll speak to the foreman,' Laveaux said.

'Why would you want to do that?'

'Because there's been a mistake. I saw what happened and this man was not to blame.' Laveaux made an open-handed gesture. 'I consider myself a good citizen, Mr Chaisson. This man wasn't in the wrong. I'll speak to the foreman on Esplanade and explain the situation to him.' He paused and nodded to Harrison. 'And if he doesn't want to listen, I'll give *him* a job.' He looked again at Chaisson. 'If he's employed he doesn't violate his parole, does he?'

Chaisson took a sliver of chewing gum from his pocket and unwrapped it. 'That's neighbourly of you, Mr Laveaux. More than neighbourly.' He broke off and scratched his head. 'For what it's worth you might want to think about what you're offering. This guy is bad news. I've had a few assholes in my time as a parole officer, but Harrison's something else. He's the kind of parolee that makes a man question his choice of occupation. You understand what I'm saying? But I got paperwork whichever way it goes, so if you want him you can have him.'

'I'll keep a very close eye on him, Mr Chaisson.'

Chaisson thought for a moment. He could sense Laveaux's mind working, chill and clinical with no clue as to what he was disseminating.

He opened the back door. 'Get out, Harrison,' he said. 'Somebody up there seems to like you.' He looked at Laveaux. 'If this turns out bad don't say I didn't warn you. I'll call your office later and we can sort out the paperwork.'

He drove off and Harrison was left by the railroad tracks that ran alongside the dock, his face to the sun looking at Laveaux in shadow. Harrison scratched the tattoo on his arm. He worked his jaws as if he knew he had to thank Laveaux but couldn't quite summon the word.

Laveaux stood there watching him, waiting.

'Thanks,' Harrison muttered.

Laveaux didn't reply.

Harrison worked the crane for Laveaux and every day he stared across the gap to Esplanade where Flunk and Digger drove forklifts. Ignace hated him and he made no secret of it. He sat in the office now, watching Harrison shifting the last of the pallets from the dock on to a curtain-sided truck.

'This feels bad,' he said. His voice had been a rasping hiss since he took a punch in the throat, years back on a shrimp boat. It was the same man who had caught Augustine with the boat hook: he ended up as bait for the shoepick. 'So Marcel says he punched out three Texyans in Angola, so what? We know nothing about this guy, 'cept he got a mouth on him worse than any. What about Junya? What about all we got going?'

His cousin spoke without looking up from his desk. 'Do you see him working your boat?'

'No.'

'Then you have nothing to worry about.'

'I see him working the dock, Augustine.'

Laveaux laid down his pen. 'You see him working *my* dock, Ignace. Right where I can see him.'

Ignace's eyes glowed like lighted coal. 'You know what I think this is about? I think you want him around because he reminds you of Etienne. Ever since you seen that tattoo you had a hard on for this guy.'

Laveaux sat for a moment, his knuckles gradually whitening where he squeezed his hand into a fist.

'Etienne's dead, Augustine. He had his dick cut off and stuffed in his mouth.' Ignace pointed a finger out of the window. 'Harrison might have been a tunnel fighter but he's a Yankee and we don't know anything about him.'

Laveaux got up and came around the desk; he was a full six inches taller than his cousin, lean and very strong. Ignace knew he could put his hands round his throat, lift him off his feet and strangle the life out of him while he kicked and squirmed like alligator gar on a stringer. He had seen him do it once out in the swamp. One of the old crew had snitched to a Lafourche Parish sheriff's deputy about a shipment of coke they were bringing in through the salt marsh, west of the Leesville Bridge. The deputy had been bought off and the snitch was invited to go fishing with Augustine and his cousin.

Augustine held him off the ground by the throat while he jerked and jumped, muscles twitching like a marionette, his face purple then blue and his tongue swelling up in his mouth till it popped out like a thick wet rag. Just before he died Ignace unseamed him like he had the Yankee and his guts flopped out in the boat. They dumped him in the bayou for the alligators to devour while they baited their hooks with intestine.

Ignace backed away from him. 'You too strung up on Vietnam, Augustine, you been that way since Etienne don't come home. Anyone to do with that place and you is too easy to fall over.'

'Ignace,' Laveaux said quietly. 'If you don't learn how to talk to me I'm going to cut out your tongue so you can't talk any more.'

Ignace stepped back. His cousin's eyes had gone dead and he knew he had crossed the line.

'OK. I'm sorry. I just get worried is all. We got a lot at stake.'

'Don't worry. Nobody pays you to worry.'

Ignace could see his cousin's hands were quivering ever so slightly. He had pushed too hard with his comments about Etienne. Laveaux worked the ends of his fingers together: another bad sign. Ignace took another step backwards.

'I'm sorry. OK? I said I was out of line.'

'I'm going to forget what you said, but get back to the swamp now. OK? Before I change my mind.'

Ignace's cellphone rang. He stared at his cousin then

switched it off. He turned to leave but Laveaux called him back. 'Where's Junya?'

'He's still on the boat with Marie. I told them to stay put till we sail.'

'You don't sail till Friday. I got business for Junya.'

Harrison parked the forklift, climbed down and stripped his worn leather gloves from his palms where they stuck with sweat. Stuffing the gloves in his back pocket, he wiped his hands on a rag. Ignace stalked across the concrete to his new Dodge pickup.

'Nice rig,' Harrison muttered.

'Don't you touch it.' Ignace bristled at him like a hunting dog. Harrison said nothing, stood his ground and went on wiping his hands. 'I catch you near my truck I'm gonna fry you ass.'

Harrison leaned and spat.

Ignace fitted his key in the lock. 'My cousin might be stupid, but I'm not. Count your days here. You ain't got many.'

They stood for a few moments, ten feet between them, Harrison gauging Ignace's next move. The tension was broken by the sound of Laveaux on the metal steps that led to his office. Ignace jumped in his truck, fired up the engine and pulled out of the warehouse. Harrison took tobacco from his pocket and rolled a cigarette. Laveaux ignored him and walked out on the dock. Harrison was left on his own, the sun going down over the west bank, casting the river in silver streaks like molten metal. He made his way to the waterfront and saw Laveaux climb aboard the *See More Night*.

Harrison stood in the doorway of the warehouse, hidden in shadows that were cast by the sun. Laveaux stood by the great cable winch they unrolled to hook up the barges. The pilothouse was set to the port side of the upper deck below the bridge and as Harrison watched he saw a figure inside the cockpit itself. Laveaux had one hand shading his eyes. He called out and the door to the pilothouse slid open. Harrison saw a young mulatto kid step across the upper deck and lean on the rail. He couldn't make out his face, just baggy jeans and sneakers and a red windbreaker jacket. Laveaux beckoned him inside.

'You still working?'

Harrison almost jumped out of his skin. He looked round where the height and width of Gumbo filled the space behind him. Gumbo was one of his fellow dockside roustabouts. He was slow-witted: some of the guys joked that his brain was like soup with loose bits floating in it, which was why he got his name. As far as Harrison could make out he was some distant Laveaux clan member from Barataria.

'Hey, Gumbo, what's up?'

'Not much. You got a cigarette, Harrison?'

'Sure.' Harrison tossed him tobacco and matches. Gumbo struggled with the paper, his thick fleshy fingers too clumsy to roll it properly. Harrison rolled one for him and he lit it. The two of them stood smoking, watching the water and the pelicans and the cars on the west bank bridge. The trumpet player started up outside the Café Du Monde. Laveaux came out on deck again and Harrison saw a young black woman behind him.

'Who's that?'

'Dat'd be Marie,' Gumbo said. 'She hang around some-time.'

'Who is she?'

Gumbo shrugged. 'Just a girl. Sometime she hang with Ignace.'

'I never saw her before.'

'She don't come round much. She look after Junya.'

'Junya?'

'Him.' Gumbo pointed to the mulatto kid who followed Laveaux on to the dock.

Harrison stepped back inside the warehouse. 'I'm done for the day, Gumbo. I'm outa here.'

'You wanna go get some red beans and rice?' Gumbo looked hopefully at him. 'It's Monday today. I always have red beans and rice when it's Monday.'

Harrison patted him on the shoulder. 'Some other time, hombre. Today I got bills and shit to take care of.'

He stood on Decatur Street and watched as the mulatto kid came cycling down the road from the wharf, standing on the pedals of his bicycle and weaving in and out of the rush-hour traffic that backed up to Esplanade. Harrison was on the corner with St Philip and he watched as the boy headed off in the direction of the House of Blues. This didn't make sense. Laveaux ran a Cajun Mafia from Barataria who hated blacks about as much as it was possible to hate them. So what was a black kid doing on the tugboat? He wanted to follow the boy to see where he went, but he was on a bicycle and even in a truck Harrison couldn't have got near him. He flipped away his cigarette and went into the Honfleur for a beer.

Laveaux saw Harrison go into the bar from behind the tinted windshield of his Suburban. He had watched Junya take the right fork where the road split. His cellphone rang: he checked the caller ID, thought about whether he wanted to answer it then put it to his ear.

'Hello.'

'What's happening?'

'I'm thoughtful.'

Silence at the other end. Laveaux could almost taste the tension he had generated.

'Why?'

'I took on a new man a couple of weeks back. He makes me that way.'

'Is there anything I should know?'

'Only that Call brought him to us.'

Again there was silence and Laveaux swapped the phone to his other hand.

146

'Call?'

'Call. Don't worry. At least, not yet.' Laveaux smiled to himself and snapped the phone closed.

Ignace crossed to the west shore in his truck, mumbling and muttering to himself, window rolled down, arm hanging out holding a cigarette between his fingers and flicking ash. He drove quickly, getting to Barataria Boulevard before the real rush hour got going. His mind was turning over like the auxiliary engine on the boat. He passed the Jefferson Parish sheriff's headquarters on his right and thought about Bill Chaisson, the cop turned parole officer, who had been looking after Harrison. Maybe his cousin liked the irony, he seemed to thrive on little details like that, but to Ignace it was just another omen. Chaisson was the cop who went after the killers of the boy in the bayou.

He had a bad feeling in the pit of his stomach, and when he had this feeling he couldn't sleep or concentrate or pilot his tugboat with the skill required to keep it off the sandbars. He drove quickly now, heading for the Barataria Bridge, the bayou and home. Only there did he feel truly safe. He smiled to himself. The Laveaux kings of Barataria, like the Lafitte brothers before them. He thought of the Temple where Jean and Pierre sold stolen slaves from pirate prizes on the black market and there was nothing Governor Claiborne could do about it. Augustine loved that story, he told it often when the two of them got drunk and mixed a little cocaine in their wine like the old days.

His face darkened again as he thought about the confrontation with the Yankee just now. Something about that man's face, something not good, something decidedly bad there, like a Roogaroo or some other mythical creature that had stalked his dreams since childhood.

He crossed the Barataria Bridge, pulled off the road and headed down a dirt track into a thick grove of cypress where the ground was marshy once you were off the gravel. He came to a broken-down cottage built six feet off the ground, with wide steps leading up to the battered veranda. His godmother was sitting in the wooden rocker he had bought last Christmas, smoking her clay pipe.

Her hair was grey and hanging loose. She would have tied it in a bun as she did every morning, but by this time of day it always looked a little wild, strands flying here and there, clustered about the wrinkles in the aged leather of her face. He parked the truck and took the bag of cherries he had bought for her in the French Market.

'How you doing, ovadaddy?' Her voice was like crushed gravel, like his only softer, age being the factor rather than a blow to the throat.

'Halo, Nannan.' Ignace climbed the steps and set the bag of cherries in her lap. She stared through him with sightless eyes, the iris blue, the pupil cotton white like the mouth of a water moccasin.

'You bring me cherries, Iggy.'

'Yeah, Nannan, I got the ones you like.'

She reached out a bony hand and gripped his arm. 'You a good boy – never fo'get you Nannan. Sit down, I get you a beer.'

Ignace stroked her wrinkled hand, where pronounced blue veins lifted in ridges from the weak and feathery flesh. 'You set there, Nannan. I get my own beer.'

When he came back he sat down on the step with the cicadas beginning to chirrup in the grass. He listened to the sounds of early evening and ripped the ring pull off the can so the beer frothed over his hand. He sucked the pale liquid from his skin.

'I need to talk to you, Nannan.'

'I know you do, boy.' The old lady sucked smoke noisily through her pipe. 'I been waiting for y'all.'

twelve

Harrison made contact with Penny at Chaisson's office during his regular parole meetings and they decided to get Call out of the way permanently. While he remained in the picture there was the possibility that Harrison might be compromised, and enough time had elapsed since the meeting in the Margaritaville to take him out now.

'I think it's time,' Harrison said. 'Laveaux has gone for the cover. In a weird kind of way he respects me. It was like Bill thought – the tunnel rat thing got to him. Ignace is a cold-eyed sonofabitch, but his cousin seems to respect me.'

'What about fingerprints?' Penny asked him.

'Not a chance, not right now anyways. Laveaux is extremely careful. I told you already, in a bar he never sets his glass down. I mean, he keeps hold of it all the time he's sipping. And he passes it right over to the bartender to wash when he's done. He clips his cigars and carries the butts with him. In his office he makes his own coffee and washes up directly. I don't get to go anywhere near his office and on the dock he wears gloves like the rest of us. If I could get drunk with him I might get something, but Laveaux doesn't get drunk.'

'What about Ignace?'

Harrison smiled. 'You mean get a set of prints? That'll take even longer. I don't get to go anywhere near Ignace.' He drummed his fingers on the desk. 'What d'you think, Matt? You ready to pop the weasel?'

'Sure. Why not?' Penny took a pinch of chew from Harrison's tin and worked it against his palm. 'There's something I wanted to mention about that kid you saw on a bicycle,' he said. 'I heard a whisper from NOPD drug squad that there's a new supply of crack hitting the Lafitte and Iberville projects. Apparently some mulatto kid with river connections is undercutting the existing dealers. Sort of scenario that usually means somebody is going to get whacked. But not with this kid, he seems to have protection.'

Harrison stood up. 'I'll bear that in mind, Matt. In the meantime, let's round up Call. The tugboat's due in on Friday.'

They used the harbour police again and Call was arrested on another parole violation. The tug was moored against the wharf and Ignace stood on deck, face red, veins bulging in his neck, with Frederico, Mesa and Podjo the engineer thrusting like dogs on a leash. Harrison and Gumbo had the crane ready to start loading lengths of pipe into the four barges lashed against the bows. Ignace waved his hand like a flag, telling them to wait. Harrison switched the motor off and rolled a cigarette, sitting in the cab with his foot against the glass. He watched as Ignace protested.

'What the hell you think you doing?' he yelled at the police officer putting the cuffs on Call. 'This is twice now. How am I supposed to run my boat?'

'Mr Laveaux,' the uniform said, 'we've got a warrant from the Department of Corrections. We don't have a choice but to serve it. We don't want to cause y'all any trouble, but we got a job to do.'

'And I'm left a man down with the tug due at Conoco 41.' Ignace drew his lips into a line.

The cop just shrugged his shoulders and piled Call into the back of the Crown Victoria.

Harrison flapped out his match and blew smoke from the side of his mouth. Nobody spoke until the police car had left the wharf and then Ignace spat. 'Now I'm a deckhand down.'

'Take Gumbo with you.' Laveaux came out of the warehouse and everyone looked round at him. 'I'll have someone else lined up by the time you get back.'

Ignace laughed out loud. 'Are you kidding? Gumbo's so clumsy he'd go overboard in a three-foot swell.' He rested his white-booted foot against the gunwale and spat on the dock once more.

Harrison pushed open the cab door. 'We gonna load this sumbitch or what?' he said.

Ignace glared at him as if at last he had a focal point for his anger. Laveaux stepped in his way. 'Load her up,' he told Harrison. He took Ignace by the shoulder and they went up to the bridge.

Laveaux took a small leather hip flask from his pocket and poured whiskey into two cups. Ignace sat in the Captain's chair and looked over the barges where Harrison was swinging the boom. Laveaux handed him the drink and leaned an elbow on the GPS monitor. He looked out at Harrison. It was exactly six weeks since he gave him the job and now Call was gone and there was a vacancy on the boat. He could feel the tingling sensation at the ends of his fingers.

'What're you going to do if you won't take Gumbo?' He turned to his cousin. 'You sail with the evening tide and you need two hands on deck.'

'I don't know what I'm going to do. I'd take Bernaud only he's in the swamp.'

'And that's where he stays.' Laveaux bent to look him in the eyes. 'You know that's where he stays.'

Ignace sipped whiskey, allowing it to lie against his tongue for a few moments before swallowing. 'We got no other men?'

'We've got men, but none I can spare. We've got boats coming in from upriver.'

'Alls I need is a deckhand.'

Laveaux turned again and watched Harrison in the pilot-house on the crane. 'Take the Yankee,' he said.

Ignace stared at his cousin. 'Are you kidding me? On this fucking trip?'

'Ignace.' Laveaux's tone was quiet. 'I think you should take the Yankee.'

'No.' Ignace stood up now, bristling all at once. 'You're mad, Augustine. You losing it.'

Laveaux's eyes dulled.

Ignace was shaking his head. 'Don't you think it's just a little funny that Call got busted? The same Call who also got busted three months ago and who just happened to bump into his long-lost friend in the Margaritaville a couple of weeks after?'

'At last you're thinking.' Laveaux turned his back to the bows and folded his arms across his chest. 'Yes, Ignace, we might have a fly in the parlour.' He sipped whiskey. 'I have to go north for a few days. I don't want that fly buzzing around where nobody knows where he is.' He smiled, and the scar puckered his flesh. 'You understand? If you can see a fly you can swat it.' He stood straight again. 'Take the fly, Iggy. Keep your eye on him. That'd make your Nannan happy, wouldn't it?' Ignace stared at him, his mouth gaping. Laveaux patted him on the shoulder. 'You know there's nothing goes on in Barataria that I don't know about.'

Ignace turned to look at Harrison through the for'ard window. His Nannan was working on a gris gris for the Yankee. She hadn't finished it yet, but till then maybe it *was* better if he was kept close. 'All right, I take the fucker,' he said. 'I'll find out who he is, but if I don't like what I find – he won't be coming back.'

They sailed downriver with the evening tide, Harrison on deck with a brush and the deck hose, scrubbing the rust on the cable winch. The wind was in his hair and he could smell the ochre-coloured river where diesel had been spilled.

Pelicans flew to his right and a dredger was deepening the channel beyond Esplanade Wharf. He was exposed now, alone on the tug heading for the gulf with four men who at best didn't trust him and at worst wanted to kill him. He scrubbed at the rust and his hands felt numb round the brush handle. There was an ache in the pit of his stomach and he couldn't get Santini's face out of his mind. Her black hair, he could smell it as if it was some reminder of the mistake he was making. The boy in the bayou was dead; he had been dead for three years and he would remain dead.

He stood up, the breath catching all at once in his chest. He gazed a hundred yards to the shore and realized then just how far away that was. A short swim, yet a swim too far. He'd drown if he tried to get off the boat. The currents and eddies were deadly. Yet the inclination was incredible: climb on the gunwale and dive in, swim for all he was worth. He had a knot in his bowels he didn't recall experiencing when he was undercover before. Chaisson's words haunted him. Glancing up at the bridge, he saw Ignace watching him as if he could guess his thoughts. Harrison swallowed, went back to his scrubbing and thought about the .45 wrapped in his kit bag.

As the new deckhand he was the lowest in the food chain. Ignace was top predator, though he spent most of his time up on the wood-panelled bridge. Frederico was the other deckhand but he was still way above Harrison in any pecking order. Reluctantly he had showed Harrison over the boat.

The deck was wide and sloping, made of steel and dominated by the massive cable rig in the stern, which they used when they were towing barges. Today, though, it wasn't in use as the tugboat had the ability to push as well as pull the barges. Some of the boats that Harrison had seen had huge flat-fronted arms, which rested against the hull of the barge they were lashed to. The *See More Night* was not flat-bowed, however. It carried the normal if stubby lines of a regular tugboat, but the prow was pronounced with a fixing ridge that slotted into grooves cut in the leading barge. Frederico said it was a better system for a seagoing vessel, because it was easier to swap the barges to the stern when they wanted to tow them, as they would when they hit the salt.

'Why don't we just tow them on the river?' Harrison asked him.

'Because we don't is all. The skipper likes to push them inland and tow them at sea. He strings them way out in back, but he don't like to do it on the river.' Frederico made a face. 'The coastguard cutters take more notice when you're towing on the river – they don't think you got as much control. How many tugs you see towing instead of pushing? We dock at the Fourchon and then we swing round and tow them out from there. You don't want barges close when you at sea. Ignace, he get in the pilothouse and string them barges out in a line from the stern. He string 'em way back then tighten up that cable. You don't want a barge busting you up in a storm.'

They stood in the bows and Harrison squinted at what looked like a metal box fixed to the deck: it was about three feet square and two feet high. 'What's in the box?' he said.

Frederico laughed at him. 'It ain't no box, you gou gut. That's a cargo hold. There ain't nothing in there that concern you ass. There's rope and shit and stuff we might need. If the Cap'n want something he get me to go get it.'

The boat was painted blue, its name *See More Night* printed below the port quarter gunwale. Frederico took Harrison in through the starboard door. Steps led down to the engine room and another door to the galley and living quarters, with a washing-machine on one side and a dryer on the other. The rest of the floor space was taken up by junk and bits and pieces of rope, life preservers and buoys.

'This here we call the fiddley,' Frederico told him. 'Below is the engine room. That's Podjo's place. Don't be getting in his way or he likely tie you to the heavy bag and whomp you. He got a speed bag down there too, but he won't let you use them if he don't like you.' He showed Harrison his teeth. 'An' he don't like you. I'm the deckhand that helps Podjo out when he's working. You don't go down there and you don't go for'ard in the hold. You dig what I'm saying?'

'Coming at me loud and clear,' Harrison said.

Beyond the fiddley was a wide and spacious galley with the cooking facilities and sink to the right of the door. There was a fixed table big enough to seat six, and to the left of it a gangway led for'ard to two cabins on either side. Directly ahead of those was a toilet and shower room.

'You sleep in here.' Frederico opened the door to the port cabin, which housed two bunks and not much else. 'I get to share with you.'

'That'll be nice for me.'

Frederico let his breath go in a hiss. 'Better you watch your mouth, brother. Nobody on this boat gives a shit whether you come back from the salt. You hear what I'm saying to you?'

Harrison looked in his eyes and knew that he meant it. Lots of hands were lost – he wouldn't be the first casualty.

'We on deck at different times,' Frederico went on. 'It's a good thing. Call used to snore. If I slept in a bunk above a man that snored I'd have to kill him.'

Harrison looked at him. 'You ever been in jail, Frederico?'

'Oh, yeah.' Frederico's eyes lit up in the corner. 'I been in jail plenty of times.'

'So what did you do – kill all of your cell-mates?'

Frederico pressed his face close to Harrison's. 'I only kilt one.'

He left Harrison alone then. There were no portholes in the walls and the cabin was closed and hot and quiet. No ceiling fan. Harrison sat on the bottom bunk, and he was back in the tunnels of Cu Chi with dirt spilling dry and dusty on his face. He crawled, elbows and knees in the earth, the light cast by his flashlight bobbing against the wall of darkness ahead. He remembered the fear, cold and clammy like fingers over his heart. He had that sensation again.

He had been in similar situations to this before. That was his edge. Experience was everything and he had been in desperate places and escaped them. He could do it again. He told himself he could do it again.

He scrubbed the deck as the tug headed out into mid-channel. The coastguard traffic signal was against them: he could see the light, blinking at the top of the tower above the wharf side. Algiers lay flat and grey across on the west bank and the French Quarter was squat and square behind them. This was a no wake zone so it would be slow going till they cleared Orleans Parish.

He checked the towing and masthead lights as they drifted past Pauline Street Wharf with the industrial canal cutting a furrow between the buildings. The water was muddy brown, heavily silted here, and it slapped against the hull in caps of white. The engines vibrated through the steel deck under his feet. Podjo hung his head out the stern door, which could be sealed to keep the ravages of the gulf at bay. Now it was clipped back, however, and Podjo stuck a cigar in his mouth and lit it, watching Harrison out of half-closed eyes.

Podjo was a tall and muscular Cajun, perhaps in his early thirties. Frederico was younger and Jimmy Mesa the mate, who wore the Confederate bandana tight to his skull, was younger still. He and Ignace were close, sharing the cabins and shower room directly below the bridge. That was another place given as out of bounds to Harrison. He was only allowed on the bridge when he was on watch, and Ignace had yet to tell him if and when that would be.

Podjo watched him now with that cold unblinking stare that Harrison had witnessed in all of them. This kind of exposure was as cold as it got, way deep with no one to rely on but himself if things went wrong. It dried the inside of his mouth. He had no means of communication with the outside world. Cellphones didn't work well on the bayous and he had deliberately left his Nextel with Penny. If one of the crew stumbled on that he would be crabmeat for sure. The voyage was four days in all, downriver to the Intercoastal canal then Bayou Lafourche. They would tie up at the Fourchon, before the sea run to the Conoco rigs. He thought that ought to be interesting with a front pushing up from Mexico.

Podjo sucked his cigar with wet lips and Harrison scrubbed the deck, dousing it off with the hose. When he was done he pushed the neck of the hose through the scuppers and water gushed over the side.

'Y'all done there?' He looked up to see the mate watching him from the rail of the upper deck.

'I reckon.'

Mesa nodded. 'There's a bunch of rope in the fiddley needs sorting. Go see Frederico. He'll show you.'

They worked Harrison till ten that night. The wind had lifted and the rain began to drift at first, blowing in flurries across the deck and bringing chilled spray off the river. Then a low tidal surge hit the bows as the front began to take hold. Harrison stood at the door to the fiddley, looking astern as they left the lights of Port Nickel behind. They would turn starboard into the industry canal and join the waterway from there. The surge was well upriver, which meant the front was really going to blow, but Harrison figured the man-made inland waterway would be calmer than the Mississippi itself.

Mesa was driving the boat, Ignace in the galley boiling crayfish in salt water and spices and garlic. Harrison had to admit it smelt good. Flipping away his cigarette, he went out on deck again to check the lash fixings. The boat was stable, though the wind and rain beat off his slicker. Glancing above his head, he could see Mesa on the bridge adjusting the starboard spotlight. Harrison thought about what Frederico had told him and looked at the for'ard cargo hold, the lid screwed down tight with turnkeys.

He checked the fixings and spat tobacco juice that blew back in the wind, then he looked up again and saw Mesa watching him like a vulture. He felt the knot in his gut, went astern once more and hung his slicker in the fiddley. Frederico was sitting at the table in the galley, buttering great chunks of French bread. Podjo came up from below, sweat on his dark-skinned face. He wiped oil from his hands on a rag then carefully washed them with soap and water and took a beer from the fridge. He brushed past Harrison and Harrison could smell the sweat on his body, feel the tingle of revulsion as the big man touched him. Ignace was almost ready with the crayfish. Harrison stood behind him and saw the bone-handled 'gator knife hanging in the scabbard at his side. He hadn't seen the knife before. Ignace hadn't worn it before. As if he could feel the scrutiny, Ignace turned to face him. 'Yankee, when we get to the any coast, you watch the bridge.' He spoke in his whispered rasp; the living areas were surprisingly quiet, well insulated from the thundering of the engines.

'What's the any coast?'

'The waterway, the Intercoastal, you dumb fuck.' Frederico looked at him as if he was stupid.

Harrison curled his lip. 'Guess if I spoke coonass I'd know, huh?' He plucked a cigarette from his pocket and headed for the steps to the bridge.

'Not now! When we get to the any coast.' Ignace checked him and Harrison turned. Ignace was staring at him. Frederico was staring at him. At the door to the fiddley Podjo was staring at him. 'I'll tell you when we get there, hafass.' Ignace tore the head off a crayfish and sucked it.

In the cargo hold Junya lay against a pile of ropes, trying to get comfortable. He hated it down here, closed in, away from the world, the only reality the stark white walls and the single light bulb that hung from the ceiling. He glanced across at Marie, who seemed to be dozing, and figured the only reason they didn't die was because ducts leading from the engine room ventilated the hold. He picked up his book of drawings that nobody knew he had, and flicked through the pages.

Everyone was in the book, from Gumbo to Augustine and the other older man he had seen only once before. Marie was there and the crack whores he had seen when he was taken from Audubon Park. He turned the pages and came to the last drawing, like the others, purely from memory, and this time only in profile. He hadn't got a really good look, but he figured he had it right. The white guy from the Iberville, who Dylan thought was a screwball. He looked at the face as he remembered it, cold and bruised with shadows.

From above his head he heard the sound of a mallet thumping the turnkeys and he stuffed the sketchbook out of sight. The hatch was opened and he felt the wind and the freshness of rain on his face. Marie felt it too and stirred where she lay, then Frederico backed down the ladder carrying a tray balanced on upturned fingers.

Harrison took his watch on the bridge while the rest of the men ate. There were two sets of steps between him and them and their conversation was lost to him. Carefully he cast his gaze round the bridge, looking for what he did not know. Everything was neat and orderly, the wood polished and clean, the charts carefully indexed and the equipment state of the art. He sat in the captain's chair, watching the revs and the temperature and the autopilot bearing. The spotlights shone ahead and he was using the radar, but the waterway was straight and they would not reach a major turn before Mesa relieved him.

The mate was as cold and suspicious as the rest of them, which was going to make life interesting. There was a time when it would have appealed to him, the tension and exposure, the utter self-reliance – but not this time. That bothered him: it might cloud his judgement or dull his senses with fear. That wasn't a word he had used about himself in a long time, but he used it now. To deny it was blasé and dangerous. He had to be careful and he had to be on his mettle more than ever before. He was older and slower and out of practice and the crew was young and wise-ass and outnumbered him four to one.

He stared through the for'ard window at the oil black strip of water that was the Intercoastal Waterway. He checked the chart, swivelling the chair to look behind him. Ignace was meticulous: the current chart was set under glass to keep it flat and free of any coffee spills; markings could be made in felt pen and the glass rubbed clean later.

The waterway took them across the top of Barataria, a sprawling mass of bayou and swamp and cypress trees, live oak and alligator. A million tiny waterways, fishing camp and islands. If you got lost in there you would stay lost for ever. No wonder Jean Lafitte had such success back at the beginning of the nineteenth century. He could watch the Gulf of Mexico from Grand Terre and send his schooners out to intercept Spanish galleons, sink them and murder the crew. Then he could slip back to his swamp with no one able to touch him. Harrison thought of Laveaux with his own vantage point on Grand Terre – perhaps one Lord of Barataria had given way to another.

He considered again why he was out here and Call's story troubled him. He could be lying about Carter's murder, but there was no reason for him to do so. He had readily admitted that he moved the boy in the bayou's body from the fishing camp to Jesuit Bend, and he had told them that Laveaux made the phone call to ask him. So why, if he had been involved with Carter's death, did he not just give them the heads up? He knew the FBI had him up a greased pole with a pit bull waiting below, so why not go the distance? There was no reason, other than the fact that to hold your hand up for moving a body was one thing, taking responsibility for murder was something different altogether.

Harrison considered the possibility that Call didn't know anything about Carter's murder. The Charleston parole officer had sworn he didn't make contact even though Carter flagged up his name. There had been two sets of prints found at the camp, and Harrison was sure the second set belonged to Laveaux. Which was the legitimate reason he had put himself here. Perhaps he ought to remind himself more often. It might give some balance to the sense of unease that plagued him. Laveaux was so very careful where he left his prints: it gave credence to the original supposition that Carter *had* found Laveaux's prints at CJIS.

But from what they had seen from his bank accounts Carter hadn't been paid on his last deal, unless, of course, he had a stash somewhere else. He would, no doubt, remove the prints from the record only when he had been paid. As soon as Laveaux's name cropped up Harrison had instructed a search of the computer but nothing came to light. If it had been Laveaux, would Carter have erased his prints before being paid? Perhaps he had been paid and they just didn't know about it. At some point it would have occurred to him that large amounts of money going into the bank aroused suspicion. He might have the payment hidden somewhere they didn't know about.

Harrison scratched his tattoo where it itched on his arm, something psychosomatic he was sure. And then it suddenly occurred to him. Felon prints were not the only ones kept at CJIS – they kept military records, too. If either of the Laveaux cousins had had any time in the service their fingerprints would be at the facility. The investigation had been so caught up with Call nobody had thought to check the non-felon records.

Footfalls, heavy on the steps, broke his thoughts and Mesa came up to the bridge with two cans of beer. Harrison squinted at him. This was something different. His hackles rose and his guard came up: he needed to watch every word.

Mesa passed him a beer and Harrison tore off the ring pull and took a long drink. The beer was cold and dry and worked against his throat. He wiped his mouth with the back of his hand.

'You been to sea before?' Mesa asked him.

'Nope.'

'What did you do? Before you was at the farm, I mean.'

Harrison looked at him. 'Not a lot.'

'You work?'

'When I had to.'

'Who you work for?'

'I worked for me. I never took kindly to no boss ordering me around.'

'Guess you had to get used to that in Angola. Them bosses up there, they just love to give orders.'

'You been to Angola?' Harrison asked him.

'One time, just for a year or so.'

'What did you do?'

'Drove my car through the window of a pawnshop – all but kilt the owner. The dumb fuck sold my best gun from under me. He knew I was coming with the money.' He paused. 'I used to know a couple of guys in Camp J.'

Harrison sipped beer and imagined the conversation round the galley table a few minutes earlier. 'Like who?' he said.

'Like Momma Cade.'

'Big Momma, huh?' Harrison looked Mesa in the eye. 'Girlfriend of yours, was she?'

Mesa stopped with the beer can to his lips and stared at him, the same look of death in his eyes that Ignace and Podjo showed.

Momma Cade was part of the brief the stagehands

162

set him up with. He was a huge black man who ran the coloureds in Camp J, called Momma because he'd had a partial sex change. His genitals had been removed but he had no breasts. He was muscular like a man, but with the genitalia of a woman. Nobody messed with him and the young black boys queued up to be his patsy.

Mesa set the can down. 'You was in Camp J, right?'

Harrison nodded. 'For a little while, but I was way too white and way too old to patsy for Momma Cade.'

'They say you didn't patsy for no one.'

Harrison shook his head. 'Like I said, too old.'

'And too mean, huh.'

Harrison didn't answer.

'You think you mean, Harrison?' An edge had crept into Mesa's voice now. Harrison didn't say anything. He sat where he was in the skipper's chair, the beer can resting in his lap.

'Maybe one day we'll find out.' Mesa jerked his head towards the steps. 'Go eat.'

Harrison took his place at the table. He half expected the crayfish to be gone or cold, but there was still a couple of pounds steaming in the wire mesh cradle. He picked up a bowl and tore hunks of bread from the loaf then ladled the piping hot crayfish into the bowl. He split them, sucked the heads and peeled the bodies out of the shells.

Ignace watched him eating from across the table. Podjo was down in the engine room with Frederico, which left the two of them alone together. It was midnight and the boat was getting closer to where Bayou Barataria flowed away from the man-made canal. Ignace smoked a cigarette, tapping the end every now and again with his index finger. Harrison ate in silence, head down, concentrating on the bread and the fish.

'My cousin likes you,' Ignace said.

Harrison spoke without looking up. 'Augustine doesn't like anyone.'

Ignace shook his head. 'He likes you.' He gestured to Harrison's upper arm and the tattoo. Harrison looked up now and saw he had his alligator-skinning knife on the table. It was bone handled, the grips well worn, and the blade was long and slim and shining. Harrison wondered if that was the knife that had unzipped Peter Thomas and left tiny fragments of blade in his skin. Ignace saw him looking and ran his index finger along it.

'Always keep it sharp,' he said. 'My best skinning knife.' He leaned a little closer. 'You ever see a 'gator skinned, Harrison?'

Harrison shook his head.

'I can skin a ten-footer in one piece, peel that hide right off the mother. Hang it up in one hit to dry.' He pressed the point of the blade against the tattoo on Harrison's arm. 'A tunnel rat,' he said. 'You got my cousin all mixed up with that. His brother was killed in Vietnam and he gets a little confused because of it.'

Harrison dropped the last of the crayfish shells into the bowl. 'Augustine confused? I don't think so.'

'Oh, it's true,' Ignace went on. 'Sometimes he does things on the spur of the moment, makes a decision and regrets it.' Carefully he slid the knife back in its scabbard. 'That's when he calls me to clean up the mess.'

Harrison scrubbed the galley till it shone. Ignace came back down from the bridge, went into the fiddley and called Frederico up from the engine room. He turned to Harrison. 'You off duty now, go get some sleep.'

Harrison took his cigarettes from his pocket. 'I'll go on deck for a smoke.'

'It's raining on deck.'

'I don't care. I like the rain.'

Ignace stepped closer to him. 'You not listening to me. I said, go get youself some rest.' He took the cigarette from Harrison's mouth and put it in his own.

Ignace and Frederico watched him go to his cabin. He

could feel their eyes on him, aware of their silence. Closing the door, he heard voices: they were muted and half in Cajun French which he would never understand. Something was going down and he was stuck on the horns of a dilemma. This was exactly why he was here, to find out what was happening. Instinct told him to open the door, creep on deck and see what was going on. He sat on his bunk and smoked a cigarette. The boat was still moving at the same speed. He would have detected any reduction in the revs and there hadn't been any, so they weren't going to tie up. The voices had died away now, but he could hear a dull thumping sound coming from the bows. It lifted over the diesel, which was more of a vibration through the floor than an assault on the eardrums. He lay back on the bunk, one arm behind his head, and smoked, quelling his natural instinct to go and investigate. They were either testing him and doing it early, or just keeping him out of the way as they had done with Marcel Call.

Junya stood on a pile of rope as the cargo hatch was raised for the second time that night, and he knew the skiff was coming alongside. He had listened for the higher pitched whine of its engine through the steel hull and detected its note way before anyone else on the boat. He had perfected that skill along with many others over the past three years. Lying down here among the ropes and boxes, there was nothing else to do. Marie spent her time singing softly to herself or sleeping, and she wasn't down there all the time anyway: like tonight, for example, already she was up in the Captain's berth. But Junya had nothing to do except listen and draw and map the intricate series of bayous in his mind.

He could drive a boat from pretty much anywhere in Barataria and get where he wanted to go even in the dark. He knew the currents, he knew where the sandbars were, which bayous you could get through in what kind of boat.

He could do it with no lights, just using the moon and the different darkness of swamp and sky to navigate. He knew the trees – the twisted knots of cypress, the live oaks, pecan and palmetto. He knew where the blue herons nested and where the alligators dug deep into the banks, fifty of them at a time in one den to hibernate. He knew all this and he was a street kid from the projects. But he was black enough to be black and mulatto enough for the likes of Laveaux to tolerate him.

He climbed the ladder to the deck where he stood in the rain with the wind on his face and whitecaps chopping the bayou. The wind blew harder, rain sheeting over him, and in a moment he was soaked. The white-hulled Lafitte skiff was on the port quarter now and he worked his way aft to where the whole crew was waiting. Ignace slipped an arm round his shoulders and brought his face close so Junya could hear the rasp of his voice against the wind. Bernaud sat behind the wheel in the skiff. He peered up at Junya and Junya could see his ski mask hanging out the back pocket of his jeans.

Junya lit a cigarette and the wind took the smoke. Ignace nodded to the skiff. 'Time to get it done. We got another cargo waiting upriver.'

Harrison felt under his mattress for the unregistered .45. The breath felt weak in his chest and he was aware of his heart lifting against his ribs. His palm was moist on the door-handle. He stepped into the corridor as if to go to the bathroom. He could no longer hear any voices. He paused and glanced over his shoulder. He could see nobody in the galley, at least not in his field of vision, and nobody in the fiddley. He took a breath and crept to the end of the corridor where the table was. There was no one there. He hesitated a moment, listening for any sound of Podjo in the engine room, but there was no sound. The door from the fiddley to the deck was open and the wind whistled, bringing with it

flecks of spray. Harrison tasted it on his skin, fresh water –
they were still on Bayou Lafourche.

He moved on the balls of his feet now, the gun cold
against the skin of his back, into the fiddley where he
paused at the top of the steps. The aft deck lights were on
and he could see the crew with their backs to him, wearing
yellow oilskin slickers. Ignace was nearest him, his arm
around the shoulders of the young black kid Harrison had
seen in the Quarter. He was talking to him, his head low
against the wind. Podjo was leaning over the side with a
rope in his hands, and Frederico alongside him. Harrison
guessed Mesa was on the bridge, driving the boat. He
watched as Frederico lifted the boy on to the gunwale then
lowered him over the side. Another boat, Harrison
thought. That must have been the banging he heard, one
hull against another.

Podjo straightened and Frederico turned. Harrison
ducked back inside. He moved quickly into the galley.

The black girl stared at him from where she leaned by the
steps to the skipper's cabin.

'Did you find what you were looking for, honey?'

thirteen

Harrison stared at the girl. He could hear the crew now and he bent to the fridge for a Coke. His hand was shaking as it encased the chilled aluminium. Behind him Ignace came in and Harrison turned and faced him. Ignace squinted at him.

'How long you been there?'

'Just now.'

Ignace glanced at the woman. 'That right?'

She made a face but said nothing.

Ignace came alongside Harrison and Harrison could smell whiskey on his breath.

'When I tell you to stay put it's for your own safety. A boat like this can be dangerous, especially at night.'

Harrison made an open-handed gesture but his mouth was bone dry. 'I'm right here, aren't I?'

Ignace went up to the bridge and Frederico disappeared in to the cabin. Podjo stripped off his slicker, ran his eyes over Harrison and slid down the steps to the engine room. The black girl sat down at the table. She drank Coke through a straw and lit a menthol cigarette. She wore jeans and a skin-tight top, which showed off her breasts, the nipples prominent where she wasn't wearing a bra. Her fingernails were long and painted crimson and she tapped the tabletop in time to the music that lifted now from the radio. Harrison watched her, his pulse evident at his temple, sure she had seen him but not sure why she hadn't said anything to Ignace. Bluff it, he told himself.

'You still staring, mister.' The girl sipped Coke.

Harrison didn't reply.

'Don't be staring at me.'

'I wouldn't dream of it, lady.'

'Make sure you don't is all.' She looked at him and there was something in her eyes but he couldn't say what, a feeling, a thought perhaps, a question.

He stepped through the door on the windward side, the air fresh on his face, the rain slanting in from the south now, the very edge of the storm. He thought about the kid leaving the tug on another boat in the middle of the night. Again he asked himself the question – what was Laveaux doing with a young mulatto boy and where was he going in the dead of night with a storm blowing in from the gulf?

Frederico had gone aft to the cable, working on the winch in preparation for when they shifted the barges round to the stern. Harrison stood where he was for a few moments, watching him and listening to Ignace in the galley. He could hear him joking with the girl. Marie, Gumbo had called her. She looked like a crack whore, though perhaps a little too calm, and not skinny enough. An ex-crack whore maybe. Anyway, a little piece of ass for the skipper to have on his boat. Why hadn't she told Ignace what he was doing? He heard them move to the stairs for the skipper's cabin. Maybe she hadn't seen him after all? Maybe she figured he wasn't snooping? Then again maybe she would recount exactly what she saw to Ignace as they lay together in his bunk.

Ignace appeared in the doorway behind him. 'Go work the cable, Yankee,' he said.

Between them he and Frederico got the cable coupling unhooked and greased and checked the massive hawser lines, which were still tied to the stern. Frederico didn't speak, they just sweated side by side in the rain till the Cajun stood back and took the hat from his head. He wiped his brow and looked up at the pilothouse. Harrison watched while he climbed the steps and went into the cab to check something. The rain fell harder still and Harrison took shelter in the fiddley. He could hear Podjo pounding the heavy bag below deck. The night was swathed in rain clouds, some very black, others a lighter grey against the horizon. They were crossing the northern rim of Barataria Bay and Harrison could see a mound of earth off to the left where gravestones gleamed in the rain. He could see the lights on Barataria Bridge and thought just how isolated the community would be whenever the bridge was out.

Research from the organized crime squad showed that Laveaux owned a lot of Barataria, purchased from the oil and gas companies who had built many of the canals, destroying a massive amount of wetland in the process.

Frederico slid down the steps from the pilothouse. Then he went for'ard and climbed to where the mate sat on the bridge. Harrison listened to Podjo working the bag some more then he went back to the galley and could smell the scent of Marie's cheap perfume hanging like a moist shroud where she'd been sitting. Two glasses stood on the table: one was hers with the Coke still in it. The other was empty and smelt of whiskey. Harrison pulled his cuff down over his fingers and picked the glass up. If he was lucky it carried a set of Ignace Laveaux's fingerprints. Carefully he wrapped it in toilet paper then stuffed it in a sweatshirt and stowed it in his bag. He racked his .45 and popped the round from the chamber. Releasing the clip, he pressed the hollow-point shell back into the top and slid the clip back into the grips. Racked once more with the safety on, he hid the weapon back in his pack. Handling it made him feel better.

In the galley he washed Marie's glass and made some coffee. He could hear her moans from the cabin above his head. Mesa came down from the bridge. 'You done for the night now, Yankee,' he said. 'The skipper says you got to go to your bunk and stay there.'

Back in the cabin he took the .45 from his pack and lay down to sleep with his hand under the pillow and the weapon in his hand.

Laveaux sat in his office with only the desk lamp burning. Spread on the desk before him were the papers from the Department of Corrections, the reports on Harrison that Chaisson had filled out. Laveaux picked up a photocopy of the Angola release papers and studied them. He laid them down again, flared his nostrils then went to his filing cabinet and pulled out a similar set of papers for Marcel Call. He laid the papers side by side and checked the dates Call had been in Angola with Harrison's. He scoured the reports for details that might raise questions. He realized then that Call's parole officer hadn't informed him whether he had been sent back to Angola. He lit a thin black cigar, snipping the end first and placing it in his jacket pocket. He stepped out on to his balcony that overlooked the wharf and the water was slack beneath the lights from the bridge. Traffic moved to and fro in the stillness. The front had yet to reach this far upriver and the air was still. Laveaux wet the end of his cigar as he drew on it, allowing the smoke to drift from his nostrils. He thought of two ex-cons and two differing parole officers from west New Orleans. All appeared to be in order, but instincts that were old and well oiled told him it was not. Taking his cellphone from his pocket, he dialled Conti, a tame bull at Angola.

'This is Laveaux,' he said when Conti answered the phone. 'I want you to do something for me.' He waited while the man got a piece of paper and pencil then told him what he wanted. 'He claims his name is Harrison. I want to know when he was in Camp F and when he was in Camp J. Check whether he had any contact with a man named Marcel Call. And check whether Call is back there now. He was picked up for a parole violation so he should be.' He

171

switched off the phone, rolled the cigar between his fingers, sensing the weight in the atmosphere that told him the storm was on its way.

fourteen

'We were met by another boat.' Harrison sat in Chaisson's office with Penny. 'I figure we were right on Bayou Barataria. The boy was loaded on to it, some kind of skiff probably. I didn't see it and I was confined to my cabin when it came back.'

'But it did come back,' Penny said.

Harrison nodded then picked up his bag from the floor and took out the glass he had wrapped in tissue. 'Have you got an evidence envelope in your car?'

Penny's eyes widened. 'Is that . . . ?'

'Relax, it's not Laveaux. It might be Ignace, however.'

Chaisson took a brown paper sack from his desk drawer. 'This'll do for the time being.' He held it open while Harrison slipped the glass inside.

'Get it dusted as soon as possible and send the results to Santini,' Harrison told Penny. 'When she takes them to CJIS ask her to get the analyst to check the non-felon records as well, see if either of the Laveaux cousins did any time in the military.'

He went back to his apartment on Frenchman Street to get some more gear together. Nobody had told him whether he was off the boat and with his feet back on dry land he felt a bit more secure. Nothing had happened with Marie. If she had told Ignace he hadn't mentioned anything or changed his behaviour in any way to indicate as such. Harrison couldn't be sure, but some instinct told him Marie hadn't said anything. The question was, *why?*

They had returned from the gulf that morning and the crew were drinking in the Apple Barrel. Harrison had looked for Marie, but he had seen nothing of her since the night when the boy left the boat. That had been before they hit the salt, two days ago. Out in the gulf it had been busy, hard, vigorous work. They had made drops to various rigs with the front battering them and seasickness welling in his throat. When they were finished Frederico took the watch and Harrison slept the sleep of the dead till they were back on the Mississippi.

He called Santini on the cellphone and she was very pleased to hear from him.

'God, it's good to talk to you, John. I have to tell you I was worried.'

'There's no need, baby. I know what I'm doing.' He told her what he had given Penny. 'We should've considered non-felon records right from the start. I guess we just got excited about Marcel Call.'

'Is he in witness protection now?'

'Call? Yeah, I guess we got him stashed somewhere.'

'Are you OK, John? I mean really?'

Harrison let go a breath. 'Yeah.'

'Are you sure?'

'I'm fine.' He wasn't, though, and he knew it. This was respite, back in the world seeing faces like Penny and Chaisson and knowing he had back-up on every street corner. But out there in the gulf he had been scared. He didn't like the feeling and he assumed it came with age. The closer a man got to the end of his life the more he wanted to prolong it.

'Are you still there?' Santini said in his ear.

'Yes, I'm here.'

'You don't sound too good.'

'It's tougher than I figured it would be, Fran. That boat is smaller than you'd imagine when you're stuck on it.'

'But you got Ignace's fingerprints.'

'I think so. I think it was his glass. We'll know if you can match them.'

'I'll get going on that right away. You take care out there on the water. Keep cool and remember why you're doing it.'

'Why I'm doing it?'

'Yeah. Don't let it get personal. When it gets personal it gets dangerous. The Jesuit Bend murder was nothing to do with you.'

Harrison stared out of the window as another tugboat steamed under the twin bridges.

'Just be careful, Harrison.'

'I will. Don't worry.' He hesitated. 'I think about you a lot when I'm out there, you know.'

'Do you?'

'Yes. Makes me wonder what the fuck I'm doing down here.'

She was quiet for a moment. 'I miss you, you know.'

'You do?'

'Yes, I do. Look, I know I keep saying it, but don't let personal feelings compromise you. You can't afford it. It's what we're always taught but it's true.'

'Don't worry. I can handle it.'

'I hope so, because the word is you're the last person who should be undercover down there.'

Harrison ground his teeth. 'Whose word?'

'Oh, the whispers I get from Somers, the SAC in Pittsburgh. Nobody can believe that Mayer backed you with the review board.'

'Mayer knows me, Fran. He knows I can cut it.'

'That's not what I hear. Everyone thinks you're too old.'

'Make me feel good, why don't you.'

'I'm sorry. Now I'm not being very professional, am I? I guess that's harder when you've slept with someone.'

'You told me it was just sex.'

'Did I? Well, I was wrong.'

175

Harrison smiled. 'Don't worry about me, Francesca. I'm going to be just fine. And don't listen to whispers.'

'Just make sure you look after yourself. I meant what I said just now. I miss you. Call me as often as you can.' She hung up and he sat for a while thinking about what she'd said.

fifteen

Ignace drove to Barataria. He had to wait while the bridge was up to let a freighter through and he sat at the wheel thinking. The first thing his cousin had asked him when he got back was how the Yankee had made out. Ignace didn't like the way he had found him in the galley with Marie, but could find no fault with his work. He had held his own out by the rigs when it was swelling fifteen feet and they were trying to hook drilling pipe on to the line dropped by the crane. He had thrown up many times, which made the rest of the crew laugh. There was nothing like a landlubber trying to work on a pitching boat.

His cousin had been checking up on Harrison while they were at sea. They had had a conversation earlier in his office while the crew unloaded on the wharf.

'Conti at Angola confirmed to me that Harrison did three months in Camp J,' Laveaux told him.

Ignace looked unimpressed.

'Would you last three months? Jimmy was out of there in a week. It's lucky we had Conti working for us. Jimmy got turned out so many times he was starting to enjoy it.'

Laveaux looked down on the dock through the window, the scar on his face pale in the late afternoon. 'There's no word yet about Camp F.'

Ignace nodded. 'You know, I been thinking. Maybe we ought to hunt Marcel down, find out if he's back at the farm.'

Laveaux looked at him. 'He's not back at the farm. He's not in the parish jail either. I don't know where he is right now.' Again he looked out of the window. 'I intend to find him, though, and find out why he's not in Angola. In the meantime, the Yankee keeps his place on the boat.'

Ignace opened his mouth to protest but his cousin silenced him with a look. 'Either he is who he claims or he isn't. I won't know till I find Call. Till then I want to keep him close.'

It was then that Ignace told him that his Nannan had said they needed to beware any stranger. But Ignace's Nannan was not Augustine's and he laughed.

'You think I care what that toothless old woman has to say? You're a fool if you listen to her, cousin. I stopped believing people were conja the day I found out about Santa Claus.'

Let him mock, Ignace thought as he pulled up outside his godmother's house. Let Augustine mock. He might live to regret it yet. He climbed the steps, aware of the wind freshening the heavy leaves of the pecan trees. The old woman was not on the veranda and he knocked lightly and went inside.

The house had the same musty smell that he remembered as a child: she had never married and had never been the cleanest of people. Everything remained in perpetual darkness, as she never pulled the drapes. She didn't need light to see and she hated the touch of the sun. Her skin was grey and flaky. Ignace found her in the kitchen, sitting with a can of beer in her hand and the gris gris she had made on her lap. She looked up with unseeing eyes.

'Is that you, Iggy?'

'Yeah, Nannan.' He sat down beside her. 'You know, you should lock you front door. Anybody could walk in here. They some bad people about.'

She smiled and showed him blackened gums from years of sucking tobacco. 'Who gonna come into my house when Iggy Laveaux be my godson?'

Ignace sat back and laughed. 'You right there. Anybody come bother you I slit their throat in no time.' He looked again at the gris gris, a charm she had made from the claw of a chicken, wrapped in a strip of alligator leather and tied with Spanish moss.

'You take that with you, boy. I finish it this morning.'

Ignace picked up the charm. 'Augustine wants the Yankee kept on the boat, Nannan.'

'With all you got going on?' The old woman spat on the floor. Wind rattled the glass in the windows and Ignace could smell the damp rising from the trees outside. 'You know, maybe you cousin got a point,' she said after a moment. 'Maybe he do.' She spoke softly now, her voice not much more than a whisper. 'Put the gris gris on him and watch him very close.'

Harrison moved his gear back to the boat, keeping the .45 in his bag. Frederico had the top bunk and he was messy and didn't wash his clothes very often, notwithstanding the perfectly good washer and dryer they had on board. The cabin stank of old socks and Harrison sprayed deodorant around as he stowed his gear.

Frederico filled the doorway behind him. 'You trying to tell me something?'

'You work it out.'

'Don't fuck with me, man. Not even in a joke.'

Harrison looked at him. He could feel the trepidation returning, mixed with a sense of hatred. He knew that he had been around people like this for too long. Santini only echoed his own fears – coming back when it was this personal was dangerous. The problem was, the sickness caught up with you. When an agent had been in deep like he had so often, the Bureau worried about losing their man to the other side. So much time in the company of the bad guy, they feared his grip on reality might falter. But Harrison was too old and too cynical for that to happen now. His biggest danger was making a mistake, getting something wrong and blowing his own cover. Every time he looked at the faces of this crew he saw the photographs from three years previously – the boy with cheese wire embedded in the flesh of his neck, eyes eaten out of their sockets, two fingers gone to alligator gar, bite marks in his flesh where other fish or birds had picked away at his carcass.

Frederico still stood in the doorway. 'The skipper wants you on deck,' he said.

They were moored next to the wharf and Harrison could see Laveaux on the phone in his office. Laveaux stared down at the boat through the window, his face still and cold, cast half in shadow. The sun was high today and it burned over the Quarter. Harrison could smell chicory from the Café Du Monde; he could hear the first few notes from a lone saxophonist in Jackson Square.

Ignace was on the upper deck, watching the dock crew unloading barges from another of their boats: coffee stacked high on wooden pallets, 'Colombian Dark' stamped with the fleur-de-lis on the side of the crates, tons and tons of the stuff. Ignace was watching him, one hand in the pocket of his khaki pants. Harrison saw Marie walk across the upper deck and stand with Ignace. He watched her, the way she leaned an arm over Ignace's shoulder like a lover. She caught Harrison's eye, flared her nostrils slightly as if she could smell an unpleasant odour and sucked on her cigarette. Ignace didn't seem to notice. His eyes moved from Harrison to the barges and back again. A pelican flew in close to the deck, banked and settled with a rush of wings but barely a ripple on the water. The pelicans had almost been lost to the delta a decade or so earlier. Before the environmentalists cleaned things up the oil industry used to dump all kinds of chemicals in the bayous and the pelican's eggs suffered. The shell wouldn't harden properly so few of the young survived. The state bird itself was almost lost to the state.

'Harrison, you go help in the galley,' Ignace called down to him. 'Jimmy is cooking. Go give him a hand.'

Ignace seemed calmer to Harrison, but in a way that only made him meaner. His face was pinched and hard, black eyes, black hair, hollow cheeks and those front teeth missing – he had false ones but he rarely bothered to wear them. A dozen years younger than Harrison, he was tall and lean, though shorter than his cousin. He was smart, though, and sharp as an open razor. Harrison knew he had to watch Ignace more than anyone else.

He went inside and Mesa glanced at him.

'You need a hand?' Harrison said.

'No.'

'Skipper said to give you a hand.'

Mesa shrugged. 'Don't need it.'

Harrison looked at the square set of his shoulders and went back on deck. Ignace stared down at him. 'I told you to go help the mate.'

'The mate don't need any help.'

'Clean the decks, then.'

'I did that already.'

'I don't see it. Do it again where I can watch you.' Ignace pushed Marie away and she half stumbled, then she looked at Harrison again and for the briefest of moment he thought he saw something in her eyes. She regained herself and stepped back with a defiant toss of her head.

Harrison went into the fiddley for the deck brush and called down the steps for Podjo to turn on the hose.

Junya was playing cards with him. He laid out a pair of aces and Podjo scratched his head. 'That all you got?' he said. 'Damn, you was bluffing me all the time.'

'Podjo, put on the hose,' Harrison called again.

That voice. Junya could feel the creep of a spider across his shoulders. Podjo got up and turned on the hose. He looked down at Junya's pensive face. 'What's up with you?'

Junya tapped the upturned card. 'Pay me what you owe.'

He beat him twice more before Podjo got fed up and punched the heavy bag. He had a very short fuse and was useless at cards. It was dangerous to play him, but Augustine favoured Junya, and Podjo wouldn't do anything to him. Even so, the boy watched his back. He liked the pleasure beating a man twice his age gave him, but he was wary enough to back off when it was time.

'Quit worrying, Podjo, you know you'll win it back.'

Podjo started the engines, and the clatter took away any further conversation. Junya climbed the steps and peeked into the galley. He was not supposed to be out and about in the daytime but they had docked yesterday and he was damned if he was going to cook all day in the hold.

The mate was washing vegetables in the sink. He had the radio going and Junya moved to the door of the fiddley. The new deckhand was outside with his back to him, washing the steel down using the high-pressure hose. He was not very tall, wearing jeans and a T-shirt, grey hair loose at his shoulders. He half turned and the boy caught sight of his face in profile. He stood for a moment and stared. He never forgot a face and he had seen this one before.

Harrison felt the weight of scrutiny and glanced up. The mulatto kid was staring at him from the door of the fiddley. They regarded each other and the kid's eyes were as cold as any he had seen on the boat. For a full thirty seconds they stared and it was Harrison who looked away first. He tried to appear nonchalant, going back to his work, but he knew the boy was still staring and sweat gathered on the palms of his hands.

Ignace came over from the pilothouse on the upper deck and looked down at Harrison. 'You done already?'

Harrison glanced up at him then looked back at the doorway. The boy was gone. He shook his head at Ignace and turned back to his work.

Junya was in the hold. His heart was pounding and he scrabbled for his sketchbook. Quickly he worked through the pages till he found what he wanted. It was the same man. There was no question it was one and the same man. He snapped the book closed and questions burned in his head. What was the white man he had seen in the Iberville doing on the *See More Night*?

He lay back on the ropes, the knots against his spine comforting and familiar. He remembered watching the way that guy had fronted those boys in the project. Nobody did that, nobody other than cops. They were the only ones to stare you down when you pulled alongside a car at the lights and eyeballed the potential jack. Tourists, businessmen, all the regular people were scared of you so they gripped the steering-wheel like their lives depended on it and looked straight ahead. That was always a give-away and they got what they deserved. The only people who'd look back in your face were plainclothes cops.

The hatch opened and Marie came slowly down the steps. Junya watched the curve of her buttocks through her jeans, felt a little stirring then looked away, disgusted with himself. Marie was like a mother to him. She got down and dusted her thighs with long-nailed fingers.

'What's with you, honey child?' she said. 'You look like you saw a ghost.'

Junya didn't say anything. He held on to his sketchpad as though his life depended on it.

'You best be putting that away now. You don't want Ignace catching you with it.'

Gently she prised the book from his fingers and slid it beneath the ropes. 'If he saw that he'd kill us both fo' sure.'

'Who's the new guy, Marie?'

'Just a deckhand. I think Augustine bring him in. Nobody seems to want him around very much.'

'They don't like him?'

'Honey, he's a Yankee. They hate him.'

She smoothed his nappy hair with her palm. 'You know, you a beautiful child.'

'I'm fourteen, Marie.'

She smiled. 'You think you fourteen. Neither one of us know for sure, now, do we.'

Junya crawled into her arms. 'If they hate him so much how come he's on the boat?'

'I don't know, honey. Like I said, Augustine want him. Ignace thinks Augustine likes him because he was a soldier in Vietnam. Ignace thinks his cousin is soft in the head when it comes to Vietnam. Ignace thinks he's gonna bring disaster down on us all.'

Junya laughed. '*Ignace* is a superstitious fuck,' he said.

'Don't you be using language like that.' Marie tapped him on the skull. 'Not in front of yo' mama.'

Junya apologized to her, then stood up. He moved about the hold. It was confined but not oppressive, the ceiling was high and he figured it was about fourteen or fifteen feet square – it wasn't so bad on short trips.

Marie watched him pacing and thought about how in saving his own life he had inadvertently saved hers. She had been clean for three years now and knew that if the two of them could hold it together she might just stay that way. But Augustine still owned them. She was a fixture on this vessel as much as Junya was, and she was a fixture in Ignace's bed. That she hated more than anything else. It reminded her of the years she had spent being trawled out to the ships in mid-river for use by the crew. Sometimes she and the other girls would be out there for days before Ignace sent a skiff to bring them back. Mercifully she had been so high most of the time she remembered very little. She had left it all behind when Augustine gave her the boy to watch over. But she still felt like a whore whenever Ignace touched her.

'What you thinking?' she said to Junya.

He didn't answer right away, his mind was turning somersaults. He could smell cop from three blocks away and it stank that night in the Iberville. He must have been wrong. What would a cop be doing on this boat? He looked round at Marie.

'What happened to Marcel?'

'He got busted again. Some violation of his parole.'

Junya gazed at the wall beyond her without seeing it.

'Why you ax?'

'I don't know. I was just thinking. Where'd the new guy come from?'

'Angola, they say. Just got out. He's on parole hisself. Ignace told me he was working on Esplanade Wharf, but got in a fight on the dock. Augustine seen the fight from his window and told the PO that he'd give the Yankee a job. None of the crew like him, though. Ignace done put a gris gris on him.'

'A gris gris?'

'You know, voodoo, a charm, spirit.'

'He believes all that shit.'

'It ain't shit, honey.'

'It's shit.' Junya took out a cigarette.

'You shouldn't be smoking, child.'

'Marie, I was smoking before you was my momma. OK?'

She laughed at him. 'OK. But you shouldn't talk like that about the gris gris.'

'Why not? What anybody do to anybody else in this life is down to them – it don't got nothing to do with no voodoo.'

They sailed downriver with empty barges riding high in the water. Harrison checked the cables at the bows and climbed on to the open-topped barges themselves, which were rusting to copper at their seams and down along the gunwales. They were pushing four of them down to the Southwest Pass where a container ship with another load of coffee was waiting for them. He walked between the barges, checking the lashings as he had been taught. If one came free on the river all hell could break loose. Ignace had never lost one and it was Harrison's job to make sure it stayed that way. He walked back to the deck, rechecking them as he went, and he thought about the woman and the boy on the tugboat with five men. It didn't make any sense. What was Laveaux's Cajun Mafia doing with a black boy and a crack whore?

The FBI had suspected Laveaux was running prostitutes, but this girl didn't look to be servicing anyone but the skipper. He had seen the boy on his bicycle on Decatur Street, and Penny spoke of a new supplier in the projects with connections to the river. The boy had ducked out of sight when Ignace spoke to Harrison earlier, but they hadn't put in anywhere, so where was he now? The same could be asked of Marie. Harrison hadn't seen her on the last trip other than the night in the galley. He looked the length of the barges to the superstructure of the tugboat. The sun was against him so he couldn't see who was on the bridge. All at once he thought of the cargo hold and Frederico's words.

They sailed from New Orleans to the gulf via the Scott Canal and Southwest Pass. They loaded crates of coffee from a container ship moored close to the mouth of the river, then carried on along the southern tip of Louisiana. Night fell and Harrison was on deck, smoking a cigarette and watching the lights of the oilrigs from where he leaned on the port gunwale. Ignace was on the bridge with Mesa and the others were playing cards in the galley. They were cruising along at eight knots, heading for Barataria Bay. One section of barge was still empty and Frederico said they would dock at Port Fourchon and load it up with coal that was coming in from Poland. Harrison thought of the mines shut down in West Virginia.

He flipped away the butt of his cigarette, thinking about Maxwell Carter and what he might have discovered. The more he thought about it the more he believed Call. Call had no reason to lie about Clarksburg. He knew he could be looking at first-degree murder for the boy in the bayou, notwithstanding his offer to implicate Laveaux by a phone call. Unless they matched his fingerprints there was no evidence against Laveaux, and with the publicity the Jesuit Bend case had received no jury would find a problem linking Call to more than moving the body. First-degree murder got him a lethal injection. All of which made it unnecessary to lie about Carter.

'Mister, I think you the man.'

Harrison heard the voice behind him and a shiver ran like static in his hair. He stood exactly where he was, adrenalin prickling the skin of his shoulders. Those were the words every undercover agent feared above all else. He had never heard them before and had never expected to. He stared across the chopping white crusts of water, the breeze blowing his hair back and salt thick in his nostrils. His mouth was dry and his blood coursing. Slowly he turned and saw the boy sitting by the open hatch on the cargo hold.

'You hear what I said, mister?' The boy spoke to him again. 'I think you the man.'

Harrison stared at him. He dulled his eyes like a dog before it bites, the way the really worst cons did in the big house before they tore someone's arm from its socket. But the boy didn't spook. He just sat where he was and smiled.

'Y'all think you might kill me, but you won't. The badge won't allow it to happen.'

The wind was stronger now but Harrison could hear every word.

The boy got up then and sauntered over to lean on the gunwale. Harrison looked sideways at him and he looked sideways at Harrison.

'I'm from the street, Mr Yankee-doodle deckhand, and I can smell the man.' The boy sniffed the air, like an animal testing the wind. 'People like me always know the man. The man wanna bust our heads, especially in New Orleans.' He spat into the wind. 'He stomp us any chance he get.' He spoke like an adult, hardened, reciting what he had witnessed. Yet he was a child, small and skinny and smooth-faced. Harrison's heart was moving against his ribs.

The boy did something then that made his stomach cramp. Reaching up, he trailed a slow finger the length of Harrison's spine.

Harrison gripped him by the throat and hoisted him off the deck. He held him with both hands, every muscle shaking, the vein pumping in his neck. The boy coughed and spluttered, fighting Harrison's wrist, the fingers pinched and clawing. His eyes were popping and his cheeks bulging. Harrison held him a moment longer, then his mind blanked and he was underground and shots were ringing out in the darkness.

'What the fuck . . . ?' Frederico came across the deck with a knife in his hand. Harrison dropped the boy, turned and pivoted.

Frederico snarled at him and rolled the knife in his hand.

Harrison's heart was pounding. 'Put it down, Frederico.'

The boy was scrabbling across the deck at his feet. The Cajun twirled the blade, his mouth hanging open like a dog's. Harrison could see Ignace and Mesa watching them from the bridge. Frederico swung wildly. Harrison fell back, the blade just missing his stomach.

'Think you wanna fuck with the crew?' Frederico spat on the deck. 'Man, I been waiting for this.' He came again and Harrison feinted and dropped back. Frederico switched the knife from hand to hand and back again. He paced Harrison like a cat, walking round him in circles, looking for his move. Then he lunged hard. Harrison dropped to one knee, caught Frederico's arm under his own and carried his weight backwards. Pushing himself up on the balls of his feet, he knocked the knife from Frederico's grip and snapped his arm across the gunwale.

Frederico screamed.

Then Podjo was there. Mesa came across the deck. Ignace was on the upper deck.

Frederico lay writhing at Harrison's feet, holding his arm where a sliver of bone was poking through the skin. Harrison stood where he was, breathing hard; his only thought – survival. Podjo took a pace towards him and Harrison lifted his palm as if to keep him back. Podjo hesitated, looked up at Ignace then stepped forward again.

'Podjo,' Ignace called down to him. Podjo stopped.

Ignace came down the steps to the deck. The boy was crouched by the cargo hold. Frederico's blade lay on the floor at Harrison's feet. He made no attempt to go for it. Ignace stood five paces from him, eyes hawked.

'Don't send a kid.' Harrison breathed heavily. 'You send a kid to finger me, I'm gonna cut off his head and show him the hole in his neck.'

Ignace stood where he was as if he was unsure exactly how to handle the situation. Harrison took his chance. He hovered a moment on the balls of his feet then shoved past Podjo. He stalked into the galley, the breath sticking in his throat. He went into his cabin, slammed the door and unrolled the .45 from his pack. Something fell out of the towel and he shrank back, thinking it was a scorpion. He looked again and saw it was a severed chicken's foot wrapped in what looked like a piece of hide. He stood for a long moment with the boy's voice in his head, the cocksure way he had spoken, with absolute certainty.

The utter vulnerability of his situation came over him. He'd have to bluff it hard now or shoot his way out. His hands were trembling.

He made a decision. Stuffing the .45 in his belt, he went on deck where Podjo was bending over Frederico. Harrison pushed the engineer aside and dropped the chicken's foot on Frederico's face.

'You want to put the gris gris on me, asshole?' He rested his foot on Frederico's chest. 'Like I'm gonna believe any of that coonass shit. Go near my stuff again, I'll kill you.'

'Junya, you sumbitch, get below.' Ignace's words cut

through the wind. 'Podjo, get Frederico inside.' He stared at Harrison.

Harrison waited, hands hanging at his sides, the adrenalin thinning his blood so his mind was cool and sharp. Instinct had taken over. Fight or flight – and there was nowhere for him to run. Ignace had his 'gator knife hanging from his belt, his right hand hovering above the sheath, the fingers twitching. Harrison faced him down with the deck rolling under his feet.

'You broke Frederico's arm.'

There was a different light in Ignace's eyes now and Harrison could sense his uncertainty.

'And I'll break his neck and every other fucking neck if any one of you coonass bastards so much as looks at me again.' He took a pace towards him. 'You think I'm a cop – *you* tell me. Got it? Don't send no fucking child.'

Ignace stared at him, eyes wide, hand resting on the bone-handled skinning knife. 'You just made your mistake.' He spat on the deck. 'This is a small boat and you got nowhere to go.' He looked at the grip of Harrison's .45 protruding from his belt. 'You think you the only one on this boat with a piece?' He snorted, turned on his heel then looked back. 'Stay away from the kid, Harrison. I catch you anywhere near him I kill you myself.'

Harrison stayed on deck, the gun still in his belt, wondering how and when Ignace would make his move. The river slipped by the gunwales as if to mock him with the proximity of the shore. The currents would drag him under before he could swim twenty yards.

He felt somebody move next to him. It was Marie: he scented her before he looked round. He knew he was trembling, knew that anyone standing close enough could feel it. He didn't look at her, didn't speak. He took a cigarette from his pocket.

'My, oh, my,' she said softly. 'You the only Yankee on a boat full of Cajuns and you break somebody's arm.'

Harrison didn't reply.

'First off you sneak out on deck, peeking at stuff you shouldn't be peeking at, then the very next trip you break somebody's arm.'

Still Harrison didn't reply. The pulse thudded at his temple now, adrenalin pumping again. He felt weak all at once as if his sugar levels were low.

'What's the matter, honey, Junya hit a nerve?'

Harrison stared at the shapeless grey of the western levee.

'That why you put on such a show? That why you didn't put him overboard when you could have?' Marie laughed at him. 'Real bad man would've drowned his nigger ass. Were you trying to be bad, mister? I met some bad men in my time. Baby, you ain't even close.'

Harrison could see Ignace above them on the upper deck.

Marie sensed him, too, and backed away. 'You just think on this, honey child. It wasn't Junya told Ignace about no cop. You done that youself.'

sixteen

Harrison was shaken awake by the sound of the anchor rolling out on its chain. The cabin was tight and black and airless. The upper bunk pressed in on him and for a moment he was underground with a punji stake mantrap willing him to stumble and impale himself. He rolled out of the bunk and thumped on to the floor, righting himself instinctively and reaching for the .45. But there was no dirt and no tunnel, only the heat of the cabin and the grating sound of the chain rattling to the seabed.

Pulling on a pair of jeans, he went into the galley. Nobody was there, no sign of anyone. On deck the dawn was breaking and he could see the flattened alluvial banks of the Grand Terre Islands. He saw the mate watching him from the upper deck.

'I thought we were headed for the Fourchon,' Harrison said.

'We were.' Mesa smiled at him but only his mouth moved. 'Till somebody step out of line.'

Harrison felt the knot begin to tighten in his stomach. He looked north again and could see they were sheltered from the sea by a sandbar. Beyond it at the top of the beach he saw a camp built on eight-foot pilings, surrounded by live oaks. The water was grey and the building stark against the sand. Very little grew this far south, the salt saw to that. Augustine Laveaux's twenty-six-foot speedboat was moored close to the shore.

The sound of an engine broke the silence and Harrison looked astern where a large flat-bottomed skiff rounded the head and bounced across the chop, sending spray high in its wake. Skiffs drew little water and could happily work in less than three feet. He watched as it came closer and realized Gumbo was at the wheel. What was Gumbo doing all the way down here when he worked on the wharf in New Orleans?

Podjo moved next to him. Harrison hadn't heard him come on deck.

'The boss invited us for breakfast,' Podjo said. 'I don't know what we're having. Some kinda meat, I guess.'

Harrison could smell his sweat; he could hear the rise and fall of his breath. Podjo patted him lightly on the shoulder and stepped back inside.

Laveaux watched their approach from the veranda of the single-storey camp. He wore a pair of white cotton pants and a loose-fitting shirt with the sleeves pushed up, to reveal the muscles of his arms and the gold Rolex that hung a little loosely from his wrist. Harrison sat in the stern of the skiff with Marie and the boy next to him. The boy eyed him darkly but said nothing. Ignace stood beside Gumbo with his back to the bows, his arms folded, staring all the time at Harrison. Frederico sat hunched in his seat, holding his broken arm to his chest.

Gumbo slowed the skiff in the shallows and Podjo jumped out and moored them to a heavy log on the beach. Ignace splashed through the surf to where his cousin was watching from the beach, the wind ruffling his hair. Harrison sat where he was for a moment, aware of the .45 in his belt. Mesa jerked a thumb at him to move.

He went ashore and paused at the edge of the sand. Laveaux stood facing him with Ignace to one side. Junya ran ahead for the shade of the wide veranda with Marie following behind. Laveaux stared from under hooded lids at Harrison who remained where he was, hands at his sides,

the weight of the gun in his belt. Laveaux glanced dis-
paragingly at Frederico who stood to one side. 'Breakfast,'
he said, and headed up the beach.

Harrison hesitated for a moment, letting the breath
escape his lips. Marie was on the veranda where a large
table had been laid. She watched him carefully and he
remembered her words from last night. He glanced back at
the skiff, wondering if he could make it, but Gumbo stood
impassively in the shallows. Harrison squared his shoulders
and walked up to the camp.

Two women served them breakfast – eggs and ham,
bacon and rolls, coffee and orange juice and bloody Marys
for whoever wanted them. Harrison sat at the corner of the
table. Conversation was minimal, the crew eating rave-
nously, Junya with his eyes on his food, Marie next to him
watching like his mother.

Laveaux spoke to his cousin in Cajun French and Ignace
nodded to Frederico, said something else then looked at
Harrison. Harrison ignored them and drank coffee. He was
out on a limb here, and he knew, no matter that he might
comfort himself a fraction with hurting a few of them, they
would kill him if that's what they planned to do. The stark
reality of his life dawned on him there in the sunshine with
the waters of the Gulf of Mexico lapping at the sand and the
rigs marking the horizon. He could have stayed in West
Virginia with Santini who undoubtedly would have been
good for him: there was something about her that he hadn't
seen in many women before. But these were foolish
thoughts cluttering his mind when a cool head was vital.
He pushed them away, steeled himself and lit a cigarette.

'This camp is right about where Lafitte had his cottage,'
Laveaux said suddenly. The others were silent. Frederico,
with his good elbow resting on the table, stared at Harrison
with hatred in his eyes.

'Jean Lafitte,' Laveaux went on, 'the Lord of Barataria.
Have you heard of him, Harrison?'

'I know he had a bar on Bourbon Street.'

'A bar on Bourbon Street.' Laveaux raised one eyebrow then nodded to the waters of the gulf. 'He ruled most of what you see here.'

Harrison smoked his cigarette.

'Junya.' Laveaux snapped at the name like a dog. 'What have you got to tell me?'

The boy stared into his own lap for a moment and Harrison could feel the sweat beginning to creep in his hairline. Podjo shifted slightly further away from him as if he were a leper and to get too close was dangerous.

Laveaux got up and walked round the table to where the boy hunched next to Marie. He rested a palm on top of his head then squeezed so his fingers were white at the tips. Marie was very still beside the boy, one hand holding an unlit cigarette. Ignace watched like a hawk.

'What have you got to tell me?' Laveaux repeated.

Junya twisted his head from the grip and glared at Harrison. 'I told him I thought he was a cop,' he said. 'Ignace been jumpy as fuck since he come on the boat. I figure that's the reason so somebody better call the sumbitch on it.'

Laveaux was looking at Harrison.

Harrison was ready to throw the table over. He was going to die here, he knew it, and strangely a sense of calm came over him. Now the moment was here, he would make a fight of it at least.

'Are you a cop, Harrison?'

Harrison stared Laveaux right in the eye. 'What do you think?' he said.

Laveaux's eyes were as dead as at any time Harrison had seen them. He pressed the fingers of one hand against the palm of the other. Ignace looked on with his brow furrowed.

'We had it confirmed you did the spell in Camp J,' Laveaux said quietly. 'Three months.'

Harrison just looked at him.

'Never had it confirmed about Camp F, though.'

'Keep looking. You will.'

Laveaux paced the veranda and looked out to sea for a while. Then he turned to Junya again. 'What makes you think he's a cop?'

Junya didn't answer him right away. He shot a glance at Harrison. 'I used to be able to smell them,' he said. 'Cops got a particular way of smelling.' He shrugged. 'But I guess if he's in Angola he can't be no cop.' He shook his head and looked up at Laveaux. 'Guess I been hanging with you too long, lost my sense of smell.'

'You mean you *don't* think he's a cop?' Laveaux looked quizzical. 'Make up your mind, boy. Last night you thought he was.'

'Last night I don't know what I'm thinking after he's trying to choke me.' Junya rubbed his neck.

I figure we best chop him up anyway and feed him to the shoe-pick,' Frederico said.

Laveaux curled his lip. 'Are *you* going to do it, Frederico? I thought you tried already.'

Mesa laughed and Podjo forced a smile. Ignace sat where he was, the knuckles of one hand pressed against his jaw. Harrison sat watching Laveaux with his hands resting on his thighs.

'Give me your piece,' Laveaux said without looking at him.

Harrison tensed.

'Give it up.'

Harrison stared at him.

'If you're clean you got nothing to fear.'

Harrison still sat there. He looked at Junya who looked back at him. Then he stood up and, reaching behind him, drew the .45 from his belt. Frederico was watching like a hawk now, his eyes balled, the fingers of his good hand bunched into a fist. Harrison held the weapon loosely in his right hand then laid it on the table, the butt facing Laveaux.

Laveaux folded his arms and looked down at the gun. Again he spoke to Junya. 'Your sense of smell,' he said. 'What's it tell you now?'

The boy sat with his hands clasped between his thighs, looking across the table into the grey of Harrison's eyes. 'What the fuck, I don't know, do I?'

Laveaux picked up Harrison's gun and released the clip from the grips. He checked the shells and raised one eyebrow. 'Hollow point,' he said. 'No second chances.' He inspected the barrel where the serial number had been filed off, the worn nature of the grips, then slid the clip home again. He racked a round into the chamber. 'This violates your parole,' he said.

'So call up Chaisson.'

Laveaux half smiled and released the round from the chamber. 'Junya's a smart kid, Harrison,' he said. 'His sense of smell might be off, but there's nothing wrong with his thinking.'

Harrison looked at his gun in Laveaux's hand. He had it rested in the crook of his left arm, the barrel pointing at him.

'I guess old Junya's been thinking about Marcel Call,' Laveaux went on. 'I guess we all have.' He smiled. 'What do you think about Call?'

Harrison was quiet for a moment then he said, 'I think he's just a coonass like the rest of you. I think he was no good in a fight and letting him buy me a drink was stupid.' He looked at the faces gathered around him. 'You know what else I think?' He lifted his eyes to meet Laveaux's. 'I think you either give me back my piece or shoot me with it.'

'He ain't no fucking cop.' Marie shook her head. 'Shit, he don't have the brains. What kinda cop's gonna beat on Junya's ass with a boat full of Cajuns setting there in the river.' She pushed her chair away from the table, scooped up her pack of cigarettes and walked the length of the veranda.

Laveaux watched her go then he sat down and thought

for a long moment. Nobody spoke. Ignace was watching Harrison. Harrison was watching Laveaux.

'You think she's got a point?' Laveaux asked him.

Harrison said nothing.

Laveaux was silent after that. He sat weighing the pistol in his hand then he stood up and handed it back to Harrison. He turned, leaned on the rail and exhaled a breath.

'You nearly strangled the boy,' he said, 'and you broke Frederico's arm. I've been patient with you, Harrison. But now I have to tell you – cross me again I'll feed you your own liver.'

seventeen

Ignace brooded on the bridge. He was sitting in his skipper's chair, gazing the length of the barges as the *See More Night* steamed up Bayou Lafourche. They had loaded the coal at Port Fourchon, and were on their way back to the wharf once more in New Orleans. He took the gris gris from his pocket and questioned whether his cousin might not actually be right. But all his life his Nannan had been conja, able to use the magic and summon the powers of voodoo. His mother had told him, his aunts had told him, every woman in the family had told him.

Twice in his lifetime she had put the gris gris on someone. A pregnant neighbour had offended her and his Nannan put the spell on her: she lost the baby and nearly bled to death in the miscarriage. Another woman from Houma had a daughter that was leading her son astray: she put the gris gris on the whole family and the girl died in a house fire.

Ignace sipped from his tumbler of whiskey and inspected the charm once more. Maybe his Nannan could only work her magic on girls. Maybe it didn't work on the Yankee. Maybe it had been defiled by the way he tossed it at Frederico, or perhaps it was nothing to do with Frederico. Maybe it was the Yankee himself. He seemed to lead a charmed life. Yesterday morning on Grand Terre was the time to get rid of him regardless of who he was. Augustine had had the chance right there and yet he hadn't taken it.

*

Harrison lay in his bunk with Gumbo snoring above him. The big man had taken Frederico's place on the boat. He was so heavy the bunk boards bowed and Harrison wondered if they might not just give way and collapse on top of him. He couldn't sleep. On the bayou there was only one man needed on watch, which meant that sometimes he and Gumbo were in the cabin at the same time.

Mesa would be on the bridge. Everyone else was sleeping so he sat in the galley with some coffee. He could hear Ignace having sex with Marie, low guttural moans, followed by the sound of a slap and then her crying. The cabin door opened and she came stumbling down the steps. She saw Harrison, faltered and wiped at the tears in her eyes.

'What you looking at?' she said.

Harrison said nothing. This woman had saved his life. Her words had stayed Laveaux's hand. Whether she believed what she had said Harrison didn't know, and yesterday he hadn't cared. Today, though, that question was uppermost in his mind. He took a cigarette from his shirt pocket and offered it to her. She sat opposite him and lit it, dabbing still at her eyes.

'Where's he at?'

'Passed out.' She exhaled smoke heavily.

'Does he always give you the treatment?'

'What's it to you?'

'It ain't nothing to me. But why put up with it?'

'Like I got a choice?'

They were quiet for a moment, Harrison studying her face across the table. She was young still and quite pretty. Her eyes were oval and dark but they gave nothing away. He thought again about yesterday and the fight with Frederico. What she had said to him on deck afterwards: she knew he was sneaking around and she reminded him that Junya hadn't told a soul he thought Harrison was a cop, he had done that himself. He wanted to know why she had not said anything to anyone when she saw him in the fiddley, he wanted to know why she had saved him yesterday, but he couldn't push it. He couldn't even mention it because he had no idea what other games were being played on this boat. Ignace seemed to have his own agenda and this woman occupied *his* bed, not his cousin's.

Marie got up and fetched a long-necked bottle of beer from the fridge. She passed it to Harrison and got herself another. Harrison twisted off the cap and beer bubbled to spill over his fingers. Marie took a long swallow and he found himself watching the skin of her throat.

'Why are you on the boat?' he asked her. 'You Ignace's girlfriend?'

'Why you axing?'

'It's just a question. Call it conversation.'

'What makes you think I want a conversation with you?'

Harrison shrugged his shoulders.

Marie pursed her lips, sipped beer and sucked on her cigarette. 'Ignace thinks I'm his girlfriend. I'm here because Augustine wants me to be.'

'You Augustine's girlfriend, too?'

'Watch what yo' inferring, mister. I ain't above putting my fist through yo' teeth. I guess y'all think I'm just a whore, a piece of black pussy for the skipper. Well, I ain't no whore, mister. You got that?'

Harrison sipped his beer. 'Nobody said you were a whore.'

'I seen it in yo' eyes – you all the same. Yankee or coonass, it don't make no never mind.'

Harrison finished his cigarette then stubbed the butt out in the ashtray. 'Why does Augustine want you on the boat?' he asked her.

She cocked her head to one side. 'You know what? All of a sudden you axing a lot of questions.'

Harrison shifted his shoulders. 'I'm making conversation is all. In case you didn't notice, I don't get a lot of it.'

'Then why you stick around here?'

'You know the deal. It's this or the pen. I got a parole officer busting my balls as it is. I blew it one time and I ain't about to go back.'

'You got Bill Chaisson, don't you?'

'You know him?'

'Honey, I know all the New Orleans POs. I had about ever' one of them on my case one time or another.'

Harrison smiled. 'They're cops. I mean, they're not paid to arrest you or nothing, but it's still Department of Corrections. Whichever way you look at it, they're chicken-shit cops.'

Marie blew smoke from the side of her mouth. 'Cops,' she said. 'Chicken shit, yeah. I guess you and me know all about chicken-shit cops.'

Harrison didn't rise to the bait. He tipped the ash from his cigarette.

'Why *does* Augustine want you on the boat?' he asked again.

'To look after Junya.'

Harrison was considering that comment when Ignace appeared. He looked at both of them, the drink showing dull in his eyes. Then he stepped into the galley and stretched. 'Looks nice and cosy,' he muttered. 'Marie, get you black ass back up those stairs.'

Marie sat where she was for a moment. Ignace bent to the fridge and took out a bottle of beer. 'Woman, I ain't gonna tell you again.'

She got up and moved to get past him. Ignace brought the flat of his hand hard across her scalp, sending her into the wall. He went to hit her again, backhanded this time, but she ducked out of the way and scrambled up the stairs. Harrison sat where he was, and when Ignace looked back at him Harrison's eyes were narrow and sharp.

'Sometimes people just don't get it,' Ignace said.

'Sometimes.'

They stared at each other for a moment, Ignace's face the

boiled red of a crab. He worked his fingers over the condensation on the bottle then went back upstairs. Harrison sat where he was, waiting for the sound of him hitting Marie, but thankfully it never came.

He hated men like Ignace, men who exploited the weakness in others, particularly that which they perceived in women. Men like Ignace caused Harrison to look at his own life and ask himself why he had chosen the path he had, twenty years working undercover for the FBI. Was it because he had this crusading passion for justice, or was it just easier to hang out with the low life instead of getting something real going of his own? As age had caught up with him it had been a question he asked more and more, and one he didn't like the answer to.

He was aware of a sense of rage now deep within himself, the kind of rage that comes after experiencing real fear. It was natural after what had happened yesterday, but the more he looked at himself the more he realized it was not a rage against others but himself. He didn't need to be here, he had the chance of that other kind of life and yet here he was. He finished his beer, lit a cigarette and went out on deck.

The night air was cool and moist, though the mosquitoes had lifted from the marsh as the sun went down and they whined about his head. He wore repellent as all the crew did, but the mosquitoes always seemed to pick out the one bit of flesh he had missed. He glanced at his watch: 2.00 a.m. He was as awake as he was mid-morning. Gumbo slept like a baby, his snores rising almost as soon as his head hit the pillow.

Simple mind. Harrison had always thought of people who slept that quickly as being overly simple: there wasn't enough to occupy the mind so the mind shut down and they slept. In reality he was just jealous. Sleep was snatched where he could get it, and even then his dreams were so naked and vivid he might as well be awake.

A movement made him look round and he saw the kid squatting on the hatch of the cargo locker as he had been before. Harrison's pulse quickened. He rested his arms on the gunwales once again. Bayou Lafourche slid by in the darkness. They were north of the Leesville Bridge now and he saw an old grasshopper nodding its head beyond the batture land, pumping what little oil was left into the tank built behind it.

They passed shrimp boats, base skimmers with huge swing arms and scoop nets, the tickle chain chinking in the wind that arced across the bayou, ruffling what few trees clung to the edge of the levee. Harrison felt the boy move alongside him.

'What do you want?' he said.

'Just getting some air, same as you.'

Harrison looked back across the water and Junya plucked the cigarette from where it burned between his fingers. 'Mister, that was a fine show you put on back there, but I don't buy a second of it.'

Harrison was cold all at once: what was this now? He thought this moment was behind them – what game was Laveaux playing?

'I might be just some nigger to you,' Junya went on. 'But I'm smarter than you and the rest of this whole crew put together.'

'And that's why you live in a cargo hold.' Harrison took another cigarette from his pocket and snapped open his Zippo.

The boy nodded to the lighter. 'Augustine's got one of them. It belonged to his brother, and his brother is the only reason you ain't dead already.'

Harrison looked round. 'Smart kid, uh.'

'Mister, I'm smarter than you'd know. Augustine's got this blind spot when it comes to Vietnam, and that's where you're set, right there in his blind spot.' He sighed, drew on the cigarette and exhaled hard. 'You know what? This crew is way too young for you to be here. I reckon down at the station house y'all figured that. Y'all knew about Etienne, though, huh? Figured the only way in was to have something in common with old Etienne. Hell, the whole of New Orleans knows what Augustine thinks about vets. Me, I just think it's bullshit, a bullshit excuse for a buncha government bullshit. But I can see how a cop might want to use it if he was after Augustine.'

He had backed away slightly and Harrison felt the nerves cramp in his gut as they had done before. This kid had balls of steel and there was a certainty in his words that knocked the wind out of him completely.

Somebody moved on the deck behind them and Podjo's massive frame appeared in the glow of the lights.

'Junya, get below,' he muttered. 'It's time I closed the hatch.' He looked beyond the boy at Harrison who stood where he was and blew smoke across the bows. He waited for the boy to say something more but he didn't. He just climbed down the ladder and Podjo secured the hatch over his head.

eighteen

The tug docked again in New Orleans, crossing the water-way from Bayou Lafourche and joining the big river at Algiers Lock. Two of the barges were tied up at Governor Nicholls Street Wharf but the one carrying the coal was destined for Third Street. Harrison helped unload on Governor Nicholls, then stood on the wharf with Gumbo as the final barge was shunted under the west shore bridge. He looked for any sign of Laveaux but his office was closed.

He took his opportunity and crossed Decatur Street to Café Beignet where he called Matt Penny. Then he walked north through the quarter all the way to Rampart Street where Penny picked him up.

'The boss wants a meeting,' Penny said.

'I don't have time. You'll have to fill him in. The tug's coming back this afternoon and I have to be visible.'

'He's not going to like it.'

'He'll understand.' Harrison stared through the wind-shield for a moment. A meeting with Mayer was his chance to quit: all he had to do was tell him what had happened and they'd pull him out. There was no way they would risk anything, with Junya still thinking he was a cop. He could walk away with his life intact. He knew he should take the opportunity: the proximity of what had happened on Grand Terre was so livid the sweat moved on his palms.

'Are you OK?' Penny asked him.

'I'm fine.' Harrison glanced at him. He should just tell

Penny. Already his life had hung by a thread. He had called him with the simple intention of getting out, packing his bag and going back to Santini, but now he was here all he could think about was last night on deck when Junya reiterated what he'd said. It contradicted his behaviour at Grand Terre. The question was, *why?*

'You don't look OK,' Penny said. 'What's been going down?'

Harrison made a face. 'I had a breakfast with Laveaux yesterday morning.'

'And?' He could see the hope suddenly in Penny's eyes.

'No chance, Matthew, the whole crew was watching me.'

Penny made a face. 'You had me going there for a moment.' He blew the air from his cheeks. 'Santini called – they ran Ignace's prints against the set at the fishing camp. It wasn't him, JB. She also checked the non-felon records. Neither cousin ever did any time in the service.'

Harrison frowned. 'So what did Carter find, then?'

'I don't know.'

'It has to be Laveaux. Carter must have found an old felon record that we didn't know about. There's no other explanation.'

'So why can't we find it – if we assume nobody paid him?'

Harrison had no answer for him.

Penny dropped him off again on Esplanade Avenue. 'Something else for your report,' Harrison said. 'They checked me out at Angola. It seems Laveaux did a little digging.'

'None of the hello lines have been called. He must have someone of his own up there.'

Harrison nodded. 'Camp J came up, Matthew, but not F. I don't know who they've got in their pocket, but I need to appear in Camp F.'

'OK.' Penny squinted at him. 'Anything else?'

'Where's Call?'

'He's in a safe house in Metairie.'

'He should be in Angola.'

'I know it. But he said if we shipped him back the deal was off. He'd take his chances with the jury and we could whistle for his testimony about Laveaux's phone call.'

'Get him back to Angola. Tell him it's temporary but get him back there. They're suspicious of Call, Matthew. If Laveaux can check me out in Angola, he can check out Call. What's he going to think if he doesn't find him?'

Harrison walked down Esplanade, crossing Royal and Chartres before he got to Decatur Street. He should have told Penny what had happened. To keep information like that from the contact agent was not only unprofessional, it was dumb. He was dumb. That had been his way out right there and he hadn't taken it. He leaned against the wall of a house and lit a cigarette. What was he thinking? Because of what Santini had learned he now needed to get closer to Laveaux than ever, which would be nigh on impossible, given what happened down in the gulf. There was little to be gained by remaining on the tugboat now. But then he thought about Junya and Marie and he knew there was something going on that he couldn't figure out. But whatever it was it seemed to be between them and him, and he didn't think either Ignace or his cousin knew about it.

He found the crew drinking in the Apple Barrel. Frederico had his arm in plaster and he looked warily at Harrison. Harrison bought himself a drink and sat on a stool while the crew huddled round a table. Mesa came up to the bar to buy another round and leaned on the counter next to him. 'We're sailing again at four.'

Harrison licked the gummed edge of his cigarette paper. 'OK.'

'You sure you wanna be there? I mean, life ain't exactly been pretty fo' you, has it?'

Harrison lit his cigarette and looked sideways at him. 'My life ain't never been pretty.'

*

Ignace had a hangover, sitting in the office overlooking Governor Nicholls Street Wharf. He had met Augustine at Third Street and ridden back with him. A harbour police car had drawn up on the dock and the patrolman was talking to one of the truck drivers who stood by while Gumbo and the roustabouts loaded his vehicle.

'We got a problem I don't know about, cousin?' Ignace gestured below. Laveaux shook his head. 'No. Everything we don't want them to see went down to Third Street.'

Ignace came away from the window. 'I want the Yankee off the boat,' he said. 'What Junya said still bothers me even if it don't bother you.'

Laveaux smiled at Ignace's troubled expression. 'Harrison's a tough little cocksucker, isn't he? It took balls to hand me that pistol.' He sat down behind his desk, took two black cigars from the top drawer and passed one to Ignace. 'I like him.' He clipped his cigar and wet the end with his lips. 'I like him where I can see him.'

Ignace looked unimpressed. 'We should've clipped him. For once Frederico was right.'

'Frederico was biased.'

'Biased?'

'Yes, it means sort of prejudiced, Ignace.'

'I know what the fuck it means.' Ignace felt in his pocket for the charm his godmother had given him.

'You still playing with that thing?'

Ignace pulled out the chicken's foot. 'You think it's stupid, don't you?'

'In this day and age, yes, I think it's stupid.' Laveaux took it from him, tore off the leather binding and tossed it in the trash can. Ignace watched in horror.

'You don't need it,' his cousin told him. 'Stuff like this is why we ended up on the bottom bunk when the old world split.'

'What you talking about now?'

'Exactly.' Laveaux rolled his eyes. 'My point proven,

cousin.' He sat forward and picked up his pen. 'Go and round up your crew. I don't want them shit-faced when you sail.'

Ignace got up, cigar clamped between his teeth, and headed for the door.

'Ignace.' Laveaux called him back. 'There's something I want you to think about.'

'What?'

'Why d'you think I gave Harrison back his gun?'

'Because he was in Vietnam, because of Etienne.'

Laveaux looked at him. 'Etienne, Etienne, all I hear about is my brother. You really think I'd let my feelings about Etienne threaten everything?'

'I don't know.' Ignace shrugged. 'Maybe.'

Laveaux shook his head. 'Sometimes you are so stupid I can't believe we're related. I gave Harrison back his gun because we don't know who he is. If he's bad then he'll think he's won something and he'll be a little bolder. If he's good we've lost nothing. So long as he doesn't get to see what he's not supposed to, it costs us nothing, having him on the boat. And we keep him where we can see him. It's also a lot easier to get rid of him if we want to.'

'We should get rid of him now.'

Laveaux rolled his eyes. 'If we do that and he *is* a cop, we don't know what that's going to bring down on us. We might be risking everything for nothing. You understand?' He stepped right up to Ignace. 'We don't move till we know what – if anything – is going down. And we won't know that till I find Marcel Call.'

nineteen

Will Bentley was looking forward to the cemetery tour organized by the Jesuit School. It was somewhere his parents had never taken him. What with his dad working on Magazine Street all week they never came into the city on the weekend. They lived in suburbia along with all the other middle-income families.

When it was announced that his class would be visiting St Louis No. 1 and 2 as part of their history project he had been delighted. The cemeteries were part of what made the city so different: the dead buried above ground in visible, sometimes accessible tombs. Will loved the idea of going to the cemeteries. Though he was only eleven he shared his father's fascination with history and the thought of seeing Dominique You's grave was incredible.

It rained in the morning, but by the time they pulled up in the school van that afternoon the sun was bright and hot and beating back off the sidewalk. Will wore a Tiger Woods baseball hat pulled down over his close-cut hair, a pair of shorts, sneakers and T-shirt. He carried his school bag on his back, and was due to meet his father at the 1st District police station on Rampart Street after the tour was over.

Junya was selling crack in the Iberville, though that was not his main reason for being there. He was up against the clock. Augustine had taken him and Marie to one side as soon as the tug docked. He had come down into the cargo hold where they normally waited till all was quiet on the dockside. Today, though, he was in a hurry. He had an order to fill and was short – something had gone wrong further upriver.

Marie had driven the van because Frederico couldn't with his broken arm, and she was parked now on the other side of the project, waiting for him. They had cruised St Thomas and the Calliope to begin with and got nothing. They would have gone to Magnolia too, but Junya had lots of enemies in Magnolia from his days running with Wendell's gang. He didn't want to be back in this part of town again as it was too close to home but, given the time constraints Augustine had put on them, he had little choice. Claiborne Avenue was too dangerous and the only other option was somewhere in Algiers. Without Frederico to back them up, Marie didn't want to go to the west shore.

It didn't take him long to get rid of his supply of little yellow rocks. He didn't sell directly to the kids but to dealers, part of the old gang he ran with. He had a roll of bills in his pocket that would keep him in boom box music for a year, but it was going in his stash with the rest. Junya had plans. He was way too smart to wind up back here, especially with the Gangsta Disciples moving in, and he was too smart to get whacked by Laveaux when the time came, as it inevitably would. No, he had his stash and he had plans that even Marie didn't know about: he just hadn't been able to figure out a way to execute them yet.

Until now, that was. Now he had an idea, an idea that made his blood run a little chill. It meant sticking his neck out so far he might just hang by it. Already it could have got him killed, and for a while he questioned his own judgement. But he had always been able to smell cop and that Yankee reeked so bad he might as well have been skunked.

He sat on the step of one of the blocks, bathing in the warmth of the sun. This past winter had been cold and spring, too, had not been what it should have. Too wet and windy – not just the downpours you expected in the south, but heavy prolonged rain, the grey kind that seeped into your bones. Shading his eyes, he saw a gang-banger watching St Louis No. 1 from the roof. They didn't rob so many people in there these days, not since the city put wire up. It was still a dangerous place for the wrong kind of person but nothing compared to when he was running with Wendell.

Will Bentley was getting bored now. Almost four o'clock and they had been to No. 2 and he had seen the grave of Dominique You and that's all he was interested in there. Here in No. 1 he had seen the crosses on the voodoo queen's stone and had been a little disappointed. He didn't know so much about her, but Dominique You was a pirate who sailed with Jean Lafitte, and fought the English at the battle of New Orleans. The history books told how he had been a favourite of Andrew Jackson, and Will would be able to tell that stuff to his dad, which was great. His dad knew much more about St Landry Parish than Orleans, which was where their family originally came from.

'Hey, Will. They got bodies buried in the walls,' Todd Weighbridge said to him. Todd was another kid from his class whose father worked for the city. He and Will had been pals for a couple of years.

'No, they don't. They only got that in mid-city.'

'Yeah, they do. They got bodies in the walls. Climb on up and see for yourself.'

Will shook his head. 'You climb up.'

'I did it already. The walls are crumbling and you can see the actual bodies, the bones, Will, the skeletons.' Todd's eyes were shining.

'You're kidding me.'

'I'm not. Look, I'll watch the teachers, you climb on up and see.'

Will looked at the crumbling white stone, with the three-storey project blocks rising beyond. They had been told never to go into the projects. He gazed between the tombs where the teachers were standing together talking, then he glanced at the walls. It would be easy to climb up without a teacher spotting him. But he still figured Todd was lying. The walls didn't look thick enough to put bodies in them, but the thought of seeing skeletons was too much to ignore and he picked his way between the tombs to the wall.

Todd kept watch while Will pulled himself up. He was right. The walls were way too thin, and though they were crumbling there was nothing to see.

'Todd, you . . .' he started, then his section of wall crumbled and he slid down the far side into the Iberville project.

Todd looked up to laugh at him but Will was no longer there. 'Will?' he hissed.

'Will?' But Will didn't answer. Over by Marie Laveau's tomb the teachers were preparing to leave.

Will picked himself up and dusted the chalk from his knees. He picked up his fallen bag and turned to find a way round the side of the wall. Four kids stared at him.

'What you doing, nigger?' One of them with squint eyes and a gold tooth came over. He had a cellphone in his hand and a pager clipped to his belt. He was big and very black and the muscles stood out on his arms. Will didn't say anything. He looked from him to the others and then to the first block where three more of them were watching. All at once he was scared.

'Nice sneakers.' The kid with the squint kicked his foot. 'You got nice sneakers, my man. Cost plenty, uh? What outfit you run with, boy? Or is yo' daddy one of them rich niggers who don't live here no more?'

The others giggled and one leaned against the wall, blocking Will's retreat. He flicked at his face with a finger. 'Yo' in the wrong place, nigger.'

Junya saw him on the wall, saw him fall and saw the gang-bangers descend on him like vultures. Most of them were already cracked out on the shit he had brought from Laveaux. He watched them toying with the plump-looking kid, poking him, treading on his feet, mussing him like a cat would a mouse. Already he was crying. Junya sat for a moment longer, the sweat moist on his hands, a tingling sensation in his gut – the same tingling he always felt when he did this. Getting up, he wandered over to the gang and their fallen victim.

Will was looking for a way to escape his antagonists. One of them had a switchblade and was spinning it in his hand, catching it by the handle no matter how many times it flipped. Tears streamed down his cheeks and he could feel the build-up of urine in his bladder.

'Let me go,' he said. 'Please let me go. The teachers will be looking for me.'

Junya pushed through their ranks and looked at the boy. He was about the age he himself had been when Laveaux scooped him up. He looked him up and down, his clothes grimy now where he had climbed on the wall.

'School ain't no place for a nigger like you,' the boy with the squint was saying. 'I think you better stay here. Yo' our nigger now.'

Junya stepped between them and took Will by the arm. 'He ain't yo' nigger, he's mine.' He winked at Will and led him through the gang, who looked on but didn't object. Junya slipped an arm round Will's shoulders and walked him across the street.

'I n-need to get back to the cemetery,' Will stammered. 'My teachers . . . I've got to meet my dad.'

Junya nodded knowingly. 'You'll get back, my man. Quit worrying. You just can't go back that way. Look at those niggers. They eat you alive, boy.'

Will looked over his shoulder and saw the gang following them now, a good thirty or forty yards back but close enough to make him pick up his step.

'You come with me,' Junya said. 'I get you back to yo'

daddy.' He led him between the buildings then across Bienville to Iberville Street where Marie was waiting in the van. She was chain-smoking and flipping the butts out the window. She saw Junya and the kid in the door mirror and flipped the catch on the back doors. Junya led Will up to the van.

'Who are you?' Will said. 'What's your name?'

'Just call me Nonk,' Junya said. 'You know that's Cajun for uncle. Just you call me Nonk and think of me as yo' uncle.' Opening the back doors, he pushed Will ahead of him. Marie started the engine.

twenty

Marcel Call protested. Penny explained to him what was happening but he protested all the louder.

'I told you fucking Feds I ain't going back to the farm. That wasn't part of the deal, man. No way, I said. No way, no how.'

Penny guided him out the front door of the house in Metairie where two parole officers were waiting to drive him to Angola.

'There's been a change of plan, Call,' Penny said again. 'Take it or leave it, buddy. If you leave it you can take your chances with the jury, as you said you would. But I got to tell you no chance is no chance and you will get the needle.'

Call looked at him with his eyes bunched up. 'Damn,' he said, and spat on the sidewalk.

Harrison was back on the tugboat, helping Gumbo with the for'ard lines as Ignace increased the revs and spun the wheel to starboard. Jimmy Mesa cast off in the stern and Harrison threw off the spring then they steamed away from the dock. He stood for a moment with the air trapped in his throat, watching the land fall away. Even these few yards offshore the water began to eddy and he knew his chance had gone. He felt a weakness in his limbs and he wondered what had possessed him. There was only one consolation and that was very small. Ignace knew he had a .45 under his pillow, but nobody knew about the snub-nosed .38 he now had strapped to his ankle.

Junya sat in the hold with Marie and Will Bentley who was sitting on a pile of old rope with his hands tied behind his back. His tear-stained face was grubby and his eyes quick and darting like a bird with a broken wing. He looked from Junya to Marie and back again.

'Where are you taking me?' he asked them yet again. 'Why am I on this boat?'

Neither of them answered him. Junya smoked a cigarette and glanced every now and then at Marie who was painting her nails. Will looked beyond them to the white-painted bulkhead and the shelves piled with boxes, the great coils of rope thick and grey like snakes. 'My dad will be worried,' he said. 'He was supposed to meet me.'

Junya lifted a finger to his lips to quiet him.' Hush,' he said softly. 'You giving me a headache.'

Will's face crumpled and the tears started to fall again. He felt stupid, foolish and ashamed. He cursed Todd Weighbridge for going on about skeletons in the wall. He had thought this boy who called himself Nonk had saved him from the others, but he should never have got in that van. Once in the van Nonk had tied his hands and blindfolded him. He hadn't taken off the blindfold till they were down here in the half-darkness. He could tell they were on a boat just by looking around. He could smell diesel and oil through the air vents and he could hear the engines and the slapping sound the water made against the hull. It was like being in an empty barrel. He tried to think positively, but he was scared now, really frightened. He had never been this frightened in his life. Every now and again Junya would stare at him and the look in his eyes was far worse than anything he'd seen in the project. He thought of his mother and father and was filled all at once with a terrible sense of dread.

*

Laveaux stood on the balcony, a black cigar between his teeth, watching Harrison on deck as the *See More Night* pulled out into mid-river. Many thoughts worked their way through his mind. Cold and calculated like mathematical equations, he ground the answers out and spat away the chaff. His cellphone rang and he took it from his pocket, checked the caller ID and answered it.

'Yes,' he said.

'It's me, Conti. I thought you'd want to know. We just got word that Marcel Call is on his way back here. He's been in the Orleans Parish Jail while his attorney fought the violation charge.'

Laveaux inhaled smoke without removing the cigar from his mouth. 'Call me when he's settled. I have some questions for him.'

twenty-one

Jordan Bentley took the phone call in his office. It was his son's school and his hands shook when they told him. Will had gone missing in St Louis No. 1 cemetery. The teachers running the trip had searched the place from top to bottom but he was nowhere to be seen: they had discovered he wasn't there as the roll was called when the children got back on the bus.

Now Bentley stood in the reception area of the 1st District police station and spoke again with Todd Weighbridge, Will's best friend.

'He just climbed up on the wall, Mr Bentley,' Todd told him. 'I tried to stop him but he wanted to see if people were buried in there like they are in mid-city.'

The tutor in charge of the trip was standing to one side, giving a statement to a uniformed police officer. She kept looking over and when Bentley looked back her lip trembled.

Bentley stepped out on to North Rampart Street with an ache in his stomach that felt like the weight of a stone. He looked towards Armstrong Park. Maybe Will had walked. He had arranged to meet him here at the 1st District because he had to see the Captain before he went home. He had asked the school to drop the boy off, but maybe Will had decided to walk here instead. But Bentley had told him never to walk, not on his own in New Orleans, particularly not round here. St Louis No. 1 was on Basin Street, which was barely a block away but far enough, given the neighbourhood. He knew there was no way Will would have walked without telling anyone.

Back inside he looked again at the teacher and she avoided his gaze. He could see by the puffy skin round her eyes that she had been crying. *She* had been crying. What on earth was his wife going to be like when he told her? Frustration was building inside him, frustration and fear.

'Can you get a cruiser to run me up to the cemetery?' he asked the officer behind the desk.

'I got one on its way round right now, sir.' As she spoke a white NOPD crown Victoria pulled up in front of the building. Bentley climbed into the passenger seat, where a pump-action shotgun rested, barrel to the roof, like a sentinel between him and the driver. A minute later they were parked outside St Louis No. 1. Another car was already there and two officers were questioning a group of kids across the street.

Bentley could tell that nobody was in the cemetery. He couldn't see between all the raised graves and crypts but the silence of the dead echoed their emptiness back at him. He called out nonetheless. 'Will? Are you in here, Will?'

There was no reply and he began to search between the stones. There was no sign of his son, however, and he stopped and gazed beyond the walls to the rising blocks of red-brown brick that were the dwellings of the Iberville project. This was where music blared all night and doors banged and guns were fired during every hour of darkness. This was where decent apartments were triple locked, and where children were born to drug-addicted mothers who would never see them grow up and whose only gift to them at birth was the AIDS virus. He stared at the barred windows, the razor wire on top of the fences, and felt new fear move in his gut.

Jordan Bentley was the United States Attorney for Eastern Louisiana, based on Magazine Street at the edge of the business district. He had grown up in a ghetto pretty much like the one he was looking at now but instead of succumbing to life on the street, his mother had ensured that he clambered his way out. Now he spent his time prosecuting federal cases, many of which were directed at people who came from places such as this. He knew better than most just how cheap life could be if the wrong person caught you alone.

He took his cellphone from his pocket and called the special agent in charge at the FBI field office. Bentley knew about stranger abductions of children. In ninety-seven per cent of cases, if the victim was not recovered within the first three hours, they were already dead.

Matt Penny drove to the Iberville, along with half a dozen other brick agents from the field office. The special agent in charge rode with him. Mayer and Bentley were personal friends. The Captain of the 1st District was on the street and he had started to co-ordinate a house-to-house investigation. That wasn't going to be easy. The people of the projects were suspicious of the police at the best of times and with this many officers on the street they would be doubly so. They just had to hope that an older member of the community had seen something, they would get nothing from the young ones.

Mayer and Penny got out of the car and walked over to Bentley. Already TV crews were gathering and the Channel six helicopter was hovering overhead. There was nothing like bad news to really travel fast.

Mayer asked Bentley exactly what had happened. Bentley told him what he knew and the three of them walked into the project together. A group of young kids, no more than eleven or twelve years old, were sitting on the concrete step at the entrance to one of the blocks. Cops were already at the other blocks. The kids told them nothing. Some of them said they hadn't seen a kid in the area at all, others just said nothing. The minutes were ticking away and Bentley could feel the panic beginning to take hold. He forced it down. To panic was to get nowhere. He told himself he was too professional to panic. He looked at his watch: already they were half an hour into the first of the precious three. He had to tell his wife before she heard it on the news.

Penny was interviewing kids at the run-down children's playground when a black Lincoln Town Car turned off Basin Street and drew up beside Bentley. He left the group of people he was talking to and walked over, pausing as David Mouton's driver opened the door for him and the Attorney General climbed out of the back seat. He tugged at the front of his jacket and flicked some dust from his arm. The TV camera crews flocked towards him.

'I didn't know the Attorney General was in town,' Penny said to Mayer as he got to him.

Mayer nodded. 'They fixed up the new wing of the courthouse. He and the governor came down from Baton Rouge to open it.'

Bentley came off the phone to his wife and the Attorney General laid a hand on his arm. 'Jordan,' he said, 'the police called my office. I am so sorry.' His face was tanned and lined, iron-grey hair oiled and swept back from his forehead, exposing the sharpness of his widow's peak. He was a good-looking man and a good lawyer and he and Bentley had worked together on many occasions. They were not friends, however. Bentley was from an old black family and the Moutons had arrived with the earliest Acadians from Nova Scotia. They only had the law in common.

'I hope you don't mind but the governor is on his way over to your house,' Mouton told him.

Bentley stared at him. 'My house? What for?'

'To bring your wife here. He thought it would help.'

Bentley compressed his lips. 'He didn't think to ask me?'

'He's trying to help, Jordan. We all are.'

'Find my son,' Bentley said. 'That'll help me, David.'

The Attorney General looked across the project where hundreds of black faces were watching them from windows, from the rooftops, from the street. Literally dozens of news crews were on the scene now, cameras everywhere and reporters talking into microphones. 'Have the police turned anything up yet?' Mouton asked him.

Bentley shook his head.

Mayer walked over. 'Charlie.' Mouton shook his hand. 'If there is anything my office can do, you only have to ask.'

Mayer looked at Bentley. 'You OK?'

Bentley made a face.

'What about your wife?'

Bentley shot a glance at Mouton. 'The governor's bringing her here.'

Mayer pushed breath from between his teeth. 'We'll find the boy,' he said. He glanced at his watch. Forty-five minutes had elapsed since the school had broken the news.

Val Mouton's car stopped outside the Bentley family home in Slidell on the north shore of Lake Ponchartrain. He waved his driver to stay where he was and climbed from the back seat. Emily Bentley answered the door with tears streaming down her face. Mouton opened his arms and pulled her to him. 'All right,' he said. 'It'll be all right. I promise you, everything's going to be all right.' He held her for a few moments while she gathered herself.

'Mrs Bentley, forgive me,' he said. 'I was in town with my cousin when I heard. I knew your husband would be at the scene so I took it upon myself to come and get you, to bring you to him, ma'am. I hope you aren't offended by my presumption.'

'Not at all. Thank you for coming, Mr Mouton. I was going out of my mind on my own here.' Emily stepped back inside and grabbed her coat from the rack in the hall.

Mouton guided her over the step and closed the front door. He pointed to the state police cruiser parked in front of his Lincoln. 'We have an escort, ma'am. We'll have you there in a jiffy.'

Bill Chaisson bit into a shrimp po' boy and wiped mayonnaise from his mouth. He was sitting in Palastina's office, watching the Channel Six newscast from the Iberville project. He saw agent Penny and he saw Jordan Bentley. He saw Valery Mouton arrive with Bentley's wife in his limo. 'Heavy shit, uh?' he said, gesturing to the screen.

Palastina sipped Coca-Cola and wiped his fingers on his napkin. 'No kidding. The governor himself involved. What I want to know is what the kid's doing there in the first place.'

'School trip,' Chaisson said. 'History lesson or something.'

'They let them loose in the cemetery?' Palastina shook his head. 'You know what, Bill? As long as I live in this town, I won't be having kids.'

Chaisson got up to pour some coffee. 'I hope to Christ they find him. You know the statistics for stranger abductions in this country.' He sat down again and sighed.

'Changing the subject, I hear Marcel Call went back to the farm.'

Palastina nodded. 'This afternoon. He'll be settled in by nightfall.'

'I bet that pleased him.'

'They shouldn't fuck with their parole, Bill, should they?'

Chaisson thought of Harrison on the tugboat. 'No,' he said, 'they shouldn't.'

Harrison was on the upper deck cleaning the lines that ran from the pilothouse to the winch cable. The sun was gone, replaced by angry-looking clouds from the southwest, and the first spots of warm rain moistened the wind. The tug was pushing four empty barges in close to a hundred feet of water. The river was grey-green here and the levee heavily fortified by bulwarks and riff-raff made from very large

225

boulders. The batture land was soaked with recent tidal flow and two brown pelicans sat together, the wind ruffling their feathers on the surface of a borrow pit. On the port side the swamp ran for mile after lost mile all the way to Breton Sound. Across LA23 the morass that was the Barataria stretched in a wilderness of unforgiving wetlands.

Harrison quite liked the river: he wouldn't have minded doing a job like this for real. Some tugboat skippers went all the way from the gulf to the source right up by Lake Superior. They would load and unload cargoes *en route* and only ever leave the boat to restock supplies. In bygone days the flatboat men from the north had floated their barges down using only the river currents. The swamp was grey here and thick with twisted-trunk cypress trees so valued because of the wood's resistance to moisture. The logging companies had stripped the Barataria bare once already, but the area was protected now, as were the alligators that lived there.

Since his fight with Frederico Harrison had sensed a subtle change in the attitude of the crew. They were still distant and sullen most of the time, but they seemed a little more respectful. Even Ignace was not in his face as much as he had been. He went below decks to where Podjo was struggling with a leaking gate valve and caught the thick scent of oil and water lying rancid in the sumps. He gave Podjo a hand and between them they fixed the valve, then he held the heavy bag while Podjo worked out. He could feel the power in the blows the Cajun unleashed. The bag swung even though Harrison was holding it, and he imagined those great hams of fists breaking ribs like sticks for kindling.

'Were you ever in the fight game proper?' Harrison asked him.

'Made Golden Gloves one year – got through a few bouts.'

'Then you got beat, uh?'

Podjo looked at him. 'There's always somebody bigger and tougher than you are.'

Harrison smiled thinly. 'So they tell me, Podjo.'

He climbed the steps to the galley. Dusk was falling now and the levee and the odd batture house he could see were cast as shadows deep in the gloom. They passed a broken-down base skimmer with its arms bent and the scoop nets rotting in the water. A jack-up was tilted at a skew angle where one of its elongated legs had found the silted bottom and the other two had not.

Gumbo was making dinner, rice and red beans and slices of sausage mixed in a broth of his own concoction. He stirred with a wooden spoon and sipped noisily. Harrison took a bottle of beer from the refrigerator and snapped off the top. It was beaded with condensation, which he rubbed into the heat of his forehead. All at once Jimmy Mesa came down the stairs, pushing Marie in front of him.

'Sonofabitch,' he was saying. He saw Harrison and stopped. For a second he looked troubled then he pushed Marie out on deck. Harrison sat where he was, sipped beer and watched. Gumbo watched him.

A few minutes later Mesa came back again only this time he was pushing Junya before him, prodding him in the back with a stiff finger. Harrison had not even known the boy was aboard. He watched as Mesa shoved him to the steps that led up to the bridge, the boy stumbling along in front of him. He could feel the sudden tension in the air: the whole atmosphere had altered.

Gumbo went back to making his soup. Podjo was leaning at the top of the engine-room steps, his face the colour of bruised plums. More than anything Harrison wanted to creep to the foot of the bridge stairs and listen. He could hear Ignace's voice above the insulated sound of the diesels but the words were unintelligible. He remained where he was, sipping beer, while Podjo watched him like a soldier on sentry duty.

Ignace had Junya hunched in the skipper's chair, cowering with his head squashed into his neck. Ignace stood over him. 'You hafass dumb fuck – you took the wrong kid. You know who that boy is down there?'

Junya could smell the whiskey caking his breath.

'Only the son of the US fucking attorney.' Ignace looked at Mesa who blocked the stairs, arms folded. 'The US attorney, Junya. You a fucking gou gut. Augustine tell me how smart y'all are, but you a gou gut, a dumb fuck, a hafass sumbitch. You took the wrong fucking kid, now we got it all over the TV.' He glared again at Mesa. 'We got the attorney general of the state of Lou'siana making appeals on Channel Six. We got the fucking governor comforting Jordan Bentley's wife.'

Augustine had called him a few minutes earlier: the disappearance of William Bentley was on every newscast, not just state-wide but throughout the whole country.

Ignace looked again at Junya, then he stared through the porthole at the thickening darkness where the rain was heavier and the wind blew hard across the water. 'You listen up,' he said. 'We gonna let you off the boat downriver. You take that kid and get rid of him, you hear?'

Junya stared at him.

'The damn US attorney, boy – you want every fucking cop in the state coming down on top of us?' Ignace nodded for Mesa to take him down. 'And keep that Yankee the fuck away from him,' he said.

Junya wasn't watching Ignace, he wasn't listening to his words. His heart was high in his chest and sweat trickled the length of his spine to run between his buttocks.

twenty-two

Bentley paced the floor of Mayer's office and cursed himself for keeping their son at school in the city instead of one in the suburbs. But until today the school had been excellent and Will's education second to none. Bentley himself had been to that school and he always attributed part of his success to the manner in which the priests had taught him. His mother had been something of a saint, doing everything in her power to keep him off the streets where they lived. Now all that work seemed for nothing: her only grandchild was missing. He looked across the office to where Mayer was on the phone. Val Mouton sat with Emily on the couch. Bentley looked away. The man was milking this for every scrap of publicity he could get. It was common knowledge he was getting the Democratic nomination for President. Then he wondered if he was being fair. Mouton had proved himself to be a good man and it was probably his own short-sighted prejudice that blinkered him.

His wife looked at him with pleading in her eyes, as if she wanted him to do something and do it now. Her baby was missing and all her husband could do was pace the floor. But what could he do? Every FBI agent in the state was on the case, every New Orleans police department, the state police and every sheriff's office in every parish south of Baton Rouge. They had been to every house within a three-mile radius but Will had just vanished, disappeared into thin air as if the ghost of Marie Laveau had risen up to take him.

Bentley pressed his head against the window, looking through the rain, which fell in stair rods now, towards the university campus. Beyond the fields and the baseball diamond was Lake Ponchartrain and their home in Slidell where Will's bedroom was empty. He was in danger of panicking again. The three hours were up and already his boy might be dead. He hadn't mentioned those statistics to Emily.

She came over to him now and touched him on the shoulder. He turned. Sweat rolled in sticky globules from his hair and trickled down his face. Emily mopped his brow with a handkerchief and he took her in his arms and held her. Mayer put down the phone.

'That was the state police,' Mayer told them. 'They're watching the major traffic routes.'

'Those kids in the Iberville know what happened,' Bentley said.

'Sure they do. But they're not about to give anything up.' Val Mouton stood up.

'Can't we just roust a few of them?' Bentley looked at Mayer. 'Jesus, listen to me – *roust a few of them*. I'm the fucking US attorney.'

'We've been on to the Department of Corrections,' Mayer said. 'They're looking at the register of sex offenders in the city – the nearest is a block north of City Park. I'm sending a couple of agents to interview him now.'

Bentley nodded.

'Try not to let it eat you up.' Mayer looked at Bentley's wife. 'You both need to keep your heads clear if you can.' He made an open-handed gesture. 'I guess that doesn't help much, eh.'

'Nothing's going to help, Charlie,' Bentley said. 'Except a call to say they've got him and he's safe.'

'He will be safe.'

'You think?'

'I hope.'

Emily Bentley started to cry and the governor took her out to get some iced water.

Bentley looked after them, still not sure whether he hated Mouton or was grateful to him. 'You know the deal, Charlie,' he said to Mayer. 'This is a stranger abduction. The first three hours are absolutely critical. I was supposed to meet Will at four this afternoon. It's now a quarter after seven.'

'Statistics, Jordan, just facts and figures. You know as well as I do they don't apply to each and every case.' Mayer rested a palm on the back of his chair. 'I've spoken to the crimes against children unit and they're checking for known offenders who might be in the area. One of their agents may want to talk to you.'

Bentley nodded, but he didn't want to hear it. Crimes against children – the phrase churned his stomach when he thought the child was his own.

Junya sat in the cargo hold and sucked hard on a cigarette. He had retied the bonds round Will Bentley's wrists and placed the black bag over his head. The boy was sitting rigidly on his coil of rope, his body stiff with fright. Junya exhaled smoke harshly and shook his head at himself. He should not have been in the Iberville, Augustine had told him to keep away from that part of town. They should never have rushed him like that, though. What the hell did they expect if they rushed him like that?

This really gave him something to think about, however. There was much at stake here, too much and too soon. He wasn't ready and he had a weird feeling in his gut that as soon as he wasted the kid Ignace would whack him. Three years he had lasted, three fucking years with a master plan in his head and now no time to pull it off. He should have run off months ago, taken his chances back on the street. But that would have been no good: people had tried to fly from Laveaux before, only to have their wings clipped permanently.

He lifted his shirt and took the piece from his waistband. It was a 9-mm automatic with the serial number filed off. He was supposed to use it to do the boy. Ignace said he could keep it afterwards. Of course he could keep it – that way the Plaquemines Parish sheriff would have no trouble booking him if that was how Augustine played it. It wouldn't be, though, he knew that. Augustine would never take that kind of chance.

He slid the magazine out and checked the number of rounds. The clip was full and he replaced each bullet before sliding the clip back into the grips. At each metallic clicking sound he saw Will Bentley twitch where he sat.

'Don't you worry, Willy boy. Everything gonna be just fine. Gonna get you off this boat real soon now.' His voice was soft and low and all the time he was speaking he was thinking. The best thing would be to dump the gun in the river afterwards, but then he stood no chance with Ignace and the crew. He stood no chance anyway. At least if he had the gun they would have to shoot him. If he was unarmed they would be nasty, they'd torture him for being such an asshole and then leave him somewhere in the swamp for the alligators to chew on. Spring was here now and the majority of them would be out of hibernation.

The saliva dried in his mouth and he replaced the gun in his pants. Lying back against the bulkhead, he lit another cigarette and watched the boy for a moment. Still Will sat where he was, only moving when his muscles twitched in fright. He should just pop the sonofabitch right here and be done with it. He mashed out the cigarette, leaning his elbow on Will's backpack. He took his sketchpad from where it was hidden among the ropes. This was *the* document, containing the history of the past three years – faces, names and places. But what good was it to him now?

He skimmed the pages in frustration till he came to Harrison's profile.

On the bridge Ignace was brooding, drinking whiskey with Mesa as the tug ploughed a furrow through the oily blackness towards the tiny hamlet of Buras. Ignace thought again of his godmother and the cackle of derisory laughter she had thrown up when he had told her of Augustine's cynicism.

'That boy wouldn't know trouble if it was sitting on the bedstead, pissing on him,' she had said. 'He always had water on his brain about Etienne, and this Yankee with a rat tattoo done sprung a leak he don't know how to plug.' She had looked sharply at him then, gazing steadily and sightlessly out of pure white pupils. 'You got to act, Ignace. You don't, this man gonna tear you down like a rotten tree in the bayou.'

And now this new trouble had blown up in their faces: Junya and his carelessness. He spent too much time ashore with rocks of crack in his pocket and kids from the projects sniffing round him like dogs. More trouble brought on them by Augustine and his foolishness. That was the trouble with Augustine, what with his Riverwalk condo and his camp at Grand Terre. He thought he was Jean Lafitte reincarnated. And he accused Ignace of superstition and dreaming.

Ignace watched his course once more. There was a towhead before the next bend and he needed to be starboard of it. He was, he should be – he had done this trip more times than he cared to remember. The towhead was visible, the channel slack and deep on the port side, which allowed the deposits of silt to build up, forming the low alluvial island. Mesa moved from where he stood at the top of the stairs as if he wanted to check on the towhead himself, and Ignace slopped more whiskey into his glass.

'What happens to Junya when this is done?' Mesa asked.

'You need to ax me that? You know what's gonna

happen, what should've happened a long time ago.' Ignace took a harsh pull at his drink and wiped his mouth with his hand. 'I ain't thinking about him.'

'What are you thinking about?'

Ignace turned for'ard once again and pointed through the window into the darkness. They could just about see Harrison's shadowy form against the gunwales, the lighted glow of a cigarette cupped from the rain in his palm. 'I'm thinking about him,' Ignace said. 'I'm thinking about how we should fo'get Augustine and take two for the price of one.'

twenty-three

The tug took the bend in the river close to the port shore, having safely negotiated the towhead. The mate was at the helm now and Gumbo was on the starboard quarter preparing to lower the dinghy, a four-man pirogue made of aluminium and powered by an Evinrude outboard motor. Harrison was at the door to the fiddley, keeping out of the rain, but he could see Gumbo's bulky movements in the stern.

'Skipper wants to see you, Harrison.' Podjo moved behind him.

'Where's he at?'

'His cabin.'

Harrison raised one eyebrow. 'He ain't bored with Marie now, is he?'

Podjo just looked at him and stepped outside, the wind catching the black bandana tied around his skull.

Harrison knocked on the skipper's door and Ignace called him in. The Cajun was lying on his bunk with one arm behind his head, looking up at the ceiling. On the floor beside him there was a bottle and two glasses. His cabin was only slightly larger than the others, but there was only the one bunk, which made it feel bigger. He had a worktable and chair fixed to the floor at the foot of the bunk.

He motioned for Harrison to sit down, then reached for the bottle and glass and tossed them across to him. Harrison didn't say anything, just uncorked the whiskey and poured a heavy slug. Ignace was smoking a cigarette and the smoke curled where he allowed it to drift from his nostrils.

'How is it you think you can just sit and bullshit with Marie ever' time you feel like it?' Ignace said in his hoarse, harsh whisper.

Harrison sipped from his glass. Whatever Gumbo was doing was not for his eyes, and this was Ignace's clumsy way of keeping him inside. He leaned the back of his head against the wall. 'That's what you think I'm doing?' he said.

'It's what my eyes tell me.' Ignace blew smoke at the ceiling. 'You got no respect, Harrison. You know that?'

Harrison didn't say anything.

Ignace laughed and shook his head. 'You got no respect but you got my cousin going fo' sure. After what you done to Frederico I can't believe you still set there. Still, sometimes Augustine can be hafass sonofabitch, sometimes he don't see what's set on the end of his nose.'

Harrison sipped whiskey.

'Me.' Ignace's face was cold again. 'I'm old family, Harrison. Frederico, he's family, too. You fuck with him, you fuck with me. That's the way it is. Just because Augustine don't kill you yet doesn't mean you safe. I told you once this is a small boat and you got nowhere to go. Every move you make I'm watching you – step out of line with Marie, I'll slit your throat.' As if to emphasize the point, he pulled the skinning knife from his belt. 'The last man who fuck with me got to see this blade.' He smiled, showing the gap in his teeth. 'I opened him up like a zipper.'

'Another Yankee, uh,' Harrison said.

Ignace stared at him.

'I was in Angola, remember.' Harrison stood up. 'Old Cristophe didn't last too long when he opened his mouth, did he?' He curled his lip. 'You know what, Ignace? I think your cousin's got the drop on you when it comes to family.'

Gumbo had unscrewed the hatch on the cargo hold and

Junya looked at Marie. He stood up and grabbed Will Bentley, hauling the boy to uncertain feet by the armpit.

'Come on, y'all,' he said. 'Old Nonk's taking yo' on a trip.'

'Where are we going?'

'You'll see,' Junya said. 'Well, matter of fact, yo' won't. You'll be blindfold, won't you?' He laughed and glanced at Marie. She watched the smoothness of his face, the dark light in his eyes, and she clenched and unclenched a fist. Junya cut the tape on Will's hands and placed them on the rail so he could feel his way up the steps.

On deck Gumbo hoisted the boy over one shoulder and whacked him on the heels to silence him when he gasped. Junya checked the 9-mm in his belt and pulled out his switchblade. Gumbo lowered Will over the side, where Podjo was already in the boat. The boy still had the thick black hood over his face and he gripped the metal gunwale with both hands as the boat slopped in the waves. The rain streamed off his clothes and the wind tugged at the hood, and as he sat there, shivering, his teeth started chattering.

'Wait a minute,' Junya said to Podjo. 'I got to get his bag.' He scuttled back to the cargo hold and stuck his head down the hole. 'Pass me his bag, Marie.'

She handed it to him and as he took it his fingers brushed hers and for a moment they looked in each other's eyes.

'There's nothing I can do,' Junya said. 'I just got to go with it.'

He made his way across the soaking deck, where Gumbo lifted him down into the pirogue. Podjo twisted the throttle open and they cut across the current to where Fort Jackson lifted like a growth on the edge of the darkness.

Podjo bumped the aluminium bows up against the riffraff and Junya grabbed hold of one of the larger rocks and held it steady.

'Get up,' he said to Will. 'Just stand up and give me yo' hand.'

The boy did as he was told, his flesh icy to the touch as Junya gripped his trembling fingers and levered him out of the boat.

'They're sharp rocks, watch yo'self.' He climbed out after him and led the way across the batture towards the levee and the gun emplacement and beyond that the fort itself. It had been built in 1822 to watch the lower river after the British had attacked New Orleans seven years previously.

They climbed the grassy mound by the fortified gun emplacement, slippery now with so much rain, and slid down the other side. Junya walked Will in front of him till they were lost from view at the river, then made him stop and took the blindfold off. He handed him his school bag. 'Here, carry this.'

Will looked through the rain-soaked darkness at him, and his hands shook as he slipped his arms through the loops of his bag. He peered beyond Junya to the wizened darkness of the fort, the walls shadowy and greyer than the night, surrounded by the outline of huge live oaks, their branches drenched with moss.

The wind whistled through the concrete gun turrets and howled about their ears. 'My dad,' Will said through his tears. 'I'm supposed to meet my dad.'

'Fo'get about yo' daddy. And quit that snivelling. Think yo'self lucky you got yo' a daddy.' Junya waved the black-barrelled 9-mm under his nose then prodded him in the chest. He looked at the fort, at the wooden bridge across the moat to the entrance that was locked and barred now.

'Come on,' he said, and prodded Will once more. He walked him across the parking lot, past the state employee van that was parked by the bridge. Junya made him stop again and the rain fell harder. He gazed to his right where Highway 23 went south as far as Venice, the last habitation before the Head of the Passes. He thought of Podjo waiting in the pirogue the other side of the levee, with the waves slapping the hull against the riff-raff. He knew he had to get on with this.

He made Will walk ahead of him again and they climbed the bank between the dripping trees to the lowest point in the walls. Then Junya stuffed the gun in his waistband and flicked open his knife. Rain glinted on the blade as he held it under Will's nose.

'We is gonna climb this wall,' he said. 'If you hesitate or try to run I'll stick you where you stand.' He made Will turn and side by side they pulled themselves over the wall.

The irony wasn't lost on Will Bentley's eleven-year-old mind. There were two places he had wanted to visit that his father had never got round to taking him: one was St Louis cemetery and the other Fort Jackson. Now in the space of a few hours he had climbed the walls of both.

He dropped down on to a raised piece of ground halfway round the wall from the entrance. The fort was built in a rough square, grassy in the middle with a yawning black maw where the tunnel led to the gate. Junya pushed Will ahead of him, down the slope to where the billets had been: all that was left were the arches cut in the walls like so many sightless eyes. He flicked his lighter to guide them and nudged Will with his blade.

'Keep going. Right in back there.'

Holding the lighter up, he could make out the long tunnel at the back of the arches that led the length of the wall. It was cold but dry in here. He heard the scuttle of rats' claws on concrete and shivered. He had always hated rats. He thought he probably preferred water moccasins to rats.

'Are you going to kill me?' Will's voice cracked as he squeezed the words out.

'Yep.'

'Please don't.'

Junya was quiet. He leaned against the wall and took out the 9-mm. It would make a hell of a bang in here. He decided to use the knife.

'Please.'

'Quit whining. It'll be quick and I promise it won't hurt.'

Will was shaking, a silhouette against the limewashed walls of the tunnel. Junya snapped his lighter again and saw the tears running down the boy's face. He thought of how young he was, the same age he had been when they scooped him up at Audubon Park. He thought about Will crying for his father, something he could never have done because nobody knew who his father was. His mother was a whore who gave birth to him at thirteen and died four years later. His old man could be any one of a hundred guys. The best thing he could say about his own childhood was that he hadn't been born HIV positive.

He couldn't remember his mother's face, only her hand as she held out her ring, a cheap dime-a-dozen thing that you could pick up in any pawnshop or thrift store. He wore it round his neck on a piece of fishing line till he started mugging tourists, then he wore it on a gold chain. He still wore it today, though Ignace had taken it once, and it was his best memory of childhood. He was sure he had watched his mother die, but had blotted it out or covered it over with the other deaths he had witnessed. Coming from where he did, killing somebody was like taking a dump – no big deal and sometimes some pleasure in it if you were left alone to enjoy it.

He racked a round into the chamber of the 9-mm and pointed it at Will. So it was loud. So what? If that van meant there was a guard on duty, Junya would be over the wall and back in the boat before he got his boots on. He aimed the gun at Will's face. Then he stopped again.

'I got to use the knife,' he said. 'This is too loud. Turn around.'

Will stayed where he was, the tears no longer silent on his cheeks. 'I'm only eleven,' he sobbed.

'Stop that fucking whining.' Junya slapped the wall. Something was staying his hand, but it wasn't pity or fear. He was tired and Harrison's face haunted his mind. 'You old man is an attorney?' he said suddenly.

Will nodded.

Junya lifted the knife to the boy's throat and held it there for a moment. He heard the trickling sound and smelt the hot flush of urine as it ran through the boy's clothes. He was weeping again, only louder this time. Junya grabbed him by the collar and shook him.

'I told you to shut up,' he said. 'God, you like a fucking girl. Can't you just quit it for a moment?'

'I'm scared . . .' Will bleated the words at him and Junya shook him again.

'What kind of attorney?'

'Federal. He's a US attorney.'

'What does that mean exactly?'

'It means he works for the government.'

'But with the cops, yeah?'

'With the FBI mostly.'

Junya lifted his eyebrows. Again he saw Harrison's face in his mind. He chewed the skin on the back of his hand and thought hard. Podjo would be getting really pissed by now. This was taking way too long and if he wasn't careful the big guy would come looking for him. Maybe he should take his chances and run now, but he'd never make it out of Plaquemines Parish without one of Laveaux's boys getting him. Besides, Marie was on the boat and he couldn't leave her to die.

'Listen,' he said suddenly. 'I'm supposed to kill you. You know that.'

Will nodded.

'Well, I ain't gonna.'

Will pissed his pants all over again.

'Oh, for fuck's sake,' Junya said. 'Get a grip of yo'self and listen up. You do this wrong and I'm the one whose gonna make fish bait. You hear me? If you fuck up they'll kill me fo' sure.'

He left Will Bentley in a concrete shed on the upper level of the fort under the spread of an oak tree. He closed the door and slid the bolt across. There was a gap big enough for the boy to wriggle out at the bottom but he was in such a state of shock Junya figured he wouldn't realize it. 'Now, you listen up,' he said. 'I'm right outside this door. I'm gonna set here till it gets light and dark and light again. You so much as whimper I'm gonna shoot you where you sit. You understand me?'

All he could hear were little choked sobs from the other side of the door. Stuffing the gun in his pants, he ran through the trees to the wall as rain-soaked Spanish moss licked the skin of his face.

twenty-four

The silence of the house was appalling. Bentley had driven home with his wife sitting next to him. They crossed the causeway and she didn't speak, just sat there rigidly with her hands fisted in her lap, her gaze fixed on the horizon. Bentley didn't know what to say. He wanted to comfort her, she was his wife, yet he felt no comfort himself and he didn't know what to say to her. Val Mouton had known what to say, David Mouton had kind and effective words when she arrived at the Iberville, but as they drove home his helplessness was overwhelming. It was all he could do to keep a lid on his own emotions, let alone support Emily in hers.

He closed the front door and they stood in the silence of the hallway, his wife with her coat round her shoulders. There was no TV, no music, no sound of Will clattering down the stairs. Bentley stood a moment fighting back his tears, looking at the house as if he were seeing it for the first time. Emily looked round at him.

'It's so quiet,' she said. 'Will it always be this quiet now?'

Bentley swallowed the lump that was forming in his throat. He took his wife's coat and hung it on one of the pegs. It slipped noiselessly to the floor and for a moment he just stared at it. His wife picked it up, hung it again then they both just looked at each other.

'I don't know what to do,' Bentley said. 'All my life I was

structured and organized and in control. But now . . .' Tears filled his eyes. 'I don't know what to do.'

Harrison saw the boat racing back across the chop as they headed downriver. He was standing at the door to the fiddley, looking across the stern. Podjo was driving. He recognized him as they got closer then he saw a second person with him, the mulatto kid Junya. The boat came alongside leeward of them: they were in a 'no wake zone' and Mesa was chugging along at less than five knots. Ignace was watching from the upper deck. Gumbo was at the gunwales. Harrison went to help him. He crossed the deck, aware of Ignace behind him, waiting for a comment, an order to go below, but it never came. His heart rate quickened. He was not allowed to see the pirogue leave but coming back was OK.

Podjo kept the boat pushed up against the side and the boy climbed the ladder. Harrison held out a hand and Junya grabbed it without looking at whose it was. Harrison hauled him over the side and it was only when his feet were back on deck that Junya looked up. For a second they stared at each other and Harrison witnessed a strange expression in the boy's eyes. Gumbo slapped Junya on the backside and he made his way for'ard.

Harrison helped Gumbo and Podjo haul the pirogue back to its platform. It weighed a hell of a lot and took the three of them straining and sweating to get it back on board. Harrison bent to his knees to catch his breath and he felt a hand fall on his shoulder. He looked up into the engineer's face and Podjo smiled at him, and as he did so he traced the length of Harrison's spine just as Junya had done. For the first time since he came on board Harrison seriously considered trying to swim for the shore. But there was no way he could make it. The Mississippi currents were perilous: this far downriver there was the salt water to contend with as well. The salt was heavier and lay under the fresh-water layer, with riptides and whirlpools coming in from the gulf. The storms and hurricanes dug great holes in the seabed, sending unspeakably powerful drags well up-river. You only had to look over the side in the daytime to see where whirlpools gathered malevolently, ready to drag you down to your death.

Podjo was waiting for him to react, to make a move on him. Harrison could see it in his eyes, Gumbo to one side, hands under his armpits, watching. Harrison shrugged off Podjo's hand and stepped away from them. Ignace watched from the upper deck, a cigarette burning between his fingers.

Harrison stalked back into the fiddley with his shoulders square and a scowl on his face, but he was scared and he was thinking hard. He had misjudged this situation badly and one by one the crew were letting him know his days out here were numbered. Nobody had forgotten Frederico and he imagined the likes of Podjo and Gumbo, Jimmy Mesa maybe, promising they would get even. If that was all it was, he might escape with a beating. Even with Ignace and his rantings about Marie, he might escape with a beating. But a beating by any of this crew could easily become a murder. He had come back, put himself on the wire, and for what? The chances of getting anything on Laveaux were nil and he knew it.

Nobody was in the galley and he went to his cabin to try and figure out what he could do.

Marie was lying on his bunk.

Harrison stood there with a hand fisted on his hip. 'What the hell d'you think you're doing?'

Marie put her finger to her lips and reached behind him to close the door. She slid the bolt across.

'This is really clever,' Harrison said. 'I just get done having my ear chewed off by the skipper and now you're in my bunk?' He unlocked the door again. 'Out,' he said. 'I got enough trouble in my life already.'

Again Marie closed the door. It was warm in the room, no air from outside and no porthole. It felt claustrophobic with two of them in there. Harrison could smell her cheap scent as he had done across the galley table and even then it stirred him. Up close he could see she had a bruise under her right eye.

'I got to talk to you, Harrison,' she said. 'Ignace is on the bridge now, he won't be calling me till later.'

Harrison shook his head. 'I want you out. He just threatened to disembowel me if I so much as looked at you.'

She looked at him with her chin high for a moment. 'He don't own me.'

'Yeah, he does. You're posted, baby. Trespassers will be cleaned and gutted.'

She looked at him and he saw the same expression in her eyes that he had witnessed a few times already, a questioning, an uncertainty, and mixed in with it somewhere – fear. Again he looked at the bruise under her eye. 'If he don't own you, why d'you put up with that shit?'

Marie said nothing.

'You could just take off in New Orleans. Not come back to the boat.'

She laughed. 'I did that once. I ended up as a crack whore.'

'And you ain't a crack whore now?'

She pursed her lips. 'I haven't done crack or turned a trick in over three years.' She lit a cigarette. 'I look after Junya.'

Now Harrison laughed. 'Like that kid needs parenting? Give me a break, Marie. He needs looking after like I need another hole in my head.'

'You don't understand. Augustine asked me to watch him, to make sure he do what he's told.' She half smiled. 'Ignace don't own me, Harrison. Augustine does. He owns me and Junya both.'

Harrison's mind was falling over itself. What was this

now, the next instalment of Ignace's little game? His way of flushing him out finally, after failing with Junya?

'Junya knows you a cop.' Marie's voice was soft at the edges. 'He can help you get what you came for.'

Harrison felt trapped, cornered like an animal. His mind wouldn't work properly. His mouth was suddenly dry. 'I tell you what,' he said, 'you go back to Ignace's cabin and tell him to back the fuck off.' He could feel pinpricks of adrenalin in his fingertips. 'You tell that coonass sister-fucker, any time he wants to play I'm ready. Tell him I really don't give a shit any more. They can take me down any time they please but this boat ain't gonna have no crew left by the time it gets to New Orleans.'

Marie looked at him with disgust curling her lip. 'God, you're such an asshole. You don't understand, do you? Junya can give you everything.'

'Out.'

She looked at him, mouth puckered as if she wanted to spit. 'You want me out, you throw me out.'

Harrison took the .45 from under his pillow and worked a round into the chamber. Marie laughed derisorily. 'What you gonna do – shoot me? Get a life, Harrison. You can't shoot me. You know fine you can't. How'd that look in your report?' She let her words hang in the air and she left.

When she was gone Harrison sat on the bunk, chin to his chest and sweat beading on his forehead. They were playing with him: he felt like a mouse trapped between the paws of a bored and overfed cat. He thought hard. He couldn't swim for it, the only way off the boat was in the dinghy, and how he'd get that in the water on his own he didn't know. The fear began to pick at him. He felt tired all at once; he felt tired and scared and old.

He must have dozed because he opened his eyes some time later and heard a cry of pain from above. He lay back, arms behind his head, and heard the scream again. Ignace must be slapping Marie. He rolled on his side and ignored it. The door opened suddenly and light played across the floor. Harrison sat up sharply. He saw Marie in the gangway. She had the dirty streaks of tears smudging her face.

'What do you want?'

'Ignace is beating on Junya. He's drunk, Harrison. And he's hurting the boy bad.' She came inside and pushed the door to with her heel. Switching on the light, she wiped away fresh tears with the heel of her hand. 'I don't care what y'all think, but none of what I said earlier was anything to do with Ignace or his cousin or anybody else. If they knew yo' was a cop they'd cut your throat. There'd be no messing, believe me. I seen them do it. You think Ignace got the brainpower to play mind games with you?'

Harrison heard another howl of pain and Marie's face crumpled. From somewhere deep inside his head Harrison heard another voice: it yelped at him through the darkness, like a dog that had been kicked. He blinked hard, trying to clear the memory.

'There's nothing I can do, Marie.' His heart thumped against his ribs. 'Whatever the deal is between Junya and the skipper, it's got nothing to do with me.'

Marie stared at him. 'You got to help him.'

Harrison sat up and shook his head. 'I don't got to help anybody. I help me, Marie. You got that? Just me.' He stared at her. 'Whatever Junya's doing on this boat is his business. I'm here on my own account, and I'm just trying to stay out of trouble. I told you already, I got enough shit with Ignace without looking for any more.' He lay back again. 'I know what you're doing, Marie. Ignace is just desperate for an excuse to whack me. Anything'll do. He tried to find one himself earlier, but wasn't up to it.' He closed his eyes. 'It ain't gonna work. I'm not going for it. Now I'm beat, Marie. Turn off the light on your way out.'

He rolled on his side and slipped one hand under the pillow where he gripped the .45.

'Fuck you, Harrison. Fuck you all the way to hell.' Marie closed the door.

He lay for a long time listening to the engines rattling away below. He listened for any more sounds from above his head but heard none. All was quiet, too quiet almost. Stuffing the gun in his waistband and pulling on a sweatshirt to cover it, he went through to the galley.

Podjo was sitting at the table, playing cards with Gumbo. He glanced up at Harrison, said nothing then returned his attention to the cards. Gumbo didn't even look up.

Harrison went out on deck. The wind was up and it whipped his hair about his face, so he took the kerchief from his pocket and tied it round his head. He took a cigarette and made his way for'ard. Looking up, he could see both Mesa and Ignace on the bridge. If they saw him they ignored him. In the bows he leaned on the gunwales and watched the shore go by, thinking about Marie and Ignace and how he could have stopped all this with one word to Matt Penny. What he had hoped to gain he had no idea, he had been working on instinct alone. But maybe those instincts were off, because he had achieved nothing and now any one of the crew could kill him at any moment. He tried not to think of Santini but it was hard. He didn't know if he loved her or not, but she represented something other than this kind of life, the one good opportunity a man gets, and he had passed his up. More than fear, he felt foolish.

A noise behind him made him start and he looked round to see Junya sitting on the hatch to the cargo hold with a cloth held to his face. Blood gathered under his nose and his right eye was swelling badly. 'What the fuck are you looking at?' he said.

twenty-five

Marcel Call could hear footsteps approach his cell. A shiver ran down his spine and puckered the skin between his buttocks. The lights were out and he had been in solitary since the Feds brought him back to Angola. That hadn't been the deal and he'd threatened to give them nothing, but it made no difference because here he was with his ass in the wind, just waiting.

And he knew the wait was over.

The locks tumbled and the door slid back and he could see the bulky frame of a guard in the half-light from the corridor. He could hear his breathing, laboured and wheezy, and he could smell the breath from where he lay, rancid like an animal that chewed bones. The guard came into the cell and Call could make out his billy and gun strapped to either hip. The door closed, the lock tumbled again and the guard stood there, just breathing.

Call lay on his back as if stricken by some disease that rendered movement impossible, freezing his tongue along with his limbs. The guard stared through the darkness at him, the rasp of breath the only sound save the shouts from the cells along the hallway. Call tried to sit up. Then he heard the electronic beep of a number being punched into a cellphone.

In bed at his Riverwalk condo Laveaux studied the naked back of the girl lying asleep next to him. She was very stoned and very drunk and had passed out as soon as he was finished. His cellphone rang where he had set it on the nightstand and he let it be while he licked the skin between her shoulder blades. She still tasted of sweat. Picking up the phone, he lay on his back looking up at the ribbons of silver cast by the moon on his ceiling.

'This is Conti,' the voice said in his ear.

Call heard the guard give his name and his stomach cramped. He tried to get up, but Conti pressed him down on the bunk with the flat of his hand. Then he passed him the cellphone. 'Somebody wants to talk to you.'

Call could feel the clammy imprint of Conti's palm on his chest. He took the phone and held it to his ear.

'Hello?'

'Hello, Marcel.'

Call had known it would be this voice. He had known it would as soon as he heard Conti give his name. It did nothing to lessen the shock, however, and the pain in his guts stabbed him now like a knife.

'Augustine.'

'How are you, Marcel?'

'I'm OK.'

'How's Angola?'

'The same.' Call looked at Conti's shadowed features through the darkness. 'What's up?'

Laveaux stared at the ceiling. 'That's a good question.' He paused for a moment as if considering his words.

Call gripped the phone that bit tighter. Conti stood over him, his back to the metal door, one hand resting on the butt of his holstered pistol.

'Harrison,' Laveaux said softly. 'I want you to tell me about Harrison.'

Call switched the phone to his other hand. 'Augustine, there's nothing to tell.'

Conti leaned forward and gripped his knee with one

meaty paw. He pinched his fingers deep into the cartilage and Call almost cried out.

Laveaux heard him wince. 'Certain words have an effect on Conti. You know that.'

'Yeah, I do. I'm sorry.' Call could feel the perspiration bead on his brow. 'It's just like I told you,' he spluttered. 'I only knew him for a little bit. In here. Conti'll tell you. He saved my ass from the Texyans.'

Laveaux was quiet for a moment. 'Now you're making assumptions. Conti won't tell me anything. He can't. He doesn't know. He thinks you might be lying. You know how he hates a liar.'

'I'm not lying, honest.' Call's voice was rising in pitch. 'Augustine, I know better than to lie to you.'

'Conti doesn't see it that way.' As if he could hear him, Conti gripped Call's knee again and worked his fingers deep into the muscle. Call almost screamed with the pain.

'Honest, Augustine, I wouldn't lie to you. I swear. Come on, you know me. I swear I wouldn't lie.'

'That's not good,' Laveaux said. 'You lie to me then you lie again, swearing you didn't lie in the first place. That's not good at all. It offends Conti's Christian sensibilities.'

Next to him the girl rolled on her back so her breasts were exposed. Laveaux leaned on his elbow and blew on a nipple so it puckered, the flesh gradually tightening and the nipple turning white at the tip. 'Talk to me, Marcel,' Laveaux said softly. 'Tell me about the Yankee.'

'I don't know anything. I swear.'

'There you go again.' Laveaux laid the phone down and took the nipple in his mouth. He sucked it, pulled at it with his teeth, licking the aureole with his tongue.

Conti lifted Call off the bunk by the collar. He held him one-handed, Call on tiptoe gripping Conti's wrist. Conti took hold of his scrotum and squeezed.

*

Laveaux heard the scream down the line and turned his attention to the other nipple. Still the girl didn't stir. He rubbed the aureole and watched the nipple grow hard, more taut and erect than the other one. He coated it with saliva.

'Marcel,' he said softly into the phone. 'I promised Conti he could take his time. You know how he enjoys his work.'

'Please, Augustine. Don't . . .'

'He's a craftsman, you know that. He likes to see that the job is done properly.'

'Augustine, please.'

Again Laveaux laid the phone down. He studied the girl once more. So drunk and stoned he could do anything he wanted to her and she would never know. But that was no fun: it would be like fucking a dead person. He heard Call scream again and knew that Conti had crushed one testicle. He got up from the bed and, scooping up the phone, he wandered to the windows.

'He's a cop.' Call's voice was a breathless whistle in his ear. 'Please, Augustine. My balls. There was nothing I could do. Please. They got my prints from the fishing camp.'

Laveaux was silent.

'The cops pulled me in. Some guy got killed in West Virginia. They thought it was me.'

'So you led them to me.'

'Yes. No. I swear I could do nothing about it. Please, Augustine. There was nothing I could do. I didn't tell them anything.'

'What did you tell them?'

'Augustine, I didn't . . . Please.'

'What did you tell them?'

'Nothing. There was nothing to tell, was there? I don't know nothing. They told me this guy in Virginia got wasted, but I don't know nothing about that. They didn't tell me what they was gonna do, they just wanted me out of the way.'

'So Harrison could take your place.'

'I don't know.'

'So they could use you against me. What did they offer in return – the witness protection programme? Did they tell you I couldn't get to you, Marcel? Was that what you thought?'

'I didn't think anything. I swear, Augustine. I don't know. I been in jail since they pulled me off the wharf.'

Laveaux was quiet. 'But you led them to me. You deliberately betrayed me.'

'I didn't. They told me they'd bust me. They made me tell the story about the Texyans.'

'So you could lead them to me.'

'No. I swear. I don't know nothing, do I? I couldn't lead them to you. I had nothing to give them. They just wanted a way of Harrison getting introduced is all.'

Laveaux drew breath audibly through his nose. He stared across the Mississippi as a foghorn sounded on one of the ships, echoing across the water.

'Did you hear that, Marcel?' he said. 'There's a fog coming in.'

Call held the phone to his ear. 'Augustine,' he said. 'Augustine.'

Conti took the phone back from him and clipped it on his belt. Call could hear the sound of somebody shouting further along the hall. Somebody else kicked a door and the metal resounded like a gong. Conti stood in front of him, his hands loose at his sides.

'Take your shirt off,' he said.

Call stared at him.

'Don't make me ask again.'

Call unbuttoned his shirt and handed it to him. Conti smiled and Call saw his teeth in the darkness. Then his bowels were suddenly loose as Conti tore the shirt into strips.

twenty-six

Ignace was on the bridge when Augustine called on the satellite phone. He listened, tensing his fingers slightly as he gripped the glass he was holding. He didn't say anything, just listened till his cousin was finished then put the phone down. Mesa sat in the skipper's chair alongside him.

'What is it?' he asked when he saw the look in Ignace's eyes.

'My Nannan,' Ignace said. 'She is conja, Jimmy.'

Harrison sat at the table in the galley with the .45 in his waistband. Podjo sat opposite, eating chilli with crackers and salt, a beaded bottle of Dixie beer at his elbow. Gumbo was sorting gear in the fiddley. Harrison sat with his back to the wall, weary but not wanting the isolation of the cabin. He wanted them where he could see them. Every now and again he would hear Ignace and the mate up on the bridge. He had a can of open but untouched iced tea on the table in front of him. Podjo was eating steadily, and saying nothing. He could see Gumbo in the fiddley, hear him moving around above the noise of the engines. He looked up and saw Ignace in the doorway that led to the for'ard steps. He looked at Harrison and something in his expression made the hairs lift on the back of his neck. Ignace went to the sink and ran the tap. The next thing Harrison knew he was pressing the barrel of a gun against his neck.

'Put you hands on the table where I can see them,' Ignace said.

Slowly Harrison rested the flat of his hands on the tabletop. He felt the flutter in his chest and stared into Podjo's black eyes. Podjo shovelled another spoonful of chilli into his mouth.

'I sound like a cop, don't I?' Ignace reached behind Harrison and plucked the .45 from his belt. 'When I talk like that, I sound like a cop to you?' He passed his own gun to Podjo, who wiped his hands nonchalantly on his thighs then levelled it at Harrison.

'We just spoke to you buddy Call,' Ignace rasped in Harrison's ear. 'You know we couldn't find him for months and then he show up again in Angola where he should have been all the time.' He smiled, showing the gap in his teeth. 'He hanged himself.'

Harrison half-closed his eyes. *Get him back to Angola. They're suspicious of Call, Matthew. If Laveaux can check me out at Angola, he can check out Call. What's he going to think if he doesn't find him?*

His heart sank like a stone. They had been ahead of him all the time. He had badly underestimated Laveaux, personal feelings had got in the way and clouded his judgement. Looking back in the cold light of this grim reality, it was bound to happen.

Ignace was leering at him. 'What we gonna do with you, uh?' He shook his head and fingered his favourite skinning knife. 'I guess I'm just gonna have to think fo' a little while.' He stepped back and ordered Harrison up from the seat. Gumbo was watching from the fiddley. Ignace waved Harrison's own gun in his face. 'I think I need a little time to enjoy this,' he said. 'I need a little time to think about how best I can enjoy it.' He looked at Podjo. 'Put him in the hold,' he said.

It hadn't stopped raining but the wind was lighter now. They were at the Head of the Passes and there was stillness in the night air that was brooding and watchful. Podjo kept the weapon on him as he walked for'ard. Gumbo opened the hatch to the cargo hold. It was dark below and Harrison climbed down the steps. They secured it again above his head. He heard them giving the turnkeys a thump with the mallet.

Unsure of his footing, he stumbled. The floor of the hold was littered with ropes and tarps and boxes. He made his way to the bulkhead and sat down, releasing the breath from his lungs.

'I guess we got company, Marie,' Junya said through the darkness. 'I told you I knew he was a cop the first time I saw him.'

Harrison didn't say anything.

'That wasn't on the boat. No, sir, I saw him before then. The first time I saw him I was setting on a stoop in the Iberville.' He laughed softly. 'My buddy Dylan, he saw a nuthouse patient walking the project with a .45 in his hand.' He flicked his lighter for a cigarette and Harrison saw the oval moon of his face. 'I never saw no nuthouse patient. I saw me a cop.'

Will Bentley sat on the concrete bench with the cold seeping into his buttocks. He was crying, his tears hot on the icy chill of his cheeks. Outside the rain still poured and the darkness was complete. He couldn't think of anything, couldn't do anything. He just sat there and cried. Twice he had wet his pants and they stuck to him with rain and urine and he was disgusted with himself. That was his first definite thought since he had been shut in here: disgust that he had pissed in his own pants. But he wouldn't tell anybody. Hopefully, with the rain no one would be able to see. Then he thought about his mother and father and knew how worried they would be. He knew where he was; he could tell them exactly where he was. If he could get out of here he could maybe get to a telephone and they would come and get him. Then he recalled what Nonk had told him, that he had to wait and not move at all. Nonk would be outside, waiting in the rain to shoot him.

That was rubbish. Rational thought was returning now, the sense of shock diminishing. Nobody would shut him in here and then sit in the rain holding a gun on him. But he knew when he did get out he couldn't let them call the sheriff. Nonk had told him that as soon as the men on the boat found out he'd let him go they would kill him. He started to cry again, realizing just how close he had come to dying himself and believing now that Nonk's life was in his hands.

When the tears stopped he shivered, thinking hard again. He would call his dad and explain to him that he mustn't call the sheriff or anybody else just yet. A weird sense of loyalty welled up in his breast and he had no understanding of why. Nonk had kidnapped him, blindfolded him then taken him all the way to Fort Jackson before making him piss his own pants with fright. Yet he believed Nonk was telling the truth. He couldn't just let him die.

But Nonk wouldn't be out there in the rain; nobody would sit out there in this rain. Will got to his feet, went to try the door and heard somebody move outside. He shrieked and sat down on the cold stone once more. 'I was only stretching,' he cried. 'I wasn't trying to get out. Honest, I was only stretching.'

Dawn broke with tendrils of grey light slipping under the door to the hut where Will lay curled on the seat. He yawned and sat up, for a moment wondering where he was, and then all at once he remembered and his fear was redoubled. Light, dark and light again: was this the second day or only the first?

Somebody bumped the door from the other side and he fell back with his hands up to his face.

'Don't shoot me,' he called. 'I was only checking.'

He stared at the door, expecting it to open and Nonk to

point a gun at his face like he had before. A sob racked his body, then he heard the sound of somebody scratching and he shrank against the wall.

At the bottom of the door he saw a dog's paw scraping the soil.

He thought for a moment, wondering what Nonk was doing with a dog, then it dawned on him that the sounds he had heard had *just* been the dog. Nonk was long gone. Will dropped to his knees and realized that with a bit of pushing the rotten wooden boards would give enough for him to crawl outside. He could see daylight and feel the moist air, and he lay flat on his belly and worked his way under the door. There was no Nonk and no gun, only a skinny-looking Catahoula cur blinking at him. He recognized the breed because his father always talked about them – real Louisianans, he called them.

The dog was just sitting there and looking at him with its head to one side, ears cocked and listening. Will stared at it and the dog stared back, then it padded over and licked the salt from the tears on his face. All at once Will started laughing.

From the hut he could see across the grassed courtyard of the old fort. In the daylight it was nothing like as daunting as it had been at night, but at night he had been prodded along at the end of Nonk's knife. Today there was no sign of him. The rain had stopped and the sun was coming up in the east. He could see the tunnel that they had gone into and the narrower one that led to the main gate, and he could see the comforting presence of a soft drinks machine in the shadow cast by the wall. The dog licked his face and Will smoothed its head then stood up and felt the warmth of the early morning. The sound of an engine starting over by the entrance made him pause.

He ran down the slope and across the grass, the hound dog gambolling at his heels. At the tunnel he paused. The main gate stood half-open and as he walked towards it he saw a door marked WARDEN on the left. He knocked, received no answer and knocked again. Still he got no answer so he made his way along the tunnel to the bridge. The van he had seen last night in the parking lot was no longer there.

Will gazed at the gun emplacement to get his bearings. He remembered that from last night when Nonk took the blindfold off. Suddenly the urgency of his situation came back to him: his life had been spared and now he felt the debt weighing heavily. If he got this wrong they would kill Nonk for sure. That would be his fault and he didn't want anyone's death on his conscience. Turning back to the tunnel once more, he knocked at the warden's door. When there was no answer he went inside.

A fire glowed in the pot-bellied stove and two worn armchairs stood empty in front of it. A television was switched on though the sound was turned down, and Will was amazed to see a photograph of his own face looking out at him. Suddenly he burst into tears. There was a telephone on the desk and, lifting the receiver, he called his father.

Jordan Bentley woke without realizing he had been asleep. He was lying on the couch, fully clothed. He and his wife had sat up into the early hours trying to convince each other that it would be all right and they would find their son alive. But Bentley woke to silence and the terrible realization that it had not been a dream. It was real. The silence of this house was as real as the hole in his gut. He saw Emily in the kitchen. She was sitting at the table, her hands wrapped round a coffee cup, tears still staining her face. He sat up and looked at his watch. It was seven-thirty: that meant Will had been missing for over fifteen hours. The phone rang and he stared at it for a moment then snatched it from the cradle.

'Will?' he said. 'Is that you, Will?'

'Mr Bentley, this is the FBI's crimes against children unit in DC.' It was a woman's voice. 'Did the special agent in charge at New Orleans tell you we might be calling?'

'He did.' Bentley shook his head at his wife's expectant face. She was beside him now on the couch. He took her hand and gripped it. 'Look, agent . . .'

'Baker, sir.'

'Agent Baker, can you call back later? I want to keep this line clear.'

'Of course. I just wanted to tell you that we've been fully briefed on the situation, sir, and anything we can turn up we will.'

'Thank you.' Bentley hung up and told his wife what the agent had said.

'Will that bring our boy home, Jordan?' Emily burst into tears.

Bentley held her, and realized it was the first time he had done so since this happened. They had not shared physically in their fear, the terrifying beginnings of grief. Each had tried to stand in their own space, as if there was strength in that and that alone. He held Emily tightly now, however, and he realized just how much he loved her.

The phone rang again.

They both stared at it for a moment.

Bentley picked up the receiver. 'Hello?'

'Dad, it's me, Will.'

'Dear God, Will.' Bentley burst into tears.

Will held the receiver tightly as his father sobbed down the line. 'Don't worry, Dad. I'm all right. I'm at Fort Jackson.'

'Where?' His father's voice was choked.

'Fort Jackson.'

The door opened and a Mexican man stood there with his hands on his hips. He wore a faded blue cap and green overalls. 'Just a minute, Dad,' Will said. 'I think the warden came back.'

'What you doing, boy?' The Mexican said. 'What you doing on my telephone?'

Will's father asked him to put the man on the line. Will looked up at the Mexican.

'This is for you,' he said. The dog sat close to his legs and Will patted him on the head. 'It's OK, Jackson. Everything's going to be fine now. Everything's going to be fine.'

The Mexican looked at the dog and then back at the boy. He picked up the phone.

'Who is this?'

'Jordan Bentley, the US attorney in New Orleans.'

The Mexican stood up a little bit straighter. 'You ain't got no business with me, sir. I work for the state. I got a green card.'

'I'm not interested in that. That boy with you is my son. He went missing yesterday. You may have seen it on the news. Please keep him right where he is. I'm going to speak to the Plaquemines sheriff's office and get them to send a vehicle.'

The Mexican looked at the boy, scratched his head then glanced at the newspaper he had just bought and saw the same face staring up from the front page. His eyes balled and he gripped the receiver more tightly. 'OK, sir, no problem. Leave it with Henrique. I take care of your boy.'

The boy tugged his arm and he handed the phone back. 'Dad, listen to me,' Will said. 'This is really important. Don't tell anyone you've found me, especially not the TV. Please, not yet.'

Bentley listened to what his son was saying, covering his joy and relief for a moment. Something in Will's voice pricked at his senses. 'All right, son.'

'I mean it, Dad. If you do, a boy called Nonk could get killed.'

'OK. I have to tell the Plaquemines sheriff, though. You stay put, you hear. Don't move and don't let that man out of your sight. Here, speak to your mom.'

Bentley passed the phone to his wife who was weeping quietly beside him. He stood up. He could have danced; he could have sung. He punched the keys of his cellphone and spoke to the sheriff's office in Plaquemines Parish. They told him they would send a car right away. Dialling again, he called the FBI. He didn't give out any details other than where Will was and that he was safe. Then he and Emily got their car and headed for Interstate 10. Until he could sit down with his son and talk properly, he wanted this played exactly as Will had asked him.

Bill Chaisson was sitting in his office off Magazine Street when Palastina came in at eleven. Palastina looked grim, the skin of his face pinched and his eyes pensive.

'You look good. What's going on?' Chaisson asked him.

'Marcel Call.' Palastina sat down. 'He was found hanged in his cell this morning.'

twenty-seven

Harrison must have slept because when he woke up the hold was filtered by daylight coming through the vents to the engine room. Junya was sitting on a coil of rope with his arms wrapped about his knees, watching him. There was no sign of Marie.

'Tell me you ain't a cop,' Junya said.

'I'm not a cop.'

Junya spat on the floor. 'Goddammit, Harrison.'

Harrison sat up. He wasn't about to admit anything to anyone – he didn't know whether Laveaux had actually got anything from Call or whether this wasn't just one final bluff to flush him out. 'Your friend was right, Junya. I'm just a dumb psycho who likes to walk the projects.'

'Then how come you're set there?' Junya stared at him. 'I watched you, Harrison. I know how you are. I see yo' brain working. You ain't a basket case, you're a cop. I know because you reek of it.' Junya fumbled in his pocket for cigarettes. 'Have it your own way, but I tell you – if you want them I can give you them all.'

'I don't know what you're talking about.'

'Harrison, I ain't gonna play games with you, you Yankee dumb fuck. You know just fine what I'm talking about.' Junya rolled the unlit cigarette between his lips. 'I can help you out. You can help me out, but only if we work together.'

Harrison leaned against the bulkhead and watched the

boy, trying to remember that he was just a boy. His eyes were sharp points of light, brow furrowed in concentration.

'In case you hadn't figured it out already, you is dead meat,' Junya went on.

'And you?' Harrison said. 'Why was Ignace busting his fists on you last night?'

Junya clicked his tongue. 'He's always does that when he gets drunk. Last night was extra because I make a mistake. When he finds out just how bad that mistake actually is, I'm as dead as you are. They'll cut me off as soon as spit. Marie, too. In case it escaped yo' attention, these boys ain't partial to niggers. They don't mean nothing by it, it's just the way they was raised.' He flicked ash on the steel floor.

'Then how is it you and Marie have been around them so long?'

'You been talking to Marie?'

Harrison smiled. 'You know I have, or rather she's been talking to me. You must think I floated upriver with the shrimp. Do I really look that dumb?'

'You need to ax?'

Both of them laughed then. It was the first time Harrison had heard the boy laugh genuinely, without a twist of cynicism on his mouth. Junya clamped the burning cigarette between his teeth.

'Marie told me she tries to look after you.'

'She does. She's the only person in the whole damn world that give a fuck about me.'

'She's a crack whore.'

'Don't be saying that. She was a crack whore. She ain't no more. She leaves that shit alone.'

'And you? What about you?'

'Me?' Junya's eyes glinted. 'I ain't never touched it.'

Harrison believed him: the boy was far too lucid, too sharp-minded to be using. In a weird kind of way Harrison liked him, notwithstanding his sassy mouth. He was far more observant than the rest of the crew despite his age and position. But Harrison wasn't going to give up anything. Right now he was a prisoner and it looked like both the boy and Marie were, too. But people played strange games when they wanted something, especially people like Laveaux, and he wasn't going to compromise himself any further.

'I can give you it all,' Junya said again. 'I know you a cop so whether you admit it or not don't make no never mind. I got them all, faces and places going back three years. But I ain't giving you zip without a promise of immunity and a place on the witness protection programme.'

Harrison laughed, rolling his eyes to the ceiling.

'You can laugh at me. I don't mind. If that's the way you want to play it. But there's a whole lot more to this shit than you could begin to know.'

The engines suddenly stopped and Harrison sat and listened to the silence. The tugboat bobbed with the current in a way it hadn't before.

'They dumped the barges,' Junya said, sweat visibly prickling his brow.

'What does that mean?' Harrison asked him.

'It means they don't want no cargo, Harrison. They don't want no cargo at all.'

twenty-eight

Laveaux watched from his office window as the car drew up on Governor Nicholls Street Wharf. His secretary buzzed through on the intercom and told him Chaisson was in her office.

'Show him in,' Laveaux said, and sat down behind his desk.

The secretary brought the parole officer in and Laveaux waved the door closed. He sat with his long fingers built in a steeple before him.

'Mr Chaisson. What can I do for you?'

Chaisson settled his bulk in the vacant chair and rested the flat of his hands on his thighs. He had left Harrison's contact agent at the FBI field office. The FBI had learned the news about Call and were very concerned for Harrison. Chaisson had come to get him back.

'Harrison violated his parole.'

'He did?' Laveaux lifted one eyebrow.

'He's been fighting in Mick's Bar on Iberville Street,' Chaisson said. 'NOPD's got a warrant out for him. Where's the *See More Night*, Mr Laveaux?'

Laveaux sat forward and took a cigar from the box on the desk. He offered it to Chaisson who shook his head. 'I'm afraid I can't tell you exactly,' Laveaux said. 'They're stuck down at the gulf somewhere with engine trouble. It's caused me a few problems, I can tell you. They had to dump the barges and I've lost the contract to another skipper.'

Chaisson looked carefully at him. 'Mr Laveaux, you have a fugitive on board.'

Laveaux spread his palms wide. 'There's not much I can do about that now, is there?'

'But you can confirm he is still on board. He's not absconded anywhere.'

'As of last night I can.'

Chaisson looked him in the eye. 'I'd like to talk to Harrison on the phone or radio, please. Make sure he hasn't taken off.'

'I'm sure you would. I'd like to talk to the skipper myself. But neither of us can, Mr Chaisson. We've got an atmospherics problem down there. Must be a front blowing in. The last contact I had with them was yesterday afternoon when they reported the engine trouble. I haven't been able to talk to anyone since.'

Chaisson felt a chill on the nape of his neck. 'OK,' he said. 'If that's the situation, I'll be handing this over to the US Marshal's office. I'll need to give them the location of the tugboat.'

'I can give you the last known location.' Laveaux went to the wall where the river charts were hanging. 'They were due to service the rigs off the North Pass and they dumped the barges at Pass a Loutre. That's all I can tell you. I guess the marshals will use the Coastguard. That saves me the bother of reporting the situation.' He smiled then and opened the door. 'Thanks for stopping by.'

Outside, Chaisson had to take a moment to calm down. He stood inside the warehouse, watching the dockside roustabouts waiting for the next cargo to come in. They eyed him and he eyed them, like a cop who might have arrested them at one time or another. In his car he punched a number into his cellphone and Matt Penny answered.

Penny hung up the phone and went straight up to the conference room where the special agent in charge was debriefing Will Bentley. The boy's father was with them. Will Bentley sat next to his dad, talking into a tape recorder. He had told them what had happened and how the boy he knew as Nonk had insisted he sit tight and not say anything to anyone. He had been free for six hours now and so far the story hadn't made the news. They were concerned about the Mexican warden, though: he might be looking to make a name for himself with the media. Bentley had told the man to keep his mouth shut, that this was FBI business. But in reality there was nothing they could do to stop him and every second phone call was some news programme or other wanting to know what was going on. Both the governor and David Mouton had called for an update that morning. Bentley had lied to him like he had to everyone else. But they could not keep a lid on it indefinitely and Mayer explained that to Will.

'It wouldn't be your fault if anything did happen to this boy,' he said. 'You must remember that. I'm sure nothing will, but we can't keep this a secret. There are too many people out there looking for you. Think of all those police officers still searching. If they knew you were safe they could be doing other important stuff, couldn't they?'

The boy nodded, but he looked suddenly frightened and clutched his father's hand. Bentley stood up. 'If y'all don't mind, I'm going to take him home now. As and when you make a statement is all right by me.'

When they had gone Penny spoke to Mayer. 'Boss, we can't locate the tugboat. Johnny Buck is missing.'

He passed on what Chaisson had told him. Mayer stared at him, his face white at the cheekbones. Marcel Call's death had knocked him sideways. 'The boy called himself Nonk,' he said, half to himself. 'That's what Will Bentley just told us. He was a mulatto kid but called himself Nonk.'

Penny looked quizzical.

'Nonk is a Cajun word. It's how they refer to an uncle.' Mayer clenched a fist. 'How many tugboats are there with young black kids working them? It's the same boat. Fort Jackson, Head of the Passes, Pass a Loutre. It's the same damn boat.' He looked round at Penny. 'Get the SWAT team rolling and get a chopper up.'

Penny left the office, already on the phone.

Mayer moved to the window and saw Bentley's car pulling out of the parking lot. He thought of where Will had been found, close to the Barataria, the Laveaux stomping ground – thousands upon thousands of square miles of swamp. Somewhere down there Harrison was missing. And then another thought struck him, one that really chilled him. The FBI had been hunting a suspect for the bombing at the Olympic Games in the hills of North Carolina, a labyrinth of hill and forest just as Barataria was a labyrinth of water. They'd first gone after him in 1997 and they were still searching.

twenty-nine

Bill Chaisson sat in his car, watching as Laveaux left his office. He knew the FBI had rolled the SWAT team and were flying two choppers down to the gulf to hunt for the tugboat. Some chance, Chaisson had thought. Even if they find it, Harrison won't be aboard. He knew what would go down. As far as the crew were concerned, Harrison was a parolee on his way back to the farm. They'd just say he jumped ship somewhere along the gulf coast and was probably in Mexico now. The boy in the bayou murder, it was like going back three years and coming up just as empty-handed.

Laveaux drove right by him and Chaisson waited till two more vehicles passed before pulling out in pursuit. He figured the feds could roll the SWAT team if they wanted – they had a far better chance of finding Harrison by following Laveaux. He had shown his hand last night by taking out Call. He must have got what he wanted, and if they were lucky he might want to kill Harrison himself.

He followed him carefully. After twenty years in the police force Chaisson was adept at surveillance techniques, though he had no doubt Laveaux was equally as adept at counter-surveillance. He kept his distance, but the traffic was slow-moving and he was able to follow him across the river into Jefferson Parish and on to Barataria Boulevard without losing sight of him. The afternoon was waning now and new rain clouds lifted in the west. The day had been hot and muggy, nothing vaguely fresh about it. Chaisson drove in his shirtsleeves, shoulder holster unfastened and lying on the seat beside him.

He had already tried to anticipate Laveaux's moves: he had a big speedboat moored at his sister's house where the Intercoastal waterway crossed the head of Bayou Barataria. From there it was thirty-seven miles due south to his home on Grand Terre Island. Chaisson had racked his brains trying to think where he could commandeer a boat without Laveaux being the first to hear about it. Whole sections of the community were hooked up to the family in some way or another. He had called Palastina at the office and Palastina solved the problem. He had an uncle who lived just north of the Barataria who kept a boat gassed up. The boat wasn't very big, just an aluminium skiff with an outboard motor, but it would take Chaisson wherever he needed to go.

The news of Will Bentley's safe return broke as Laveaux headed for Barataria: he was listening to the radio when the programme was interrupted by a newsflash and an interview with the warden at Fort Jackson, who told how he found the boy shivering in the grounds of the fort itself. Laveaux's eyes dulled as he took in the details. He counted down the minutes till his cellphone rang.

'Yes.' He spoke softly.

The voice in his ear was agitated. 'He's alive.'

'So I hear.'

'What happened?'

'I don't know yet.'

'He can ruin us.'

'No, he can't. He's only seen the boy.'

'Deal with it.'

'It's already being dealt with.' Laveaux hung up the phone. Amateurs, why had he ever hooked up with amateurs? He punched a number into the phone.

*

Ignace gazed through the for'ard windows at the darkness that enveloped Barataria Bay like a fist. They were moored over the oyster beds north of Grand Bank Bayou. Two skiffs owned by his cousin were alongside and in the shallows a ruined oyster boat listed badly. The scoop was rusted now and the boat lay in the water to her gunwales. Blue claw crab had made their homes in the breaks along her hull.

The wind had picked up and the first spots of thick, black rain began to fall against the glass. Ignace took a bottle of whiskey from the closet, poured a large slug and drank deeply. He worked it out again in his mind, congratulating himself while at the same time chastising Augustine's foolishness by ignoring the words of his Nannan. Augustine would never admit he was wrong, but that didn't matter. Ignace knew he was. He had been on the phone just now, telling Ignace that the Bentley boy was still breathing and that the cop from the boy in the bayou murder was tailing him.

Ignace downed his whiskey then took Harrison's gun and slipped it into his belt. In his cabin he found Marie still lying on the bunk where he had told her to stay. For a long moment he looked at her. She had been good, very good, for a while. Much as he hated to admit it, he liked black flesh, although Marie was much more mulatto than black. He figured her parentage had mixed with Creole somewhere along the way, ending up with the smooth darkness he liked so much in her.

Being an ex-crack whore, she knew all the tricks and she always came back for more even when he beat the shit out of her. He looked at her now, thinking how he would like one last go at her, but even the whiskey he had drunk couldn't fuddle his brain that much.

Marie saw the look of death in his eyes and a stone moved in her belly. She had been dreading this day ever since she had stared into Junya's face before the boat picked them up by the levee. She hadn't thought she would see the boy again after that day, and when she did she felt there was something like hope in the world. Augustine told her what he wanted and after that she was no longer a crack whore. She was a prisoner, though, more accountable than she had ever been, and somehow she'd known that this moment would come. Quietly she got up, pulled a T-shirt over her head and fastened the buttons on her jeans.

Ignace motioned her down the steps ahead of him and she paused at the galley table, catching Podjo's glance where he played cards with Mesa. Gumbo was leaning in the doorway to the fiddley and he looked longingly at her. Nobody spoke, there were no words, they all just knew. Ignace pressed her lightly on the shoulder and bent to Podjo.

'Take the pirogue and get one of the skiffs,' he said. 'Gumbo, you go with him.'

Harrison heard the turnkeys being hammered loose above his head and he rested against the bulkhead and looked up. Sweat crawled on his leg where the ankle holster lay heavy all at once, and he considered making his move now. He waited, watching as the hatch was lifted and two figures were framed against the plum colour of the sky. He decided to wait, he was at too much of a disadvantage down here. They didn't know he had the .38. They had seen the .45 often enough and assumed it was the only weapon he carried.

He recognized the shape of Marie's hair and heard Ignace's low and rasping voice commanding her to climb down.

All was darkness in the hold after the hatch was secured above Marie's head. No light from the engine room, but plenty of heat finding its way through the vents. Harrison's jeans stuck to his thighs and he had discarded his shirt completely. Junya had fallen quiet this past hour but he sat up now as Marie settled on a pile of boxes.

Harrison heard a sigh lift from her, then a lighter snapped and he saw her face shadowed in the orange glow. The smell of smoke drifted across the cargo hold towards him.

'Well, Mr Yankee, you better be a cop because we all in shit street now.'

Harrison peered through the darkness at her. 'What's going on?'

'Ignace just sent the boys for a skiff.'

'He did?' Junya said. 'Shit.'

'What's the problem with that?' Harrison asked.

'A skiff is to take us into the swamp,' Junya told him. 'We won't be coming back.'

'They know,' Marie said. 'I heard him talking to Augustine on the telephone.'

She snapped her lighter once more and Junya's face broke the darkness. 'You let him go, didn't you?'

Junya didn't reply.

'Let who go?' Harrison said.

Marie looked at him. 'Will Bentley.'

Harrison was quiet then. Junya sat down heavily. 'Mister, quit jerking us around and tell us who you are.'

'You already know who I am.'

'Marie, pass me yo' lighter.' Junya turned the flame up high then struck the flint and peered into Harrison's eyes. 'You know Will Bentley, don't you, Mr Yankee-I-ain't-a-cop-asshole. He's the son of the US attorney.' He paused for a moment. 'Ignace told me to kill that boy, but I let him go. I let him go because you was on board this tugboat and I know yo' was a cop.' He shook his head. 'Take a look around. You really think this is just a game to flush you out? Your cover ain't that difficult to penetrate, baby. I had yo' down as the man when I saw you in the project and now Augustine got to Marcel Call.' He lost his grip as the lighter burned him and darkness enveloped them again. 'We can give you everything. You understand what I'm saying? There's been shit going down like you wouldn't believe. I seen it all. I'll give it up, Harrison. But first you got to promise immunity and witness protection.'

They all heard the sudden jabbering of an outboard motor and Junya gripped Harrison's shoulder. 'We don't got much time, Harrison. That's the pirogue going to get a skiff.' He thought for a moment. 'I figure we're moored over the oyster bed on Grand Bank Bayou. That's where Ignace always hang this thing when something big's going down. It's where we hide while the trawlers and the really fast skiffs head out to the gulf.'

'Why do they go out to the gulf?' Harrison asked him.

'To get cocaine, of course. Where were you born, mister? You figure this is just a reg'lar tugboat, a bunch of racist coonass sailors who just happen to make an exception for one black kid and his momma?'

He explained how at an appointed time the skiffs raced across the salt to where a mother ship was moored. They loaded shipments of cocaine. Some of it was in coffee, some of it was in coconut oil and some of it was just in packages. The mother ship lay among the rigs like any other supply vessel, about twenty miles offshore. Most of the coke was put on to a fast trawler with the compartments built under the shrimp store. When the Coastguard put dogs on they couldn't sniff through the seafood and their handlers didn't like their paws being cut to ribbons on the shells.

The trawlers supplied a bunch of Lafitte skiffs that could carry half a ton each and still make sixty miles an hour across the bayou. A small amount of the stuff came aboard the *See More Night* as coffee, which was unloaded along the harbour wharfs in New Orleans.

Harrison listened but didn't say anything. He still didn't know if he could trust what he was being told. 'Fuck it,' Junya said. 'That's only the half of it. But you got to come through for us. I got proof of who is involved and I'll sit down in any court in the country and testify. But you got to get us out of here and you got to give us immunity.'

'He's telling you the truth,' Marie said.

'You do know who Will Bentley is, don't you?' Junya asked. 'Or you know who his daddy is.'

Harrison still sat where he was, thinking hard. 'What did you mean when you said you let him go – why did you have him in the first place?'

'We ain't saying no more.' Junya twisted round to peer at Marie in the darkness. 'Marie, don't be saying nothing else.'

Marie sucked on her cigarette and blew smoke at Harrison. Through the hull they heard the reverberation of an engine.

'That's the skiff coming back,' Junya said. 'Like I told you, we're at Grand Bank Bayou. That's only a little bitty distance from Grand Terre Island, where Augustine got his house. We got about four minutes till we're on that skiff and then we alligator bait.'

Harrison stood up, but as he did the hatch was lifted and a powerful flashlight blinded him. He heard the sound of a pistol being racked and then Ignace's voice hissed at him. 'Got me a nice .45 hollow point here with a serial number filed off.' The beam moved from Harrison's face to his arms. 'Get them hands over you head, Harrison, and get you ass up this ladder. Junya, you and Marie stay back. Any of y'all try anything dumb I've a mind to shoot you where you stand.'

Again the light played on Harrison's face. He couldn't see a thing and to go for his gun now would be suicide. Pulling on his shirt, he gripped the rail and climbed up to the deck. Ignace kept the torch on him every step of the way and when his head drew level with the hatch he felt the barrel of his own unregistered weapon pressed against his scalp.

'Nice and slow now, Mr po-lice officer, nice and slow.'

Harrison climbed out and Gumbo gripped his arms, pinning them behind his back so he couldn't move. The next thing he knew, silver duck tape was binding his wrists and he thought of Maxwell Carter. Junya and the girl were brought up after him. Junya saw Harrison with his hands taped behind his back and a look of disgust crept across his face.

Ignace lined them up in the stern while he paraded in front of them like some macabre sergeant major. Harrison watched his eyes by the deck lights, dull and glazed with alcohol, eyes numbed from all normal human feeling. They reminded him of a contract killer he had worked alongside while undercover in Florida. To the average citizen he looked like a normal regular guy, but when you got up close and looked into his eyes, they were as dead as all of his victims.

Lying alongside now, he could see a flat-bottomed skiff with a canopy over the pilot's console. Podjo sat behind the wheel with the engine idling, and tied to the stern the dinghy bobbed in the wake. Ignace looked in Harrison's face. 'Nobody told me what kinda cop you are, Harrison. You NOPD or harbour or what?'

'I'm the kind that'll haunt you night and day.'

For a moment Ignace blanched.

'I know you're a superstitious sonofabitch,' Harrison said. 'So be real prepared.'

Ignace pressed the barrel of the .45 against Harrison's chest. 'Oh, we prepared,' he said. 'You dumbass buddy Chaisson is tailing my cousin right about now. I figure he's thinking Augustine can lead him to you. Apparently he's sending the US marshals in after you, too, seeing as how you such a bad felon and all.'

'Give it up, Ignace,' Harrison said. 'If Chaisson's looking for me then so is the FBI.'

'So you a Fed.' Ignace lifted his eyebrows. 'I never kilt me no Fed before.'

Harrison breathed in his face. 'You better think about that one. We're the meanest gang out there. Take one of us down and you got twelve thousand more on your ass. Twenty-four seven, partner, every day of your life.'

Ignace shook his head. 'I don't think so. Me, I'm just a reg'lar tugboat cap'n, stuck down here because of engine trouble. And there's a storm blowing in that's gonna send a tidal surge upriver that'll set all kinds of currents tearing up the place. I'm just setting out the storm and by the time you friends get down here we'll have the engine fixed and me and the crew will be on about our bidness.' He laughed. 'You, on the other hand, will be highballing it to Mexico. I mean, you ain't gonna stick around, are you? You only got the farm to look forward to.'

Gumbo manhandled them down into the dinghy, strung out on its line behind the skiff. Ignace obviously figured that if they were towed behind they couldn't make any trouble. The rain was falling hard now and the surface of the bay was lit with spouts of foam where the drops were large and heavy. Within a few minutes there was whiteout and Harrison sat in the dinghy with his hands tied behind his back and a gun strapped uselessly to his ankle. He watched, hair plastered to his scalp, the wind ripping up the surface of the bay, as first Marie then the boy were handed down beside him.

The world was grey and white where the rain fell in sheets and every now and again the sky was torn by lightning. For a second the landscape was illuminated and Harrison could see the vast expanse of water that was Barataria Bay, flat and grey and empty. To the west was the bayou itself, passing through swamp and island till it hit land proper at Barataria. To the east there was just swamp, a thousand and one tiny waterways and banks of unstable mud where only cypress grew with any confidence. A man could float a boat in there one day and never find his way out again. Harrison had only been into the swamp on one occasion before and he knew that everything looked the same. He also knew there were alligators and poisonous cottonmouth snakes that curled round the branches of trees to pluck frogs from the water.

Junya sat down next to him, the rain on his face making him blink where he couldn't wipe it away. Marie sat for'ard of them on the other seat and Harrison looked beyond her to where Podjo was revving the engine on the skiff. Both Gumbo and Ignace climbed aboard, Ignace taking his place in the shelter of the pilot canopy while Gumbo, seemingly oblivious to the rain, sat in the stern with a pump-action Remington trained on the dinghy. From the deck of the tugboat Mesa handed down two 'scoped rifles; all the men wore camouflage fatigues for hunting. Ignace nodded to Podjo then swivelled round in his seat and grinned through the rain at Harrison.

'Y'all hold tight now,' he called.

Podjo jumped on the gas.

thirty

Matt Penny stood on the rain-soaked tarmac of the field office parking lot while the pilot of the Coastguard Black Hawk informed them what the weather centre had reported.

'There's a major storm blowing in from the gulf,' he said. 'We're catching the tail end of Hurricane Juanito that hit Mexico last weekend.'

Penny bit his lip. The hurricane hadn't been the worst, but Mexican buildings were not the best and many homes had been destroyed along the Yucatan Peninsula. Fourteen FBI agents were assembled waiting to roll in two separate choppers, blue and gold teams, seven men in each, including sniper observers.

'Can you fly in it?' he asked. It was all he needed to know. 'We got an agent missing.'

'Yeah, I can fly in it.' The pilot showed his teeth. 'I guess I've flown in worse. The gulf coast, you say?'

'Somewhere between the mouth of the river and the Fourchon. Could be into Barataria Bay, we really don't know.'

'How many choppers have you got?'

'Just you and one from the National Guard. Their pilot told me the same stuff about the weather only he didn't want to fly.'

The pilot nodded to the open door on the fuselage. 'Get your boys saddled up and let's roll.'

*

Chaisson was sitting in the boat he had commandeered, watching a pelican perched on the pilings of Laveaux's sister's house. His speedboat was still moored at the alligator dock in front, across the bayou from the mound where the graves were very white against the oak trees. A great egret stood on the riff-raff stones that kept the graves intact, like some silent sentinel to the next world. Somewhere down in the swamp he knew Harrison was facing execution, if he wasn't dead already.

His cellphone rang, which surprised him. This was about as far south as it would work. It was Penny from the seat of a Black Hawk. Chaisson had told him he was tailing Laveaux.

'What's going on, Bill?' Penny asked him.

'Not much. I don't know if he's on to me or not. But he's not moving.'

'I just rolled the SWAT team.'

'Let's hope you can find him.'

'Let's hope.' Penny had to shout above the noise of the chopper. 'You want any back-up?'

'Are you kidding? I'm just set here in the rain. What good is back-up gonna do me?'

Harrison was thrown on to the floor of the dinghy as Podjo opened up the skiff and they tore across the bay, the wind buffeting them from the southeast. The rain and spray were indeterminable from one another and Harrison tasted both salt and fresh water in his mouth. His head was pressed against the seat, feet pushing at the bulkhead, when he felt something sharp in his back. Carefully he used his feet to lever himself round so he could sit up, and when he did he saw a shard of aluminium that had peeled from the seam in the floor.

Marie was still perched precariously on the seat in front, partially obscuring Gumbo's view from the skiff that towed them towards the salt marsh and the swamps west of the

Mississippi. Junya was squatting close to Harrison and Harrison nodded his head at the piece of aluminium.

'You figure you can do anything with that?' he yelled.

The boy didn't reply. He just rolled on his side and worked his way round till the shard was under his wrists. He was bumped and thrashed by the speed with which Podjo dragged them across the bay. He banged his head on the seat and swore out loud. Already they were beyond Cat Bay and coming up fast on Crane Island. Harrison watched him working at the binding on his hands. Suddenly Junya grinned at him, rain and spray littering his face. He started to laugh where he lay in the bottom of the boat, but the wind took any sound as soon as it left his mouth. Then he brought both hands round in front of him. Harrison glanced ahead and saw Gumbo no longer watching them but taking shelter under the canopy with the others.

The line between the skiff and the dinghy was about thirty feet long and fixed with a shackle. Harrison had already decided what he was going to do. He knelt in the bottom of the boat while Junya ripped the tape from his hands. Harrison felt for the gun at his ankle.

'Just full of surprises, ain't you?' Junya said when he saw it.

'Untie Marie. I'm going to loose that rope.' Harrison slapped Junya on the back and moved for'ard.

Gumbo looked round, looked away again then looked back, bringing up the gun as he did so. The boom resonated across the bay, tearing a hole in the wind. Marie screamed close to Harrison's ear. She fell heavily against him, almost knocking him off balance.

Harrison eased her down into the bottom of the boat, her hair streaked by the rain, fear standing out in her eyes. Then he crawled to the prow and unhooked the shackle that bound them to the skiff.

Already Podjo was hauling the skiff around, sending up a

huge white wake that threatened to tip the dinghy where it bobbed in the surf.

Harrison weighed the .38 in his palm. It would be useless from this distance. It would be useless unless they got really close, but with only five bullets he had no intention of letting them get really close. Junya was holding Marie, her facial muscles taut now, and as Harrison moved towards the stern he saw blood on her shirt.

'How bad?' he yelled over the wind.

Marie bit her lip and he clambered beyond them both and squeezed the fuel pump ball that fed the Evinrude engine. Pulling open the choke, he hauled on the starter line. The engine coughed but didn't fire and he squeezed the ball again. Across the bay the skiff was coming about and Ignace was lining them up in the sights of his rifle.

Only vaguely did Harrison hear the report, but a wave spat close to the boat and then another. He hauled on the line again, but still the engine wouldn't fire. He cursed aloud. The skiff was fully about now and Podjo had the throttle wide open, the bows high, sending a wake all the way to the islands.

Junya scrambled to him and pumped the ball again. 'Haul on it now,' he yelled. 'Haul on it as I pump.'

Harrison yanked on the line and the engine coughed, sputtered then rattled into life. Crouching down, he took the tiller and twisted the throttle grips open. Junya almost went overboard as the bows lifted and the boat bucked forward.

Ignace fired a second shot and a third that pierced the gunwale above the water line, ricocheting past Harrison's head. Ducking low, he tried to steer as the dinghy lurched and bounced across the waves in the direction of the swamp. He knew there was no way he could outrun the skiff – their only hope was to lose it in bayous.

thirty-one

Mayer sat with the Bentleys at the family home on the north shore of Lake Ponchartrain. Since Will had been found safe and well, he had requested some statistics from Washington on missing children in the Mississippi delta. What he learned had disturbed him and he was probing Will as gently but effectively as he could.

'Don't worry about the news breaking, Will,' he said. 'There's nothing to be bothered about. It's not your fault. You had to tell us what you did. The TV people found out by accident. That's just the way it is sometimes. The important thing is that you're safe and well.' He smiled his encouragement. Will sat between his father and mother and nodded.

'I did what he asked,' he said. 'That's all I could do.' He was still in shock and had had no time to recover and none of the rest that the doctors said he should get. But he was the only link to the boy and the boat, almost certainly the same boat that Harrison was aboard.

'Did he tell you anything else, Will?' Mayer asked him.

Will bit his lip, trying to remember exactly what had happened two nights ago or whenever it was he'd landed at Fort Jackson.

'He was very interested in the fact that my dad is a US attorney,' he said. 'But that's all he really said.'

He looked beyond Mayer and was back in the tunnel with the rain falling outside and the fort shrouded in the kind of darkness he had only witnessed in dreams. He could feel the chill of his own urine sticking to his legs.

'Listen to me.' Nonk's face was very close to his. He still held both the knife and the gun and Will's eyes were fixed on them. 'I'm gonna let you go. But you got to help me. You hear?'

Will nodded. He couldn't speak, couldn't form any words, his mouth was too dry.

'You tell yo' daddy, I want immunity and protection. Tell him if I get out alive that's what I want and in return he gets the lot.' He paused, scratching his scalp with the barrel of the gun and thinking. 'Tell him I might be a dumbass sumbitch, but I think there's a cop on the boat and I been looking for a cop for three fucking years.' He seemed to be talking to himself now, rather than to Will, and he looked beyond him as if he looked into the future or maybe the past. 'I don't know why I'm doing this, you little shit. You got everything I never had. I ought to kill you and be happy with it, just like they axed. I could. And I mean like that.' He snapped his fingers under Will's nose and the boy's bladder emptied again.

'Goddammit. Quit doing that. You know how bad that stinks. You tell yo' daddy he's got to come through for me, though I don't know how the fuck I'm going to get out of this thing. Tell him I'm giving you this chance, tell him he's lucky you is somebody worth keeping alive. The others, they just street litter, trash for the garbage man, like I was.'

'The others.' Mayer brought Will back to the present, to the warmth and comfort of his home. 'What others?'

Will shrugged. 'He didn't say, Mr Mayer.' He looked at his father. 'Will he get what he asked for, Dad?'

Bentley lifted his eyebrows. 'I don't know, son. It depends on a lot of things.'

Will got up then and walked to the window where the

storm was buffeting the banana trees in the yard. 'It doesn't matter,' he said. 'He's probably dead now anyway.'

His mother got up and slipped her arm round his shoulders. Turning to her, he buried his face in her breast and she held him, feeling his warmth, the life in him that she thought had been lost for ever.

thirty-two

Harrison drove the boat with one hand, the other clutching the .38. Podjo worked the skiff round behind them and opened her up again. They were being baited, the skiff slowing down and speeding up, cutting across the stern while Ignace loosed off rifle shots. Only the wind and the bucking motion of both boats stopped him taking clear aim and plugging one of them. He was enjoying it. The three of them were laughing and whooping and yelling over the wind. They had a spotlight on the boat and every time they made a turn Ignace's target was laid bare before him.

Marie was lying in the bottom of the boat with Junya supporting her head. Her skin was grey and she had lost blood and Harrison had given Junya his shirt to try and staunch the wound.

Junya left her for a moment and scrabbled across the seats. 'Got to get us into the bayous,' he said, 'We won't outrun them from here.' Looking over the gunwales, he seemed to get his bearings. 'Look after Marie. I'll drive the boat.'

Pushing Harrison out of the way, he took the tiller and crouched low to keep Ignace's shots off him. He looked across the bay then turned due north, heading straight for the lesser grey of the salt marsh that he knew would give way, in time, to swamp and float top and trees. Places they could hide.

Harrison lay down in the bottom of the boat, partially

protected now by the gunwales. Marie lay in two inches of water, the spray and the rain combining to half sink them. She lay on her back, looking up at the sky as the rain spattered her face and soaked her hair till it sparkled with globules of water. She lay still and her breathing was harsh and laboured. Harrison could hear it, coming in short gasps through the wind.

'I'm going to try and turn you,' he said. 'I've got to look at the wound.'

As carefully as he could, he eased her on to her side. Her back was a bloody mess, the shot having punched a hole the size of his fist in the skin and soft tissue. It had penetrated just below her left shoulder and the material of her top had meshed into the wound itself. He had nothing to bind it with. There was nothing other than the soaking, bloodied shirt Junya had already used.

Harrison kept her on her side now, trying to keep the wound out of the water. He could see the shock standing tall in her eyes. She didn't speak to him. Her lips looked bruised and puffy, her skin breaking in sweat.

There was nothing he could do and the frustration boiled and with it his hatred of Ignace Laveaux. The wind suddenly died and he looked back at Junya, slouched so low in the stern he could barely see over the gunwales. Harrison lifted his head and saw the skiff fifty yards back. They were entering a bayou. He had no idea where, but Junya ran the boat straight up the middle with the throttle fully open. Harrison watched as the spotlight from the skiff picked them out. Moments later another shot rang out.

'Slow down.' He moved next to Junya.

'What?'

'Do it. They can hit us any time they please all the time they can see us.'

'I know where I am,' Junya said. 'I can lose them.'

'Not with a searchlight on us you can't. Slow the boat down.'

Junya did as he was asked and the bows dipped, and as they did Harrison lay in the stern, his face dangerously close to the steaming engine casing.

The skiff came after them, not slowing, the searchlight panning back and forth over the hull. Harrison lay still, the .38 in both hands. He counted down five seconds and saw Gumbo take shape in the prow. He fired one shot. The light exploded and then they were in darkness. He could no longer see Gumbo or the skiff and heard Podjo throttle back hard as the blanket of night was thrown over his eyes. He leaned close to Junya. 'Now you can get us out of here.'

Junya had been in these waters many times over the last three years; he had routed through different bayous from different points of Barataria whenever Bernaud pulled alongside the *See More Night* in his skiff. The two of them had crossed the mud bank and marsh, the plairie as the Cajuns called it, picking their way among the tiny inland waterways and across the float top, muddy land where you could walk without incident for ten minutes then sink so fast you'd drown a minute later. Always to the same place. Its location was imprinted on his mind, as he knew it would be for ever. He could run a boat through these bayous at night because that was all he had ever done. He had lost count of the times he had made the trip – in with a cargo then out with the boat empty, back in empty and out again loaded up to the gunwales.

Already he had put some distance between them and the skiff as Podjo floundered without lights. Ignace would have to rely on his own instincts if he wanted to catch them. All at once Junya felt the promise of light at the end of his own particular tunnel. Glancing down into the gloom, he saw the prostrate form of Marie, the only person he had cared anything for in as long as his memory served him. She was young enough to be his sister yet old enough to be his mother. 'Hang on, baby,' he whispered. 'We can still do this thing.'

Harrison sat down next to him; Junya had throttled right back now. 'How much gas have we got?' Harrison asked him.

'I don't know. But I reckon they keep it topped up.'

'Can you get us out of here?'

Junya looked sideways at him. 'I can get us in here first, which is what matters. Laveaux controls this bayou, Harrison. Right now Ignace gonna be on the wire telling him to shore up all the exit routes between here and the any coast.'

Harrison peered into the darkness. The rain had eased and the wind had died down, and the engine seemed very loud in his ears. He kept his eyes on the stern, staring beyond the boy at the tiller, looking for any sign of the skiff.

Junya tiptoed north. Every now and again he would drop the revs to an idle so they could listen. Behind them they could still hear the engine note of the skiff.

'Shit.' He spat into the wind. 'That's Ignace on the wheel. He knows this plairie better than I do.' He cursed again. 'I hate this fucking salt marsh. We need trees, Mr FBI man. What we need is trees.'

Behind them Ignace had sent Podjo to try and fix the spotlight while he took the wheel in one hand and the satellite phone in the other. Somewhere overhead he thought he heard the dull whirring of a helicopter's rotors but he might have been mistaken.

Laveaux sucked crayfish heads and dipped his fingers in warm water and lemon juice. His sister Sylvie looked after the Barataria house and skinned his alligators for him during hunting season. She was arguably a better hunter than he was himself, setting her hooks just the right height above the water so the 'gators took the chicken and hook right into their stomachs when they leapt. She knew just how to hold them under the jaw so they didn't bite her hand off when she took in the line, and she could plug them in the soft spot between the eyes with absolute precision. Often, though, she held them while he shot them. She knew the instant the head was out of the water whether the 'gator was big enough to take, and if it wasn't she'd cut the line. An alligator would dissolve an iron hook in two to three weeks in the stomach, human bones were gone in a matter of hours. Sylvie steamed crayfish like no one else and her brother ate with her every Friday.

When Ignace called him from the skiff and told him what had happened, Laveaux clenched his fork so hard the metal bent and he dropped it, ruined, on to the table. He hung up and called his sister – she had taken the pots to the kitchen. She came through and wiped her hands on a towel.

'Come with me,' he told her. 'We've got to take the boat south.'

It was ten-thirty when Sylvie fired up the speedboat and set the engine on idle while Augustine brought his guns. He handed her a rifle and two handguns, including a cannon of a .44 Magnum. He cast off in the stern and they chugged out into the bayou as a tugboat pushing four barges came up alongside. On Augustine's instruction they stayed in the lee of the barges all the way to the bridge, then Sylvie opened the speedboat up and they headed south for the bay.

Bill Chaisson watched as the tugboat rumbled under the bridge then swung his night-sight glasses back to the house. Laveaux's boat was missing. The sound of a V8 inboard made him curse and he swung the glasses south again and saw the wake as they hit the bayou.

On the Coastguard Black Hawk Penny juddered and thumped against his seat, the Kevlar armour and weaponry only adding to the blows to his body. He peered through the glass at his feet as the searchlight picked out the rolling breakers that ripped chunks out of the gulf coast. They were flying low and the wind buffeted the chopper so the pilot fought with both cyclic and collective in turn.

'You better pray this engine keeps going,' he yelled at Penny. 'You wouldn't want to see me auto-rotate in this.'

'Just a laugh a minute, aren't you?' Penny shifted the plug of chew against his cheek and looked again at the coastline.

thirty-three

Salt marsh gave way to cypress swamp, the trees suddenly taking shape against the grey and rain-washed horizon like spectres of trees, primordial, as if allowing a glimpse of how things had once been. Harrison looked astern but couldn't see the skiff. He could hear it, though, and it was still too close for comfort. He looked back at Junya who kept his eyes fixed on the prow.

'You still know where you're at?' he asked.

'Yeah, I know where I'm at. Don't worry about it, Harrison. Do what you can for Marie.'

'Kind-hearted sumbitch all of a sudden, aren't you?'

Junya didn't smile. 'The deal is still on, Harrison. If we get out of this, I want immunity and witness protection.'

'Immunity from what?' Harrison leaned closer to him. 'From where I'm sat, you two look like the victims.'

'Is that how it looks?' Junya lifted his eyebrows. 'Well, you just keep that in mind.'

The engine sputtered suddenly and Junya looked down. 'Pump the bubble,' he said. Harrison dropped to his knees and pumped. But the tank was empty, nothing but air resisting the pressure of his hand. The engine missed again then died completely and suddenly there was only the wind and the rain and the sound of the skiff coming steadily closer.

Harrison checked the tank. 'A round must have breached it,' he said. Carefully he climbed over Marie's prone body and felt under the seat for paddles. He tossed one to Junya. 'Ditch the engine,' he said. 'We don't need the extra weight.'

Deftly the boy uncoupled the Evinrude and it slipped beneath the oil-black surface of the bayou with barely a ripple. Harrison bent close to Marie and felt her breath on his face. It was ragged still, but even. He checked her wound and found it had begun to congeal. She wouldn't bleed to death at least.

Junya sat on the seat alongside him, already dipping his paddle. 'We've got to get off this bayou,' he said. 'They'll be swarming all over us in no time.'

How Junya had any semblance of a bearing Harrison didn't know. Yet thirty years ago deep underground in Cu Chi other men had said the same thing about him. Rain ran off his face, the wind lifting through the moss-sodden trees to blow harder again. They left the main bayou for a much narrower channel where cypress overhung the water very close to the boat.

'Watch them branches,' Junya said hoarsely. 'We don't want no congo falling into the boat.'

'Congo?'

'Water moccasin, Harrison, poisonous fucking snakes.'

Harrison watched the trees and paddled on, keeping close to the bank but careful not to brush the overhanging branches, particularly those laden with Spanish moss. Moss gave moccasins the perfect cover for hunting.

Marie moaned where she lay and Harrison bent to her once more. Junya sat on the for'ard bench and paddled hard. Harrison touched Marie with light fingers and she opened her eyes and recognized him.

'I'm cold.'

'I know. I'm sorry.' The rain rolled off Harrison's hair and down his face and naked shoulders. 'Junya,' he called softly, and the kid looked over his shoulder. 'Where are you taking us? Marie needs shelter and I need to look at her wound.'

'A few miles further.' Junya looked down at Marie. 'You hold on now. We got a couple of miles is all.'

They paddled on through the narrow bayous. Harrison's night sight had settled now and he could see the water and the weight of the trees, the soaking vegetation that grew on land that might not actually be land, merely floating islands of quicksand. He had no idea where they were. They had been paddling for a couple of hours at least and he could no longer hear any sign of the skiff. But the boy did not falter once and Harrison began to see him in a whole new light. He wasn't just some kid from the street, some would-be gang-banger hanging out with the big boys. There was a strength about him with this talk of protection and purpose. He watched him now, sitting in the prow, working his paddle and leading them deeper into the labyrinth.

Ignace slowed the skiff till the engine just idled and the wake dropped away behind them. The wind had lifted again and was rippling the surface of the bayou, sending up little twisters of spray, which danced to the banks and disappeared into the low-growing palmetto. Podjo stood under the tarpaulin canopy that had kept the bulk of the rain off them, and waited. He knew better than to try and prompt anything from his skipper when he was thinking. The satellite phone rang where it was stowed beneath the console. Ignace picked it up.

'Yeah?'

'Where are you?' His cousin's voice in his ear.

'A little south of Grand Bayou.'

For a moment Laveaux said nothing. Ignace heard a rush of static, then, 'You following them still.'

'Uh-huh.'

'South of Grand Bayou?'

'Yeah.'

'Maybe you're thinking what I'm thinking.'

Ignace was fingering the gris gris he still carried in his

pocket. 'There's nowhere else to go. Gumbo shot Marie. They need someplace to take her.'

'I've spoken to the others, there's no way they can get out.'

'Where's Bernaud?'

'Bernaud is watching. Listen, Iggy. Get rid of them quickly. No games now, just do it and dump them.' Laveaux laughed in his ear. 'Like the old days, uh, hunting and being hunted in Barataria.'

Ignace furrowed his brow. 'Who is being hunted?'

'Me. That parole officer is still on my tail. I think there's a helicopter up there somewhere, too. But don't worry, cousin. All is well. Just get rid of them now. And I mean *all* of them, Iggy.'

'What about the contract?'

'We can start it up again when the dust has settled. I'm going to the tugboat, then Grand Terre. I'll see you later.' He hung up and Ignace eased the revs a little higher, pointing the boat northwest towards the swamps of Live Oak Bay.

Laveaux lost his tail halfway down Bayou Barataria, seeing the lights disappear as he threw up a wake large enough to shower those houses closest to the levee. His boat had a V8 engine that could generate over one hundred miles an hour if he needed it. It was thirty-seven miles from the waterway to the gulf and he knew exactly where Ignace had anchored the tugboat. When he left the bayou and hit Barataria Bay he really opened her up. The storm was blowing itself out, moving east along the coast towards Gulfport. Vaguely in the distance he heard the rotors of a helicopter and saw lights crossing the bay some distance north of him. He smiled widely and tapped his hands on the wheel. They would find nothing in this weather and they would find nothing when the weather shifted and the sun came out to warm the backs of the reptiles. There were hundreds of thousands of square miles of swamp and it all looked the same from the air. They could trawl the bayous for ten years in a hundred different boats and still not find anything. He, on the other hand, could find anything he wanted at any time: this was his turf and, like Lafitte before him, he would not give it up easily.

Jimmy Mesa threw them a line when they got to the tugboat. Sylvie tied on at the bow while he secured the stern. They were windward still but secure enough. Laveaux did not plan to stay very long.

'Jimmy,' he said as they went into the galley. 'Pour me and my sister a whiskey then we search this boat from top to bottom. Get rid of all Harrison's stuff. If the police find you, tell them he ran off, jumped another boat and was headed for Mexico. If they come before Ignace gets back, tell them he and the others have gone for help with the engines. OK?'

The mate nodded. 'What about the boy?'

'The boy is history. The boy made a mistake and now we have the Feds down on top of us.'

Mesa lifted one eyebrow. 'Heat like that gets you killed.'

'Worse, it puts you in jail, and I have no intention of lowering my pants for some hairy-assed hillbilly with one tooth to his name.' Laveaux swallowed whiskey. 'When they find where we're moored at, which they eventually will, we'll have them swarming all over the vessel. I want every trace of them erased. Go through Ignace's cabin and get rid of anything that puts Marie on this boat.' He paused then turned to his sister. 'On second thoughts, Sylvie, you do that. You'll do a better job.' He spoke to Mesa again. 'You take the cabins, give me all Harrison's stuff. I'll take it to Grand Terre and burn it.' He paused for a moment. 'Where was the boy?'

'In the cargo hold.'

'Anywhere else?'

Mesa pursed his lips. 'The bridge for a time. Ignace give him a little pat.'

Laveaux left them to their tasks and went on deck again. The steel was slippery with spray and he picked his way carefully to the cargo hold. The hatch was secured and he took the mallet to the turnkeys then swung himself down. Feeling in the darkness for the light switch, he blinked in the sudden glare. He stood very still and took in every aspect of the hold: every piece of rope, every box, every spare oil filter and valve for the engine room; every life jacket and whistle, the spare emergency position-indicating radio beacon.

He could see how the ropes had been shifted around to make better seats and bedding. Ignace had had them down here a long time and they had tried to make themselves comfortable. He took a coil at a time and wound it round his arm then tossed it back as it would have been tossed before. Picking up a length of hawser from where it lay by the bulkhead, he saw an empty pack of cigarettes. Carefully he checked the box then dropped to one knee, resting an arm on his thigh. The boy had been very good, and Augustine had underestimated him. He should have listened harder when Junya said Harrison was a cop. But Harrison had been good too, very cool under fire. But, then, he was a veteran of countless sorties underground, in the most inhospitable fighting conditions imaginable. Pity he turned out to be a Fed. Under different circumstances he would have made a useful ally.

Satisfied that any search of the hold would reveal nothing out of the ordinary, he climbed the steps to the bridge, checking first on Sylvie who was going through the skipper's berth with a fine-tooth comb. On the bridge he checked the chair and chart table and Ignace's whiskey closet. Sylvie came up and told him Ignace's cabin was clean. Mesa already had Harrison's gear in a bag out on deck.

Laveaux went back to his boat, his sister climbing down before him. 'I'll be on Grand Terre,' he called up to Mesa as he cast off. Sylvie fired the engines and backed away from the tugboat. 'You remember what to say?'

Mesa nodded, a crooked grin on his face. 'Of course. The Yankee jumped ship for Mexico, no one has seen him since.'

thirty-four

Junya lifted his paddle and laid it across his knees; behind him Harrison was watchful. They were close to a low bank now, a sloping beach of mud deep in the swamp where the wind had ceased to blow and the rain was no more than spittle in the trees. Marie moaned softly and Junya turned and laid a hand across her mouth. She looked up with fear printed on her face. He stroked her forehead lightly and looked back at Harrison, the whites of his eyes glinting in the partial light from the moon.

The water was still, dark but for the silver fragments of moonlight breaking through the moss. Harrison could hear the croaking of frogs and the ripple in the water where an alligator moved away from the bank. Junya lifted a finger to his lips and pointed through the broken trunks of trees. Harrison's eyes followed where he pointed but saw nothing. Junya lifted his paddle again and took them deeper into the cypress, funnelling a path along a trainasse no wider than the boat itself. Harrison could hear every dip of his paddle now, the tempest well behind them, and he had his ears pricked for any sound of an engine. But he heard nothing but frogs and cicadas and the occasional plopping sound of fish breaking the surface of the water.

Junya took them right into the float top then the boat came to a stop and he laid his paddle under the seat. He slid down next to Marie and touched his palm to her brow.

'She's hot,' he whispered to Harrison. 'We need to get her inside.'

'Inside where?'

'There.' Junya pointed over his shoulder and Harrison peered between the cypress and the silent live oaks and gradually he made out the shape of a ruined fishing camp fifty feet back from the water. He looked harder and saw it lifting skeletal in the gloom, two storeys, the windows in the roof punched out so they looked like eye sockets where the flesh had been eaten away.

'Help me get her up.' Junya had half lifted Marie, and was struggling. Harrison took her other arm and between them they got her to her feet. Harrison checked her wound and was relieved to see the bleeding hadn't started again. Very carefully he supported her while stepping over the gunwales on to soft and fleshy ground.

'Walk where I walk,' Junya hissed through the darkness.

He led the way, while Harrison supported Marie, who somehow managed to get one foot in front of the other. Junya looked carefully about them, inspecting the shadows amid the foliage for any hidden watcher. He moved with great care, easing aside the fronds of palmetto, which clustered at the feet of the oaks, ducking his head so as not to disturb so much as a strand of moss. Then he stopped in a clearing where the ground was that bit firmer and cast his eye over the old fishing camp. Harrison held Marie to him, looked where Junya looked and saw that the camp stood on pilings, which were covered over with boards right across the front. The steps up to the decking were completely rotten.

'Be very careful where you tread, it's pretty bad in places.'

Junya led the way round to the back, where the bayou lapped almost to the building itself. He pointed to another set of steps that led up to a firmer section of decking. Harrison realized that from this angle the place didn't look

302

so bad. The porch was intact, as was the door and the window. Junya climbed the steps and twisted the white enamel doorknob. Harrison picked Marie up now and carried her. She was heavy and her limbs were loose and he knew they had to get her to a doctor soon. He climbed after Junya and as he did he thought he heard someone whisper in the darkness.

The hairs lifted on the back of his neck and voices from the past came rushing through the stillness. He stood for a moment and listened but heard nothing more and he knew the voices were in his head, voices of the night that only came to him from deep impenetrable darkness.

Junya led the way inside and Harrison moved past him so he could close the door. He set Marie on her feet again but held her and her head lolled against his shoulder. All was still. Harrison felt dry boards under his feet and could smell dust and dirt and the moisture off the swamp.

'The front is never used,' the boy told him. 'They like it to look old and spooky because it keeps prying eyes away. Not that there are any. The whole place is posted, Augustine's land.'

Harrison frowned in the darkness then blinked as Junya lit an oil lamp. He kept the wick low but bright enough to outline a room with a couch and a table and chair. He moved Marie to the couch and laid her on her side. Junya disappeared into a room at the back and came out with a bottle of water and a first-aid kit.

'Where'd you get that?'

'Oh, this place is stocked.' Junya handed him the first-aid kit. 'I hope you're an EMT, because I don't know shit about mending people.'

'Just breaking them, uh?'

Junya didn't smile.

Again Harrison thought he heard someone whisper and sweat crawled in his hair.

'This place haunted or what?' he said.

Junya looked back at him. His eyes had glazed and he seemed to be lost somewhere inside himself.

Harrison turned his attention to Marie, easing aside the shirt where he had strapped up her wound. He was naked from the waist up yet he wasn't cold and didn't remember being so, too much adrenalin pumping, paddling through the bayous in the dead of night with one ear cocked for Ignace. And where was Ignace? It occurred to him that if Junya knew about this place then Ignace must, too.

Junya was by the front door now, peering into the gloom. Again Harrison heard the sound of somebody whisper. It came from under his feet and he looked down at the boards.

'Maybe I'm just getting old,' he said, 'but this place is spooking me.'

'It should.' Junya was staring at him now, his eyes hidden in shadows. 'It's that kind of place.'

Harrison opened the first-aid kit and inspected the contents for alcohol and bandages. He poured water over cotton wool and began to bathe Marie's wound: it seeped blood and she opened her eyes and groaned.

Junya was by her side in a moment, clutching her hand like the child he actually was.

'It's OK, Marie. It's OK. You gonna be fine. We gonna get you out of here and into witness protection. No more Augustine and no more nights with Ignace.' He looked up at Harrison. 'That's what we gonna do, Mr FBI man, that's what we gonna do.'

Harrison dressed the wound and when he turned Junya was playing with a gutting knife he had got from the kitchen. Harrison took out his .38, checked the cylinder for the four remaining rounds and snapped it closed again. Junya got up and went through to the kitchen. 'Gonna get some more water,' he said. 'I'll be right back.'

Across the float top where the land dissolved into mud and marsh and quicksand more deadly than any predator, a boat was moored to an oak tree. A single-seat pirogue, a shadow on the water. A figure sat in the prow very still and upright, a pump-action shotgun resting across his knees. Far in the distance he could hear the sound of a Lafitte skiff moving through the bayous.

Junya was gone a few minutes. Harrison checked the bandage on Marie's shoulder and wiped the perspiration where it had gathered again on her brow. He found an old blanket lying in one corner, shook it down and covered her up with it.

'You're doing OK,' he said. 'Try and sleep, we'll have you out of here in the morning.'

Marie reached for his hand. 'Thank you,' she said. 'I mean it, really. Thank you.'

Harrison smiled and stroked her hair, easing it back from where it fell across her eyes.

'Will things work out, do you think?' Fear stood out in her face now, her eyes sharp again where some of the fever had left her.

'Course they will.'

'I mean with the protection and immunity and everything.'

Harrison wrinkled his brow. 'I don't know, Marie. It depends what you can tell us. I guess it depends on what you've done.' He tried to smile. 'You both keep talking about immunity – immunity from what exactly?'

She opened her mouth as if she wanted to say something and then closed her eyes, the lids fluttering for a moment or two before she opened them again. 'Why were you on the tugboat?' she asked him.

'Because we're looking to nail Augustine for the boy in the bayou murder.'

Marie's eyes widened, and she looked beyond Harrison. He turned and saw Junya standing behind him. His face was cold and his eyes looked suddenly old beyond his years. Harrison stared at him for a moment then looked back at Marie, and he could see sleep overtaking her.

'Harrison,' Junya said softly. 'There's something I got to show you.'

He led the way to the side door and peered out again. Then Harrison followed him to the front of the camp where the floor was rotten, the door broken down and the windows punched out.

'We'll hear anybody coming that way for sure,' Harrison said. Junya nodded, took him by the arm and led him to the little kitchen. He paused to check on Marie and laid the knife down beside her just in case. In the kitchen he lit another oil lamp, and Harrison saw a propane burner, boxes of tinned food and crates of bottled water stacked against one wall.

'You hungry?' Junya said. 'We can eat.'

Harrison shook his head. 'What did you want to show me?'

For a moment Junya stood there as if deliberating with himself. Harrison waited, one ear listening for sounds of movement outside. Earlier he had thought he caught the note of a distant engine, but he might have been mistaken. Junya stared up at him then he bent and lifted a floorboard right at his feet. Harrison watched as he removed another and then another, and felt the pulse thicken at his temple. A short ladder led straight down to where more boards were laid across the mud. He could see mush and water seeping through the gaps. He closed his eyes, the breath caught in his throat and he was back in Cu Chi, staring down at a spider hole, which had been camouflaged from above. The hole was where two Viet Cong snipers had popped out of a tunnel and opened fire on a patrol, killing two young GIs. The rats had been summoned and Harrison was about to go down and investigate.

All at once he realized Junya was holding his hand – not just holding it, tugging it.

'Come on, we can't leave Marie for long. What's the matter with you?'

Harrison gazed listlessly for a second.

'You OK?'

No, he wasn't OK. Harrison was trembling and the sweat ran on his brow. Junya started down the ladder. Harrison regained himself and climbed down after him. The drop was no more than six feet and he could see that the boards were crudely thrown on the mud. He had to be careful where he put his feet.

And then he heard the whispers.

They came at him through the darkness, assaulting his senses, voices hushed yet there. And he heard another sound, this time from inside him, a single child crying. Junya flicked his lighter. Harrison blinked in the sudden glare of the flame then stood still and stared. Five yards ahead, hidden by the boards that had been built across the pilings, was a metal cage. Black-skinned hands gripped the bars and three pairs of eyes stared back at him.

thirty-five

Chaisson followed the wake from Laveaux's speedboat. He might be twice as fast, but if he left twice the wake you could follow it for miles. Chaisson had fished this area most of his life and he could read the signs. He held the tiller and twisted the throttle, riding right up the centre of the wake left by Laveaux. He followed him down the bayou till it opened into the bay and he headed south towards Grand Terre and the passes. Once out of the bayou the wake dissipated more quickly, but Chaisson could see Laveaux's lights racing south towards the oyster beds at Cat Bay. He followed, always watching the lights, aware that there was nothing to hit. The rigs were further east and anyone that could hit a platform in the dark shouldn't be out in a boat.

He moved south over the chop, the lights from the big rigs visible out in the gulf now, like low stars against the horizon. The wind had dropped, the front moving away, and there was no rain in the air, only the spray kicked up from the bows to lick his hands and face. He touched a toe against the pump-action sawn-off he still kept from his days with the Jefferson Parish sheriff. It was comforting, as was the Casull nuzzling his armpit under his windbreaker.

He eased back on the throttle as the lights from Laveaux's boat appeared to slow up ahead. They remained stationary long enough to get a bearing and then they died. Chaisson was piloting *his* boat with no lights, but the islands of the Grand Terre showed up as shadows now, lighter than the bay itself and directly under the moon. He moved closer and closer to where he thought the lights had been and then he killed his engine and waited, just bobbing with the roll of the waves.

He remained there for fifteen, perhaps twenty minutes before the lights came on again and the boat moved away from its mooring. Chaisson watched as it headed east for the bayou before shifting south. Laveaux was going to Grand Terre.

He was no longer bothered where Laveaux was going, however: he was much more interested in where he had just been. He could make out the grey hulk of the vessel through the darkness as he lifted the paddle from its housing. The new wake from the speedboat rippled out to rock him where he sat, and he waited in the darkness for silence to return. Then and only then did he dip his paddle into the waves.

Closer and closer he moved, working the small craft through the water till he came up alongside the bigger boat. Clearly now he could see the marque painted on the port quarter. *See More Night*. He had found Ignace's tugboat.

For a long time he sat in the dinghy, windward of the tug, watching the deck lights above his head. He heard no sound, saw no movement, nobody came out on deck, and all the time Chaisson had the sawn-off resting on his knees. When he was satisfied he paddled to the stern and caught the line, which hung down from the cable tie. He secured the dinghy then, using the line for leverage, climbed up on deck, with the shotgun stuffed inside his jacket. He halted at eye level to the gunwale, breath coming hard now, limbs trembling where he supported his two-hundred-and-thirty-pound frame. There was no sign of any movement on deck, nobody between him and the open door to the fiddley.

Chaisson had been on many tugboats in his time and he had been on this one, too. When Harrison had been taken on as a deckhand he had made his customary inspection as parole officer. He pulled himself up the last few feet and dropped on deck, hidden from view by the massive cable winch. He could smell oil and diesel now, though no engine vibrated under his feet. Sliding the Remington loose from his jacket, he held it in one hand and, crouching, crabbed his way across the deck.

At the door to the fiddley he halted and listened, hackles high. But he heard nothing. He could smell food, though. Somebody was cooking soft-shell crab in garlic, and Chaisson realized just how hungry he was. He heard the low tones of a radio playing somewhere above his head and he stepped inside the fiddley. The engine room was down the steps below him. He could smell salt water in the sump and oil thick in his nostrils. He moved to the door between the washer and drying machines. One man stood in the galley with his back to him, working away at his meal. Jimmy Mesa, the mate. Chaisson would know the back of his head anywhere. He had spoken to him a long time ago when he was working the boy in the bayou murder. He had spoken to lots of Laveaux's men and had got the same silence from all of them.

He drew himself up to his full height and very deliberately pumped a double-ought shell into the chamber of the shotgun. Mesa stiffened, then swung round with a kitchen knife in his hand. Chaisson looked at the knife then at his gun and finally into Mesa's eyes. 'You're not a betting man, are you, Jimmy,' he said.

thirty-six

Harrison stared at the cage, fighting the myriad images that flashed through his skull.

'Hey, mister, let us out of here.' The voice was small and frightened and it spoke English, which for some reason shocked him even more.

'Hey, Nonk. Let us out, man. Come on, you one of us, brother. Let us out before that Bernaud come back.'

Harrison saw the terror in the other faces as the name Bernaud was mentioned.

He gripped Junya's shoulder. 'Who is Bernaud?'

Junya didn't reply.

'Who the hell is Bernaud?'

Junya looked up at him, something ugly about his eyes now. 'He's one of Augustine's men. The jailer. He likes the perks that go with the job.'

Harrison stared at the cage. Three black children, all male, none of them more than twelve years old. They were crouched on rotting wooden boards, which were cracking over the float top. They reminded him of POWs in Vietnam: bent double, half-naked and terrible fear in their eyes. 'We've got to get them out of there,' Harrison said.

'You try if you want to. I ain't got no key.'

Harrison looked at the cage again. It was constructed of heavy ironwork, like that which they scrolled in the French Quarter, only naked and cruel and cold. 'Where is the key?'

'Bernaud's got it.'

'And where is Bernaud?'

Junya shook his head. 'I don't know. Sometimes he's here, sometimes he's not. He lives alone in the swamp.'

Harrison made his way along the loose boards to the cage where he bent down and gripped the bars with both hands. He tensed as if he meant to prise them apart and one of the boys gripped his fingers where they encircled the metal.

'Who are you?' Harrison asked him. 'What're you doing here?'

The boy didn't answer. The others didn't answer. They just blinked at him through the darkness.

'We've got to go back upstairs,' Junya said. 'We can't stay down here and we can't get them out without the key.' He moved to the bars. 'Y'all stay quiet now. We come to get you but y'all got to wait a bit longer.'

'Why you bring us here, anyway, you fucker?' the first boy snarled through the bars.

Harrison was staring at Junya, who lifted a hand to silence the speaker. 'Yo' stay quiet now, y'hear.' He pointed at Harrison. 'Me and him got to figure out what we're gonna do. If y'all make a noise you'll bring Bernaud back and none of us will get out. You hear what I'm saying – Bernaud will come and kill you.' He took hold of Harrison's arm. 'Come on. We got to get back to Marie.'

Harrison didn't know what to think. A part of him wanted to blast away at the lock with his .38 till those boys were free, but he knew that would bring everything down on top of them. The whispered sound of their voices haunted his thoughts as he went back up the ladder and Junya reset the boards. They stood together in the little kitchen and Harrison looked him squarely in the eye. 'So now I know why you want immunity,' he said.

Junya shook his head. 'No, you don't.'

Marie was soundless on the couch and Junya looked down at her with fear in his eyes till Harrison indicated the rise and fall of her chest. They stood side by side and watched her for a moment then Junya went to the front windows and peered through broken shards of glass dusted with spiders' webs. He listened to the frogs and the cicadas and pricked his ears to listen for anything else.

Harrison moistened a piece of cloth and dabbed at Marie's forehead where perspiration prickled. Junya sat down at the table and took out a cigarette. It was soaking wet and he just sat there picking at the threads of tobacco. Harrison sat down at the table with him. He took a watertight tin from his back pocket and set it before Junya then he took the .38 from his ankle rig and set that down also. Junya took the tobacco makings and rolled two cigarettes, one of which he handed to Harrison. 'They picked me up on the levee by Audobon Park,' he began.

Dusk was falling when he fled the scene of Wendell's murder on Canal Street. February, and the bleachers were out on St Charles Avenue in readiness for the parades: Fat Tuesday was another fertile time for an eleven-year-old kid who hadn't seen the inside of a school in years. He had been looking forward to it, discussing the possibilities with Wendell. Wendell had 'owned' the bricks on two blocks of the Iberville, but Wendell had just got his head blown off and now those 'bricks' were open.

Junya had been packing since he was seven years old, but wasn't packing today. The cops in this part of town were very serious, what with headquarters being in the Garden District. He never carried a piece in this part of town and certainly not when his gang leader just got wasted. He could talk his way out of most situations or use his knife, or he could run if he really had to.

He met the crack whore outside the park: she was quite pretty and she talked to him in a way that reminded him of his mother. She tottered along on high heels and tried to climb the levee by The Leake. She said she had never seen it and there the city was so much lower than the river, or so she had been told, and she really wanted to climb it. But she was high as a kite and her laugh was almost maniacal, just like his mother's had been, and for some reason Junya helped her up. Darkness was complete by then and a thick fog curled in from the river, casting the levee grey and hazy, softened only by the orange glow of lights from the street behind them. The crack whore slipped on her backside, legs in the air. She laughed out loud and Junya sat down beside her.

Then she fumbled in her purse, looking for a cigarette, and pulled out a one-inch .38.

'Now keep yo' mouth shut and do exactly what I tell you,' she said.

Junya looked at the gun. 'Whatever you say, lady. What click you run with anyway?'

'I don't run with no click.'

'What's yo' name?'

'Marie . . . Never mind my damn name.'

'What you gonna do – rob me? If you do that, I'll find you and kill you.' He looked her in the eye. She drew back the hammer.

'OK, rob me if you want to. I won't come looking for you.'

A boat drifted up to the levee barely visible in the fog: it was full of black women like Marie. She prodded him with the pistol. 'Get yo' ass over there, honey. And be quick about it.'

He sat in the boat surrounded by half a dozen crack whores, heading for the big ships. Junya knew most cops turned a blind eye to the traffic – some of them were on a kickback and it saved bringing lots of drunken sailors into the city. There was a man driving, a big guy with the dark hair and skin of a Cajun. He took them out into the middle of the river where a skiff drew alongside. The women pushed Junya to the gunwales. Another Cajun man wearing a Confederate flag bandana on his head reached down for him. As he was hauled on board Junya looked back at Marie and just for a moment he could see the sadness deep in her eyes.

The man in the bandana ran his hands over him, took the knife and the roll of money from his pockets then pressed him down on the floor. A mile or so further on they came alongside a tugboat that was moored next to some rusting lash barges off on the west bank. The boy was hoisted over the side.

Before he knew what was happening somebody had picked him up and marched him inside the boat. A tall Cajun with a thin, rasping voice inspected him as if he were an animal. He reached inside the boy's shirt and broke the chain from round his neck with the ring his mother had given him attached to it. The boy looked at him, looked at the chain, but said nothing. He was thinking hard and fast and noting every detail of the tall man's face. The man pocketed the ring, placed a hand on his shoulder and turned him around and around. He crouched and looked in his eyes, then ran his hands down his flanks and Junya felt his flesh pucker and a sickness clog in his gut. The man straightened up again then marched him to the bows and the open cargo hold.

'Climb on down and keep your mouth shut.' He took out his knife and showed Junya the serrated edge of the blade. 'You make one sound and I open you up like a kang.' He made a rending motion like a tin being opened and lifted the boy on to the ladder. Junya climbed down, stepped on to what felt like a coil of rope and immediately fell over. Somebody kicked him where he lay then a match flared and a dozen pairs of eyes peered at him through the darkness.

Junya looked across the table at Harrison. 'They come from all over,' he said. 'Always black kids like me and always from close to the Mississippi. Some of them couldn't remember when they'd been taken, but they'd been on the boat for ages, on another boat before that and another before that. I reckon the youngest was about seven and the oldest about my age. This was three years ago.'

Harrison stared at him. 'How old were you then?'

'About eleven, I guess. Maybe ten, I don't know. Ain't never had a birthday.'

He had no idea how long he stayed in that cargo hold, but it was hot and sweaty, a dozen of them crammed together among the ropes and boxes, the only air that which came through the vents in the engine-room bulkhead. It was dark all the time, so he had no concept of night or day: they were given some bread to eat and water to drink at odd intervals. One boy kept crying and there was no way anyone could shut him up. One of the crew stuck his head down the hatch and warned him but he just wouldn't stop, then a crewman with a sock-style hat hanging down his back climbed down and carried him off. They never saw him again.

Some time later, after Junya had slept for a while, he felt the revs drop right off and the tugboat shuddered to a halt, with water slapping against the steelwork of the hull. He looked above his head as a mallet thumped the turnkeys that secured the hatch and saw moonlight in the sky, way above the deck. The boys were ordered out of the cargo hold and placed in flat-bottomed skiffs that had run up along-side. The thin-faced man with the rasping voice got in another skiff ahead of them.

Then they were racing through the night, deep into the swamp, and he had no idea where. The skiff slowed as they got into the narrower channels, leaving the main water and man-made canals behind. The moon was high overhead and the night as still as glass, not cold as some nights were in winter but warm and sickly, the air thick with the sound of frogs calling each other to mate. Up ahead he saw the dim lights of a fishing camp and the shape of three men standing on the deck that ran all the way around. Two of them he saw clearly, but the third disappeared into the shadows as the skiffs drew alongside.

The twelve black boys were herded like slaves then forced up a gangplank to the deck. Another Cajun, even taller than the one with the rasping voice, ushered them inside. A scar split his cheek from eyebrow to jawbone.

Inside, the camp was one long room with a low ceiling and chairs pushed back, a raised alcove separated by a handrail right at the back. The scar-faced man stepped into the shadows of the alcove as if he was talking with someone. The boys were shunted into the middle of the floor and Junya looked round at each and every one of their faces. His heart was pounding, his bladder full, and he could see no way of escaping. At the alcove two other men leaned with their backs to the rail. They looked Spanish, maybe from South America somewhere, fat faces, one with a drooping moustache, the other clean-shaven but his cheeks indented with pocks. Junya looked at them and they looked back at him, sizing him up like livestock.

The Cajun with the rasping voice came over and told them to take their clothes off. He crouched in front of the smallest boy who had tears brimming in his eyes. 'Cut that out or I'll kill you.'

None of them moved right away. Junya stood behind two others out of view of the South Americans. Then a man stepped out of the shadows as if to get a better look. He was white with greying hair, oiled back from his forehead. He wore a well-cut grey suit and gold cufflinks in the shape of the fleur-de-lis. He was no more than ten feet from Junya, only visible for an instant then melting back in the shadows as if someone else beckoned him. Junya watched and saw a hand grip the rail – the same white cuff, the same gold cufflinks.

'Take you damn clothes off, you little mother.' The voice scratched in his ear. Junya looked at the Cajun and saw a length of cheese wire with two wooden handles hanging from a hook on his belt.

Naked, they stood shivering in the sudden cold: twelve young black boys not yet at puberty but each one of them holding both hands over his genitals. Junya watched as the two South Americans moved among them, looking them over like cattle at an auction. A voice he hadn't heard before rose from the shadowed section at the back. It was low and flat-toned and full of lust. 'They're perfect for you. Right now they're pretty, but if they ever grow up they'll breed and kill.' He paused then added, 'Bring that one over to me.'

Junya watched as the small boy who had been crying was taken into the alcove. His heart bumped against his ribs. The man with the wire was standing against the wall nearest him, his hands on his hips. Junya heard the young boy squeal, then he was aware of one of the South American men standing right behind him. The man took his arm and turned him where he stood; he looked him up and down as if trying to find a defect.

Junya knew he had to do something: there was no other way out of this. Steeling himself, he swaggered over to the man with the rasping voice and the wire.

'This is bullshit,' he hissed.

The man looked down at him. 'What?'

'I'm saying this is bullshit.' Junya threw out a hand. 'Call this a scam? Fuck, I could do better in the projects with a dozen cops looking over my shoulder.' He leaned against the wall, still naked but with his hands behind his back. 'So far I seen you and them.' He pointed to the South Americans. 'I seen yo' boat and two more of yo' crew. I seen about a half-dozen crack whores and a guy taking them out to the ships. What kinda bullshit is that?'

The man was frowning now. 'What you talking about?'

'I'm talking about how visible this is, man. Some of them boys tell me they come from way the fuck up north. They all seen you just like I have. Takes just one kid to get away and yo' whole operation is blown the fuck outa the water.'

The man was staring at him.

'Why you use crack whores, man? Because they girls?' Junya shook his head. 'A crack whore gonna be the first to snitch. They sell their own mother for the price of a rock, especially if they getting beat on by a cop.' He shook his head. 'What yo' need is a kid. You want to steal kids? Get yo'self a tame one, mister. Let him do the stealing for you. That way all yo' got is one face. Then if one get away that's the face you close up for the night. You hear what I'm saying to you?'

The man looked at him for a long moment, one eyebrow heavily arched, then he pushed himself away from the wall. 'Wait here,' he said, and disappeared into the shadows. Moments later he reappeared with the scar-faced man. He crouched down and looked Junya in the eye. 'You sound like you want to trade,' he said. 'I like a man who likes to trade.' He swept the room with his hand. 'That's what we got here, a little trade going on. You want to be that kid you told my cousin about just now?'

'Sure I do.'

'Then what you got to trade with, Junya?'

'That's when I got my name.' Junya relit his cigarette. Harrison sat on the other side of the table from him with his arms folded, his face grave. A fishing camp, twelve naked boys and a Cajun with a cheese wire.

'The first one was Ignace,' Junya said, 'the other Augustine. The South Americans, I don't know names, but they're Colombian and they got the cocaine scam going, like I told you, mixed in with coffee and that.'

Coffee again: something about coffee in Harrison's head, something he had seen. The fleur-de-lis stamped on the sides of crates lining the dock. He looked back at Junya. 'What happened then?' he asked.

*

Ignace crouched beside him and let his fingers trail his spine. Junya tried not to squirm. He looked at the other boys, trembling and sobbing in their turn, eleven of them paraded like naked buck slaves before a purchasing crowd.

'These niggers are going south,' Ignace said. 'I mean way south. You understand what I'm saying?'

Junya nodded.

'All except that one.' Ignace pointed to the smallest boy, the one who had been taken into the shadows, the one who had been crying. 'He's too small. *Tros petit*, you dig?' Then he handed Junya the length of cheese wire. 'You do a good job now, boy, and we'll see if we can trade.'

He moved back to the wall and waited till the South Americans had finished looking over their stock then the room descended once more into silence. All Junya could hear were the night birds calling from outside and the slight creak of boards when somebody shifted their weight. He could smell the mud and tannin from the swamp, the aroma of humus disturbed from the bed of the bayou by a paddle or an alligator or just the shifting current. Ignace nodded to him and before he could think about what he was doing he had crept up behind the smallest boy and slipped the razor-sharp wire round his neck.

He crossed the wooden handles over one another and jerked down hard. The boy gagged and choked, hands to his throat, the fingers coming away bloody. Junya hauled on the wire for all he was worth, closing his eyes, limbs trembling, muscles quivering involuntarily. The wire bit deeply and easily. The boy was lifted up on his toes and his back pressed against Junya. Blood spurted from his neck, tumbling over Junya's hands. He twisted so hard his arms shook. Opening his eyes, he gazed beyond the dying boy to the shadows. One last strain on his wrists and the boy was just nerves twitching. As he went limp, Junya let go and he slid to the ground, the blood hot and wet where it formed a pool at his feet.

*

Harrison sat with his chin on his chest and his eyes closed.

'Those other kids,' Junya went on. 'They was loaded on to a skiff and they gone.' He sucked on his cigarette. 'They were taken to the mother ship and then to Colombia. Ignace told me they were going to make movies.'

Harrison looked up at him.

'Just one each, mind.' Junya rested his chin in his palm. 'Ignace told me how much money those films make, how much more they're worth when little black Sambo squeals in English before they snuff him out.' He pressed his fingertips together as if he was putting out a candle.

Harrison stared at him and Junya stared back, only his eyes seemed dull and listless, sightless for a moment as he looked through his own dirty window on to the past.

'What about you?' Harrison said. 'What happened to you?'

Junya made an open-handed gesture. 'Here I am, brother. Setting in camp with you.'

'How many have you taken since then?'

'You mean lured away from the street, you mean stolen, Harrison?' Junya rolled his eyes. 'I don't know, thirty maybe.'

'From New Orleans?'

'No, not from New Orleans – only one or two from there. I been all over. The furthest north they sent me was somewhere near St Louis.' He spat a tobacco thread on the floor. 'I'm the Pied Piper, Harrison. A whole fucking procession of them.'

'How did you bring them down here?'

'We'd load them in the van and drive. Sometimes they'd go on one of the other tugboats, but they all ended up here. Bernaud watches over them till they're shipped out in batches.' He let breath hiss from his cheeks. 'It ain't a big deal to Laveaux, just a sweetener for the cocaine. He gets the best price and nobody else gets supplied. There ain't no coke in New Orleans that don't start out with Laveaux.'

Harrison moved to the couch and gazed down at Marie's closed eyes. It felt strangely unreal: after three long years he knew who had murdered the boy in the bayou. It wasn't Augustine Laveaux at all. Junya had killed him: this young kid from the projects, sitting here in the middle of the swamp and asking for immunity.

'So now you know,' Junya said, as he sat down again.' I only did it to save my own life. I been a prisoner ever since, the only one they have to get rid of if something goes wrong.' He flicked dirt from his fingernails. 'And now something has. I took that Bentley kid and he was the wrong kid. But I let him go, Harrison. And I had the balls to call you out when I did. I been looking for you ever since I kilt that boy in the camp. I wanted out. I wanted a reg'lar life. I don't want to be no dealer, no hustler, no child-stealer no more. I want off the street, I want to try and grow up without getting shot in the back of the head.' He crushed out his cigarette. 'I got proof of who is involved. I got a sketchbook with all their pictures in it. I can draw, see. I'm good. I drew you when I saw you in the Iberville. I drew everybody who was in that camp. I drew Ignace and Augustine and the one guy with the cufflinks.'

'Where's the book?'

'I got it safe. You get me immunity and I get you the book. Then you put me on the stand and I give you everybody. Marie gonna back up my story.'

Harrison was staring at him but didn't see him. Outside he could hear something, but he couldn't place what it was. Junya knelt beside Marie. 'This is the Marie who was on the levee with me,' he said. 'Augustine give me to her to keep an eye on. She got herself clean and stopped turning tricks, almost become like a momma. I want her out and I want me out, Harrison. That's why I been talking to you.'

Harrison wasn't listening. He stood at the table, his

fingers tightening about the grips of his .38. He knew what
he could hear now, the faint noise a paddle makes when it's
dipped into the bayou.

thirty-seven

Chaisson used his old Jefferson Parish handcuffs to secure Jimmy Mesa to the leg of the table. It was fixed to the floor and Mesa had to sit down with his arms stretched in front of him.

'There ain't nobody else on board,' he said. 'Don't you think I'd holler if there was?'

'Where's Harrison?'

Mesa didn't reply. Chaisson pursed his lips as if he had a sudden bad taste in his mouth then he kicked Mesa hard in the stomach. 'Think on that,' he said, and climbed the steps to the bridge. He used the VHF to call the Coastguard who patched him through to the Black Hawk and Matt Penny. He gave them the location of the tugboat and by the time he went back down the steps he could hear the chopper's engine in the distance.

'That's the FBI,' he told Mesa. 'You in a lot of trouble, boy.'

'I ain't in no damn trouble. Y'all the one that's in trouble. You wait till I tell Augustine's lawyers how you cuff me and kick me. Your boy done run off is what he done. What the fuck you expect? You was hauling his ass back to jail.'

Chaisson shook his head. 'Jimmy, do me a favour and shut up with your bullshit. Try and talk sense now and tell me where Ignace took Harrison.'

Mesa glowered at him but said nothing. Chaisson

brought the butt of his shotgun down on to his instep. Mesa screamed in pain.

'You hear that chopper, Jimmy? That's a bunch of ex-soldiers all pumped up and ready to go. Think what they're going to do with all that adrenalin when you start blowing smoke up their collective ass.'

Mesa's face was flushed red at the jaw, his eyes bunched tight. He let go a stiff breath and tried to sit up without banging his head on the underside of the table.

'Where are they, Jimmy? Where'd Ignace take Harrison?'

'Harrison lit out. I told you that already.'

Chaisson shifted the shotgun from one hand to the other. Outside, the sound of the chopper was louder than ever. He glanced at the clock set alongside the barometer on the wall. Nearly four in the morning: he was tired and he was hungry. Harrison was out there somewhere, maybe dead already, and here he was wasting time with a piece of shit like Jimmy Mesa.

He went on deck, a hunk of French bread in his hand as the chopper hovered lower and lower. Two fast ropes dropped at the same time and two black-suited FBI agents slid to the deck, followed quickly by two more. The first two, crouching, levelled carbines at him with red-dot laser sights criss-crossing his chest. Penny put his weapon up and took off his ballistic helmet. 'Any sign of Harrison?'

Chaisson shook his head. Above them the chopper hovered, the downdraft blowing a hole in the water. Chaisson led the way into the galley and Mesa looked up at the four heavily armed agents in full combat gear. Penny looked down at him and spat tobacco juice in the sink.

'He the only one here?' he said.

Chaisson nodded. 'Spinning me a line that my parolee took off for Mexico.'

'Is he now?' Penny looked at Mesa again who was looking less sure of himself. 'You figure he knows where the rest of the crew took him?'

'Yep.' Chaisson hefted the sawn-off so the barrel rested against his shoulder.

'I tell you what, Bill,' Penny said. 'Give him five seconds to tell you and if he doesn't – pop him. Nobody's gonna hear you. As far as I'm concerned, we never saw him. None of the crew were on board when we got here.'

'Sounds fair to me.' Chaisson looked at Mesa. 'What say, Jimmy? Sound like a plan to you?'

Mesa was staring at Penny.

Penny winked at Chaisson. 'See you back in New Orleans.' He walked out on deck and told the winch man to stand by in the Black Hawk.

Chaisson already had a round racked in the Remington. He held it in one hand, unclipped Mesa from the table leg and marched him on deck. Penny had his back to them; the other agents leaned on the gunwales with their weapons easy. The helicopter was two hundred feet above them again. Chaisson marched Mesa past the winch and made him duck under the cable and the rope that lashed it down in the stern. Then he told him to stop and with one hand on his shoulder raised the barrel to the back of his head.

'Last chance, Jimmy. I don't give a fuck if you live or die. No one will know the difference.' He fired the round over the top of Mesa's head and the man fell to the deck with his hands covering his ears.

'OK. OK. I'll tell you,' he cried.

thirty-eight

Junya saw the first shadow melt into the float top close to where they had moored the boat. 'We got to get out of here,' he said. 'They'll pick us off, no problem.'

'We can't,' Harrison told him. 'We leave and those boys below are dead.' He was thinking hard – only the .38 and four rounds between them. 'You can get outside from down by that cage, can't you?'

Junya nodded.

'OK.' Harrison handed him the gun. 'Stay with Marie. If they come in, shoot them. Can you do that?'

Junya curled his lip. 'What do you think?'

Harrison left him and went into the kitchen where he took a carving knife from the drawer. Lifting the floorboards, he slithered down the ladder till his feet touched the wooden planks below. He felt his way to the cage. 'Any of you guys make so much as a sound we're all dead,' he whispered. 'If you're quiet I might just be able to get you out of here.'

He didn't wait for a reply, but worked his way across the boards, beyond the cage to the front of the camp where the planks dropped eight feet from the veranda. He moved on the balls of his feet, taking care with each step, testing the boards for sound and stability where they were laid directly over the mud. The darkness wasn't total – the moon was out and pale slivers of light found gaps here and there, aiding visibility. He paused halfway across as he thought he heard a voice through the darkness. It was a hoarse whisper that might have been close and might have been far away, the sound amplified by the water. He recognized it, though. Ignace.

At the front of the camp he put his eye to a gap in the boards. At first he could see nothing. The field of vision was limited and he had to move his head to see in any kind of an arc. He made out the twisted trunks of trees, the thatched palmetto growing round the live oaks, the grey nature of the muddy float top and beyond it the dark ribbons of water. Frogs croaked, cicadas called, lending a deeper intensity to the night. Then he saw somebody move out from between the trees.

They would fan out. He figured there were only three of them, maybe four if they had hooked up with the man called Bernaud. But they would fan out and come at the camp from different directions. One man was making his way towards the front, only fifteen yards away, picking a careful and silent path between the cypress and the oak.

The trees were thin and tall and ragged, palmetto and bunch grass growing between them making it even more difficult to see. Harrison only had a knife in his belt and there were four guns against him. Two would flank the house and one would work his way round to the back. He decided to take out the one man he could see. If he could take his rifle he had a chance with the others.

There was a gap in the boards to his right, which would give him room to manoeuvre round behind the assailant. He bent to the mud and caked his face and torso where he wore no shirt. Then he moved with stealth, crossing under the camp on the balls of his feet, being careful where he stepped. He paused for a moment then slipped outside and felt the breath of the night on his face.

The faintest of breezes had risen now, fluttering the moss and rustling the topmost branches of the trees. Harrison was outside and side-on to the man in front of the camp. He had stopped, was standing still with the rifle levelled at hip height. Harrison froze in the lee of an oak tree so no image would be cast by the moonlight. The man was listening and Harrison listened too and heard the slop of heavy feet in the mud right behind him. He remained absolutely motionless, watching the man in front who was looking directly at him now, or at least his head was twisted that way. Silently Harrison slid the carving knife from his belt and held it close to his leg so the blade wouldn't reflect the moonlight.

He could hear breathing now, heavy, laboured breathing, and the feet in the mud were so close they were almost upon him. He dared not move, dared not turn his head even a fraction. The man in front stayed motionless, facing him so the weapon was lost in the bulk of his shadow. If he fired he would hit Harrison for sure and Harrison had no idea whether he had been spotted or not.

Gumbo moved alongside him, stopping within a foot of where Harrison was melted against the tree trunk. He peered into the gloom, looking towards the front of the camp like a man who was lost. His breath was sticky and stiff, coming almost in a grunt. The mud squelched as his boots sank into it.

Harrison rammed the knife into his chest with all the force he could muster. Gumbo cried out like a child. The other man fired and Gumbo was lifted off his feet, toppling back into a trainasse that cut the float top. Harrison rolled to one side and lay in the mud, hidden by palmetto and bunch grass. He could see Gumbo's fallen gun, the glint of blue metal as the barrel stuck up from the mud. It was sinking slowly, the stock already embedded. He didn't want a weapon with its barrels jammed with mud. He reached for it, fingers brushing the cool metal. It came loose with a wet sucking sound and he fell back against the tree trunk.

Carefully now he worked himself round the back of the oak tree so he was facing away from the house. He inspected the weapon in the moonlight: a pump-action shotgun. The odds were evening up. Then he heard the man in front of the camp head for the shelter of the boards.

Harrison cursed under his breath. If he got to the cage first he would kill those children.

Junya had stayed close to the front windows where he picked out the man making stealthy progress directly up from the bayou. He knew who it was: he would recognize that waddling gait in the deepest blanket of darkness. Bernaud, the one who liked to avail himself of the boys locked in the cage. It was why Laveaux kept him on guard. He would do anything to keep that particular job and for three years nobody had got within a mile of the camp without Bernaud redirecting them. He barely spoke, gave nothing away and knew every trainasse, every alligator hole in the bayou. Junya saw him moving towards the house. He heard somebody cry out and Bernaud fired into the darkness.

Junya looked round at Marie.

Podjo held a pistol against her temple.

Ignace stood in the kitchen doorway.

thirty-nine

Harrison moved back to the camp. Already the man in front was at the boards and moving round to the right where Harrison had seen more gaps. He moved left, carefully checking for any signs of the others. One down, three to go, and now he had a weapon.

He eased through the gap in the boards and was under the camp before the other man, which gave him the advantage. His heart was thumping in his chest and he could feel every muscle, every sinew working. He was aware of each movement, no matter how tiny, every minuscule sound, just as he had been thirty years ago. Now he waited, listening, watching, his eyesight good in the darkness. He could sense movement on the far side of the camp. A gap in the boards shadowed as somebody turned sideways and slipped through. Harrison had moved left, making sure his body didn't block the grey of the gap, as he had just witnessed. Above his head he heard the fall of heavy feet.

'Harrison.' Ignace's rasping voice peeled across the bayou. The man under the camp stopped moving and listened. Harrison was in a crouch ten feet from him, unseen in the gloom.

'We got the boy, Harrison.'

'Ignace.' Harrison heard the man mumble the name in the darkness. He lowered his weapon to his side and fumbled in his pocket for keys.

Harrison racked the Remington. 'Make the wrong move and I'll put a hole in you the size of Alaska.'

The man was half-bent, weapon at his side, the keys dangling from his hand. Harrison had the shotgun trained on the very middle of his shadow. 'Don't even think about it,' he whispered. 'I got nothing at all to lose.'

He could see the man's eyes now, the flat, square face in the shadows. He could see the pale skin at the sides of his head where the hair was shaved above his ears. This had to be Bernaud.

Bernaud let his weapon fall to the mud but still held the set of keys. Harrison moved at a crouch and pressed the barrel of the shotgun against his balls. 'Unlock the cage.'

'Harrison.' Ignace's voice came again, louder this time, straining the vocal cords where he shouted.

'Unlock the cage.' Harrison dug the barrel deeper into Bernaud's groin, and the man bent to the lock and opened the door of the cage. Harrison motioned for the three young boys to come out. They did, soundlessly. He then ushered the Cajun inside and locked the door. Now he bent for the fallen weapon: a Magnum hunting rifle, good for at least six hundred yards. He looked at the tallest boy, who stared back, his face no longer frightened, eyes wide and blinking.

'I guess you know how to use this,' Harrison said.

The boy stared at Bernaud. 'On him? Are you kidding me?'

Harrison handed the gun to him. 'If he makes a sound shoot him.'

'You bet.' The boy hefted the gun and aimed it at Bernaud's chest.

Ignace's voice came again from above their heads. 'You Yankee asshole, you got ten seconds to come out then I slit the boy's throat.'

Harrison passed the shotgun to the second boy who followed him across the boards to the gap on the left-hand side of the camp. 'I've got to go up there,' Harrison said, pointing above his head. 'You go outside, count two minutes then start pumping rounds over the top of the camp. Can you do that?'

The boy held the weapon like a veteran. 'Oh, yeah,' he said. 'Just a pity it ain't a chopper.'

Harrison smiled and stepped outside again. A chopper was street slang for an AK47, the preferred weapon in the projects of New Orleans. He stood in front of the camp with the knife in his belt at the back. 'Ignace,' he called. 'Ignace.'

He saw someone step across the broken window. At the same time the boy with the Remington moved behind an oak tree. 'I'm coming in,' Harrison called out, and with his hands flat on his head he made his way round to the back of the camp.

Podjo stood at the door with an automatic resting over the crook of his arm. He moved back to let Harrison up the steps then pushed him into the room. Harrison stumbled, and as he regained his feet Podjo whipped the knife from his belt. Ignace sat at the table with Junya directly across from him, the .45 pointed at his chest.

'You enjoy youself out here?' Ignace said coldly.

Harrison didn't say anything.

'You led us quite a dance. You know, I figured you was fonchock the first time I clap eyes on you. You fooled Augustine, but you don't fool me.' His eyes darkened. 'Where's Bernaud?'

'Bernaud's dead. So's Gumbo.' Harrison jerked a thumb at the blood on the blade of the knife.

Ignace curled his lip. 'You should've lit out, brother, taken the pirogue and gone. You give youself up for a boy and a crack whore?' He nodded to where Marie lay prostrate on the couch. 'That don't make sense to me.'

Harrison just stared at him.

Ignace got up. 'You still think you got a chance but you don't.' He gestured at Marie and the boy. 'When I kill them,

333

you got nothing. And when I kill you, you buddies at the FBI got nothing.'

'That's true.' Harrison said. 'But you know what, Ignace? They're going to know what went down here just the same. Your life – your cousin's life – ain't gonna be worth a rat's ass.' He leered at him. 'It's almost worth dying just to think how they'll come for you.'

Podjo was standing close behind Harrison, and Harrison was counting down the seconds in his head, just as he hoped the young kid was, out there by the oak tree. Dawn would be breaking soon: already the darkness was thinner and the night had that chill of death just before sunrise.

Ignace looked at him and shook his head. 'Say you goodbyes to Junya.' He raised the .45 and put it against the boy's temple. 'I'd like to take more time over this, but it's getting light outside.'

'Ignace.' Marie's voice was weak and sounded lost, but her eyes were open and she lay with one hand under the blanket. 'Ignace,' she whispered again, and the Cajun looked round.

'Hold on a minute, honey, I'm coming to you next.'

'Ignace.' She called more urgently this time and he cursed, lowered the hammer on the .45 and got up. 'Set there,' he said to Junya. 'I'll be right back.' He grinned at Podjo, and bent low over the couch. 'What is it, baby? I got one for you, too.' He showed Marie the barrel of the gun. Marie smiled at him, her eyes suddenly shining. Ignace leaned closer to kiss her and she brought up her fist with all the force she could muster.

Harrison heard the clunk as it thumped bone.

A shotgun blast ripped through the rafters.

Harrison heel-kicked Podjo in the groin. He doubled up and lost his grip on the rifle. Harrison punched him as hard as he could in the face. Another round burst above their heads and Harrison grabbed Podjo's fallen rifle, turned to the couch and saw Ignace, standing upright, his gun hand loose and trembling at his side. The knife that Junya had given Marie was embedded to the hilt in his sternum. Blood pulsed from the wound in gobs, and the expression in Ignace's eyes was one of complete surprise.

Harrison flipped the rifle in his hand so he held the barrel, and with one smooth action he hit Ignace full in the jaw. The bone splintered and Ignace was on his knees, his jaw smashed, teeth on his lip, bits of bone and tissue hanging over the broken skin and blood spotting the wooden floor. Harrison pointed the rifle at Podjo's head now, and Podjo looked on as Ignace swayed a little then slumped forward and lay on the hilt of the knife.

forty

Harrison sat on the deck as the sun lifted over the bayou and the cypress whispered in the breeze where it grew straight up from the water. He watched a great blue heron stalking fish on long spindly legs before settling on a single broken tree limb. Penny came out of the camp, talking on the radio, and above their heads the Black Hawk hovered and the cable was lowered for the stretcher.

The SWAT team medics had patched Marie up as best they could and she was strapped on a stretcher, waiting for the cradle to take her up to the chopper.

Harrison drew cigarette smoke into his lungs and held it before exhaling stiffly. Junya came over to where the stretcher was being hooked up and took Marie's hand. He looked in her eyes, smoothed the skin of her face and glanced at Harrison. They both watched as the winch man hauled the stretcher back to the chopper.

'They ain't taking her to Charity Hospital, are they?' Junya said. 'She deserves better than that.'

Penny shook his head. 'This is Jefferson Parish, son. They'll take her to the Memorial.'

Junya went back to where the other kids were squatting on a log, sharing smokes and talking.

Penny sat down next to Harrison.

'You were late,' Harrison said.

'I'm always late, man, you know that.' Penny nodded to

the kids on the log. 'Besides, I don't think it mattered. You had quite the army here.'

Harrison leaned back on his elbows and let the sun play across his face. He looked through the trees where the sun reflected off the bayou and the water shimmered in bands of white gold. He saw a trout jump and the ripples expanded to brush the reeds at the float top. Sweat pooled in the hollows above his collarbones. His shirt had gone with Marie. Junya was staring at him and Harrison stared back, thinking of the pictures of the boy in the bayou with the cheese wire cutting his throat.

'So what happened exactly?' Penny nodded to Junya. 'We know that kid was stealing throw-aways for Laveaux. But that's it so far.'

Harrison put out his cigarette. 'I'm tired, Matthew. We'll talk back in New Orleans.'

The other members of the SWAT team had taken their gear off now and were resting in the shadows cast by the old fishing camp. Podjo and Bernaud were sitting back to back under an oak tree, their hands cuffed together, one agent watching them with a carbine across his chest. They were waiting for the Coastguard cutter to pick them up.

Penny had told Harrison that the mate of the *See More Night* had spilled his guts when Chaisson fired the round over his head. He had given up the location and with a bit of persuasion the rest of the story would be gleaned from him and the other members of the crew.

'I wouldn't count on that,' Harrison said. 'He might have given up where we were at, but he won't be spilling any more about the family.' He glanced at Junya once again. 'He's the witness, Matthew, the main man. He's the one they want dead. I tell you I never met a kid like him and I hope I don't again.' He tapped the ash from his cigarette. 'What's happened to Laveaux anyway?'

'We sent the rest of the team to Grand Terre and put the stack into his place on the beach.' Penny spat juice. 'Got zip,

337

Harrison. He'd cleaned the place out. His boat was gone and so was he. No sign of him anywhere. Probably halfway to Mexico by now.'

Chaisson arrived in a skiff to take them to the bay where the cutter was waiting. Junya sat in silence a little apart from the other boys and watched Harrison as he stood at the pilot's console.

Late that afternoon they landed back in New Orleans. Deputies from Jefferson Parish, together with welfare officers, had already taken charge of the three boys who had been incarcerated, but Junya insisted on staying with Harrison.

'I want to go see Marie,' he said. 'And you and me got to talk.' Both of them were exhausted. The Coastguard dropped them below the harbour police headquarters at the Third Street Wharf. The special agent in charge was there and he took Harrison to one side. 'Are you OK, John? You took a hell of a risk out there.'

Harrison made a face. 'I had one chance, Charlie. I took it.'

Mayer laid a hand on his shoulder. 'We'll talk later. I'm just glad we got you out in one piece.'

Harrison lit a cigarette. 'We smashed the Cajun Mafia, Charlie. Make sure you tell them in Washington.'

Mayer put his hands in his pockets and gazed across the muddied chop of the Mississippi, towards the broken-down west bank wharfs where two rusted hulks of cranes dominated the skyline. 'I've been talking to police departments up and down the river,' he said. 'This thing is making a lot of sense to a whole lot of people right now. How many kids did they take?'

Harrison shrugged. 'Thirty maybe.' He looked across the wharf to where Junya was watching him. 'Laveaux is still out there,' he said. 'He'll be coming after the boy.'

Mayer nodded. 'Jimmy Mesa is blaming Ignace. According to him, Ignace ran the show. Augustine had nothing to do with it.'

'That figures. Blame the dead guy and leave the living to come after the only person who can testify against them.' Harrison flipped away his cigarette. 'The kid says he's got drawings, sketches of everyone involved. Pictures, Charlie, faces. He hasn't told me where, but he told me they were safe. He says they're good enough for us to identify people and indict them.' He looked at Junya once more. 'I want to keep him with me.'

'He needs to be in protective custody, John.'

'He will be – mine. Laveaux can reach out to a lot of people in this part of the world. We found that out with Call. I want Junya close. That way I know he'll be safe.'

Mayer thought for a moment. 'We'll talk about it. Right now I guess both of you could use some sleep.'

'Get us a room in the Parc St Charles,' Harrison said. 'Post a guard on the door if you want to.'

forty-one

Laveaux stood on the steps of the Shell Oil building on Poydras and St Charles, watching as two black Chevrolet Suburbans pulled up outside the Hotel Parc St Charles. A streetcar came to a halt at the stop below him and he joined the queue. Climbing aboard, he dropped some money into the slot by the driver and made his way to the rear of the carriage. He stood holding the strap above his head as they clanked across Poydras. He saw the Feds on the sidewalk. Harrison was with them: he would recognize that Yankee face anywhere. And then he saw the boy. He was shrouded by somebody's coat but his size gave him away. Laveaux's cellphone rang and he inspected the screen, recognized the number and switched it off without answering. The entourage was now in the lobby and Laveaux sat down with his back to the window and pondered his next move.

He figured Harrison would keep Junya with him: that's what he would do in Harrison's shoes. Harrison would only trust himself to do the job right. Laveaux had heard that Ignace and Gumbo were dead and the rest of the crew had been taken. He had no fear of that, rather the contrary. The crew knew he could reach out to them any time he wanted and they knew better than to snitch on the family.

The FBI only had something while they had the boy and he wasn't sure how that would stand up with a grand jury. It was Junya's word against his, the only proof anecdotal and Junya was a crack dealer. With the right attorneys it wouldn't even get to trial. But not everybody had Laveaux's nerve and there were those in this game who wanted the loose ends tied, and tied quickly. His cellphone rang again, the same number as before, and again Laveaux blocked it. He really didn't need anyone telling him what to do right now.

He got off the streetcar at Lee Circle and jumped the next one coming back, taking it all the way to Canal Street this time. He had an apartment down a side street that nobody knew about, somewhere he could go and think. He had been by the condo at Riverwalk and seen that it was already staked out by the FBI. Grand Terre was out of the question.

He had to deal with the boy. He considered going after Harrison too and decided he would avoid that if he could: there was nothing to be gained by it now. Ignace had gone up against Harrison and lost. That wasn't surprising, Harrison had ice water running in his veins and Ignace had always been superstitious and emotional. Laveaux thought about the gris gris and laughed in the back of his throat. Maybe he'd tell Ignace's Nannan personally what had happened to her godson.

forty-two

Harrison woke with the dawn and lay on his back for a few minutes. He could hear traffic on Poydras Street outside the bedroom window and light filtered under the door from the hall where agents were rotating the guard. He leaned on one elbow and looked at the clock beyond the other bed where Junya was huddled like a child. Harrison looked at his face, a shaft of daylight across his cheek where it pierced the gap in the drapes. He was a child, barely a teenager. Harrison had to stop thinking of him as a grown-up.

Child. The word plagued his mind. Someone young enough to have some kind of trust in adults – too young to fight, too young to die, too young for anything except growing up in innocence, getting an education and looking forward to the rest of his life.

He washed his face in the bathroom, running the water through his fingers as he rubbed at the lines in his face. His eyes were grey and they looked very old there in the mirror looking back at him. He felt old again all at once – weary, as if the ache was deep in his bones.

Junya wanted immunity from prosecution yet he had murdered the boy in the bayou. He would claim he'd done it to save himself, but that was no defence. His age was possibly a factor: Junya thought he'd only been eleven at the time. The legal age of culpability in Louisiana and therefore the age where a suspect could be tried as an adult was twelve. The youngest person actually tried, however, had been fourteen, but that might not necessarily help. Junya's crime was heinous. On top of that he was a crack dealer and as a throw-away his level of innocence generally was greatly reduced. One thing was certain: no judge in the country was going to grant him immunity. All of which meant they had no case against Laveaux even if they caught him. That was a double whammy in itself because all the time he was loose Laveaux would be after the boy. If he refused to take the stand Laveaux would still have him killed.

There was no immediate solution, but Harrison would keep the boy with him. He wanted a look at that sketchbook and he had to talk to people about what they might or might not be able to do in return for testimony. So far he had told no one what Junya had done. They knew from Will Bentley about the abductions, but that was as far as it went.

The bathroom door opened and Harrison looked round to see Junya standing there, wearing the pyjama bottoms they had bought for him. 'Yo' phone rang just now. That funky one that's got a radio as well.'

Harrison made a face. 'I didn't hear it.'

'It woke me.'

'Who was it?'

'I don't know, I never answered it.'

Harrison followed him through to the bedroom and pressed the redial button on the Nextel. Santini's voice answered and Harrison took the phone back into the bathroom. It was the first opportunity he had had to talk to her since he got out of the swamp.

'How you doing?' he asked her.

'I'm sorry to call so early. Were you sleeping?'

'No. I was in the bathroom. I didn't hear the phone.'

'I was worried about you, Harrison. When're you coming home?'

Home. That was a good word to hear. It sounded good on Santini's lips. Harrison sighed. 'Soon. There's some stuff I got to clear up down here first.'

'Are we any nearer solving Carter's murder?' Santini asked him. 'His mother's called me a couple of times.'

'I'll go and see her when I get back. My money's still on Laveaux. He was definitely at the fishing camp and I'm positive Carter got to him through Call. I can't prove it yet, we won't until we get a set of Laveaux's prints, but I do have a witness who will testify to him being in that camp. The trouble is, he wants immunity from prosecution in return. And that isn't going to happen.' He sighed. 'I'll fill you in properly as soon as I get back.'

Santini was quiet for a moment. 'If you know Laveaux was at the fishing camp, does that put him in the frame for the boy in the bayou's murder?'

Harrison didn't reply right away.

'John?'

'I'm still here.'

'Did you hear what I said?'

'Yes.'

'Well, does it?'

'He ordered the killing, Fran. He didn't do it himself.'

Junya was dressed when he went back through to the bedroom. Harrison clipped the Nextel on his belt and pulled on the rest of his clothes.

'Who was that on the phone?' Junya asked him.

'Francesca Santini.'

'Yo' girlfriend?'

Harrison squinted at him. 'My partner at the FBI.'

'Oh.' Junya flicked on the TV set. 'So what happens now?' he asked.

Harrison fastened the ankle holster under his jeans. 'Now you tell me where that sketchbook is.'

Will Bentley had been off school for two days and he was itching to get back so he could see Todd Weighbridge and tell him all that had happened since he tricked him about bodies being buried in the walls of St Louis cemetery.

Today, however, was Saturday and he wouldn't be going back to school until Monday. He wasn't even sure he would be returning then. He had heard his parents arguing about it: his father's raised voice about negligence and stupidity and endangering his son's life. He said it was time they moved Will to a school there in Slidell. Will didn't mind. Maybe a school on the north shore would be better, given what had happened.

He heard the doorbell ring downstairs and then his father called up to him. Leaving his bedroom and his computer, Will went to the top of the stairs.

'Have you got a minute, son?' his father asked him. 'The Attorney General would like to speak to you.'

Will's eyes widened. He had met the Attorney General before. His dad worked quite closely with him, although he was based in Baton Rouge, but he had never really spoken to him.

David Mouton was in the living room. 'How are you, Will?' he asked. 'Everybody was so worried about you. I was just heading back to Baton Rouge but I couldn't go without stopping by to make sure for myself you were OK.'

'I'm fine.'

'Say thank you to Mr Mouton, Will.' His father stood behind him.

'Thank you, sir.'

'That's OK. You had a pretty rough time. But I hear from the FBI that they got that other boy out so you don't have to worry about that. I have to tell you, though, Will, much as I admire your loyalty, it isn't very well-founded. From what I hear, that boy is responsible for an awful lot of bad things that have been happening.'

Will didn't say anything.

'Anyway, I must be going.' Mouton smiled down at him. 'My cousin the governor has taken a special interest in this, son. He spent some time with your mom and dad. He sends you his very best regards and he's looking forward to

345

meeting you. I don't know if you've heard but you're being put forward for a bravery award, possibly even a "Colonel of Louisiana".'

Will's eyes lit up.

'That'll mean a trip to the governor's mansion and a party, TV and everything.' Mouton shook his hand. 'You've been a brave boy, Will. You're a credit to your family and an example to other boys your age.'

What you mean is colour, Jordan Bentley thought to himself. He's an example to other boys his colour. He gripped his son's shoulder. 'Thank Mr Mouton for coming, Will,' he said.

forty-three

Harrison sat in the passenger seat of Penny's Impala with Junya in the back. They pulled into Jordan Bentley's quiet suburban street where a black Lincoln Town Car was parked in front of his house. Harrison sat forward, resting his hand on the front seat. 'I guess we're not the only visitors today.'

Bentley was at the door with David Mouton. Penny drove the car to the end of the block then swung round in a circle. As they headed back down the street Mouton walked up the drive.

'The Attorney General,' Harrison muttered.

'He's been pretty high profile in this case,' Penny told him. 'So has the governor. They were opening the new wing of the courthouse when your boy here stole Will Bentley. The governor himself drove Mrs Bentley to the Iberville.'

'Old Val's looking to be President,' Harrison said. 'He's going to show up wherever the cameras are.'

Junya stared out the window at Will Bentley's spacious home, with its lush green lawn, tarmac driveway and basketball hoop over the garage. He looked up at the two-storey house with its wooden balcony reaching out from the upstairs rooms, huge windows and glass doors. Every other house on the block was as perfectly manicured as this one.

Mouton rested a hand on the sill where Harrison had his window rolled down and chatted briefly to the two FBI agents. Junya didn't even glance at him: he was far more interested in the life he had given back to Will Bentley.

Maybe if he got into the witness protection programme he and Marie could get a place in a neighbourhood like this. Harrison was still talking with Mouton. Junya watched the man he assumed was Will's father still standing in the driveway.

'Anyways, got to run.' Mouton drummed his fingers on the window-sill. Junya looked round and caught sight of his hand, the shirt cuff white and starched and fastened with gold links in the shape of the fleur-de-lis. Mouton walked back to his car, grey hair slicked back, and when he turned to climb in, Junya stared at the face in profile.

'You OK, Junya?' Harrison leaned over the back of the seat. 'You're awful quiet.'

Ahead of them the Lincoln was pulling away with a hiss of tyres on the gravel.

They got out of the car and Bentley came up the driveway to meet them. He was staring at Junya. Junya stared back at him, his chin thrust truculently in the air. From his bedroom window Will recognized Junya and felt the heat all at once in his bladder. There he was in his baggy jeans and red jacket, looking scruffier than ever, dirt on his sneakers and a gold chain hanging outside his T-shirt. Will had never thought he would see him again, even when he knew they hadn't killed him. He could still smell the rain. He could see Fort Jackson in shadow and the black barrel of the pistol that Junya pointed at him.

Junya looked up, shaded his eyes from the sun and stared right at him, the cold stare that Will had witnessed in the tunnel at Fort Jackson. The same feeling of terror came over him again even though he was safe at home in his own room with his mom downstairs and his dad right out in front. Junya seemed to peer inside him, and Will had the feeling he would be able to do so even if there were walls and doors between them.

Bentley looked at Junya. 'So you're the boy. You're Junya.'

'That ain't my real name. It's what Laveaux called me.'

'What is your real name?' Bentley asked him.

Junya shrugged. 'I don't remember.'

Bentley looked at him and saw what he might have become himself, what Will might have become, if his mother hadn't been so utterly wilful and got them out of the city.

'Did y'all get my message?' Junya asked him. 'The one I give to yo' boy?'

Bentley nodded.

'So what's it to be? I ain't hanging round here if we ain't gonna cut a deal.'

Bentley glanced at Harrison. 'We can talk about it later,' he said.

Junya laughed, hands stuffed in the pockets of his jacket. 'No, sir, we can't. We either cut a deal or we don't. There ain't no bullshit. We ain't gonna talk no bullshit.'

Bentley was suddenly bristling. 'You know what?' he said. 'You don't have any choice. You should be in custody. You're the guy that walked my son across the Iberville and threw him in the back of a van.'

Junya looked evenly at him. 'That's right,' he said. 'I'm also the guy who could've slit his throat and dumped his ass in the bayou.' He looked across the lawn and saw Will now standing on the porch. 'But there he is right there. You got him back, Mr US attorney. You got yo' boy back. Now you think about our deal while I go say hi.'

Bentley stepped in his way, but Harrison laid a hand on his arm. 'It's OK, Jordan.' Still Bentley blocked Junya's way. Will had stepped off the porch. 'It's OK, Dad,' he called.

'Will, my man.' Junya stepped around Bentley. 'You gave the message like I told you. That's good, brother. Good.'

Bentley got some cold drinks while Will took Junya inside. His mother went with them.

Harrison sipped lemonade on the porch. 'What did David Mouton want, Jordan?'

349

Bentley twisted his mouth down at the corners. 'Oh, the usual – a sound bite, photo opportunity. His cousin's got his eye on the White House.'

They sat for a moment, nobody speaking, just enjoying the peace of the morning and the sunshine. Bentley squinted at Harrison. 'So tell me,' he said, 'what was life like on Ignace Laveaux's tugboat?'

'The *See More* – oh, it was a real barrel of laughs.'

'See more?'

'*See More Night*, Jordan. Funny name for a boat. I guess they figured you could see more from the deck or something.'

Bentley was quiet for a moment, staring at the concrete step between his feet. From the open upstairs window the sound of the two boys' voices drifted. He looked again at Harrison. 'How was that spelled exactly?'

Harrison raised an eyebrow. 'As it sounds. *See More Night*.'

Bentley got to his feet.

'What's up?' Harrison said.

Bentley looked at Penny. 'Would you go and keep an eye on my son, please?'

'Sure.' Penny went indoors.

Bentley put his hands in his pockets and stared for a long moment at the cars parked on the street. 'I always thought it was funny,' he said quietly, 'how history repeats itself. You know – how nobody ever learns and nothing really changes. People just go on with the same fears and prejudices they've always had, making the same mistakes over and over again.' He looked round at Harrison. 'The name of the boat might spell as it sounds, but that's Laveaux's joke.'

Harrison scratched his head. 'Sorry, man, you lost me.'

'It's "Seymour Knight".' Bentley sat down next to him again. 'As in the name "Seymour" and "knight" like knight of the realm.' He was quiet for a moment, gazing across his lawn and not really seeing anything. 'You know the Laveaux family came from St Landry Parish, originally I mean, generations back. Opelousas. It's where my family came from.' He paused again then said, 'Let me tell you something about history repeating itself, Harrison. History's my pet subject.

'In 1868 the Presidential election was fought between Ulysses Grant for the Republicans and Horatio Seymour from right here in Louisiana. We, I mean the blacks, were a free people by then, enfranchised for the first time in our history. Down here we outnumbered the whites, just like we do today. We were Republicans, of course we were – they were the ones who gave us our alleged freedom.' He looked at Harrison. 'The Democrats couldn't stand the thought of us voting, because if we did the Republicans would almost certainly carry the state. Imagine that. In the so-called period of reconstruction, the slave population taking the state from the white, land-owning Democrats.

'It was never going to happen. They made sure of it. Vigilante groups were formed to stop it happening. "Committees of vigilance" – that's what "respectable" people called them. They were the white folk's way of ensuring that us newly enfranchised blacks didn't exercise our vote. One of those groups was called the Seymour Knights.'

Bentley was quiet for a moment. 'My middle name is Emerson,' he went on. 'I don't know if I ever told you.'

Harrison shook his head.

'My mom had a sense of history, too – I guess that's where I get it. I wasn't the first Emerson in our family. There was my ancestor Emerson Bentley, who lived in St Landry Parish during the period of reconstruction. He was an educated man, at eighteen years old he was teaching at a Negro school. He was also the English language editor of the *Progress* newspaper, and very outspoken about the way the Democrats were trying to turn back the clock. He was so outspoken that one morning close to polling day in 1868, six riders from the Seymour Knights showed up at his school on horseback. They made an example of him, showed all those niggers what happened to people who spoke out. They horsewhipped him in front of his students.' He paused for a moment, his face set as if he remembered from personal experience. 'You know who led those six riders, Harrison? A man called Gabriel Laveaux.'

Harrison stared at him.

'Oh, it's true, believe me. I know my history, especially when we're talking about my family.' He stared across the street once more. 'So now you see what I mean about history repeating itself. The Laveauxs attacked my family back in 1868 and they're still doing it a hundred and thirty years later.

'They were a big Acadian family back then,' he went on, 'not upper-tier society exactly, but near the top of the lower tier. Acadiana split in two when it was settled down here – those who wanted to progress with the new capitalism and those who wanted to stay with the old ways, trapping, fishing, self-sufficiency, and so on. The Laveauxs were in between, I guess. They never quite made the upper echelons – that was the domain of the Broussards and the DeBlancs.' He pointed to the street where the Attorney General's Lincoln had been parked. 'It was the domain of the Moutons.

'Call me dyed in the wool,' he said. 'Call me an inverted racist bastard if you want to, but the Attorney General's family and mine haven't exactly been close over the years. The Seymour Knights was just a splinter of a much bigger vigilante group, the biggest of them all, in fact. They were founded by – among others – the Moutons.'

'What were they called?' Harrison asked him quietly.

'The Knights of the White Camelia.'

forty-four

They drove down LA23 to Fort Jackson. Junya had hidden his sketchbook in Will Bentley's bag and Will told them where he had left it. He knew he had lost it somewhere, but up until that point he couldn't even recall having it when he got off the boat. Junya told him that he had gone back to get the bag from the hold and had left it with him in the hut. Will had crawled under the door and Junya figured he couldn't have done that with the bag on his back, so the bag must still be in the hut. They thought about calling the warden to go and check, but he had broken the story to the media and he might fancy himself as a treasure hunter. So they drove down the highway to get it themselves.

As they passed through Buras and the old boatyard Junya turned to Harrison. 'You can have the sketchbook,' he said. 'But I ain't saying nothing about nothing till I get that immunity. I don't care what that US attorney or anybody else tells me, I'm cutting a deal.'

Harrison looked at him but didn't say anything.

'I know what yo' thinking an' all,' Junya went on. 'I done some pretty bad things, I know that. I don't expect nothing to be easy. But I've got cards to play and I ain't setting them down till I know what the dealer is doing. You understand what I'm saying?'

Harrison shook his head slowly. 'You know, sometimes I look at you and I see a kid, other times I don't know what I see.'

'Then don't look too hard and don't look too long.' Junya worked his shoulders into his neck. 'But I got information fo' you, and I mean information.'

Penny pulled up in the parking lot with the fortified gun emplacements and the river to their left. Harrison got out and the humidity of the afternoon hit him after the air-conditioning of the car. The sun was a burnt orange in the heated blue of the sky; there was no hint of cloud and nothing in the south to indicate anything moving up from the gulf.

As a precaution Penny quartered the perimeter and Junya took Harrison across the footbridge and past the warden's room, which was open but empty. A radio played salsa music so he couldn't be far away. There was no vehicle in the parking lot, however, and Harrison figured he must have run to the store for something.

Junya led him across the open courtyard with the billets on the right and the raised section that led to the gun turrets and battlements. The hut where he had imprisoned Will was still locked and he bent to the rotten wood at the bottom of the boards.

'I guess he crawled out under here,' he said. Straightening up, he slid back the bolt and there on the concrete seat was Will's red school bag.

Harrison moved to get past him but Junya picked up the bag and held it to his chest: this was his only bargaining tool. Harrison held out his hand, and when Junya hesitated he snapped his fingers at him.

'You don't have a choice,' he said. 'Not if you want a chance.'

Junya still held the bag. 'I don't want no fucking chance. What I want is immunity.'

Harrison dropped his hand to his side and looked him up and down. 'You're a real piece of work, you know that? You kill a boy in cold blood and just assume that because you got something to bargain with you'll walk.'

Junya curled his lip. 'What you saying?'

'I'm saying you committed murder, Junya. Homicide. No matter how you look at it, it was homicide. You murdered that boy and you admitted it to me.' He leaned against the wall of the hut. 'The FBI can get immunity for a witness on occasions, but you killed somebody. How do you figure I'm going to square that particular circle?'

Junya still held the bag. 'You'll find a way.' He hesitated. 'You ain't told nobody yet, have you?'

Harrison stared at him. 'Believe me, it's only a matter of time.'

He flicked through the pages of the sketchbook as they drove back to New Orleans. The boy was good – very good, in fact. The likenesses were excellent: Junya had drawn faces, sometimes two or three to a page. Harrison recognized Laveaux and Ignace and Podjo, Gumbo, Frederico and Bernaud. There was page after page of young black faces all etched perfectly, sometimes as many as six to a sheet. He glanced at Junya. 'Are they all here?'

He nodded. 'Every one I ever lifted, Harrison. Every single one.'

'Why did you do this?' Harrison asked him. 'I mean, draw them like this.'

Junya breathed deeply, audibly through his nose. He looked out of the window and shifted the weight in his shoulders. 'I don't know exactly. I knew I was in trouble after . . . well . . . after you know what . . .' He shrugged again. 'I guess I was working on a bit of insurance.'

'You intended to go to the police?'

'I don't know. Maybe. I don't know what I intended. I think I only decided to get out fo' good when I saw you on the boat. I took it as a sign, I guess, after I see you walk through the Iberville.'

Harrison looked back at the pages and flicked through the last few. He came to the drawing of himself, saw the expression in his eyes and couldn't believe Junya had captured his emotions so perfectly.

'You know, you're really talented,' he said. 'If you took this up properly you might get somewhere with it.'

Junya looked at the sketch. 'I ain't bad, am I? I only saw you fo' a minute or two.' He smiled. 'Marie's always telling me like you just did. She's the one who wanted out so bad, Harrison. She told me I could do stuff with my life – I had a brain that hadn't been fucked over with dope. She told me if I could get us out then we'd hang together sort of like a family.'

Harrison was still leafing through the pages.

'That's why I want this thing. Not so much fo' me but Marie.'

'Don't bullshit me, Junya. You're trying to save your ass.' Harrison looked sideways at him. 'I don't blame you. You figure you got something to trade so you trade. I'd do the same thing if I was in your shoes.'

Junya narrowed his eyes. 'Those shoes are getting tight, Harrison. They don't fit me so good any more. You know what I'm saying? It's time to talk turkey.'

Harrison wasn't listening to him. He was staring at a page where two pictures were drawn, one of a man in profile, his hair slicked back, good-looking in a clean-cut manner. The other was of a hand holding a rail. All it showed was the hand itself, a bit of jacket sleeve and shirt cuff. The cuff was fastened by fleur-de-lis links.

'Recognize him?' Junya said, leaning over the seat. 'Y'all should, you just been talking to him.'

Harrison felt the flesh pucker on his cheeks. Camelias in Santini's garden. Maxwell Carter's computer room where too many pages had been torn off a notepad. He thought of non-felon fingerprints and coffee, coffee being unloaded on Governor Nicholls Wharf.

'Stop the car.'

'What?' Penny looked round at him.

'Matt, stop the car.'

Penny pulled over and Harrison got out. He paced a few yards then gazed across the width of the Mississippi. A tugboat blew its horn and he stared at the lash barges it shunted, holding the sketchbook as he rested his hand on his hip. Penny got out of the driver's seat. 'What's up?'

Harrison passed him the book. Then he looked at Junya. 'Where did you see him?' he asked quietly. 'Where was he when you made that drawing?'

'I ain't telling you that, not till we sit down proper with Will Bentley's old man.'

Harrison looked at him with his head slanted to one side. 'Don't fuck around, Junya.'

Junya folded his arms. 'You got the terms of my deal. I told yo' how it was gonna be.'

Harrison took a pace towards him, but Junya laughed in his face. 'You gonna threaten me? What with?'

Harrison stared at him and the sweat stood out on his brow. Penny laid a hand on his shoulder. 'Take it easy, JB.'

Harrison turned and spat tobacco juice in the dust. He took a cigarette from his pocket and lit it, cupping both hands to the flame.

Penny looked at the picture again and whistled. Harrison looked back at the river where the tugboat was coming to the bend. A speedboat with a pirogue loaded on the side came out from under the stern. The sun glinted off metal and blinded him for a moment then he heard a zinging sound by his ear. For a second it didn't register, then he was hauling Junya behind the car and tearing his pistol from its holster. Penny rolled in the dirt on the far side of the car; he came up with his own weapon drawn. Dust spat a foot to his left and he took cover again. Another round tore a hole in the roof.

Penny popped the trunk with his remote. He scrabbled with his key. Unlocking the chain that held it half-closed, he reached for his drag bag. Junya lay in the dust on the other

357

side of the car with Harrison covering him. They were below the height of the levee now and couldn't see anything. Penny slid his sniper's rifle from the drag bag. Harrison stayed where he was, still covering Junya.

No more shots were fired. They stayed where they were for a long time, Penny sighting through the scope on his rifle, but the speedboat was screaming upriver.

Harrison's mind was working, but Junya was ahead of him.

'That'd be Augustine,' he said. 'Guess Mr Mouton told him we were at Will Bentley's house. Fuck it, Harrison. I'm doing yo' job for you.' He half sat up, holding his upper left arm. Only then did Harrison see the trickle of blood that ran between his fingers. 'Fucker never could shoot.' Junya spat in the dirt.

'Don't move.' Harrison grabbed the first-aid kit from the car. Penny was still training his rifle on the river. Harrison took the first-aid kit and attended to Junya. 'High in the arm,' he said, half to himself. 'Looks like it only nicked you, but we better get to a hospital.'

'Jefferson Memorial is nearest,' Penny said.

Junya lifted his eyebrows. 'It's one way of getting to see Marie, I suppose.'

Penny put his rifle up. Harrison dressed the arm then lifted the boy into the back of the car. Penny got behind the wheel. He placed a magnetic blue light on the roof and hit the siren. Junya shifted where he lay across the back seat. 'Shit,' he said. 'If Wendell could see me now.'

forty-five

Harrison watched Junya through the glass partition in the hospital where he lay sleeping. Marie was in the next room, which meant the FBI agents and the sheriff's deputies who rotated the guard were never stretched.

'It isn't going to happen, John. No way, no how.' Charlie Mayer, the special agent in charge, stood next to him. Behind them in the corridor Jordan Bentley leaned against the wall. Harrison was still staring through the glass at Junya.

He had told them the full story after Junya had been admitted to hospital. Mayer had come over to Jefferson Parish with Bentley.

'Junya told me this traffic in kids is only a sweetener for the real gig,' Harrison had said. 'Coke coming in with the coffee. We unloaded crates of coffee at Laveaux's wharf with the fleur-de-lis stamped on the side.'

'A lot of Louisiana companies use the fleur-de-lis on their logo,' Mayer had told him.

'They do, but David Mouton wears it on his cuffs.'

Harrison looked again at the sketch Junya had made. He looked at Mouton's face drawn in profile just like his had been. He looked at the hand, gripping the rail, with the fleur-de-lis cufflinks.

He called Santini in Clarksburg and asked her to get the analysts at CJIS to see if Mouton had done any military service: if he had, they were to run an ident match with the second set of latent prints from the fishing camp.

*

In the corridor Mayer laid a hand on Harrison's shoulder. 'We're gonna get some coffee,' he said. 'We'll see you downstairs.'

Junya had his eyes open and Harrison went in to see him.

'What's happening?' Junya asked him.

'Nothing. You've been sleeping, that's all.'

Junya tried to sit up and winced. 'No, I mean what's going on? That was Bentley's old man I saw out there.'

'Nothing's been decided yet, we're still talking.'

Junya looked at the high windows, the confines of the room. 'How long do I have to stay in here?'

'You took a bullet, Junya. Ease up, will you?'

Junya twisted his mouth down at the corners. 'It's like being in jail.'

'It's like being in hospital. Marie is in the next room. This way you get to see her.'

Junya looked at him, experience beyond his years showing in his eyes.

'You think I don't know what's going on? I give you the main man and now yo' gonna hang my ass out to dry.' He looked as though he could spit. 'You a cop, Harrison, yo' all the fucking same. Don't be telling me different.'

Harrison leaned over the bed. 'Listen, asshole,' he said. 'You killed one boy and probably sent thirty others to similar deaths in some hell hole in South America. What do you expect – a Presidential fucking pardon?'

'I expect you to do what you said you was gonna do. I expect you to keep yo' word.' Junya poked himself in the chest with his thumb. 'I kept mine, didn't I?'

Harrison looked at him then. 'I am keeping my word. I'm talking to the US attorney. That's all I said I could do. Don't you go remembering things that never happened.' He broke off, angry with the boy, angry with himself. 'The only thing you got going for you is your age. You say you were eleven

360

when you did it – that might cut you some slack with the judge.'

'Judge? What do you mean, judge? There ain't gonna be no judge.'

'Of course there's going to be a judge. It's not up to us. It's not up to the US attorney. Anything you get will be up to the sitting judge.' Harrison paced to the window and looked out across the parking lot, where two sheriff's deputies were patrolling. 'Responsibility, Junya, you ever hear of the word? Sometimes in life you have to accept a little bit.'

Junya wrinkled his brows. 'Fuck responsibility, Harrison. I'm talking about surviving. Tell the fucking judge I was ten if it'll help.' He struggled out of bed and gripped the pole where his drip was attached. 'Give me a hand here, will you? I want to see Marie.'

Marie was awake and stable. The wound in her back was healing and she was propped against her pillows. Tears filled her eyes when she saw Junya.

'Hey, big man, what you been doing to youself?'

'Got shot, didn't I.' Junya jerked his head at Harrison. 'That's what happens when you hang out with the Feds.'

Marie glared at Harrison. 'Who did this to him?'

'We think it was Laveaux.'

'You supposed to be protecting him? What kind of protection is it gets him shot?'

'We're protecting him now. We're protecting both of you. Nobody can get at you in here. There are agents standing guard on the door, and deputies all over the building.'

'Get me my own gun,' Junya muttered. 'Protect myself is what I'll do.' He wrinkled his lip. 'The FBI don't know shit, except how to blow smoke up people's ass.'

Harrison left them and went downstairs. Bill Chaisson had been sitting with Mayer and Bentley and he came out of the coffee shop as Harrison walked the length of the hallway.

'You figure the kid's going to be OK in here?' Chaisson said.

Harrison nodded. 'Better here than anywhere else – we got agents on the door and Jefferson Parish sheriff's staked the place out. Laveaux won't show up unless he's very stupid.' He blew the air from his cheeks. 'Bill,' he said, 'there's something I haven't told you.'

'You don't need to.' Chaisson stepped out into the parking lot, the sun full on his face. 'He did it, didn't he? Junya killed the boy in the bayou.'

forty-six

David Mouton was on his way back to Baton Rouge on Interstate 10 when his cellphone rang. The driver had the partition raised, which soundproofed the back of the car. Mouton checked the number on the screen before he answered. It was his secretary from the New Orleans office, a woman he was having an affair with – one of several his wife and grown-up children didn't know about.

'Hello, Carrie,' he said. 'What's up?'

'I thought you'd want to know. Two FBI agents have just been here looking for you.'

Mouton rubbed his palm on the thigh of his trousers. 'What did they want?'

'They didn't say.'

'Did you know them?'

'No, but one was clean-cut. The other was older and scruffy. He wore jeans and his hair was long.'

Mouton felt the heat flush through him. 'What did you tell them?'

'That you were on your way back to Baton Rouge.'

'And what did they say?'

'Nothing.'

'OK. Thank you, Carrie.'

'Is everything all right, David?'

'Everything's fine.'

'Can we meet up again? I really miss you.'

'Not right now, but soon.' Mouton hung up the phone

and worked at the knot of his tie. He sat on the leather upholstery for a moment, feeling the sweat gather at the seat of his pants, then he picked up the phone again and punched in a number.

'Hello.'

'We need to talk,' Mouton said.

'What about?'

'The FBI, they were looking for me in New Orleans. My secretary just called and told me.'

For a moment there was silence. 'Where are you now?'

'In the car on my way home.'

'OK. Go home and stay there. If they come by they come by. You've got nothing to worry about. You're a top lawyer, remember, you can handle a couple of Feds.'

The phone went dead and Mouton threw it down on the seat. That's easy for you to say, he thought. He realized his driver was watching him in the rear-view mirror. He stared at him. The driver looked away.

Laveaux stuffed the cellphone back in his pocket. He was dressed as an orderly standing by a drinks machine at the hospital. He had watched Harrison bring the boy in and had been watching when he came out of surgery. They placed him in the room next to Marie, which made his job easier. He should have killed Junya with the shot from the speed-boat, but Harrison had got in the way. Junya was wounded, though, so he would be here for a while. In the meantime, there was a more pressing matter to deal with and it occurred to him that this was another of life's unexpected bonuses. If it was handled correctly it might close the chapter on the whole situation and allow him to slip away. There might be no need to go after the boy. But he knew he would, regardless. Dealing with Junya was personal.

Mouton decided he would deal with the FBI at his house. He called his secretary at the Baton Rouge office and told her he was going home and to pass that information on to urgent enquirers only. His wife was away until tomorrow, visiting her sister in Opelousas, which meant he had the place to himself. Normally that allowed him to entertain a lady or two, a real kick when the little woman was out of the house. But tonight he would have to contend with the FBI.

Home for David Mouton wasn't so much a house as a mansion. It was built in the colonial style with a huge façade and pillars, an upstairs balcony that reached all the way around. The grounds were about twenty-five acres, where he bred some of the best quarter horses in the south; the pool area was palatial, as was the office facility he had built out the back. That was where he went now after he dismissed the driver. He thought about a dip in the pool, but decided to leave it till after the Feds had been. He took off his jacket and loosened his tie, then sat at his desk and checked to make sure there were no papers lying around that he wouldn't want them to see. Lastly, quite why he wasn't sure, he opened the top drawer and checked the clip on his 9-mm.

Then he sat and waited. He waited and waited and around four o'clock he heard a car pull up outside. That was a little odd: nobody had buzzed him from the gate to inform him of any visitors. That would have given him a few minutes to fully compose himself. No matter, he could handle it. Whoever had not done their job properly would pay with it later. He got up and straightened his tie. Somebody knocked on the door in a brusque, businesslike manner. I can handle the FBI, Mouton told himself. He opened the door with an easy smile on his face. Augustine Laveaux looked back at him.

forty-seven

Penny drove up Interstate 10 towards Baton Rouge with Harrison sitting next to him. They were in St John the Baptist Parish, south of Lake Maurepas with the radio channels of the Louisiana state police murmuring in the background. They were engaged in a heavy discussion about Junya, and what they thought they could get for him by way of a deal. Penny wasn't optimistic. 'You know how these things go, JB. It'll come down to the judge. Culpable age won't be anything to do with it, not in a case like this. I'd bet my pension they'll try him as an adult.'

Harrison nodded grimly. 'That's what I reckon, too. The thing is, I figure I owe him something.'

'You don't owe him anything. You can't think like that. It doesn't matter what he brought us, he killed somebody.' Penny glanced in his mirror at a car that was getting a little too close. 'Junya put your neck on the block for you when he challenged you on that tugboat. He wasn't doing you any favours right there, was he?' He paused for a moment and twisted the dial on the radio. 'You hear that?'

Harrison shook his head.

'Some trooper mentioned David Mouton.'

Harrison picked up the handset and called the state police. 'This is special agent Dollar of the FBI,' he said. 'Me and my partner are *en route* to David Mouton's house. Is there something going on we need to know about?'

The dispatcher paused for a moment. 'What's your interest with Mr Mouton?'

'We're going to tell him he won the lottery,' Harrison said. 'Hey, buddy, anybody ever tell you we were on the same side?'

'OK. Whatever. Somebody reported a gunshot at his house. We got troopers attending now.'

Harrison lifted the blue light from the well at his feet and Penny flipped on the two-tone.

David Mouton lay on the floor, one leg tucked under his chair where it had crashed over on its side. He had twisted as he had fallen and he lay on his left with his eyes wide open. Blood had rushed to form a crimson pool, discoloured to pink in places where it mixed with the dye of the carpet. Blood spattered his neck and white shirt, soaking it on one side. Flecks littered the leather couch and the bureau. The weapon, a 9-mm automatic, was still gripped in his right hand.

Harrison and Penny, shields open in their pockets, stepped beyond the blue and white tape and Harrison was reminded of Maxwell Carter's computer room. This was far more opulent, but the smell was the same and the blood-stains looked similar. It was fresher, though. The body was still warm and the blood still wet round the exit wound where his eye socket had shattered. Two uniformed troopers were standing beside the body, making their obvious death determination.

'Stupid, isn't it?' one of them said. 'Got to wait for the doc to tell us he's dead. I mean, does he look like he's breathing?'

Harrison studied the desk where a single sheet of paper, spattered with little dots of blood, lay on the leather blotter. Being careful where he stepped, he moved round till he could see what was written on it. Four words, no signature. The fountain pen lay alongside with the top fixed over the shaft.

'Looks like a suicide note,' the cop said. He raised his eyebrows and glanced at the furnishings in the office. 'This room is worth more than my whole house put together. What did he have to be sorry about?'

Harrison laid a hand on his shoulder. 'Some of us have ghosts, my friend. The room's no good if there are ghosts in every corner.'

Penny was on the phone, standing by the door. Harrison walked over to him. Outside, two cars pulled up, detectives and evidence response technicians from Baton Rouge. Penny switched off the phone. 'That was his office in New Orleans,' he said. 'His secretary was very upset.'

'Understandable.' Harrison glanced over his shoulder.

'She called him in his car,' Penny went on. 'Told him we'd come by.'

'He saw us at Jordan Bentley's. He would've seen Junya in the back.' Harrison tapped his tin of Copenhagen against his thigh. 'Somebody takes a desperation-style shot at the kid and now this. It all hangs together.'

They waited for the medical examiner to arrive and watched as he pulled on surgical gloves and began to make his preliminary investigation. The Baton Rouge detectives helped turn the body over. The entry wound was small and apart from the eye that side of his head was pretty much intact, though bloated now like a rubber mask from the compressed air of the cartridge. Harrison saw the powder burns, like a speckling of blackheads at his temple. The ME rocked back on his heels. 'I'm always reluctant to make rash statements,' he said, 'but it does look like he shot himself. The angle is good, I can tell you that as an initial impression. And the barrel was pressed against the skin. Either suicide or a very professional hit.'

Harrison got the evidence technicians to take a set of

Mouton's fingerprints for him then they went back to the car.

'What do you think, JB?' Penny asked him.

'I don't know.' Harrison spat juice on the tarmac. 'I guess it makes sense if he thought we were coming.'

'He wouldn't be the first. Better than public humiliation.'

Harrison nodded. 'They're an old family.'

'You don't sound convinced.'

'I'm not sure I am.'

forty-eight

Junya watched the news on television in his room. The door was locked and the windows were closed and a Jefferson Parish deputy, who had relieved the FBI agent, was eating doughnuts outside. Junya saw the scenes at the big house in Baton Rouge and listened as the newscaster told how David Mouton, the attorney general for the state of Louisiana, had been found dead in his office. The first reports indicated that it might be suicide. A statement from the FBI confirmed that they had been on their way to interview Mr Mouton about his involvement in a child abduction ring, and that a joint FBI/DEA investigation had been launched into the family coffee business. His cousin the governor was said to be extremely shocked and disturbed, both by the apparent suicide and the revelations from the FBI.

Junya banged on the door till the deputy opened it. 'I need a telephone,' he said.

Harrison had just stepped out of the shower when his phone rang. He picked it up. 'Harrison, it's me. I been watching all that stuff about the Attorney General on TV. Convenient suicide, wasn't it?'

Harrison sighed. 'He knew we were coming for him, Junya. The Moutons are an old respected family. Some people just can't handle the shame.'

'Shame. Yeah, right.' Junya paused for a moment. 'I suppose you gonna tell me it's a done deal now.'

'Unless we catch Laveaux.'

He heard Junya curse. 'I knew you'd say that. Fuck it, Harrison. It ain't done by a long way. What about me?'

'I'm going to do what I can.' Harrison sat down on the bed, a towel wrapped round his waist. 'I already told you that. Nothing changes, Junya.'

'Everything changes, you asshole. With him gone y'all don't need me any more.'

Harrison was still. The boy was right. It was the first thing that had occurred to him when he saw Mouton lying dead. Since then he had been back to the field office and discussed it with the SAC. The crimes against children unit was beginning to delve into the paedophile ring, and one word about the coffee house had set the local DEA agents tingling with anticipation. Unbeknown to the FBI they had been watching a plantation in Colombia for months.

'You there?' Junya said.

'Yes, I'm still here.'

'What you gonna do about me?'

'Junya, I'm not responsible for you,' Harrison said. 'You're not the victim here. You understand me? At some point you're going to have to face this thing and take some responsibility for what you did.'

'Bullshit I am.'

'We all have to, Junya. When you get right down to the corn, that's the way it is. We do what we do and then we take the rap. You did what you did and you have to face the consequences. It's the way of the world, bubba, the same for everybody.'

'Fuck you, Harrison. I put my neck on the line for you and you leave me pissing in the wind.' Junya slammed the phone down and Harrison shook his head. He sat there for a moment and then he dialled Santini's number in Clarksburg.

She met him at Benedum Airport and he had never been so

pleased to see another human being in his life. He held her and she smoothed his hair back from his eyes and kissed him hard on the mouth. Junya was still in the hospital, where he would remain till he was well enough to be moved to protective custody, though Harrison doubted whether Laveaux would go after him now. Penny was writing up his final 302 reports for the US attorney's office, not that there would be any major prosecution unless they arrested Laveaux. Harrison had thought long and hard about the Cajun. Mouton's death certainly looked like a suicide and according to the initial reports from the medical examiner that was how it was going to come out. But Harrison was pretty sure he knew who had shot at them from the boat on the river and he was pretty sure he knew where the sniper had got his information. Maybe when Laveaux couldn't clear up the Junya loose end, he decided to take care of the other one.

Santini opened the car door for him and he settled into the passenger seat. 'Harrison, I got to tell you,' she said. 'I ran a check on David Mouton at CJIS. He wasn't in the military and the prints you sent don't match the latents at the fishing camp.'

Harrison thought about that. He had looked carefully at Junya's picture. The hand he had drawn matched the layout of the unidentified prints in terms of how the hand gripped the alcove rail.

Santini guessed his thoughts. 'Lots of people wear fleur-de-lis cufflinks.'

None of it mattered. Harrison figured, as he had right from the beginning, that the second set of prints belonged to Laveaux, though he'd never prove it now. He had never seen him wearing cufflinks but that didn't mean he didn't have any. He was just as proud of his Cajun heritage as David Mouton. The fleur-de-lis was as Cajun as it got. There must have been a record of him at the facility, which Carter had subsequently erased, and Carter must have money stashed somewhere they hadn't found. Harrison didn't know. He wasn't sure he cared. He was tired.

Santini took him to her place. He didn't want to return to the emptiness of his cabin out in the hills: it was bare and cold even with summer beckoning. Santini's house was full of warmth and life and it smelt fresh and clean and above all it smelt of Santini. The case was over, he had survived on his own for five months, and now he wanted warmth and light and he wanted Santini.

His supervisor gave him a few days off and he spent the time just sitting in the house. He washed the breakfast dishes, dusted and polished – he even did something about the pile of ironing in Santini's closet. He just relaxed, emptied his mind and chilled right out. Each night when she came home he had dinner ready, the wine open and candles over the mantelpiece. He was ravenous for her, emotions woken from the deepest places, and he roved her body till he was satisfied and lay back in exhaustion.

Santini watched him sleeping with the sheet twisted round his leg, his body lean, his hair overlong again and his face ravaged, even in his sleep. She stroked his brow with delicate fingers, the weight of her breast against his ribs, and she kissed his eyelids and listened to the rise and fall of his breathing.

Harrison was in the swamp, stuck in quicksand up to his waist; alligators moved on muddy banks where the cypress grew out of the water, their branches hung with moss that drifted in the breeze. All was darkness, airless. He moved his chest, worked his lungs, but there was no air to breathe: the weight of the sand was slowly crushing the life in him. Cottonmouths moved in the lowest branches of the trees. He could hear them in the moss as they curled their bodies round the flimsy limbs, adding too much weight to the already weighted down. Every now and again the mud would bubble as something moved past his legs. And across the bayou the fishing camp stood on rickety pilings, the knocked-out windows only adding to the totality of darkness. Yet he could see the house and through the rushes and the weeds he could make out tiny figures trapped beneath its weight. Iron bars criss-crossed his mind and he could hear their voices, far off and muffled but screaming all the same.

He sat bolt upright, the sweat rolling off his skin so he was at once clammy and cold. Santini sat up next to him, one hand on his shoulder, and he shied away from her, rolled sideways out of bed and came up in a crouch.

'Jesus, Harrison, you're scaring me.' She stared at him through the darkness. He could see the whites of her eyes and where her hair framed her face. His chest was tight and his throat dried to a crisp.

He sat in the edge of the bed and Santini reached for the lamp. 'John,' she said softly, 'this whole thing is so personal to you it's intense.'

Harrison didn't say anything. He plucked a cigarette from the pocket of his shirt and lit it with his Zippo. He held the flat square lighter in his shaking hand and closed his fingers around it.

'You never had any counselling, did you?' Santini said. 'I mean, after going in deep. You had a debrief each time and that was it. You always refused proper counselling.' Harrison looked at her, drawing heavily on the cigarette, sucking in his cheeks so they formed hollows in his face.

'Talk to me, Harrison,' Santini said. 'It's way past time.'

The summer of 1969 he was nineteen years old and on his second tour of Vietnam, having conducted his first as a draftee grunt. Now he was a volunteer with the 1st Engineer Battalion Tunnel Rats, a squad of thirteen men split into Alpha and Bravo units who worked the network of tunnels in the Cu Chi region northwest of Saigon. The tunnels had been there as long as there had been conflict, which had started way back with the French. By the time Harrison joined the rats they were the elite of the elite, a few single-minded individuals who faced the kind of danger most mortals only experienced in dreams.

The day was oppressively hot and the jungle sweated, vegetation dripping with moisture after another torrential downpour. Harrison wore just his boots and lightweight pants, a six-shooting revolver strapped on his hip and a red lens torch on the ground at his feet. Lieutenant Coombs, who commanded Alpha Squad, was peering into the spider hole where the snipers had been reported. On one side was a narrow, dark entrance to a tunnel.

An infantry division had been dropped in an air-mobile insertion, and two VC snipers had gunned down two GIs who were unaware of their presence. The subsequent fire-fight had been brief and Charlie had disappeared. Fifteen minutes later what was left of Alpha Squad was flown in by chopper: only three men – the other four were already underground ten miles further north.

Harrison was waiting for orders, aware of the tingling in his palms and the hairs standing up on his neck as they always did when he was confronted with the darkness.

'OK.' Coombs looked back at him. 'Saddle up, Johnny. Martinez will take the point to the first trapdoor then I'll take over.'

'With respect, LT,' Harrison said, 'protocol says officers don't go down the holes, never mind take the point.'

'Screw protocol, partner, we're down to three men and I'm taking the point.'

Martinez, already a veteran of three tours, came alongside Harrison. 'Next time, kid,' he whispered.

Ray 'The Probe' Martinez always took the point when he went underground, and if he had his way he wouldn't give it up. He was like no other man in the unit. He lived to kill communists and if he could do it by himself so much the better.

He went down first. The tunnel entrance was carved into

the lower wall of the spider hole or sniper firing post, and Martinez crawled inside, red lens flashlight held high on a piece of wire, his revolver in his other hand. Five yards behind, Coombs went in after him. Harrison brought up the rear.

Coombs would reload for Martinez and Harrison for Coombs. That was how it went: if they made contact the point man would only fire three rounds of his six before swapping pistols with his second. That way he was never out of ammo and the VC didn't get any more of an advantage than they had already. The VC knew the tunnels, and they were built for men like them, two feet wide and only three high, narrower and lower in places. Consequently the tunnel rats were all slightly built men, but since they had been going underground the tunnels seemed to have become narrower still.

Harrison could see the red beam from Martinez's flashlight on their right: Martinez was left-handed. He crawled to where the tunnel forked, not left and right but up and down. Experience told them the upper fork would lead to a concealed trapdoor at ground level. The other dropped away into darkness.

They regrouped at the head of the drop and Martinez shone his torch. The bottom of the shaft was perhaps ten, maybe twelve feet below and it was the perfect place for a booby trap. Nothing was immediately visible, but that didn't mean it wasn't there. Using his hands and feet on the sides of the hard baked earth, Martinez lowered himself down, gun holstered again now, knife between his teeth. Harrison crouched with Coombs, weapons at the ready. Martinez got to the floor of the lower tunnel and gave them the all-clear. Harrison's breathing was stiff: it felt even more airless than normal down here, as if the very tension itself sucked the oxygen out. Carefully now Coombs descended, Harrison close behind.

The tunnel below was black and still, no light whatever

penetrating this far down: they were reliant on the beam of their torches and their hearing. Harrison worked himself forward on his elbows and knees, and now and then packed earth fell away in dust above his head. He watched for the little black spiders that could reduce a man to paralysis in a matter of hours and he watched Coombs's boots just ahead of his face.

Martinez moved without fear: it was a word he didn't understand and most of the others were happy to let him lead. He had been doing this job longer than anyone else and he had been nicknamed 'The Probe' by his former commanding officer.

Harrison worshipped him. Taller and leaner and older, Martinez kept himself to himself, but occasionally he would speak to Harrison, give him some pointers, the odd bit of advice, admiring Harrison's courage in volunteering for a second tour. Most GIs were grateful just to 'hit back in the world' in one piece. But Harrison had lost his best friend, Eli Footer from Chicago, to a VC in a spider hole, and that was why he was here.

The underground insertion team moved in unison, with the second man five yards behind the point so if the point man got blown up by a grenade his body would shield the second. The tunnel opened into a small chamber, the floor space wider and the roof higher above their heads. It might have been used as a forward aid station for the VC wounded, but it was deserted now. The tunnel leading off it narrowed again and went deeper underground before it levelled out and they came to the first trapdoor. The door was at an angle in the floor, which meant the tunnel system went deeper still. This was the most dangerous part of being underground, short of actually rounding a bend and coming up against Charlie in person. Most trapdoors were circular and wooden, bevelled into the earth and booby-trapped. The only safe way to move through them was to blow them up first.

They had used grenades till they realized just how much oxygen a grenade sucked out of the tunnel, so now they used dynamite. Martinez set the charge and they all moved back. The door blew and Martinez, ignoring Coombs's intention to take the point, crawled forward again.

The tunnel dropped away then levelled out once more, the drop acting as a blast wall. Harrison could hear Martinez and Coombs ahead of him, their breathing clear in the silence after the vibrations had died away.

All at once a burst of automatic gunfire shook the tunnel. Harrison lay flat.

Martinez loosed off three shots. Coombs passed up his weapon and then Harrison heard Martinez cursing. The next thing he knew Coombs was back-pedalling, dragging Martinez with him.

'He took one in the shoulder. We got to get him out.'

Between them they moved back, easing Martinez along the tunnel without hurting him too much. Dust fell in their eyes where earth had been loosened first by dynamite then the gunfire. They made it to the forward aid station and Coombs took a look at Martinez, who was cursing and swearing and telling them he was all right. He wasn't all right, though: he had taken a round in the shoulder and was losing blood fast. Quickly now they moved him through the larger area to the ten-foot vertical drop where the GIs lowered a ladder. A few minutes later they were in the relative safety of the spider hole. Martinez had the round lodged in his shoulder, and he was spitting venom at the lieutenant for bringing him out when he did.

'Fuck it, LT, I've fought with worse than this.'

'Not in my outfit, you haven't.'

'But we got Charlie pinned down.'

'Let it go, Martinez. I'm not losing my best point man like this.' Coombs tore open a first-aid kit and began to work on the shoulder. Martinez looked at Harrison and worked his eyes towards the hole. Harrison stared at him and Martinez gestured again. Coombs was busy with the wound. Harrison inched his way across to the spider hole and dropped underground.

Now he was on his own, a cardinal rule broken but one that Martinez broke regularly – and Martinez always came back. Harrison went down to the forward aid station and crawled back up the tunnel towards the trapdoor they had blown, his red lens torch above his head and his revolver gripped in his right hand. He had three spare cylinder clips stuffed in his pockets and a bayonet on a strap over his shoulder.

He made it to the blown trapdoor with no incident and there he paused. The sweat had built on his naked torso and rolled off him now, soaking through his fatigues so he was damp and moist and the dirt clung to him. Very carefully he checked the rim of the hole and the shards of wooden trapdoor to make sure that no secondary device had been laid after they had retreated with Martinez.

He found nothing and he crawled through the hole and down to where the tunnel straightened out. This was where they'd been ambushed and Harrison's heart beat so loudly it seemed to echo in the tunnel itself. He moved slowly now, the light from the torch his only comfort, yet it cast the darkness ahead with a crimson hue that was unnatural and eerie. The tunnel dropped still further and Harrison moved on, nobody above him, nobody in the dips where the VC dug deeper to protect themselves from grenades, and nobody round the corners. Then all at once the tunnel rose vertically above his head, perhaps four feet to another trapdoor and the next level.

Harrison crouched, listening intently for any sound from further in the labyrinth. He heard nothing but the racing of his pulse. Unlike Martinez, he knew the meaning of fear and he felt it now, alone after a foolish rush of blood, some ill-thought-out desire to gain approval or take revenge or whatever. He told himself he was down here for the two GIs whose parents would be getting a letter from the infantry, he was down here for the slug lodged in Martinez's shoulder and he was down here for Eli whose wristwatch he had found on his disembodied hand.

He had no dynamite: another mistake. He prised open the trapdoor with his knife, seeking a trip switch, some kind of safety arming device attached to a grenade. He found none, lifted the bevelled wood and crawled on, his heart in his mouth, the sweat mixed with dirt now in his eyes, making him blink with dirty tears. He moved on his elbows and knees, the tunnel bearing left then narrowing once again. Up ahead was a Y-junction where the tunnel split. Normally in a three-man team one would remain at the Y to maintain the bearings for the others and make sure they didn't get trapped if Charlie was lurking in one tunnel when they took the other. But there was no one to back Harrison up and he would have to rely on instinct alone when he got to the split. He slowed his pace now and shut off the light, waiting a moment for his eyes to grow accustomed to the blackness, to get his breathing under control. The airlessness seemed to rush at him when the light went out.

He heard rats scurrying behind him and he looked back into darkness. There was no sound ahead and he made his decision, flipping the light on once more and plumping for the right fork. He crawled on, gun cocked and ready, careful where he placed his knees and elbows. He checked ahead for pits where Charlie left poisonous snakes and sharpened staves of bamboo upended in the dirt. There were no snakes, though, and no mantraps. Harrison crawled deeper into the system. No sound from above now: too far underground to hear tanks crossing or the aircraft screaming over.

And then he swore he heard voices. Round the next bend. The red glare of his flashlight would not reach that far, but he snuffed it out as a precaution and lay with his ear to the ground and listened. He could definitely hear voices and he felt his heart thump the earth like a frightened rabbit warning the warren of danger. He checked his weapon: all six rounds intact, the chamber spinning freely and no dirt lodged in the barrel.

The infantry commander from the mobile-insertion team had told them there were two snipers and Harrison could hear two voices. They would know they had wounded at least one man, and wouldn't be expecting anyone else for a while. As quietly as he could, he inched to the bend in the tunnel wall and waited. He could still hear them, hushed whispers, no more than twenty yards ahead. He inched forward again, rounding the corner, keeping his head low and moving in perfect darkness.

As he got closer he made out the dull glow of some kind of light directly ahead. It looked too dull to be a flashlight and it was yellow like a candle. Sometimes the VC had candles to light the sleeping chambers they cut into the wall, or the tiny field operating theatres they set up and dismantled as seamlessly as someone might move a tent. Harrison waited. No sound now. The silence grew deeper and he realized they knew he was there.

He fired two shots, double tap in quick succession, heard a grunt and the light went out. Then somebody blazed away at him with automatic fire, bullets ripping into the earth above him. He lay flat until the firing stopped then loosed off two more rounds. All was silent ahead.

For a long time he lay there, working fresh ammunition loose in his pocket. He could hear his own breathing coming thick and fast now, breath after breath, and he felt sure they could hear him, too. Reloaded, he waited – five minutes, six, seven – but no more shots were fired. Still he waited and then he heard a sound he couldn't quite make out, like a whimper, a whining almost, like a whipped dog. The whimper became a sobbing sound, distinctive and human, rising in pain and fear. It sent a shiver right through him.

Still he remained where he was. The VC were notorious for luring men into traps. He waited for a further ten minutes then loosed off two more rounds and switched the torch back on. Slowly he worked his way forward. The tunnel was opening out – he could no longer feel the sides against his elbows, he could see the floor getting wider. And then he saw the first of the snipers hunched over his AK47. He was half sitting with one leg underneath him, the other thrust straight out so his body was slumped forward with the weapon supporting him. Harrison levelled his pistol at him but the man didn't move. Harrison stayed where he was, pistol trained on the VC's head, but as he looked closer he could see blood in the dirt between the man's legs.

From behind the sniper someone sobbed again. Harrison listened to the plaintive, pitiful voice, which assaulted all of his senses, and suddenly he realized why. The voice was that of a child.

He still had his pistol pointed at the sniper. He was almost to him now and he could hear the weeping clearly from behind the man. He whipped the rifle away and the man lolled forward. Harrison could see the hole at the base of his throat.

Lying against the wall with his hands pressed to his stomach, a young Vietnamese boy was staring at blood, which bubbled between his fingers.

Harrison just knelt there, looking for the boy's gun but not seeing one, looking for an explanation of his presence but not finding one. And the boy looked up at him and the tears ran on his cheeks and every time he moved the wound leaked a little more. Two snipers, they had said, but all Harrison saw was the man with the gun and this child, mortally wounded and weeping. He put away his pistol and moved forward on hands and knees till he was beside the boy, the red beam of his flashlight shining down on his wounds. The boy shrank against the wall and raised a hand as if to ward off a blow.

Harrison had nothing to bind him with, no kerchief, no shirt, nothing to staunch the flow of blood. He reached for the dead sniper, meaning to rip off his shirt, but as he did the boy's voice gurgled in his throat and Harrison looked back and saw bubbles cluster in red at his lips.

He knew then his lungs were gone.

The boy looked at him, hand still raised, soaked in his own blood. Harrison realized he was no older than his sister's son, his own nephew who would be in school right now. The boy was getting weaker and his eyes were glazing, the pupils beginning to dilate. Harrison raised his hand to do something, he didn't know what. And as he did the boy grasped his palm. His bloody fingers slid off Harrison's but Harrison tightened his grip. The boy mumbled something, words lost in the mucus that stained his mouth like macabre make-up, running. Harrison held his hand and the boy's eyes focused and fixed and he tried to get up. The blood ran from the wound in his stomach. He lost his grip and he died.

forty-nine

Harrison looked at Santini. 'He was just a child. He might have been the sniper's son, a player from an underground theatre troupe, I don't know. But he was about ten or eleven and he was unarmed. I went into that hole like some desperado. I ended up sitting in the darkness bawling my eyes out with a dead child in my arms. Six weeks later I fucked up on the point. I loosed off all six shots and Martinez hauled me out. That was it – my time with the tunnel rats was over.'

He lit another cigarette and sat down on the bed. 'I never told anybody. Not then, not since. But I killed a child, Francesca. Innocent, unarmed, someone who shouldn't even have been down there. To this day, I don't know why he was.'

Santini held his hand.

'I've seen that boy's face every day of my life ever since,' Harrison went on. 'I've seen him when I've been under-cover. I've seen him in my dreams and three years ago I saw him in a bayou at Jesuit Bend.'

'Which is why this became so personal.'

Harrison nodded.

'I've known it all along. I just never got around to admitting it to myself. It's like I buried it, never took any responsibility, not for myself or for what I did.' He sat down again. 'You know, I bawled Junya out for not accepting the fact that he killed somebody – and I don't think I did myself.'

He got up again and walked to the window where he rested his forehead against the glass. He looked at his trembling hands. 'You know, you think it doesn't matter. You think it was war and that things happen in war. You think this Vietnam syndrome, this post-traumatic stress disorder or whatever they call it, is bullshit. But it's not, Fran. It really fucks with your head.'

Santini watched him, hunched against the window. 'It's why the Bureau has counsellors, John. It's why there's such a long period of downtime when an agent kills somebody. It's why there's an evaluation process afterwards, and why undercover agents talk to people when they surface again.'

'You think I ought to talk to someone?' Harrison asked.

'Of course I do. I'm flattered you talked to me and it's a start but, yes, I think you should. The suits are looking for you to teach recruits what it's like to go in deep. If you don't deal with this part of it you're not giving them the whole story, are you?'

Junya couldn't sleep. The room was eight feet square: he had paced it. Never in his life had he felt so cooped up, so trapped. He sat on the bed, he sat in the chair, he sat on the floor, stood on the bed, bounced on the bed, dragged the chair over to the window so he could stand on it and gaze at the sky.

He considered his situation and knew that Harrison was dumping him. The US attorney wouldn't cut him a deal now, not with Mouton out of the game: he had nothing left to give them. Bentley wouldn't forgive him for stealing his son, even though he gave him back without harming so much as a hair on his head. The relief of a victim's relatives very quickly gave way to anger, and that's what had happened with Bentley, he saw it in his eyes when they showed up at the house. He would probably do everything in his power to see to it that Junya went down for good, maybe some federal pen somewhere or – if he could swing it – a state hole in the ground. Vengeance was vengeance and Southern vengeance was the worst kind, especially black on black.

He flicked through the TV channels and came up with the news. He looked at the clock. Only 1.00 a.m., hours till it got light. He sat up straighter as he saw the governor on the steps of the Legislature building in Baton Rouge. He looked a little like his cousin, though he was shorter and fatter round the middle, a little heavy in the jowls. The press were gathered around him and he stood at the rostrum like the President giving a State of the Union speech.

'Ladies and gentlemen, I want to make a brief statement,' Mouton began. Junya watched him carefully now. 'I just want to say how utterly dejected, how completely taken aback I am – shocked is the word, yes, shocked – about the revelations from the last few days. As you all know, we Moutons have the state of Louisiana carved in our hearts, we love this country. We came with the Acadians when the British took Canada and we have built our lives here.

'I am, as you know, a God-fearing man, and I pray that with God's help the authorities will get to the bottom of this whole sorry tale.' He paused, gripped the rostrum with both hands and hung his head. 'Which brings me to my cousin, the former Attorney General, a man I am ashamed to admit was family.' He looked at the camera. 'But he was family. He was a Mouton just like me, even though he has brought disgrace to this name and suffering to many people. Because he was family, I feel a responsibility to the people he has hurt, an obligation to recompense in some way, to pay for the sins committed under the family name.

'The family coffee business, of which I am no longer a part, having sold my shares some ten years ago, appears to have been nothing more than a front for the trafficking of cocaine. That is perhaps an even greater abhorrence to me than the other unspeakable activities my cousin was engaged in because, although the interference with children is heinous, the ripple effect of drugs goes much wider.'

He looked directly into the camera now. 'I have built my governorship on law and order. I have prided myself on being at the forefront of the achievements of the police departments throughout the state, but particularly in New Orleans, where we have achieved such magnificent results. I tell you all, I take this as a personal affront. It is the worst form of betrayal, to be betrayed by your own family. I might add I have considered resignation and only the will of the Louisiana state legislature has stopped me from standing down.' He bowed his head as if he was fighting with tears. 'When I think of those poor children, when I think of young William Bentley . . .' He shook his head. 'Perhaps I *should* resign, but to do that would be to admit defeat in the face of adversity.'

Junya closed his eyes. This was worse than ever, nothing like the governor himself to set the blood of the people boiling.

'We have certain people in custody,' the governor went on, 'and you have my word that others will be apprehended. You also have my word that everyone convicted of being involved in this most horrific of crimes will suffer the full weight of state or federal law. You may be assured that we will seek the most severe penalties that can be handed down by the courts.'

Junya switched off the TV and sat where he was. The governor would influence Bentley who hardly needed it anyway. There would never be any deal. They'd put him in prison, toss away the key and forget he ever existed. He had given them all he could. There was no other card to be played. And then a thought struck him: except one maybe.

Harrison looked across at Santini and the relief that he had finally told someone was immense. He felt lighter, easier, more at peace with himself than he could remember. He touched her face, cupping her cheek with his palm.

His Nextel shrilled at him where it lay beside the bed. He smiled and picked it up.

'Harrison.'

'Hey, what's up?'

Harrison sat on the edge of the bed. 'It's late, Junya.'

'I know it. Couldn't sleep.'

'What do you want?'

'The way I look at it, I'm fucked, right?'

Harrison didn't say anything.

'Not just fucked, fucked over. You know what I'm saying?'

Harrison blew out his cheeks. 'Don't start with that shit again. I'm not in the mood.'

'You're not in the mood.' Junya's voice sounded like he had a bad taste in his mouth. 'I just seen the news, man. Old Val Mouton's gonna stomp on this nigger till there ain't no more nigger to stomp.'

'I heard what he said. But it's not up to him, Junya. It's a federal case.'

'You telling me that good old boy don't got no influence? Give me a fucking break.'

Harrison sighed. 'It's late, Junya. What's your point?'

'You told me it was a done deal unless we got Laveaux.'

'It is.'

'So how about I get you Laveaux?'

fifty

A week later Marie was feeling better. The doctors had told her that the wound was healing nicely and she could move around with care. A deputy remained outside her room, which adjoined Junya's. Marie told him she wanted to use the bathroom. He told her that she would have to wait till his partner got back, but Marie said she couldn't wait and there was no bedpan in the room.

'OK, lady.' The deputy took her arm. 'I'll come to the bathroom with you. I guess the boy will be OK for a second.'

Junya was dressed, standing just inside his door and listening. For seven days he had been lying in here making the most of his wound, knowing that once he was in jail Laveaux could get to him. He needed to be back on the street where he at least had a chance. His arm was painful, but it was healing well and he knew in a few days he would be transferred to jail. Marie was in no real danger. It was him that Laveaux wanted, but the greater the distance he put between himself and her the safer she ought to remain.

He heard the deputy tell her he would go with her to the bathroom and from that he took his cue. Twisting the doorhandle, he peeked out and saw that the corridor was clear: the deputy was thirty yards from his door, walking towards the ladies' room with Marie. It was now or never. Junya slipped outside, turned right and sprinted down the corridor.

Laveaux was waiting in the next ward, dressed in the

green overalls of a surgeon and pretending to inspect a patient's chart. The deputy was leaning against the wall by the ladies' room, with his back to him. Laveaux watched him then moved into the corridor.

Junya glanced back at the deputy and saw Laveaux come out of the ward. Pushing open the fire door, he headed down the stairs.

Laveaux went into Junya's room, feeling for the knife he had hidden under his shirt. The bed was empty: rumpled and used, but empty. Junya was gone. Laveaux stepped outside again and Marie came out of the toilet.

She saw a surgeon in green overalls and rubber boots come out of Junya's room, a skullcap on his head and a mask hanging about his neck. He was very tall with dark skin and though he had used make-up to cover his scar, she would know his face anywhere. She screamed. The deputy looked up. Laveaux walked briskly down the corridor and out through the fire doors.

Marie shuffled towards Junya's room, dragging her drip and limping. She was breathless, holding the deputy's arm and trying to make him understand that the man in the surgeon's clothes was Augustine Laveaux. She got to Junya's room, but Junya wasn't there.

Junya got to the ground floor and headed for the parking lot. He was in Jefferson Parish, way off his bricks, with no money and no means of transport. A lady with a shopping bag bustled in through the main doors and Junya bumped into her. He came away with her pocket book, which contained twenty dollars and change. Now he wasn't poor any longer. He spotted a bus pulling out for the crescent city connection and he ran out in front of it. The driver stamped on the brakes and the passengers lurched where they sat. Junya climbed aboard. 'New Orleans,' he said to the driver. 'Anywhere will do.'

*

Marie's initial panic was receding. Junya was gone but she was sure Laveaux hadn't got to him. Yet she knew it was only a matter of time. She asked the deputy to get her a phone and she dialled Harrison's number. He answered almost immediately.

'Junya's on the street,' she said. 'Laveaux come after him.'

Harrison was quiet for a moment. 'But he didn't get to him.'

'Not yet, but he will, Harrison. You know that he will. He do, I'm gonna hold you responsible. You understand me?'

Harrison landed at the airport in New Orleans and Penny picked him up. 'Any word?' Harrison asked him.

Penny shook his head. 'Not a whisper, nobody's seen him. We've got Jefferson Parish deputies and NOPD out looking for him.'

Harrison tapped a tooth with his knuckle. He should have stayed down here until Laveaux was either caught or his disappearance confirmed.

'Don't go getting a complex,' Penny told him. 'You got a right to a life. Besides, if that kid had stayed put he would've been safe.'

'You figure? Augustine Laveaux up against one JP deputy? I don't think so.'

Harrison gazed out of the window. 'Where'd they get off reducing the guard anyway?'

Penny shrugged his shoulders. 'Nobody figured Laveaux would bother going after the kid. Mouton's dead, the deal is all but done with.'

It was true. Harrison himself had been complacent. 'You're right,' he said. 'But we should've known better than to think he'd leave any loose ends. He's not that kind of guy.'

Junya got off the bus on Poydras Street across the road from a diner called Mother's and sat down on the kerb. His shoulder was throbbing and when he eased back the material of his T-shirt, he could see blood against the bandage. Setting his arm across his knees, he took out a cigarette and popped a match one-handed. The summer heat was intense, the humidity almost total and the whole city felt as though it was melting.

He had known Laveaux would come. Right at the beginning he had told Junya never to cross him. If he did he would come, no matter how unlikely, no matter the odds, he *would* come after him. Laveaux would guess that Junya had given Mouton to the FBI and that would disturb him. Flipping away the butt of his cigarette, he headed down Canal Street towards the aquarium and a payphone. When he got there he called Harrison.

Harrison was at the field office, talking to Penny and Mayer, when his phone rang. He looked at the caller ID and raised one eyebrow.

'New Orleans payphone,' he muttered, and answered it. 'Harrison.'

'Still gonna stiff me? Still gonna hang my ass in the wind?'

Harrison looked at Mayer. 'Where are you, Junya?'

'I ain't no place.'

'You on the street?'

'You know that I am. You know Laveaux come for me, just like I told you he would.'

'Tell me where you are. I'll come and get you.'

'No, you won't. I know how you look after people, Harrison. I don't want you looking after me. I can look after myself. Shit, I done it for fourteen years before you come along.'

Harrison heard him spit.

'I'm gonna give you one last chance to come through for me. Like I told you in the swamp, I want a reg'lar life. I'm sick of this running shit. But you fuck me over like yo' did the last time – I'm outa here. I ain't sure what I'm gonna do yet, but when I am I'll let you know. Just make sure you ready.' Junya hung up.

Harrison looked at the others. 'He's in New Orleans somewhere. I'm heading downtown. Going to put myself about a little bit, see what I can find out.' He looked at Mayer. 'You got a vehicle I can use, Charlie?'

'The old surveillance pickup's still in the garage.'

Harrison thanked him and left.

Junya put the phone down and looked up the street. This was his city and he could survive here, but it was also Laveaux's city and he had any number of people who could reach out for him at any given time. Junya just had himself, and now he had absconded from the hospital every cop in town, as well as every hood affiliated to Laveaux, would be looking to burn his ass. There was only one place he would be safe, but it was a long walk and he might not make it unscathed.

He left the aquarium area and headed back to Canal Street. He would walk all the way up Canal to North Rampart: there were bad guys all along those blocks but there was also a good chance he might meet a couple of homeys. All the brothers liked to strut their stuff in that part of town and it was his safest bet if he wanted to keep away from Laveaux.

Harrison drove to the French Quarter and parked on Decatur Street across the road from the French Market and Governor Nicholls Wharf. It was late afternoon. Harrison leaned against the door of his truck and rolled a cigarette. Where was Junya? Where would he go if he wanted to avoid Laveaux? There was only one place. Harrison got back in the truck.

Junya lay on a stinking mattress in the burned-out apartment that Dylan and his crack-head buddies had made their

393

own. His arm hurt, though the bleeding had stopped, but the wound throbbed now in a way it hadn't before. He could feel sweat on his brow and he wasn't sure if it was just the heat of the day or something worse. Dylan for once wasn't cracked out. He sat against the wall with his sneakers untied and looked at Junya through the heat haze.

'So how much money you make?' he asked.

'Shit loads.' Junya tried to sit up. His arms ached right down to his hand.

'You spend it?'

'Shit, no. I got it stashed, brother.'

'What you gonna do now?'

'I don't know. Don't ax me that now. I got to think, man. I can't think with you axing me a bunch of stupid questions.'

Dylan made a face. 'You got any rocks, man?'

'No, I don't got any rocks. You wanna quit that shit, brother, before it kills you.'

Junya got himself upright and leaned against the wall. His mind was tumbling over. He hated this place, this room, this foul-smelling mattress and Dylan's crack-induced shaking. He wanted out. He had wanted out for a long time. It was why he had risked his neck on the tugboat. But that bastard Harrison had hung him out to dry. He pushed himself up straighter.

'Gimme your phone.'

'What?' Dylan squinted at him.

'Gimme your goddamn cellphone.'

Laveaux's phone rang. He was sitting in his apartment off Canal Street, looking at the woman in the building opposite as she arranged flowers behind the scrolled ironwork of her balcony. He watched her but didn't see her, his mind on other things. The phone interrupted his thoughts and for a moment he ignored it, then picked it up and studied the tiny screen. It displayed a number he didn't recognize. He laid it down again and pressed the points of his fingers together under his chin. The phone rang and rang. He curled his lip and finally picked it up. He didn't say anything, just listened.

'Augustine, you big white pussy. I know yo' there.'

Laveaux narrowed his eyes. 'Junya.'

'How are yo', asshole?'

'I paid you a visit this morning.'

'I know.'

'Discourteous of you not to be there.'

'I ain't gonna meet up on yo' kinda terms, Augustine. You know I ain't stupid.'

Laveaux was quiet.

'And don't ax me where I am neither.'

'I know where you are.'

'You might. But you still couldn't find me.'

'What do you want, Junya?'

'I want to make a deal.'

Laveaux laughed, only his voice had a merciless quality to it.

'I'm serious, man. I got yo' off the hook.'

'I was never on the hook. I've never been on a hook in my life.'

'No, you the great Augustine Laveaux, ain't you. Regular Jean Lafitte. Man, I don't know how you live with all that celebrity.'

Laveaux's eyes were cold now. He stared across the space between the buildings as the woman on the balcony took all the flowers from one pot and set them in another.

'You don't think you was in a spot, big man? Ax the FBI. They gonna tell you how it was.' Junya was silent for a moment. 'I gave them David Mouton. You know why I done that?'

'To get yourself a deal.'

'Augustine, how the fuck am I gonna get a deal? You seen to that, brother. I kilt that nigger. Remember? I deal crack on the Iberville. I stole the US attorney's kid. What yo' think he's gonna do – give me a reward for letting him go?'

'Why did you let him go? Why didn't you kill him?'

Junya sighed. 'Because killing him was bad news, man. All he saw was me. That's all anybody's ever seen. I figured I kill the kid and the whole fucking world gets dumped on us. He don't know what boat he was on. He don't know nothing apart from that it was me what took him. I could handle that. How the cops gonna find me? Where they gonna start looking? You got all that tied down.

'You know what, Augustine?' he went on. 'Yo' acted too soon, too fucking hasty. I guess that was old Mouton getting all fired up. Not used to the action, was he? You wouldn't have the Feds on yo' ass at all if Ignace hadn't tried to waste the Yankee.' He caught his breath as if he were in pain. 'There was no need to shoot me either, you asshole. None of what's happened got anything to do with me.'

Laveaux was thoughtful. 'You expect me to believe this?'

'You know what? I don't give a fuck. But you killing me gets yo' nowhere you ain't already. Me giving up Mouton gets you out from under the hammer. You know that it does. The Feds are setting pretty. They got the main man. You setting pretty, too – because the main man is dead.'

'And you want me to thank you, is that it?' The sarcasm was thick in Laveaux's voice.

'No, asshole, I want you to pay me. Fifty grand, Augustine. Five-O and I disappear fo'ever, that way you got nobody to put the finger on you. FBI is only gonna put me in jail anyhow. I don't want to go to no jail.' He broke off for a moment. 'You know how I like to talk, Augustine. I go to jail I just might sing out a little bit. Fuck it, you tried killing me once. I ain't got shit to lose.'

Laveaux gazed at the woman across the way and wondered if she was aware of his scrutiny. 'Meet me and we'll discuss it,' he said.

*

Harrison drove into the Iberville, slowing the truck right down. Here the roads were potholed, the tarmac split and broken. Wire fences blocked off certain sections to stop joy-riders tearing up and down the project. As he cruised slowly through, faces lifted his way – gang-bangers on the steps of the tenements, faces at windows and on the rooftops over-looking St Louis No. 1. His phone rang where it lay on the seat next to him.

'Harrison.'

'You Yankee sonofabitch.'

Harrison stopped the truck. 'Where are you?'

'Where are you?'

'Probably the same place as you.'

'What you driving?'

'Blue Ford pickup.'

Junya paused for a moment. Harrison could hear him breathing. 'I see you. Beat-up-looking vehicle, Harrison. You trying to go incognito again?'

'Let's talk.'

'Let's not. Just be at the cemetery there in the morning.'

fifty-one

Augustine Laveaux cruised slowly along Basin Street past the entrance to St Louis No. 1 cemetery, watching for any sign of a trap. He could see nothing that made the hair tingle on the back of his neck and he swung round the block and came back. This was the second time he had made the circuit. Two hours previously he had parked on North Rampart and walked up here wearing a shabby old coat and a hat pulled over his eyes: he looked like a hobo and he sipped from a bottle wrapped in a paper bag, while standing in the doorway of the building across the street. He watched for ten minutes then shuffled across and wandered the cemetery as if he were looking for a place to crash. He was checking meticulously for any sign of the FBI.

There were few places to hide in the cemetery unless you actually broke into one of the graves, and he doubted that even the Feds would violate the dead. Still he was thorough, moving among the tombs and stones and miniature mausoleums, lurching slightly as if he was half drunk. He found nothing to indicate that anyone had been there. He sat on a bench and scanned the crumbling walls and the buildings of the Iberville for SWAT team snipers. He sang softly to himself, swigging water from the paper-wrapped bottle where he held a tiny mirror so he could turn his back on the projects and still check the windows for any glint of the sun on metal.

He lurched onto the sidewalk, caught his breath against

the wall of the cemetery and inspected the buildings across the street, watching the drapes for disturbance or the tell-tale silver disc of a surveillance camera.

Back in the truck he quartered the area again and only when he was finally satisfied did he park up and wait. Junya had played both sides against the middle before but now Laveaux believed he really was clutching at straws. He thought about the boy and he watched the street, few pedestrians, not many vehicles and no police cruisers. The 1st District was only a couple of blocks towards the river and that added to the thrill that rushed now in his veins.

He had decided that this was to be his final job in New Orleans: when Junya was out of the way, he had plans in other pastures. It was a shame to leave such a good deal behind, but nothing lasted for ever. Like his historical mentor, he would seek his pleasure and business opportunities in other parts of the world.

When the time came he opened the truck door and stepped on to the sidewalk. The hobo's coat and hat were discarded, and he gazed up at the savage blocks of stone that formed the Iberville. Wouldn't it be interesting if a couple of gang-bangers came down to mug him while he was in the cemetery: he was well dressed now and could easily be mistaken for a tourist. He felt for the 9-mm stuffed inside his waistband.

Junya sat on the voodoo queen's grave and smoked a cigarette. He was sweating badly and his arm hurt like hell. A different pain than before, the wound was burning up. He assumed that somewhere across the street Harrison had snipers lined up: no doubt there was a panel van in a side street with a SWAT team champing at the bit. He didn't care: he was way past relying on Harrison or any other cop to get him out of a hole. He had been in this by himself from the start, he had his own set of rules and he was playing by them alone now.

He saw Laveaux walk into the cemetery with a swagger in his shoulders just like he walked everywhere, as if he really believed he was untouchable. He wore dark glasses and a baggy shirt over black jeans. He stood very tall and his scar was a livid line in his face.

Harrison saw Laveaux come into the cemetery from where he lay in a broken tomb. He had discovered it when he had set up the SWAT team snipers in the building across the street. He had left it till the last minute to occupy the grave, partly because he knew Laveaux would come early and partly because he had no desire to spend the night with the dead.

Junya had called and told him he would be at the voodoo queen's grave and Harrison's battered tomb was barely five yards to the left. He had spent the last hour lying alongside a set of whitened bones wrapped in rotting clothes. Carefully now he eased himself on to one elbow, ready to rise up from the grave like one of the un-dead.

Laveaux moved between the stones and stopped in front of Junya. 'Have you no respect?' he said, indicating the grave. 'No fear of the dead?'

Junya shook his head.

'You don't believe in the gris gris, then.' Laveaux laughed, his hands behind his back. Junya watched his eyes.

Harrison began to ease himself out of the grave. Laveaux was partially hidden now by a white marble crucifix that blocked the view.

Junya looked at Laveaux. 'You bring my money?'

Laveaux lifted one eyebrow so his face puckered and the scar wrinkled deeper into his skin.

'What do you think?' He brought the 9-mm round from behind his back.

'I think you're an asshole.'

Laveaux laughed softly.

Harrison was out of the grave.

Laveaux whirled to his right, grabbed the boy and held him as a shield. 'Harrison, come out where I can see you or I shoot him right now.' He glanced at the buildings across the street then sat down on the grave so Junya was between him and the entrance. 'And call off the ninja. I know they're over there.'

Harrison stepped into view from the other side of the cross. He had his arms extended in front of him, gripping his Sig Sauer. 'Can't believe you fell for it, Augustine,' he said, 'walking into a trap.'

Laveaux kept his head low so the boy was still between him and the street. It would be a brave man that took a clean shot. 'I'm walking out of here, Harrison. Put the gun down.' He held the 9-mm to Junya's temple. The boy didn't say anything. His arm hurt. He looked sharply at Harrison. 'Put it down, asshole. I ain't looking to get shot.' Harrison stared at him. He stared at Laveaux then he held his palm high before he set the gun on the ground.

'Now tell the hound dogs to back the fuck off.' Laveaux got to a crouch. 'Walk ahead of me Junya, one step at a time.' He pushed Junya slightly and moved away from the grave.

Junya lifted his hand and scratched his left ear.

Automatic gunfire erupted from the housing block behind him.

Laveaux twisted and twitched like a marionette, ropes of blood springing from his chest and neck and head. He stared incredulously at Junya.

The firing stopped and Laveaux collapsed in a heap at the foot of his namesake's grave.

Junya looked down at him then up at the blocks of the Iberville. 'Assholes,' he muttered, 'could have gone right through him.'

Sirens wailed. A van pulled up and black-suited SWAT

team members piled into the cemetery. Behind them the gunmen in the Iberville would already be long gone, weapons stashed for the shakedown.

Junya stood where he was, and Harrison could see that he was unarmed. He lit two cigarettes and sat down next to him. 'Taking a chance weren't you.'

Junya leaned and spat on Laveaux's corpse where it leaked blood on the stones. Harrison jerked a thumb at the project. 'I suppose you're going to tell me that was nothing to do with you.'

Junya still stared at Laveaux. 'Harrison, what those kids do in their own time is up to them. Don't be looking at me to answer for them.' He staggered then, his knees almost giving way. 'I got Laveaux for you, didn't I. Now get me back to the hospital, I think I got a fever.'

fifty-two

Junya was back in hospital: his arm had become infected and he did have a fever. Harrison checked to make sure he was OK and that Marie had access to him, then he went back to the field office to sign off his report before he went home to West Virginia. Santini was waiting for him and he was tired of leaving her.

The special agent in charge called him up to his office and the secretary ushered him in. Penny was seated on the couch with Mayer and Val Mouton, the governor.

'There he is.' Mouton got to his feet, his face one big smile, and gripped Harrison's hand. 'The very man himself. What can I say but congratulations on a job well done.'

'Thank you, sir.' Harrison glanced at Penny.

'I was in town,' Mouton said. 'I saw the reports this morning and had to come by. Job done, I think. Excellent work, excellent.' He smiled again and put his arm round Harrison's shoulder. 'Takes that old military precision, huh, to get the job done.'

He shook hands with Mayer and Penny. 'I have to go now, but I expect to see you all at the governor's mansion in a few weeks. I want the three of you to have dinner with me and my wife.' He paused at the door. 'Oh, before I forget – young Will Bentley, I'm giving him a state bravery award at his house next Friday. I'd love it if y'all could be there. We'll have the TV cameras and everything. I was going to do it in Baton Rouge, but his parents think his routine's been messed up enough lately.' He beamed again. 'We're going to surprise him when he comes home from his new school.'

'We'll be there, Val,' Mayer said.

'Good man.' Mouton saluted Harrison and left the office.

Harrison got off the plane at Bridgeport and climbed into his truck. He drove downtown to the resident agency, where Santini greeted him in the parking lot. She had bought coffee and doughnuts from the country kitchen and they sat in his truck just talking for a few minutes.

'I missed you,' she said. 'Again. It's becoming a habit.'

'I missed you, too.' Harrison held her hand and blew on his coffee. He felt weary, more tired even than when he came out of the swamp.

'I'm glad you got Laveaux.'

Harrison nodded. 'It was down to Junya. He gave us both him and Mouton. That's got to cut some ice with the judge.'

'When's the arraignment?'

He shrugged. 'Junya's back in the hospital. He's due to meet with Jordan Bentley when he's well enough. Hopefully they'll be able to figure something out, but I'm not taking any bets.' He looked sideways at her. 'I brought a set of Laveaux's fingerprints with me.' He smiled, raising one eyebrow. 'Took the guy to get dead before I got close enough to lift them.'

Harrison drove up to CJIS, leaving Santini back at the office. He took Laveaux's prints and passed them to the special processing unit so they could scan them into the system and run an ident check with the second set of latents from the boy in the bayou murder. A murder that was solved now. There was nothing to be gained evidentially from running a match. They had Junya's testimony and there was only the crew to go to trial. Laveaux was dead and David Mouton was dead, the biggest cocaine ring in New Orleans had been taken down. But the prints were a loose end and Harrison needed to know who the second set belonged to.

He went outside for a smoke and when he went upstairs again twenty minutes later the analyst shook his head. 'No dice,' he said. 'I'm sorry. It wasn't him.'

Harrison sat down for a few minutes, trying to figure it out. He had been sure the prints would match. It made no sense. But in the end he had to ask himself if it mattered. The deal was done, those who could be arrested had been and the others were dead. He got up and went back to his truck.

In the office he told Santini. 'Don't let it bug you,' she said. 'If there is a paedophile ring we can assume those prints belong to one of them. If the crimes against children unit can break it, we'll find out.' She touched him lightly on the arm. 'Laveaux killed Carter, Harrison. Because Carter got to him through Call.'

'Call.' Harrison sat back. 'He'd still be alive if I hadn't had him sent back to Angola.'

'Maybe.' Santini laid a hand on his shoulder. 'Quit torturing yourself. You've done enough of that already. Call was a bad guy. Bad guys have to take their chances.'

'Yeah, you're right.' Harrison scratched his head. 'I'd like to be able to tell Mrs Carter who killed her son, though.'

He took out his notes again and leafed through them. A thought struck him and he picked up the phone to the Jefferson Parish sheriff. He wanted the detective in charge of the Jesuit Bend cold case to talk him through their file.

'I've been through this a dozen times already,' the detective, a man called Clayton, said when Harrison got hold of him. 'What is it with the FBI? The case is closed now, isn't it?'

'There's still a couple of details I need to tie up,' Harrison said. 'Come on, partner, one more time. Humour an old soldier, will you?'

'Whatever.' Clayton exhaled audibly. 'You know this isn't the only cold case we got down here. This is bayou country, remember.' He paused. 'OK, let's see, the card we made up of the latent prints from the fishing camp was sent up to CJIS by Detective Muller before he retired. We'd done that every now and again over the period since Bill Chaisson first worked the case. When CJIS was established their database wasn't what it is now – you know it's constantly being updated. Anyways, when Chaisson originally looked for a match in '98 there wasn't one. I guess Muller figured, given all the new technology they got up there, it was time to try again.'

That made sense to Harrison. Marcel Call's Louisiana rap sheet only went back a couple of years and that was in New Orleans.

'Like I said,' Clayton went on, 'the original card was sent up, which is how they like to get it. They scan it into their system, I guess, and keep the hard copy on file someplace. They told us there was no match and we got a copy back.'

'Carter sent it back.'

The detective thought for a moment. 'I guess. Like I said, this was all done by Muller and he's gone now.'

Harrison bit his lip. 'So you're telling me nobody who actually spoke with Carter is working for the department right now.'

'No, sir.'

Harrison blew out his cheeks. 'OK. Look, can I ask you a favour? I want one of our organized crime squad agents to come over and have a look through the file. Would that be OK with you?'

'I guess. But there's nothing to find that I haven't told you about already.'

'Thank you, Detective.' Harrison hung up and told Santini what Clayton had told him.

'That's pretty much what I got back in December,' she said. 'There was nothing out of the ordinary in the file, just a regular cold case.' She pushed back her chair. 'You want to go get some lunch, John?'

Harrison followed her to the door then his phone rang and he went back to answer it.

'Detective Clayton here again, Jefferson Parish.'

'Detective.'

'Before y'all get an agent over here I've picked up on something. I don't suppose it matters much but I guess you might not know about it.'

Harrison sat down. 'Go on.'

'It's a scribbled note, something Muller must've written. I guess it slipped out of order and I didn't pick up on it till you got me looking at the file again just now.'

'What is it?'

'Muller noted that he spoke to Maxwell Carter at the special processing unit at CJIS, and Carter confirmed the latents as non-ident. Carter also told him the original we sent up wasn't good. He had enhanced the image on the system and was sending back a freshly printed copy. The previous copy at JPSO was destroyed. There'd be no point in hanging on to it with a better one on file.'

'Thanks, Detective,' Harrison said quietly. 'I won't be bothering you with that agent after all.'

They sat in the country kitchen and ate lunch. 'It doesn't make a whole lot of difference,' Santini said. 'All it does is confirm what we suspected anyway. Carter doctored the prints on the system so nobody could ever make a subsequent ident. That's why there's no match with the prints you took from Laveaux. It makes sense now. Carter had Laveaux's prints on file at CJIS like we originally figured. He got an ident with the latents from Jefferson Parish and blackmailed him. Then he altered the file and sent them back to JPSO. He then removed Laveaux's rap sheet from the system and waited to get paid.' She made an open-handed gesture. 'Only he didn't get paid, did he.'

'And what's he got as back-up if Laveaux won't pay him?' Harrison said.

Santini stared at him.

'I mean, if he's proving to Laveaux that he's destroying all the evidence before he gets paid, he's dumber than we know him to be. He's leaving the way open to get whacked.' He stood up. 'I'm going to take a run up to the crime scene. I'll see you back here later.'

He drove back to Maxwell Carter's house where the whole thing had begun. *En route* he called in at the Bridgeport police HQ and collected a key from Detective Proud. 'You want to take another look?' Proud asked him. 'There's nothing there you haven't seen already.'

'You're probably right, Tom. But I'd like to swing by anyway.'

Proud handed him a key. 'Be my guest. By the way, you might want to have a word with the old lady when you get a moment. She's keen on somebody from the FBI telling her what's going on.'

'What's she been told so far?'

'Nothing, other than the fact that we haven't caught her son's killer yet.'

'It was Augustine Laveaux,' Harrison said. 'I just can't prove it.'

The July day was hot, the sky clear and the atmosphere very dry. Harrison had always preferred mountains to the flatlands of places like Louisiana or Mississippi. Here the mountains were not as high as out west, but the elevations were still pretty good, and you didn't have to travel far along Highway 50 before you could stop and gaze at the blue ridges stacked against the sky. Sweat gathered at the nape of his neck and he switched on the air-conditioning in his truck, a far cry from the last time he had visited Carter's house when the snow had been a foot deep in the yard.

The house was quiet and still smelt to him of the murder.

The edgy metallic scent given off by dried blood hit him at the foot of the stairs. Everything was still as neat and untouched as it had been at Christmas, only now a thick layer of dust covered the furniture.

At the foot of the stairs he paused and took a pinch of chew from his tin. The place reminded him of David Mouton's office just as that place had reminded him of this. The way things looked, Laveaux seemed to answer to Mouton. But Harrison found that a little hard to swallow: it was much more likely to be the other way round. He wouldn't bet against Laveaux having been there when Mouton 'killed' himself. The UV scanner showed that Mouton had been holding the gun when it was fired, but that didn't discount the possibility that Laveaux was about to cut off his balls as he did so.

Harrison climbed the stairs to Carter's computer room where the brown stain smudged the landing through the open doorway. To the left was the desk with the computer. The history book on Louisiana lay where it had been before and Harrison leafed through the pages. Somehow Carter had come across Laveaux's prints and then he had done some research. It would not have been hard to find out that the tugboat his cousin captained was called the *See More Night*, and from there he could get to The Knights of the White Camelia.

He stopped and thought about it. Carter scribbling down the words 'white camelia' created a tacit association with the Mouton family. Had Carter known about Mouton? He had no way of getting his fingerprints. Mouton hadn't served in the military and he had no criminal record. Perhaps Carter was just demonstrating the depth of his research, his way of proving to Laveaux he was serious.

Harrison didn't know. He would never know. He left the book where it was and looked at the desk, coated in dust as everything was. He glanced at the keyboard and the monitor and then he looked at the filing cabinets standing alongside.

He noticed there was a furrow in the carpet beside one of them. He touched the indentation with his fingertips and realized the cabinet must have been moved at some time. He hadn't noticed it before. Perhaps it had been Carter cleaning very thoroughly maybe. Perhaps it had been the evidence response team. Another thought struck him. Perhaps someone had moved it when they were looking for something.

He sat at the desk and contemplated his dull reflection in the blank computer screen then he looked down at his feet where the bloodstain pushed out in a dried puddle all the way to the landing. It was a very messy, very unprofessional way of killing someone. If it had been Laveaux he had been way out of his territory. Experience told Harrison that taking a killer from their home turf to make a hit somewhere else made them nervous. Any job they had to do would be done quickly and then they would be gone. Bridgeport was a small town: a man like Laveaux would stick out a mile, what with his height and the boat-hook scar on his face. If that was the case, speed being of the essence, why garrotte Carter's leg? It took him so long to die. And then it dawned on him – unless Laveaux was torturing him.

He looked again at the filing cabinet. He looked at the book on Louisiana history. Everything pointed to the fact that Carter was a bright man: they said as much at CJIS. He was meticulous and careful. Would a man like that destroy all the evidence before he got paid?

Outside, birds sang in the apple trees in the yard, a pair of starlings gossiping to one another. Harrison climbed into his truck and lit a cigarette then he drove back to the highway.

He drove out to Maple Lake and the pretty blue house where Carter's mother lived. The last time he had been there the lake had been frozen solid, and now children were leaping off the diving boards, their screeches echoing across the valley. Mrs Carter was tending her roses in the front yard. They climbed a trellis that had been erected over the porch since Harrison had seen it last. The roses were cherry-coloured, some in full bloom, others just coming out, their scent thick and heady in the stillness.

Mrs Carter looked older than she had done the last time he had seen her. She stripped off her gardening gloves and thanked him for coming.

'I was going to make some tea,' she said. 'I make it English-style, Twining's breakfast tea with milk and sugar. Would you like some?'

'That sounds perfect.' Harrison followed her inside.

'I suppose you've come to let me know how it's all going,' Mrs Carter said as she showed him into the lounge.

'Yes.' Harrison turned to face her. 'The investigation was expanded somewhat.'

'So I heard on the news.'

'That's the way things go sometimes. We have a pretty good idea who killed your son, though we can't actually prove it.' Harrison told her about Augustine Laveaux and afterwards she was silent.

'Maxwell was involved in some bad business, Mrs Carter. I'm sorry about that, and I'm sorry he ended up the way he did. But at least the man we think killed him can't kill anyone else.'

The old woman looked at the floor. 'You know, Maxwell always was dissatisfied with his lot. Greed is a dangerous vice. I always told him. Food, beer – he consumed too much of everything. I suppose in a way his greed killed him.'

Harrison didn't say anything. He sat there for a moment, thinking about the filing cabinet in Carter's computer room. 'Mrs Carter,' he said. 'He didn't give you anything before he died, did he?'

'Give me? No. Why?'

'I mean something to look after for him.'

She shook her head. 'No, I'm sorry, he didn't.'

'OK.' Harrison smiled.

'I'll make that tea.'

He sat on the couch while she busied herself in the kitchen. Santini was right: he was looking for stuff that wasn't there and stuff that didn't matter anyway. Laveaux killed Carter because Carter was blackmailing him. David Mouton was a bonus, one they wouldn't have got without Junya.

The boy plagued him, another face that would be imprinted on his mind for ever. After what the governor said on television it was going to be even harder for any judge, federal or circuit, to make a deal. David Mouton's suicide would suit the governor – at least it saved the family the public excruciation of a trial and showed some semblance of honour. The tugboat crew would probably plea bargain now that their leader was dead and couldn't reach out to them. That would be the end of it, case closed, another sordid little chapter in Louisiana's chequered history.

He looked at the clock on the mantelpiece. Nearly four-thirty. He would have tea then chase down Santini.

A Christmas card was displayed on the shelf by the clock, incongruous in July: he recognized it as the one he had seen on Carter's cabinet in the computer room. It was about nine inches high and padded, depicting a cherry black rose like those growing in the garden. It seemed an odd choice of card for his mother. Harrison picked it up and looked at the inscription. He remembered it now from when he saw it the first time.

To my mother, keep safe, Maxwell.

He put it back on the shelf and turned as Mrs Carter set a tray on the table. 'You still have the Christmas card.' He pointed to the shelf.

'Oh, yes, I always keep his cards.' Mrs Carter poured tea. 'Quite why he gave me one with a rose on it is beyond me, though. It's more like a Valentine's card. If I'm honest it's a little embarrassing, but it's the last thing he gave me and I'll keep it for a while longer yet.'

Harrison nodded. 'Memories are important.'

'They are, aren't they? Just because somebody is gone it's important we don't let them die – in our hearts, I mean.' She looked at the card again and clicked her tongue. 'I never did like those awful padded things, mind you – they're so tacky. Not like Maxwell at all.'

Harrison sipped tea and looked at her weathered face, the worn look in her eyes. She shook her head, lost for a moment in some private recollection. Harrison figured it was time to go. He would leave her to her memories.

Outside he rolled a cigarette and lit it with a split match. He thought about his conversation with Santini and was glad, glad he had spoken to her, glad he had got things off his chest, or begun to at least. Climbing into his truck, he started the engine. He sucked on the cigarette and clipped the end, leaving the butt in the ashtray. He put the truck in reverse and began to back out of the yard.

A padded card depicting a rose for your mother at Christmas. *Keep safe*, it said. Not *Be safe*. He stared at the blue house with roses climbing the trellis, like something out of a fairy-tale. People told each other to *be safe*, not *keep safe*. The hairs lifted on the back of his neck.

Mrs Carter answered the door. 'Hello again,' she said. 'Did you forget something?'

'I'm not sure. Do you think I could take another look at that Christmas card?'

'Of course.' She led the way to the lounge.

Harrison studied again the inscription on the card. Then he looked at the padded front and turned the card over in his hands. The half that backed on to the padding had nothing written on it. He looked closer still and saw there was a gap at the spine, a tight opening like a sleeve under the padding. Tilting the card to the light, he tried to prise open the sleeve but he had no nails. Unclipping his knife from his belt, he flipped open the blade and slid it behind the padding. Then gently he twisted the blade and he could see there was something inside. The blood began to pulse in his ears. A piece of green card about six inches by four, he eased it out with the knife. It was stamped 'Jefferson Parish Sheriff's Office' and the prints of four fingers and a thumb were marked on it.

fifty-three

Harrison called Santini and told her what he had found. She agreed to meet him at CJIS and he waited for her in the lobby.

'You just can't let go of something when you grab a hold. Can you, JB?' she said, smiling.

He held up the fingerprint card. 'Maxwell Carter's insurance. I need to put it to bed. All of it, Fran – you know what I mean?'

'Yeah, I know what you mean.' She touched him on the cheek. 'I guess it's part of the John Dollar rehabilitation process, isn't it?'

She followed him up to special processing and he sought out the same analyst who had run Laveaux's prints the last time.

'Your file copy of the second set of latents is a fake,' he told the analyst. 'It was altered on the system.' He handed him the Jefferson Parish card. 'This is the original. I think you'll find you have an ident with Augustine Laveaux.'

He and Santini went downstairs to get some coffee. The news was showing on television: Val Mouton was about to officially accept the Democratic nomination for President and the cameras were waiting for him outside the governor's mansion.

Santini shook her head. 'You'd figure with a criminal in the family Mouton wouldn't stand a chance. But there he is, large as life and buying a ticket to Washington.'

Harrison looked up at the screen. 'He's a powerful man, Francesca. He's got most of the Democrats in his pocket. And you have to admit he's got charisma. Besides, it's so late in the day the party would look foolish if they dumped him.'

His phone rang. It was Matt Penny from New Orleans.

'I just thought you'd like to know,' Penny told him. 'One of the guys from crimes against children has uncovered what they think might be the beginnings of something on the Web. An organization called White Camelia. They purport to be a botany society, but so far we've discovered all the members are men.'

Harrison thought about the traces of seminal fluid found in the boy in the bayou, and what Junya had told him about the kid being summoned to the alcove at the back of the fishing camp. He felt sick to his stomach. The danger would have thrilled the paedophile that took him. He would have got a massive kick from the experience. Harrison had interviewed one or two child molesters in his time and they got excited just talking about it. Whoever he was, he just wouldn't have been able to resist being there.

'They're doing some more digging,' Penny told him. 'I'll keep you posted.'

Harrison was quiet for a moment, watching the television screen above his head.

Santini had gone to get a bagel.

'You there, JB?'

'Yeah.'

'Don't forget about Friday,' Penny said.

'What about Friday?'

'Jordan Bentley's son. The boss promised Val Mouton you and I would be there, remember?'

'Oh, yeah. Of course. I'll see you there.'

Harrison hung up and looked back at the TV screen. Mouton was on the steps of the mansion now, about to begin his press conference. He would be looking to draw attention away from his cousin now that he'd performed his public act of contrition on behalf of the family. He stood at the lectern, his jacket sleeves pushed up a fraction, revealing the starched white of his shirt. The cuffs were fastened with gold fleur-de-lis.

The analyst came out of the elevator and crossed to their table. Santini was paying for her bagel. Harrison stood up. He caught the expression on the analyst's face and spoke before he did. 'They don't match, do they?'

fifty-four

Harrison parked the blue Ford pickup outside Jordan Bentley's house where TV crews from all over the state were camped on the lawn. He was late. The ceremony presenting the bravery award to Will would be over.

Penny was on the step with Mayer and both of them looked his way as he climbed out of the truck and picked his way between the film crews.

'You're late, Harrison,' Mayer said.

Harrison popped a pinch of chew into his mouth, sucked juice and spat.

'There he is.' Mouton stepped out of the house, with his arm round Will Bentley's shoulders. 'You almost missed the party.' He left Will and came over to Harrison, his hand extended. Harrison took it, aware of the sweat on the governor's palm. Almost out of instinct he squeezed, crunching Mouton's knuckles. Mouton stared at him, pain all at once in his eyes. He withdrew his hand, flexing the fingers.

'My, but you got a grip.' He turned to Mayer. 'Charlie, if it's all right with you I'd like to introduce your agent here to the media. After all, he was the one that brought down Laveaux's racket.' He smiled at Harrison. 'That's right, isn't it?'

'That's right,' Harrison said. 'Knocked them all down. Fell like a house of cards.' He turned to Mayer. 'Boss, I'd rather not be introduced if it's all the same to you.' From his jacket pocket he took a folded report and handed it to Mayer. He took Mouton by the elbow and strolled across the lawn. Jordan Bentley was on the balcony, looking down.

'I wanted to ask you something, Governor,' Harrison said.

'Go right ahead.'

'How did you know I'd been in the service?'

Mouton lifted one eyebrow. 'I didn't.'

'Sure you did. You mentioned it in Mr Mayer's office the other day. Remember? Military precision, you said.'

'Oh, that.' Mouton smiled. 'That's just a figure of speech.'

'Oh, I see.' Harrison glanced at Mayer who was reading the report and frowning heavily now. The TV cameras were following the governor and himself as they crossed the lawn. 'I guess it came to mind because of your own military service,' Harrison said.

'I don't know. It's possible.' Mouton was looking puzzled now. 'Look, it's been good to see you but if you'd excuse me I have to think about getting back up the road.' He turned, but Harrison gripped his elbow a little tighter.

'You don't think you knew because Augustine told you?' he said. 'Augustine knew I was in Vietnam. I figured maybe he told you.'

Mouton stared at him, mouth open, a trace of saliva on his lip.

Harrison looked at him with his head to one side. 'What's the matter, Governor? Did I say something wrong?'

Mouton opened his mouth and closed it again. Sweat stood shiny on his brow.

'You know, you nearly walked,' Harrison went on quietly. 'You probably would have if you hadn't made that crack about the military.' He took Mouton's hand, spreading the fingers with his own. 'You should've worn gloves. Or kept your hands to yourself. Like Augustine did – he was always careful what he did with his hands.

'You left your prints on the alcove rail, Governor. Remember, after you called that young kid on up there, the one that Junya strangled with cheese wire? Junya drew your hand on the rail. He's observant like that. Got a good memory. We thought it was your cousin's at first, but now I know it was you.'

Mouton recovered himself slightly. 'I have no idea what you're talking about.'

'Sure you do. That old fishing camp. You really should never have gone down there. Not a man with your political aspirations. But you can't help it, can you? People like you. It's the thrill, I guess. The power. You just can't get enough.' He looked Mouton in the eye. 'How many of you are there – Knights of the White Camelia?'

Harrison took his arm again and steered him towards Mayer. 'Max Carter picked up your prints when he ran a check with the non-felon records at CJIS, and discovered you'd been in the Marine Corps. Then he blackmailed you so you had Augustine kill him. I guess you wanted the original fingerprint card but Augustine was in a hurry. He started to torture Carter with the cheese wire, but then I guess he got bored and just decided to leave him. I bet you spat blood over that when he told you.'

Mouton was crumbling, shaking now. He looked from Harrison to the TV cameras and then at Mayer, who still held the report Harrison had given him.

'You know what we're going to do now?' Harrison said as they got to Mayer. 'We're going to take a sample of your DNA and see if it matches what they found in the boy in the bayou.'

Mouton went white.

'You want to give me odds on that one, Governor?'

Harrison took a pair of handcuffs from his belt, pulled Mouton's arms behind him and fastened the cuffs. He turned to Penny. 'Matthew, I'm done with this piece of shit. Read him his rights, would you?'

Penny stared at Mayer. Mayer folded the report, glanced at Mouton and nodded.

Harrison took a cigarette from his pocket and rolled it between his fingers. He squinted up at Bentley. 'What do you think, Jordan? History got a way of working itself out?'

fifty-five

Late the following afternoon Harrison sat in an FBI car outside the US attorney's office on Magazine Street. Junya was in the passenger seat, Marie and Bill Chaisson in the back. Valery Mouton was in custody and the Democrats were looking for a new Presidential candidate. The previous evening Junya had been released from hospital and he and Marie had stayed in the Parc St Charles Hotel, with Harrison in the next room. At 1.00 a.m. Harrison had answered a knock on his door. Junya had stood there, dressed in his T-shirt, jeans and sneakers.

'What's up?' Harrison asked him.

'Responsibility.'

Harrison folded his arms and leaned against the doorjamb. 'What about it?'

'I wanted to ax you what it's like. I ain't never seen it or felt it or nothing.' Junya wrinkled his brow. 'Is it something that's there all the time or does it just creep up on you?'

Harrison pursed his lips. 'It can be both ways.'

Junya nodded slowly. 'You want to take a drive with me, Harrison?'

They stood side by side under the pale light of the moon in the tiny cemetery at Jesuit Bend. Junya had his hands clasped loosely in front of him. He didn't say anything. Harrison didn't say anything. They just stood and looked at the small grave with a white stone and a little pot of fresh flowers that somebody had changed every week since the funeral. There was no name on the stone, but an inscription had been carved.

The Boy in the Bayou
May his rest be peaceful, free from the care of his waking.

Junya leaned an arm on the back of the car seat and looked round at Marie. 'You ready to do this thing?' he said.

She nodded. 'If you are.'

'I know I'm gonna do some time.' Junya pursed his lips. 'I can handle that. You just stay clean and wait for me on the outside.'

Inside the building Jordan Bentley was waiting, together with the defence lawyer that the court had appointed for them.

'Go do some talking,' Harrison said, laying a hand on Junya's shoulder. 'See what y'all can figure out.'

Marie got out the back and Junya waited on the sidewalk and they stood together for a moment. Harrison nodded through the windshield at Junya and Junya nodded back. When they were gone Chaisson got into the front seat. 'What d'you figure will happen?' he said.

Harrison lifted his shoulders. 'The boy'll do some time. No judge is going to let him walk. I don't think they'll try him as an adult, though, not after what he gave us.' He started the engine. 'So long as he gets parole he's got a chance.'

'That's what I figured.' Chaisson rubbed his jaw with a palm. 'Oh, well, I guess he's got it covered. You want to get a beer in the Margaritaville, Harrison? Gary Hirstius is playing.'